PRAISE FOR
ONE NIGHT RODEO

"Her sexy cowboys are to die for!"

> —*New York Times* bestselling author Maya Banks

"Sweet, seductive, and romantic, *One Night Rodeo* is an emotional ride filled with joy, angst, laughs, and a wonderful happily-ever-after. Lorelei James knows how to write one hot, sexy cowboy."

> —*New York Times* bestselling author Jaci Burton

PRAISE FOR OTHER NOVELS
BY LORELEI JAMES

"The down-and-dirty, rough-and-tumble Blacktop Cowboys kept me up long past my bedtime. Scorchingly hot, wickedly naughty."

> —Lacey Alexander, author of *Bad Girl by Night*

"Hang on to your cowboy hats, because this book is scorching hot!"

> —Romance Junkies

"Lorelei James knows how to write fun, sexy, and hot stories."

> —Joyfully Reviewed

"Think it's impossible to combine extremely erotic and sweet? Not if James is writing."

> —*Romantic Times*

"Plenty of steamy love scenes that will have you reaching for your own hottie!"

> —Just Erotic Romance Reviews

"Smokin'-hot cowboys [and] lots of Western charm."

> —Fiction Vixen Book Reviews

One Night Rodeo

A BLACKTOP COWBOYS® NOVEL

LORELEI JAMES

A SIGNET ECLIPSE BOOK

SIGNET ECLIPSE
Published by New American Library, a division of
Penguin Group (USA) Inc., 375 Hudson Street,
New York, New York 10014, USA
Penguin Group (Canada), 90 Eglinton Avenue East, Suite 700, Toronto,
Ontario M4P 2Y3, Canada (a division of Pearson Penguin Canada Inc.)
Penguin Books Ltd., 80 Strand, London WC2R 0RL, England
Penguin Ireland, 25 St. Stephen's Green, Dublin 2,
Ireland (a division of Penguin Books Ltd.)
Penguin Group (Australia), 250 Camberwell Road, Camberwell, Victoria 3124,
Australia (a division of Pearson Australia Group Pty. Ltd.)
Penguin Books India Pvt. Ltd., 11 Community Centre, Panchsheel Park,
New Delhi - 110 017, India
Penguin Group (NZ), 67 Apollo Drive, Rosedale, Auckland 0632,
New Zealand (a division of Pearson New Zealand Ltd.)
Penguin Books (South Africa) (Pty.) Ltd., 24 Sturdee Avenue,
Rosebank, Johannesburg 2196, South Africa

Penguin Books Ltd., Registered Offices:
80 Strand, London WC2R 0RL, England

First published by Signet Eclipse, an imprint of New American Library,
a division of Penguin Group (USA) Inc.

First Printing, August 2012
10 9 8 7 6 5 4 3 2

LIBRARY OF CONGRESS CATALOGING-IN-PUBLICATION DATA:
James, Lorelei.
One night rodeo/Lorelei James.
p. cm.—(A blacktop cowboys novel; 4)
ISBN 978-0-451-23684-5
1. Cowgirls—Fiction. 2. Ranch life—Wyoming—Fiction. I. Title.
PS3610.A4475O54 2012
813'.6—dc23   2012012937

Set in Tanson MT STD

Printed in the United States of America

*For the readers who worried
that Kyle wouldn't find his happily
ever after . . . it's finally here*

One Night
Rodeo

"*S*on, your father is dying."

Kyle Gilchrist pulled his cell phone away from his ear, staring at it as if it had grown horns. "Ma. What the hell are you talkin' about? You've always told me I was an immaculate conception. Or that you found me in the cabbage patch. Or that you were hit by a sperm donor truck."

"Kyle Dean Gilchrist, for once in your life don't be sarcastic. You need to come back to Wyoming as soon as possible. He wants to see you."

"Who?" he demanded.

"Your father."

"All of a sudden I have a father? Who is he?"

"I can't tell you." A tiny sigh sounded. "Look. He wants to meet face-to-face. Talk to you in person. Explain a few things."

Kyle's resentment flared and he attempted to keep his tone even. "So why didn't he call me himself if he's suddenly all fired up to take on his daddy responsibilities to a grown man?"

"He doesn't feel you two oughta hold this conversation over the phone. Plus, he's on a respirator."

"And why should I give two shits about him? Isn't like he ever gave a damn about me."

"Believe it or not, he does care about you. He always has."

"Why should I believe that?" He couldn't keep the skepticism from his tone.

She blurted, "He's leaving you an inheritance and he wants to discuss it with you."

Kyle's beer stopped halfway to his mouth. "Come again?"

"He's leaving you everything: the land, the cattle, the buildings, whatever cash is left over. Everything is yours. He had no other children. You're his only heir."

His father. An inheritance. This was beyond surreal. And Kyle had thought last night was an epic mindblower.

"Son? You still there?" his mother said, prompting a response.

The hotel door opened and she sauntered in. His pulse skipped a beat, or seven, as it always did whenever he saw her.

She stopped by the bed and asked, "Kyle? Is everything all right?"

He shook his head, still trying to wrap his brain around the bizarre news.

His mother demanded, "Who's that with you?"

"My wife," Kyle drawled, keeping his eyes focused on the woman wearing his ring.

"Your wife? Since when do you get married and not tell me?"

"Don't go there, Ma. Not when you've dropped a bombshell about my alleged father."

"Who is she?" His mother again demanded an answer.

"I'll make you a deal: I'll give you her name if you give me my father's name."

Silence.

"That's what I thought. I'll be in touch soon. Bye." He hung up and tossed the phone aside, never breaking eye contact with the woman standing next to him.

"You gonna tell me what that was about? Especially blabbing the *my wife* part to your mother?"

"You *are* my wife, and it looks like we're goin' to meet the family sooner than we expected."

"Oh no. Oh *hell* no." She cocked her hands on her hips and glared at him. "We both agreed this Vegas marriage was a drunken mistake and we'd get it annulled as soon as possible."

Kyle gave her a very slow, very thorough once-over, letting the heat in his eyes serve as a reminder of their wedding night. "You know, I've had time to think, and I don't wanna get this marriage annulled." He toasted her with his beer. "So pack your bags, kitten. We're headed home to Wyoming. Tonight."

❦

Twenty-four hours earlier...

Kyle raced down the hospital corridor until he spied the woman pacing across from the emergency room doors. "Tanna?"

She whirled around. "Kyle. Thanks for coming."

He loomed over her. "Thanks? That's the first thing you say to me? Jesus. I've been out of my fuckin' mind the last twenty minutes. How could you call me to get my ass to the hospital and not give me a single damn detail about what happened to her?" He had visions of her in surgery or in traction. Bloodied up and unconscious. Broken in body and spirit.

The feisty barrel racer jabbed him in the chest with her finger. "Don't you snap at me first thing, Kyle Gilchrist."

"Then start talkin'. Now."

"I told you on the phone. She fell off a horse."

Kyle frowned. "Her horse Mickey ain't even here."

"Not *her* horse. *A* horse. She landed on the steer cockeyed after she launched herself at it. I think she ended up with a hoof or a horn to her head 'cause... ah... there was some blood."

"What the hell was she doin' with a goddamn steer?"

"Bulldoggin'." Tanna's eyes darted away.

Somehow he kept a lid on his temper. "Still waiting to hear the full story."

Her defiant brown gaze met his. "You know how Celia is, Kyle. Someone tells her that she can't do something and she goes out of her way to prove them wrong."

"Who's *them?*"

"A couple of bulldoggers from Nebraska. Cocky bastards, talkin' shit to us about how easy barrel racin' is compared to bulldoggin'. The next thing I knew, Celia was ponying up a hundred bucks to prove that steer wrestling ain't that hard. Then the bulldoggers got permission from the event staff so we could have us a little race."

"You've got to be fucking kiddin' me. Celia is in the damn hospital because of some stupid bet? Why didn't you stop her?"

"Because I agreed with her and tossed in a hundred bucks of my own to teach those pompous pricks a lesson," Tanna shot back. "Celia drew the short straw to ride first."

Kyle caught a whiff of Tanna's boozy breath. "Christ. How much had you guys been drinkin'?"

"Some."

Unbelievable. "How'd you get to the hospital?"

"The bulldoggers dropped us off. Celia said she was fine and walked in on her own, so I don't think her injuries are life threatening."

"Celia would tell you that even if she had two broken arms, two busted legs, and her eyes were bleeding. Damn stubborn woman." But he hoped Tanna's assessment was right.

The emergency room doors opened and Kyle glanced up as a nurse approached Tanna. "You're with Celia Lawson?"

Kyle intercepted. "Yes. How is she?"

"She's had a chest X-ray and a CT scan. You can come back and wait with her if you'd like."

They followed the nurse to the end of a wide hallway. He stepped around the curtain.

Celia was on her back, her lower half covered with a blanket. Her slim torso appeared fragile, swimming in the floral-patterned hospital gown. Her lips were a flat line. Her eyes were shut. Kyle's gut clenched when he saw the bandage on the upper left edge of her forehead and the bruises on her cheekbone. His gaze traveled the long, thick blond braid lying beside her on the bed; the end of it brushed the middle of her thigh.

Ridiculous, probably, to watch the rise and fall of her chest to assure himself she was breathing.

On impulse, he placed a soft kiss between her eyebrows. When he lifted his head, he found himself staring into her eyes.

Those smoky gray eyes narrowed very quickly. "Kyle? What the devil are you doin' here?"

"I called him," Tanna said, scooting in to squeeze Celia's hand.

"Why?" Celia demanded.

"Because you asked for him," Tanna replied softly.

Celia's startled gaze quickly hooked Kyle's. When he smirked, she said, "Don't go getting that look or I'll wipe it right off your face."

"Sure, you will." Kyle smirked again. "Just as soon as you're not flat on your back in a hospital bed, knocked loopy."

Tanna laughed. "So how *are* you feeling, bulldoggin' queen?"

"Sore. Pissed I lost a hundred bucks."

"You don't remember they paid up?" Tanna asked. "I guess if you bleed you win by default."

Celia snorted.

"Has the doctor been in?"

"To give me stitches and to give me hell," Celia grumbled. "He poked me, muttered a lot, and then shipped me off to X-ray. I tried to tell him my ribs are just sore, not broken. Guess he didn't believe me."

"You're a few years short of a medical degree to be makin' a diagnosis," Kyle said dryly.

"This ain't my first rodeo," she retorted. "I've been hurt before."

"What ever possessed you to tangle with livestock when you'd been drinkin'?"

"It wasn't like we were shit-faced, Kyle. We each had one shot." She frowned. "No, two shots."

Tanna held up four fingers.

"Four? Really? Huh. Didn't seem like that many."

"How's your head?"

"Hard, but you knew that. The doc was worried about a concussion, so they X-rayed my melon too." Once again those icy gray eyes zipped to him. "Not a word about them finding my head empty, Gilchrist."

He'd had enough of her tough-girl attitude. "Knock it off. I get that you're scared."

"How do you know that?"

"Because, kitten, you hiss and claw when you're afraid." Kyle picked up her hand, rubbing her cold fingertips against his jaw. "So hiss and claw at me. I can take it."

"You need to shave," she snapped, jerking her hand back. "And I'm not scared. I'm annoyed."

The curtain fluttered and Devin McClain strolled in, although the country music star was barely recognizable in a ratty ball cap and sunglasses. "Hey, brat. Whatcha gone and done to yourself now?"

"Devin? How did you . . . ?" Celia blinked at him in confusion.

"Kyle called me in a complete panic. Had me thinking I'd find you on your deathbed. I wasn't sure if he wanted me here to hold your hand or his."

Kyle muttered, "Shut it, asshole."

Devin raised his eyebrow, peering over his shades at Celia. "Seems you've had a miraculous recovery."

"Why won't anyone believe that I'm fine? I just got the wind knocked out of me."

"Darlin', you were knocked out cold," Tanna drawled. She offered her hand to Devin. "Nice to finally meet you, Devin. I'm Tanna Barker. I've heard lots about you from Celia, bein's you're a family friend and a Muddy Gap homeboy."

"A true pleasure to meet you too, Tanna. Great run last night."

"Thanks." She blurted, "Omigod, I can't believe I'm standing here with Devin McClain! I'm such a huge fan. Your song 'Chains and Trains' is one of my all-time favorites."

"I never get tired of hearin' that. Thank you."

When Devin granted Tanna that million-dollar smile, Kyle could have sworn the rowdy Texas cowgirl swooned.

"So what's the diagnosis?" Devin asked Celia.

"Still waiting for the X-rays to tell us."

"Have you called her brothers?" Devin asked Kyle.

Immediately Celia grabbed a fistful of Devin's sweatshirt, grimacing as she pulled herself upright. "No. And I swear to God I will beat you bloody if you do." She leveled the same venomous look on Kyle. "That goes for you too."

"But, Celia, they need to—"

"No. Do you hear me? Janie is in the last two weeks of her pregnancy and I won't upset her or Abe for anything. And Hank and Lainie are leaving for Boulder for the consult for Brianna's eye surgery. They need to focus on her and each other, not me. Promise me you won't tell them."

Surprised by her tears, Kyle bent closer. Sweet, fierce Celia wasn't upset about being beat to shit; she was just worried about her family's reaction to it. "I won't tell them as long as you promise to call them within a day or two."

"Okay. Thank you."

He raised an eyebrow. "No arguing with me? Really? That's one for the record books."

"I don't always argue with you."

"Yes, you do."

"No, I don't."

"See? You're still doin' it."

"You started it."

"As much as I'd like to stay and hear another round of your bitchy sexual foreplay—*not*—I need to get ready to ride tonight," Tanna said.

"Now that I know you're recovered enough to bicker with Kyle," Devin said, "I'll head back to the event center for final sound check."

"Would it be too much trouble to drop me off at the arena?" Tanna asked Devin. "I'm without a vehicle."

"No problem at all."

"You're both just leaving me?"

Tanna rolled her eyes. "You keep insisting you're fine, remember? Besides, Kyle will take better care of you than I have today." She squeezed Celia's arm. "I'll see you later."

"So, brat, you still comin' to the concert tonight or what?" Devin asked.

Kyle said *no* at the same time Celia said *yes*.

"Good luck with this argument. We're outta here." Devin held the curtain for Tanna and they disappeared.

"Don't give me that look, Kyle."

Kitten, you'd blush to the tips of your toes if you'd noticed how I've been looking at you the last two years.

"What look?"

"The bossy one."

"Tough, because I have every intention of bossing you tonight."

The curtain rolled back and a young male doctor stopped at the end of the bed. "Good news. No concussion. No broken or cracked ribs. No ruptured organs. You'll be sore for a few days, and I imagine more bruises will appear. My advice is to take it easy, alternate ice and heat with the sore spots. But I'm well aware you rodeo-ers don't often follow medical advice. So the best I can do on a medical front is to prescribe painkillers."

Celia shook her head. "I hate the groggy way they make me feel."

"That's how you're supposed to feel. Like you oughta be laying down resting," Kyle pointed out.

"That's rich coming from the bull rider who's ridden with a sprained thumb, a sprained wrist, a sprained ankle, a pulled groin muscle, and a mild concussion...all in the last year. You refused pain meds and I didn't see you *resting* any of those times."

He had no response for that. Mostly he was surprised she'd taken note of his injuries.

"I'm writing you a scrip for pain meds. Up to you if you fill it," the doctor said. "The stitches need to come out in a week. Any other questions?"

"Nope."

"Good. No more mixing bulldoggin' with drinking Mad Dog whiskey, okay?"

"If you insist."

The doctor laughed. "You can get dressed. The nurse will be in with your discharge papers shortly."

Celia sat up and kicked away the blanket, dangling her legs off the bed.

Kyle's eyes drank in every inch of those ridged calf muscles covered by smooth, pale skin. His gaze traveled up slowly, stopping at the equally sexy curve of her knee.

"Stop gawking at my legs like you've never seen 'em before."

He didn't bother banking the admiration in his eyes. "Hard not to stare when you're sporting such a fine pair."

"You just noticed that?"

"No."

The air between them vibrated.

Kyle invaded her space. This close to her he felt that one-two punch of something stronger than lust. "Would it be so bad?"

"What?"

"Letting me watch over you tonight?" An internal debate warred in her eyes. Kyle braced himself for a smart-ass rebuttal.

"Watch over me like a brother would?"

"The last way I think of you, Celia Lawson, is like a sister. And you damn well know it." He pressed his lips to her forehead. "I'm glad you came to Vegas, Cele. I was afraid you wouldn't show up."

"Kyle."

"Mmm?" He placed another kiss on the edge of the bandage.

"Can we talk about this later?"

"Define *later*." The skin below the bandage needed a kiss as well.

"Right after we leave here. At my hotel. You need to skedaddle so I can get dressed."

"In a second." He smoothed flyaway strands from her face. The honeyed scent of her hair filled his lungs and he seemed to breathe easy for the first time since he'd heard she was hurt. He left one last soft smooch on her lips. It totally flustered her, which was odd, given that it wasn't the first time he'd kissed her.

"Umm . . . Hand me my clothes."

He dropped the pile on the bed. "I'll be right outside."

"No peeking," she warned as he ducked out.

Kyle paced the length of the privacy curtain. On his fifth pass, he heard her gasp. Worried that she'd strained herself, he poked his head back in. "What's wrong?"

Celia clutched a wad of fabric to her chest. "It was my favorite shirt. My lucky purple shirt. Now it's covered in blood and completely ruined." A little hiccup escaped. "I can't wear this."

"Are the jeans ruined too?"

"No. Just a few splotches of blood."

"Tossing that shirt in the trash ain't no big loss in my mind. I'm thinkin' its luck ran out. Never looked that great on you anyway."

Celia lifted her head, probably to snap at him. Before she opened her mouth, Kyle gently wiped her tears. "Come on, kitten, I was kiddin'."

"Pretty stupid to be so upset over a blouse, huh?"

"Somehow I don't think it's just about the blouse. And given that you're in the hospital, you're entitled to a few tears. You don't always have to act so tough, you know." Kyle popped the buttons on his long-sleeved western shirt. "Although I wouldn't mind seein' you in just your sexy bra and them tight jeans, I don't think you wanna flash the entire ER when I bust you outta this place. Wear this." He draped his shirt over her pillow and tucked his white T-shirt into his jeans.

"Uh, thanks."

Interesting that Celia couldn't take her eyes off his chest. "My pleasure." Kyle kissed her forehead. Twice.

"What's with you kissin' me all the time now?" she asked crossly.

"I hardly think a couple of pecks could be considered me kissin' you all the time." His eyes searched hers. "But I could ramp up the kisses to spark your memory from a few weeks back, if you'd like."

"In your dreams."

Kyle chuckled. "I'll be outside if you need anything."

❧

Like a total chickenshit, Celia was hiding in her hotel bathroom.

From Kyle.

Kyle. The guy she'd known since she was six years old.

What the hell was wrong with her?

Because the Kyle waiting for you is not the same Kyle you've known your entire life.

She dabbed concealer over the bruise on her cheekbone. Contrary to her sister-in-law Janie's claims, Celia hadn't been in love with Kyle Gilchrist since her childhood—she'd simply loved to annoy him.

Even when Kyle was a teenage boy, it took a lot to rile him, unlike her brothers, who were easily provoked. Armed with childish logic, Celia made it her mission to get under Kyle's skin as often as possible.

She'd drawn hearts emblazoned with her name on every one of his school notebooks.

He'd retaliated by stringing up her My Little Pony collection from a tree.

She'd pushed him into the stock tank.

He'd held her down and tickled her until she peed her pants.

She'd put a snapping turtle in his gym bag.

He'd tied her to the tire swing and spun her until she puked.

All harmless pranks that demanded retaliation.

The problem was—Kyle still brought out every combative instinct she owned. Her first impulse was to goad him into an argument, or to fight back when he goaded her, which happened frequently since he'd never outgrown that juvenile behavior either.

But that had all changed three weeks ago with a kiss. An incredible kiss.

Tanna had dragged her to the annual New Year's bash at rodeo legend Del Montoya's ranch outside of Stephenville, Texas. Celia hadn't known many people, so she'd been secretly happy to run into Kyle the first day of the two-day party.

Maybe it was the free-flowing alcohol, but she and Kyle hadn't sniped at each other once. The lead rope tied around the door handle of Tanna's horse trailer meant her friend was getting lucky that night, so Kyle let Celia crash in his camper. They'd talked and laughed until the wee small hours.

The next day Kyle and Tanna were competing in the private rodeo, leaving Celia at loose ends. In the late afternoon she'd headed to a small pond to watch the sunset. It'd struck her how alone she felt most the time, no matter whether she was surrounded by people, on the road, or in the arena—or even at home in Muddy Gap.

Kyle had tracked her down and somehow sensed her melancholy. The ease of the previous day's conversation lingered, especially when they talked of home. Of frigid nights and miles of snow. Of the splendor of orange and purple Wyoming sunsets splashing across a pale gray winter sky.

When she mentioned the New Year's Eve festivities, Kyle asked, "Have you picked a cowboy to kiss when the clock strikes twelve?"

"I've had enough drunken, forgotten kisses to last me a lifetime."

"If that's the case, you could always lay a hot, wet one on me," he'd said silkily. "I guarantee an unforgettable kiss."

"Like I said, Kyle. Been there, done that."

"But not with me," he insisted.

"Been there, done that with you." Celia locked her gaze on his. "You were the first guy who ever kissed me."

Kyle shook his head. "Trust me, I'd remember that."

"Trust me, you forgot. After a night out partying with Hank, you stumbled into my room instead of the guest bedroom. You stripped naked in front of my sixteen-year-old virgin eyes and crawled into my bed. When I tried to move, you grabbed me and kissed me. With tongue and everything."

He wore an appalled look. "I did?"

"Yep. Then you rolled off me and started snoring. I snuck out and crashed on the couch upstairs. You weren't in my room the next morning. You never said a word about it, which meant you didn't remember, because we both know you'd've been a total dick if you had. But that doesn't change the fact you were my first kiss."

"Jesus, Celia. I don't remember."

"It's not like I could forget. Besides, it's over and done with." She tried to turn away but Kyle didn't allow it.

His hands cupped her face. "Let me make it up to you by kissin' you at midnight tonight."

"But—"

"I'll be totally sober, I promise. And this kiss?" He'd lazily, erotically traced the outline of her lips with his thumb. "Will blow your mind."

And it had. Holy shit, had it ever.

Celia shivered, remembering being wrapped in his arms. His mouth so sure on hers as the clock struck twelve.

Four loud raps on the bathroom door startled her out of her trip down memory lane.

"Celia? You all right? You've been in there half an hour."

"Yeah. I'm fine. Be right out."

She exhaled a slow breath and studied her handiwork in the mirror. She'd tried to play up her boring gray eyes, adding black eyeliner, drawing attention away from the bruises that liquid face makeup couldn't camouflage. Extra blush brightened her pale skin. Bronze lipstick highlighted her mouth. She couldn't do much about the white bandage on her forehead, unless she gave herself bangs. Since her three and a half feet of blond hair was her best feature, that wasn't happening.

She popped a mint in her mouth and opened the door.

Kyle turned from the window and inspected her head to toe. When he continued to stare at her, without uttering a word, without a single change in his facial expression, a tiny kernel of dread bloomed in her gut.

"What? Do I look like death warmed over or something?"

"Not hardly."

"Then why are you staring at me?"

He crossed the room, stopping a foot from her. "Seems I've known you forever, Celia. Then other times, I look at you and I feel I don't know you at all."

"So I don't look like a hundred-and-fifty-pound steer got the better of me today?" she joked, unnerved by the male heat darkening his eyes.

"Nope. You ready?"

"For what? The concert doesn't start for three hours."

"I meant are you done in the bathroom? I need to get cleaned up. I'm not exactly in concert attire."

Kyle preferred dressing in traditional western shirts, so his upper-body physique wasn't obvious . . . until those long sleeves were stripped away to reveal his muscular arms. His biceps and triceps were beyond simply well defined. Yet his truly spectacular forearms always drew her attention.

"Celia?"

Her gaze met his. Kyle's eyes were an unusual hue, somewhere between summer-grass green and pine green. With gold flecks that reminded her of dappled sunspots reflecting off a crystal clear mountain lake.

"You feelin' okay?"

What was wrong with her? Salivating over his arms? Becoming mesmerized by his eyes? Maybe she had knocked a screw loose when she'd smacked into the ground today.

Right. Keep telling yourself that. He's the reason you came to Vegas. You haven't stopped thinking about him or what that kiss meant for the last three weeks.

She cleared her throat. "I'm still a little wonky. So if I say anything weird"—*like compose an ode to your tight little butt*—"chalk it up to a head injury."

Then he was nose to nose with her. "I shoulda forced a damn pain pill down your throat so you'd be sacked out instead of planning on goin' out."

Happy that snappish Kyle was back, she poked his shoulder. "I'm not missing Devin's concert. I'm not missing the private after party at the casino either. So if you're determined to be my keeper tonight, Kyle, you'd better keep up."

"Remember you said that, kitten. I'm not letting you out of my sight."

Yeah, we'll see about that.

A minute after she heard the shower kick on, she snuck out.

✆

Kyle couldn't believe Celia had ditched him.

To add insult to injury . . . she'd left him a fucking note.

Meet you at the concert ~ C

For chrissake, she shouldn't be going to the damn concert with ten stitches in her head. He half expected to find the bloody bandage in the garbage.

Reckless damn woman. Made him want to paddle her butt again. But bare-assed this time. Not in a roomful of people either, like last year in Breck's hotel suite on the eve of Celia's birthday.

They'd been drinking heavily after the monthly poker game. Some new friend of Breck's tossed off a nasty comment about women being the weaker sex, which sent Celia into full attack mode. She'd challenged the guy to a wrestling match and the dumb ass had taken her up on it.

She'd had him in a headlock within a minute.

And so it began. The other men wanted a shot at besting Wyoming cowgirl-tough Celia—none succeeding—while Breck egged her on. She'd whipped up on three guys. Then it was down to Breck and Kyle as the only ones who hadn't answered her challenge.

Breck had refused, claiming he'd never live it down if his girlfriend beat him.

Kyle had refused to tussle with Celia because he'd been pissed about Breck's treatment of her—like a pet to entertain his asshole friends. But Celia, being Celia, used that smart mouth of hers to question Kyle's manhood, forcing him to give her the Muddy Gap smackdown.

What the onlookers hadn't known, and Celia herself had forgotten, was he'd been grappling with her since they were kids. Kyle knew all her moves; hell, she'd stolen most of them from him, and she'd never bested him.

Not once.

In the spirit of sportsmanship, he'd allowed her to believe she'd gotten the upper hand, and then he'd pinned her, demanding her submission.

No surprise Celia had refused to give it.

So he took it.

Her shrieking, thrashing, and threats were to no avail, because Kyle, drunk on victory and cheap scotch, turned her over his knee to dole out the birthday spanking she deserved.

Except during the test of wills, the feel of her muscled flesh warming beneath his stinging hand and the seductive way her body writhed on his lap became an erotic interlude, not a punishment.

Round about spank fifteen, she surrendered.

Round about spank sixteen, Kyle had a hard-on that rivaled steel.

Breck had cracked jokes immediately after Kyle delivered Celia's last birthday blow. But neither Kyle nor Celia had laughed. They'd barely looked at each other, unsure how to react to the sexual tension arcing between them like heat lightning.

That night Kyle realized Celia's relationship with Breck wasn't making her happy. Maybe it never had. He became a man on a mission—getting Celia to see she deserved better than Breck. He'd never suggested becoming her replacement lover, no matter how badly he'd wanted to.

After the breakup, Kyle had seen the suspicion in Breck's eyes, as if Kyle had encouraged the breakup because he'd wanted Celia for himself.

Which wasn't entirely inaccurate.

Celia Lawson stirred something inside him. Given their tumultuous past, he'd initially believed the feeling to be frustration. Yes, he'd lusted after her for the past two years, but the pull between them had always been more than merely physical. Everything about her spoke to him on the most basic level. How she could look both innocent and sexy almost at the same time. How she moved both on and off her horse. The fire in her eyes. Her pensiveness. Her sweetness. He'd never cared enough to examine another woman's body language and quirks so intimately, which spoke volumes about his feelings for her.

Feelings that had her running scared and had him chasing after her.

He'd given her three weeks to think about the next step between them after that life-changing kiss in Texas. Now that she'd shown up in Vegas—as she'd promised—it was time she accepted that this thing between them wasn't going away.

Kyle intended to pull out all the stops tonight to make her his.

✎

After spending a few hours hanging out in the casino trying to win a little extra cash and partaking of free drinks, Celia wandered to the event center. She slipped on her all-access backstage pass and headed through the arena to the stage area. Two beefy security guys checked her pass, looked inside her purse, and waved her through. At the next backstage doorway, two more security guards blocked access. They scrutinized her pass, giving her a lewd once-over that suggested a thorough patdown. When thick-necked goon number one asked what had happened to her forehead, she almost said, "Knife fight," but amended it to "Baking mishap." Not as much fun, but that response didn't trigger a strip search.

Celia smiled when Devin approached her. "If it isn't the superstar man of the hour. How are ya?"

"Damn glad you're here, brat." Devin led the way down a long hall lined with people, but no one intercepted him.

"Who are all these people?" she whispered.

"No fuckin' idea."

"Why aren't they talking to you?"

"It's a stipulation in my contract that no one talks to me for two hours prior to a performance. Unless it's an emergency."

"Sometimes I forget you're this big country music star beloved by millions and not just the meanie who used to hang me upside down from the barn rafters."

"That was Kyle, not me."

"You used to hide in the basement closet and jump out and scare me."

"I had no part in that. Blame—"

"Kyle. I get it. Just a reminder that he's always been horrible to me."

"He didn't seem horrible to you today at the hospital. In fact, he was straight up freaked out when he called me."

"Guilt, I'm sure. Afraid my brothers would find some way to put the blame on him for my accident."

"Accident?" He lifted a brow. "That's stretching it. But you didn't seem to mind his attentions, Cele."

Don't respond. Be cool.

Devin's private ready room resembled a pricey hotel room, with a plush sitting area and a fancy bathroom complete with a lighted makeup mirror and a stylist's chair. A small bar dominated one corner. Privacy screens blocked off an area behind the living space. Probably a makeshift bedroom. Guitars, notebooks, water bottles, and articles of clothing were scattered across the sofas, coffee table, and chairs.

Devin plopped down on the couch. "You are coming to the postconcert blowout at the Trade Winds Casino?"

"I guess. Why you having it there?"

"Because it's a total dive. Cheap drinks, haggard cocktail waitresses, a crummy wedding chapel, a greasy-spoon diner, all with a honky-tonk theme straight from the fifties. It's perfectly retro and I'm feeling nostalgic."

Devin grabbed an acoustic guitar and propped his bare feet on the coffee table. He strummed a haunting melody. He'd stop, scribble in a notebook, then pick up where he left off—both the conversation and his guitar playing. He'd always done that, talked while he noodled with the strings and wrote music when it looked like he was screwing around. Sometimes it was hard to reconcile Devin the scrawny, happy-go-lucky kid with Devin the songwriter who penned such dark songs about love, lack of it, and no redemption.

"What's been goin' on in your world?" he asked.

"Same old same old. Trying to win enough money in barrel racing to justify doin' it for another year."

"What will you do if you don't?"

"Maybe enroll in trade school and get a degree as a vet's assistant, since I know a lot about livestock. Fletch has always said I could go to work for him."

He stopped playing to jot something down. "I take it you're not going home much?"

"Did Hank or Abe say something to you?" she asked sharply.

"No. I've sensed restlessness in you the last couple of times we've talked. What's keeping you from ditching the rodeo life and settling down in Muddy Gap?"

"And do what? I'm the odd one out in the Lawson family. I've got no place to live. My brothers are married with families of their own. Harper and Bran are married. My new buddy Tierney married Renner Jackson. Tanna is the exception, which is why she insists I spend my off-tour time with her in Texas."

"Weren't you seeing some guy, kinda seriously?"

"Breck and I were hook-up buddies and it wasn't exclusive." At least not on Breck's end. "I'm not looking to get married. What about you?"

Devin snorted. "Not hardly. I don't lack for hook-up offers, and that's fine by me. Touring is a bitch. But I ain't bitching because this career is fickle. I can have a song at the top of the charts, sell out big venues, and the next year won't land a recording contract. It happens all the damn time, and it will happen to me eventually, so I'm gonna ride this ride as long as I can. Then maybe I'll find a woman who ain't impressed with the celebrity and just wants a simple country boy from Wyoming."

"Tell you what, Dev. If your career hits the skids and I'm still trying to find my place in the world, I'll marry you. I know you from the days you sported a mullet. I saw you barf after gutting an antelope. And I'm thankful for the cool cred you gave me my first year on the Cowboy Rodeo Association tour when you showed up after an event and whisked me off to dinner in your tour bus."

"We had fun that night, huh?" Devin gave her a considering look. "All right. If in a couple of years we're both unhappily single, we'll tie the knot."

"Although, sex might be weird. Vaguely—"

"Incestuous," they finished simultaneously and laughed.

"Not to mention her brothers would fucking kill you," Kyle drawled behind her, "but it'd probably be worth it."

Celia whipped around to see Kyle exiting the screened-off area. "Why do you always have to scare me half to death?"

"Like you scared me when I left the bathroom and found a fucking note on the bed?"

Shit.

"At least she left a note," Devin pointed out.

"I don't appreciate bein' ditched, Celia," Kyle said in that deep, sexy rasp of his.

She stood, hoping neither man noticed her body swaying from the drinks that were catching up with her. "Being forced to hang out with me has to cramp your style, bull rider."

"That might be true if I had a style. And you can't force me to do anything. I wouldn't be here if I didn't wanna be."

Devin sighed. "No fighting. I need only good vibes in here, okay?"

"We'll just go over here," Kyle said, directing Celia to the bar. He filled two shot glasses with three fingers of tequila.

"So we callin' a truce?" Celia murmured.

Kyle's eyes pinned hers. "I thought we'd called a truce on New Year's."

"Kyle. Don't. Not now."

"You promised we'd talk about this and we haven't. So we're gonna talk about it now. Why did you come to Vegas?"

"For Devin's concert," she said way too fast.

He got right in her face. "Really?"

Stop being such a chickenshit. Celia threw her shoulders back and met his heated gaze head-on. "No."

"At least that was honest." Kyle inched even closer. "What are you so afraid of?"

Tequila truth serum had her blurting out, "You. And me. What if that kiss...that weekend we spent together...was a fluke?"

"What if it wasn't?" he countered softly.

Flustered, she had to glance away.

Kyle tipped her chin up. "Tell me you don't feel this."

"I do feel it. I don't know what to do about it."

"Give in to it. Just for one night. What's the worst that could happen?" He held his shot glass up for a toast.

Celia clinked her glass to his and downed the tequila. "Fine. I'll give in to it. But you'd better keep me from doing anything stupid."

Chapter One

Present day

*C*elia stared at Kyle lounging on the bed, admiring his wedding ring. "Wrong. We are not going to Wyoming. We are marching down to that wedding chapel right now, telling them it was a mistake, and getting an annulment."

"No."

"No? I had a fucking head injury yesterday! You cannot believe for one second I was in my right mind when I agreed to marry you!"

"You signed the papers. With little hearts by our names, if memory serves. So some part of you wanted to marry me, Celia."

Her jaw dropped. He was wrong. Completely, totally, utterly wrong wrong wrong.

Wasn't he?

His hungry gaze took full measure of her body. "I'll bet the scent of my cologne is still all over your skin."

Celia fought the urge to blush because he'd been saying sex stuff like that since the moment she'd woken up. She stubbornly repeated, "I don't remember a damn thing from last night."

"Don't matter. I have this"—he jerked aside his shirt collar to show a small purple hickey—"to prove it."

Holy crap. She'd done that?

"What's the last thing you do remember?" he prompted.

She tried to sort through her hazy memories, rattling off, "Us drinking tequila in the cab on the ride to the Trade Winds after Devin's concert. I went to find Tanna and I took…a couple or three painkillers because my head and ribs hurt."

Kyle's eyebrow winged up. "Three painkillers? Did you wash them down with booze?"

"I don't know." Man, she'd been full of stupid decisions last night. "So at what point did we exchange vows of eternal devotion and cheap-ass rings?"

"Hey, I checked the receipt this mornin'. The rings were a hundred bucks a pop, so they ain't completely cheap."

He had a receipt? "Do *you* remember everything from last night?"

Kyle leveled that damnably charming smile at her.

Dammit. "Who else knows we had the clichéd, quickie, soon-to-be-annulled wedding in Sin City?"

"Evidently Devin and Tanna were our witnesses."

Oh fuck. Celia slumped in the chair. This was seriously not good.

"I take it you haven't talked to Tanna today?"

"No. I was a little busy trying to wrap my head around the fact that I woke up naked, hungover as hell, and wearing your wedding ring!"

His phone rang. He muttered, "I figured she wouldn't like me hanging up on her."

Celia had been so concerned about dealing with the bogus marriage issue, she'd lost focus for a few minutes about the terse phone call she'd interrupted. "What did you mean when you said she dropped a bombshell about your alleged father?"

The teasing smile on his face vanished. "That's exactly it. I don't know what she meant. She mentioned some kind of inheritance, my father wanting to see me right away, and then she clammed up. When I demanded the full truth, she got pissy. Then I got pissy." The phone stopped ringing.

"Don't you want to know what this is about? Obviously she's anxious to talk to you."

His eyes were conflicted. "Maybe. It's freakin' me out. That, coupled with your near hysteria from last night's..." He looked away and his jaw tightened. "Never mind. It ain't your problem."

Seeing Kyle morph from mocking to morose so quickly triggered an odd need to soothe him. For once Celia didn't dissect the feeling. She just gave in to it and sat down next to him on the bed. "So make it my problem. Talk to me."

"You haven't exactly been civil to me since you woke up at the crack of two this afternoon."

"Blame it on the shock at discovering I'd been intimately involved in a civil ceremony last night."

"You're not blaming me?" Kyle asked skeptically.

"For us getting hitched? Yes, I'm blaming you." Celia jabbed at him with her finger. "You were supposed to keep me from doing something stupid."

He studied her. Pointed at her with his beer bottle. "Well, I don't think it *was* stupid."

His calm acceptance caused her to blurt out, "I don't even know what the hell to say to that."

The phone rang again.

"We're in the same boat because I don't know what the hell to say to her. About my father. Christ." He chugged the rest of his beer. "Talk about bizarre."

She patted his thigh. "Kyle. It has to be hard for her too. Talk to her."

"This oughta be fun." He answered his phone. "Mom. Yeah, I *am* sorry. No. I don't understand. Why now?" After a minute or so, Kyle stood and paced, holding the phone with one hand, gesturing wildly with the other. "If you think I'm gonna haul ass all the way to Wyoming so you can have the dramatic edge of dropping his name on me in person, think again. Either give me his name right freakin' now or I'm hanging up."

Kyle froze. Every bit of blood drained from his face. Then he aimed his focus on the carpet, listening to whatever his mother was saying without argument.

Celia watched his hand curl into a fist, his knuckles turning white. She had the strangest compulsion to open that tight fist and thread her fingers through his. To ease his tension. To let him know she was right there if he needed her.

"Yeah. I understand. I'm sure. No. I get it. Probably a few hours. Okay. Love you too. Bye." Without another word he locked himself in the bathroom.

Great. What was she supposed to do now? Beat on the door and make him talk to her?

Use his distraction to push for an annulment?

Celia's cell phone vibrated with a text message from Tanna. *Good afternoon, Mrs. Gilchrist! Call me. I just hit the road for TX and wanna know your plans.*

Tanna could shed light on what had happened last night. Celia put the security latch in the door to keep it from shutting and snuck into the hallway.

Tanna answered immediately, busted out "Single Ladies," and then laughed. "But that doesn't fit you anymore, does it, Mrs. Gilchrist?"

"Ha ha, T."

"Can I just do my I-told-you-so dance? I knew it was only a matter of the right timing before you and Kyle publicly admitted your feelings for each other."

The right timing? After way too many tequila shooters?

"Despite the fact you were both pretty hammered, it was romantic how he swept you off the dance floor and yelled, 'I'm marryin' this woman right now before any of you bastards try to take her away from me' and then ran with you to the chapel."

Oh no. Oh no, no, no. Kyle had yelled that? And they'd been dancing?

Tanna kept blathering on, as she was prone to do. "I couldn't believe you guys already had the paperwork filled out and the rings chosen by the time I tracked Devin down and we showed up to be your witnesses. The whole thing, from Kyle's declaration on the dance floor to the official pronunciation of man and wife, took twenty minutes tops. And I'm impressed you still had time to write your own wedding vows."

She'd written her own wedding vows? She sank to the floor in the hallway, tempted to beat her head into her knees, until she remembered she had stitches in her forehead.

"Although your *love* and *dove* rhyme wasn't particularly original, nor was Kyle's use of *ass* and *class* appropriate, the rest was really sweet and heart-felt. Like you'd both been holding your feelings inside for a long time. And that kiss." Tanna sighed. "It was beautiful, but surprisingly raunchy. I've never seen you so happy, Celia. God. You were giddy with joy."

How was it she couldn't remember anything? And was it lucky or un-lucky that Tanna did?

"Cele? You there?"

"Ah. Yeah." Celia changed the subject, lest Tanna figure out just how much she didn't remember from her own damn wedding. "Just wondering what you and Devin did after Kyle and I took off?"

"Drank some. Then two fan-girl chicks horned in and offered to blow him, so the man-whore whisked them to his tour bus. For all I know they might be on their way to Portland with him right now."

"As you can imagine, I've been out of it today. Did you call Lainie and tell her that me and Kyle ... ?"

"Yes! She's so excited for you guys. But I made her promise to wait to tell Hank until she got the okay from you two. But I wouldn't put it past Devin to blab far and wide, so if I were you, I'd start making calls." She muttered something. "Sorry, C, gotta go. Traffic is a bitch on this road so I need to concentrate on my driving, bein's I lost my traveling partner to the hottest bull rider on the circuit. Call me later."

Celia studied the floral-patterned carpet, trying to force any memory at all to the surface. Maybe she was trying too hard. Maybe if she let it ... jell, it'd all come back to her.

Her phone buzzed in her hand with a text message. From Lainie.

I can't believe you and Kyle got married last night! I haven't said a word to Hank, but this isn't a secret that'll keep for long. Be best for your brothers to find out from you. In person, not over the phone. I expect you'll come home ASAP.

As much as Celia loved Tanna, she'd seriously fucked up this situation by blabbing. Wait a second, Kyle had told his mother too. How many people had she told? How many people had Devin told? In the last thirty minutes Celia had lost any chance of getting a quiet annulment.

What was she supposed to do now? How could she tell Hank and Abe her marriage to Kyle was a drunken mistake? They already treated her like a flighty kid who couldn't make up her mind. She rolled to her feet, returning to the room to find Kyle gazing out the window. His tension was obvious in the tight set of his shoulders.

"What did your mom say?"

He didn't respond for the longest time. Then he said, "She told me my father's name. I've been asking her since I was five years old and she finally told me today." Another long pause. "Marshall Townsend is my father."

"The name isn't familiar to me. Do you know who he is?"

"Yeah. I've crossed paths with him a couple of times, but it's not like I know him. The summer after your folks died, this rancher named Marshall Townsend called Hank out of the blue and hired us to hay for him. We both thought it was weird at the time, since he didn't know Hank or me, but we figured he must've known your parents. Anyway, he wasn't friendly at all. He was cheap. He paid us the bare minimum but promised us hunting rights for the fall. When we tried to collect on the hunting rights, he said he'd changed his mind and chased us off his land."

"That's harsh."

"What an asshole, right? And come to find out, that asshole is my father."

Her heart broke for him. Celia went to him without thinking. She rested her cheek on his shoulder, hating to hear happy-go-lucky Kyle so resentful, although he had a right to be. "What can I do?"

He stiffened. "Don't take a shot at me right now, Cele. I couldn't handle another fuckin' thing today."

It hurt that he assumed she'd kick him while he was down, so she stepped back.

He remained quiet for a few moments. Then he sighed. "It's easier for us to snipe at each other, isn't it? Here I've been telling you it doesn't have to be that way between us and what's the first thing I do? Snap at you."

Slightly mollified, she said, "This news about your father is a big shock for you, Kyle, so I'll let it slide ... this time."

"So noted," he murmured.

It bothered her that he hadn't turned around to talk to her face-to-face, almost like he expected her to get fed up and leave. So naturally, she dug her heels in. "So, what else do you know about him besides his assholish tendencies? Where does he live?"

"West of Rawlins. About thirty miles from your place. As far as what I know about him? Nothin'. Except my mom says he wants to see me because he's dying." He shook his head. "He's acknowledging me as his sole heir on his deathbed? That's TV-movie-of-the-week bullshit."

"Kinda like us getting drunk and ending up hitched in Vegas, huh?" Kyle snorted.

"So what will you do? Blow him off like he's blown you off?"

"What can he possibly say to me that'll make any difference now?"

Celia warned herself to be patient with him. He was confused and hurting, and she'd snapped at him plenty of times in the hospital yesterday when she'd been in the same scared and frustrated frame of mind. "Don't you want to find out? Why slap his hand when he's finally reached out to you?"

A full minute passed before he spoke. "Pains me to admit you're right. They've only given him a couple of weeks to live at best. So I told my mom I'd go. But..." His sigh was long and loud—a sound of pure frustration. "Fuck. I don't know what I'm supposed to do." He shrugged tightly. "I'm sure I sound like a whiny prick. Forget I said anything."

"Don't slap my hand away either," she said softly.

"I'm not. It's just...Christ, Celia, I feel like a five-year-old kid. I'm afraid of facing him. What if I walk into the VA hospital in Cheyenne..." That fist clenched again. "Or worse, what if I can't even walk into the room?"

Hearing the uncertainty in Kyle's voice broke her heart. "What if I came with you? Would that help you take that first step?"

Kyle slowly turned around. "Why would you do that?"

Because I've never seen you like this, so damn vulnerable. Because I have the urge to be there for you the way you've been there for me the last year. Because there is something growing between us, something that gets stronger whenever we're together, and it scares me half to death but I'm not strong enough to walk away from it.

When she didn't respond, Kyle said, "After all your insistence on getting this marriage annulled immediately, why would you put that aside and come with me to Wyoming?"

She tossed off a breezy, "Because... hello. My ride left and I'm running low on options."

His face shuttered at her flip response and she felt like an ass for skirting the truth.

Before Kyle retreated, Celia reached for him, running her fingers over the dark stubble coating his jaw and pressing her hand in the center of his chest. "Because I owe you."

"Because we're married? It's not real, as you've pointed out. Repeatedly."

"Will you stop being a dickhead and listen to me?"

Kyle's eyes flashed remorse. "Sorry. Shit. I don't know what's wrong with me today."

Celia didn't have to tell him he was lashing out because he was scared. Kyle already knew that, even if he wouldn't give voice to it—to himself or to her. "I owe you because you were the only one who treated me normally after my parents died. Everyone else felt sorry for me. Felt sorry for my brothers getting stuck raising me."

"Celia. That's not true."

"It is true." She fussed with the buttons on his shirt. "Everyone treated me like a lost waif. Everyone but you. You riled me. Poked at me. When you found me crying in the shelterbelt, rather than coddling me, you scooped up an armful of wet leaves and kept covering me in a layer of nasty slime until I got mad and started fighting back. I chased you into the bull's pasture. We ran around until my legs gave out and I fell to the ground."

"Right into a pile of manure, if I remember correctly," he murmured.

Celia met his gaze. "That was the first time I felt normal after they died. I've never forgotten that. I've never said thank you."

"You said thank you every time you pulled some shitty prank on me. That was when I knew you'd be okay."

"So it's time for me to pay it forward. Will you let me?"

He seemed to consider it and abruptly changed the subject as he took a step back. "Who were you talkin' to a little bit ago?"

"Tanna. She's on her way back to Texas. She was anxious to recap the events leading up to our nuptials." Celia paused and cocked her head. "Evidently we wrote our own vows?"

Kyle half squinted at her. "We did?"

His surprise surprised her. "You don't remember?"

"Nope. To be honest... most of the details are sketchy for me too."

"But you told me... that we..." *Had a smokin'-hot wedding night.*

"I was yanking your chain, Celia."

Completely floored, she said, "Why?"

"Because that's what you and I do to each other, remember?"

"We're beyond that juvenile behavior, remember?" she shot back with saccharine sweetness. "Isn't that what you keep reminding me?"

"Well, us rolling around naked, sucking face like horny teenagers until we both passed out... without having sex on our freakin' wedding night is sort of an anticlimactic end to the wild-night-in-Vegas tale, don'tcha think?"

She opened her mouth to tell him to quit being an ass, but he beat her to the punch.

"And there I go again, being a dick to you. But, dammit, you oughta know I'm not the kind of man to take advantage of a drunk and injured woman."

Of course he had to throw in his chivalrousness. So she threw hers right back at him. "I'm not the type of woman to bail on a friend in need either. I offered to go home with you and the offer stands. Since we didn't consummate the marriage, we can still get an annulment after we deal with your family thing in Cheyenne. Provided..."

His gaze turned shrewd. "Provided... what?"

Provided my brothers don't kill you. "Okay. Here's another wrinkle. Apparently Tanna, ah, told Lainie that you and I got hitched last night."

"Shit. So your brothers know about us?"

Celia shook her head. "Lainie swears that she won't spill the beans.

But I—we—have to tell them. In person before they hear it from anyone else."

He groaned. "I'm a fucking dead man."

"Maybe they'll think it's funny," Celia offered. "Especially since we haven't had sex."

Kyle scrubbed his hands over his face. "Or maybe they'll cut my dick off to guarantee that never happens."

"A bit paranoid, aren't you?"

"Not after all the times they warned me away from you."

Celia put her hand on his wrist. "What do you mean after all the times they warned you away from me? When did they do that?"

"When you were seventeen I made a comment about you filling out and I thought Hank was gonna throw me through the wall. Abe basically said you're their princess and I'm a toad who's not nearly good enough for you."

Princess? Yeah, right. They treated her more like a stableboy than a princess.

"And they told me if I ever touched you, they'd string me up. By my toes because they would've already cut off my hands."

Her mouth dropped open. "Are you serious?"

"Completely."

"Maybe I won't tell them we tied the knot," she said with a huff. "Maybe I'll just tell them that you fuck like a dream and I'm moving in with you until we get sick of nonstop kinky sex."

Kyle smiled for the first time in an hour. "That works too. We would've had to tell them something anyway since we talked about traveling the circuit together. And we sure as hell wouldn't have been just...friends."

Unsure how to respond, and feeling strangely shy, Celia sidestepped him and looked out the window to the Vegas skyline.

"I'll get packed."

"My stuff is still at my motel," she reminded him.

A quick zip sounded. "We'll stop there on our way out of town. But before we leave here you'd better check on the other side of the bed to see if you forgot anything."

Celia stepped over his bag on the floor and crawled across the mattress.

"I doubt there's anything because I'm wearing—" And she found herself flat on her back, staring into Kyle's amazing green eyes.

"Thank you, for not running out screaming today. My mood swings, from happy to nasty, from sarcastic to silent, were annoying the piss out of me."

"Most days you are pretty even-keeled."

"Except when it comes to you. You make me crazy, Celia. In so many ways I can't even begin to explain to you."

Her heart jumped into her throat and she couldn't speak.

"It's getting to be a habit with us, sharing kisses one or both of us forgets. But I intend to fix that right now and make damn sure you remember this one. On the bed where we spent our wedding night."

He lowered his face to hers. But he didn't swoop in and blow her circuits with a kiss packed with tongue-thrusting power. No. He took his time. Whispering soft breath across her jaw. Letting his full, damp lips barely graze hers. Each almost connection of their mouths increased the rapid beat of her heart. Her breathing became erratic as her lungs emptied of air.

Kyle's roughly murmured "Breathe" was far sexier, far more in tune with her body's response to his than she'd imagined.

Then he rocked her to her core with a kiss so hot and sweet, so fierce and soothing, so completely unrestrained. She'd never been kissed like this. With all-consuming hunger. With pure eroticism. With a promise of total sexual fulfillment. Every pulse point in her body throbbed with anticipation.

Kyle used nibbling kisses to ease the disconnection of their mouths. He pushed up and hopped off the bed.

His cocky grin—completely justified—appeared quickly. "Come on, kitten, let's hit the dusty trail."

Damn him for acting like he had the upper hand. Damn him for melting her brain and her resistance with those molten kisses.

She slipped her purse strap over her shoulder. "We're still getting an annulment."

⮞

Kyle was so lost in thought about Celia's contradictory actions—reminding him of their friendship in one breath and then taking his breath away with such a passionate kiss in the next, that he didn't notice Breck and his buddies hanging around the concierge stand until Breck started toward them.

Kyle said, "Let me handle this."

"I don't need you to speak for me."

"Then follow my lead, so we don't get stuck in a pointless argument with him." Kyle set his hand in the small of her back and brought her closer, expecting Breck would treat her as roughly as he always did, clamping his beefy arms around her, squeezing her in a bear hug, tossing her in the air like a rag doll. He wasn't letting that happen.

But Breck stopped five feet from them. His focus was concentrated on Celia's head. "Sugar pie, what happened to your beautiful face?"

She touched the bandage with her right hand. "Minor mishap with some livestock."

"But you're okay? Where else are you hurt?"

"My ribs are sore, but besides that, I'm fine."

"Good. You still look great." Probably out of reflex, he reached for her hand. "I miss you."

"Breck. Don't."

Breck only then seemed to realize Kyle was standing next to Celia. "Gilchrist. I'm surprised to see you here, bein's you didn't finish high enough in the standings in December to compete in the Country Showdown Expo."

No surprise Breck tossed out a barbed reminder of Kyle's lackluster finish in the American Finals Rodeo—AFR—the previous month. "Guess I didn't know I needed an official invite to come to Vegas."

Breck's gaze zoomed between the two of them. As if something wasn't quite right.

Although Kyle had no idea how this Vegas marriage would play out, he wanted to rub it in Breck's face that Celia was his, even temporarily.

So he did just that. Kyle used his left hand to brush a hair from Celia's shoulder. "You've got so damn much hair, woman."

Breck's eyes narrowed first on the ring on Kyle's hand and then on the matching band on Celia's. "You've gotta be fucking kidding me." He looked at Celia. "Say it ain't so."

Celia glanced at Kyle. He brought her hand to his mouth and kissed her ring finger.

"How long has this been going on? While we were together?" Breck demanded of Celia.

Immediately incensed, Kyle got up in Breck's face. "Don't put your shitty morals on her. Celia ain't like that and you know it. Apologize to my wife, right now."

"Kyle—"

"He isn't allowed to insult you, Celia, ever. I've watched him do it enough over the last two years and I couldn't do anything about it then, but I can stop it now." He didn't move an inch. "So apologize to her."

"Jesus. All right, all right, I'm sorry."

Only then did Kyle back down.

"How long have you two been—"

"Married?" Kyle supplied. "Since last night. We're just on our way home to Wyoming."

Breck's face distorted with an ugly sneer. "Last I knew you didn't have a pot to piss in. So where are the newlyweds gonna live? In your shitty camper? Or Celia's horse trailer? Or are you sponging off Celia's brothers?" He focused on Celia. "I asked you to marry me. And you turned me down for him? A guy who has nothing?"

Jesus. That stung. Was that really how Breck saw him?

Isn't that how you see yourself?

Celia stomped closer to Breck. "I turned you down because we have vastly different ideas of what commitment means. I'd spent enough nights wondering why you preferred Michael in your bed more often than me."

Breck glanced around, but Celia had said it in a low tone so no one had overheard. "But Kyle, Celia? Really? One of my best friends? It's like a knife in my heart."

"Now you know how I felt every time you were with Michael."

Breck looked stricken. "But . . . I never hid that from you, sugar pie."

"Being honest about the nature of your relationship with Michael didn't excuse it." Celia faced Kyle. "We're done here."

She definitely didn't need Kyle speaking for her. She'd proven she could handle herself just fine.

Celia was quiet on the ride to her motel. Kyle didn't push it—they would have a solid fifteen hours together in the truck, enough time to talk a lot of things through.

Chapter Two

$\mathscr{A}$ knee to the head woke Kyle from a sound sleep. Groggy, he sat up and squinted at Celia. "What the hell?"

"You snore like a freakin' bear. And you sleep like the dead, which ain't a fun combination at all."

He scrubbed his hands over his face. Then he looked out the window. They were on I-80 almost to Cheyenne. He'd slept a solid six hours. "You okay?"

"No. I want a goddamn cigarette. This is why I hate bein' on the road. I get so fuckin' bored all I can think about is firing up a smoke. And don't suggest sunflower seeds. They don't work."

"Didn't for me either. I had to get a big bag of Dum-Dum suckers."

"Chewing on plastic straws was the only thing that worked for me." She shot him a sideways glance. "Speaking of chewing… when did you quit?"

"About six months ago. Bet with my mom as an incentive to get her to quit smoking."

"Did it work?"

"Has so far. We both chewed about a million packs of nicotine gum. Did you use pills or gum or anything?"

"Nope. I quit cold turkey. Three days after I broke up with Breck. Might sound stupid, but I starting smoking with him, so it seemed like I oughta quit when we called it quits. Been a lot tougher to give up than I thought."

Kyle looked at her. "Cigarettes were tougher to give up? Or Breck was tougher to give up?"

"Cigarettes." Celia tapped her fingers on the steering wheel. "Although there was a lot I liked about Breck or I wouldn't've stayed with him." She let a beat pass. "Thanks for what you said to him."

"I meant every word." It was the perfect opportunity to bring up the marriage issue. "So we're telling everyone who knows we stumbled down the aisle...that we're getting an annulment?" He knew his voice sounded disapproving.

"I thought we agreed on that."

"No, you informed me of your intent to get an annulment. I didn't argue. But that's not agreeing with you, Cele. Not by a long shot."

"Well, let's compile a list of who knows about us getting hitched. Tanna. Who's only told Lainie. Lainie, who says she won't tell anyone. Devin. Who told...who the hell knows all the people he's told. Breck. Who's probably told everyone on the damn circuit. Your mom." She looked at him. "Who all has your mom told?"

"How the hell would I know?"

Kyle's cell phone rang and they both jumped. "Speak of the devil. Hey, Mom. We're just starting the descent into Cheyenne."

"I've been trying to call you for the last four hours."

"What's up?"

When his mom didn't answer right away, he knew. He closed his eyes. "When?"

"About twelve hours ago. Right after I told him you were on your way to see him." She sniffled. "Evidently his death came as a shock even to the staff. Marshall didn't have anyone listed as next of kin, but one of the nurses after shift change had my number and she called me. I just got off the phone with his lawyer. He's set up a meeting tomorrow morning at nine."

Kyle didn't know what he was supposed to feel in response to this news. He'd been afraid to meet the man and now he would never have the chance. The resentment he'd tamped down earlier reared its ugly head again.

"Are you staying with me and Rick tonight? Because I made up the guest room."

"No." He wouldn't give in to her guilt. "What's the lawyer's name?"

"Bill Ruttan. His office is downtown. Do you need directions?"

"I'll look up the address when I get to the motel. Are you gonna be there tomorrow?"

"No. It's just supposed to be you." She hesitated. "And your wife, if you want."

"Jesus, Mom, you told the lawyer I was married?"

Celia groaned.

"I assumed it was all right."

He bit off, "Do me a favor. Don't assume anything. Don't talk to anyone about any of this, okay? My marriage, whatever the hell this inheritance is supposed to be about. You think you can handle that?"

"Kyle Dean Gilchrist. Stop being an ass."

"Funny, that's what my wife says to me too. I'll call you when we're done at the attorney's." He hung up, mired in that place between regret and anger. Wondering what the fuck happened next.

"Kyle? What's going on?"

"Marshall died. So there's no need for us to rush to the VA."

She covered his hand with hers. "I'm sorry."

"Yeah, me too. Pick a hotel you wanna stay at tonight."

Celia didn't speak until the truck stopped. "How's this place?"

Kyle squinted at the sign. Fairfield Inn. "This'll work."

As they entered, the front desk clerk was nauseatingly chipper. "Good afternoon. Welcome to the Fairfield Inn. My name is Trudy. How may I assist you today?"

"We need a couple of rooms."

Celia tapped his shoulder. "Why are you getting us separate rooms?"

"Because I'm in a lousy mood and I want to be alone."

Her mouth grazed his ear. "Tough shit. You're stuck with me." She gave the clerk a cheeky smile. "Sorry. Temporary marital dispute. One room."

Marital dispute? Was she serious? She was going to acknowledge their marriage . . . now?

"King-size bed or two queens?"

A challenge floated between them. Kyle said, "Two queens."

Celia dropped her gaze.

If Kyle hadn't known better, he'd have said she was disappointed.

Fuck. That was the last thing he needed to worry about: mixed signals from the woman who claimed she didn't want to be his wife.

After they were settled in their room, Celia said, "I need a shower. Food. And sleep. Food first?"

"Just as long as it's steak."

"Deal."

They opted for Golden Corral. Hitting the buffet line at different times limited their conversation, which suited Kyle fine. Although Celia kept sending him strange looks.

He dropped her off at the hotel. "While you're showering I'll track down the lawyer's office." And a liquor store.

When he returned, an hour later, Celia sauntered out of the bathroom in a skimpy camisole that matched the silvery color of her eyes and a pair of flannel pajama bottoms that hugged her ass.

Her hair was unbound. A mass of blond that brushed the lower curve of her butt. Kyle had only seen it in a braid the last couple of years. No wonder she always tamed it. With it untamed, she was a goddess. He had the overwhelming urge to bury his face in those fragrant tresses. Feel the silken strands sliding across his skin. Twined around his body. Christ. This was a bad idea. Maybe he oughta sleep in the truck.

"Hey. What's that?" She peered in the package and her hair brushed his arm. "You bought beer? And whiskey? We having a wake or something?"

His eyes connected to hers. He fought the need to consume her mouth in a heated kiss. But the scent of her, the sight of her, the inability to have her, might just drive him out of his fucking mind.

He turned away, setting the package on the small table. After ditching his boots, he snagged a cup, ripped off the plastic packaging, and poured himself three fingers of whiskey. Grabbing the remote, he flopped on the bed closest to the TV, offering an offhand, "Help yourself."

Celia took the ice bucket. She returned a few minutes later and poured herself a whiskey on ice before plopping cross-legged on *his* bed. "So..."

Her shoulder blocked his view of the TV; he shifted to the right.

"Kyle."

"Hmmm?"

"Don't you wanna talk?"

"About?"

"Your father dying. How upset you are with your mom. What'll happen at the attorney's office tomorrow."

"Nope."

Celia tipped her head so it was right in front of the TV.

"What?" he said irritably.

"Talk to me."

"Don't got nothin' to say. Now move. I'm watchin' this."

But she didn't move. "I'm serious."

"So am I."

"Why don't you—"

"Why don't you understand? It won't make a lick of difference if we dissect this fuckin' thing nine ways 'til Sunday. I won't know anything until tomorrow. For tonight, I wanna forget about it with some bad TV and some good whiskey." Kyle allowed his gaze to roam over her face, down her chest, and back up to her eyes. "Unless you're offering another way to make me forget about it, because, kitten, I'm all over that."

Celia's skin turned a beautiful shade of pink, from the roots of her hair to the center of her chest. "That's not what I was suggesting."

"I didn't think so. Pity. Now move."

She flounced off the bed.

Kyle flipped through channels. Poured himself another glass of whiskey. Tried not to stare when Celia braided her hair. Tried not to fantasize about demanding that she unbraid it.

When Celia climbed beneath the covers, he turned the TV down, not off, because he was wired. He downed his fifth shot and he still wasn't feeling the effects.

His thoughts were a jumbled mess. He just wanted to get some sleep but his damn brain wouldn't cooperate.

Hours passed. Late-night TV bored him. Tired of staring at the ceiling, he got up and parted the curtains. Great view of the parking lot. The edges were piled high with snow from the last storm. The streets were a muddy gray color that matched the sky. Dreary damn night.

Welcome to January in Wyoming.

"Kyle?" Celia said sleepily, startling him. "It's three o'clock in the damn morning."

When he didn't respond, he heard the swish of bedding, followed by her soft footfalls on the carpet. Her breath teased the back of his neck and her arms came around his waist. She held him for the longest time.

And he let her. He wondered how long she'd stay with him. Would she take off right after they told her brothers about the impending annulment? How soon did she want to meet with Hank and Abe anyway? Tomorrow? Right after they left the attorney's office? Where would she go? Back to the circuit?

When Kyle sensed her retreat because he hadn't responded at all to her sweet comfort, he squeezed her hand, then rubbed his thumb over her knuckles. "Thanks."

She murmured, "It'll be okay."

"You sure?"

"No."

No bullshit. That made him smile.

Tiredness finally overtook him after she'd returned to bed. He stripped and crawled between the sheets.

✌

The smell of coffee brewing woke him. Kyle stretched and whipped back the covers.

"Oh my fucking God, you're naked."

He cast a bleary eye at Celia perched on the bed across from his. "Yeah. So?"

"So put that thing away."

Kyle glanced down at his erect dick and grinned. "Nothing personal, kitten. Just a little morning wood."

She muttered something about it not being little at all.

"Sorry, I didn't hear what you said."

"You weren't meant to hear it. For God's sake, Kyle, cover yourself."

He didn't. He rummaged in his duffel bag for clean clothes. Celia averted her eyes pretty damn fast when he turned around. "Need to do anything in the bathroom before I shower?"

"No. Since I'm decent and you're not, I'll head down to the complimentary breakfast."

While he was shaving, trying to get his head in the right place, he realized he hadn't verified with Celia whether she planned to go to the lawyer's office with him. He stepped out of the bathroom, in his jeans, his shirt unbuttoned. "I forgot to ask if you wanted to come with me this morning. I'd understand if you don't, since—"

"God, Kyle, do you have to walk around half freakin' naked all the time?" Celia marched up to him and started snapping the buttons on his white western shirt. "I swear you're just strutting around like this to test my willpower."

Willpower? What the hell? He tried to read her expression, but she was too busy smoothing out wrinkles and straightening the piping alongside the buttons, just like a wife would.

She is *your wife*.

Feeling an odd sense of possessiveness, Kyle put his finger under her chin, forcing her to look at him.

Pure heat shone in her eyes, turning the soft gray the color of steel. He held her chin, uttering a gruff "Stay still" when she tried to jerk it away.

Celia went motionless and kept her eyes on his.

Interesting how well she responded to commands.

Kyle ran his thumb over her bottom lip. "Little wifey mine, you like what you see when you look at me, don't you?"

Again she tried to jerk out of his grip. Again he didn't allow it. "Stay. Still." Another teasing stroke across her lips. "Answer the question."

He expected her to lie. To utter a cutting comment. He didn't expect her to say, "Yes, you are gorgeous and built like a goddamn dream, Kyle, but you don't need me to tell you that."

A compliment? That threw him off.

"I'm sure all the bunnies lined up after an event always tell you the same thing," she added.

And there was the snark. But her sarcasm was covering up something else. Fear? Interest in getting naked with him? Regardless, Kyle wouldn't let her get away with it. He leaned close enough to feel her breath on his lips. "Makes me all tingly that you see me that way, kitten. Anytime you wanna do more than look? Alls you gotta do is ask." He smooched her nose and stepped back to tuck in his shirt. "Now back to the other question."

"Umm. What other question?"

He'd completely flustered her. Good. "Do you want to go to the lawyer's office with me?"

"I thought I would. Unless you don't want me to go."

"I want you to be there. I just didn't want to assume." He slipped on socks and his boots. He grabbed his coat and gloves off the chair. "Since my mother told the attorney we recently strapped on that ole ball and chain, we're gonna have to act like this marriage is real, okay?"

Celia studied him. "Just for today?"

Kyle said, "Yes," even though he wanted to say he wanted longer than just a damn day with her.

"Deal." Then she bestowed the sneaky smile that charmed the hell out of him. "But I do believe it's your husbandly duty to warm up the truck so I don't catch my death of cold." She batted her eyelashes.

He laughed. "Nice try. But I'll make you a deal. If you get overly chilled, I'll show you all the ways I can heat your body back up."

⤳

Kyle paced like a caged animal before they were called into the lawyer's office.

"Kyle?" A woman approached. "I'm Stacy, Bill's assistant. He's ready if you'd like to follow me."

He looked over at Celia. She took his hand and didn't let go until they were ushered into a good-size office lined with books.

A tall, thin man, probably in his early sixties, offered his hand across the enormous mahogany desk. "Kyle? Bill Ruttan."

Kyle made introductions. "This is my wife, Celia."

"Pleasure to meet both of you. Please have a seat."

They settled into comfortable leather chairs that sat a good foot lower than Bill's desk.

"I'll admit this case is out of the ordinary. I'm sure you have many questions, so let's start with the basics. Were you aware Marshall Townsend was your biological father?"

"No, sir. Not until my mother called me on Sunday."

"Did your mother tell you about the DNA test, confirming you are Marshall's son?"

Confused, because it was the first he'd heard of it, he said, "What DNA test? When did she...?"

"The timing of the test was fairly straightforward. Evidently you were in a serious motorcycle accident when you were almost eighteen?"

Celia muttered, "I'd forgotten about that."

Kyle remembered that after he woke up from surgery he'd asked the doctor if he'd be able to ride bulls again. The rest was a blur. "I was in a lot of pain. They kept me drugged up, and some nurse was always poking me for a blood sample or making me pee in a cup." He frowned. "That's when Marshall came forward and demanded a DNA test?"

"Only at your mother's urging. She wanted to ensure that you received the best medical care, so she contacted Marshall for financial help. He insisted on a paternity test first."

Kyle said nothing. But resentment flared. Why hadn't he known any of this? For all intents and purposes he'd been an adult. "Is that why there weren't any medical bills?"

The lawyer nodded. "I've been Marshall's attorney for twenty years, and he was quite shocked to discover he'd fathered a child. He and his wife, Inez, never were able to have children. At the time I encouraged Marshall to make contact with you. But he..." The lawyer sighed. "I'll be blunt, Kyle. Marshall Townsend was an odd duck. He did things his own way, in his own time frame. I don't know what he was waiting for, in regards to contacting you, especially after he changed his will."

"Changed it how?"

"He'd intended to leave everything to the State of Wyoming as a land trust. But four years ago he came in and named you his sole heir, his sole beneficiary. Because we already had the paternity test results on file, there were no legal issues as far as inheritance because you are his blood descendant, whether or not you knew it."

Kyle said, "My mom said Marshall left me everything. What does that mean?"

"That you are a very lucky man. I assumed you'd want a list of your current assets." He passed over a piece of paper.

Kyle's hand shook so hard he couldn't read the words. Celia threaded her fingers through his, grabbing the opposite edge to hold it steady.

Land: 7083 acres, detailed in the attached plat, in Laramie County, Wyoming

Dwelling: 1900 sq ft ranch house, and all contents

Outbuildings: 2000 sq ft barn, 3000 sq ft metal bldg, assorted outbuildings

Ranch equipment: detailed on separate page #4a section 1

Livestock: app 170 cow/calf pairs, 12 bulls, 4 horses

Mineral rights: all

Water rights: all

Optional state, federal grazing permits: subject to reapplication

Liquid assets: all bank accts

Bill handed him three other sheets of paper. "These are the most current bank statements. But keep in mind there will be medical expenses to be paid out of these accounts."

Kyle squinted at the number, then his eyes went wide.

"I'm sure this is overwhelming—"

"You're goddamn right it is. He left me all this"—he waved the first batch of papers—"and this?" He shook the bank statement. "This says there's half a million dollars cash in this account. Half a million. Five hundred thousand dollars and change in this account."

"Yes. And it's all yours."

He looked at Celia, utterly dumbfounded.

"It's okay." She squeezed his hand and repeated, "It'll be okay."

Once he'd collected himself, he glanced at Bill. "What's the catch? Change my last name to Townsend, or prove my ranching acumen for one year, or some other weird strings?"

Bill shook his head. "It's really simple. You inherited it. Everything on those lists is yours now."

This couldn't be happening. Since the first time he'd set foot on Lawson land at the tender age of eleven, Kyle had wanted a ranch of his own. He'd dreamt of it. Scrimped and saved the last five years to make that dream come true. And now? Everything he wanted—boom!—had just been handed to him?

While he sat there completely poleaxed, Bill began talking again. "As per Marshall's instructions, there won't be a funeral, a memorial service, or an obituary. He requested cremation and his remains will be inurned at the Wyoming military cemetery."

The lawyer continued. "There are two pieces of urgent business. The first being the livestock. Marshall's neighbor, Josh Jones, has been dealing with Marshall's livestock the last two months. Calving season is closing in and Josh doesn't have the manpower to handle additional birthing bovines. So you'll have to deal with that this week. Second, one of those bank accounts—"

"There's more than one?" Kyle blurted out.

"Yes. One is earmarked as back pay for child support. But there is a catch. Marshall was very clear on this point. It's up to you to determine whether your mother receives the money or if you keep it."

"How much we talkin'?"

"A little over one hundred thousand dollars. Which I believe is what financial experts claim it takes to raise a child to age eighteen."

"And she'd get it all?"

"Yes. Naturally she'd have to pay taxes on it."

"She deserves it. After all she's done for me, by herself." Even when he was mad as hell at her, he would never have denied her a windfall that she had more than earned. He took a deep breath. "I'll tell her. But not now."

"That's fine. I'll bring all the paperwork into the conference room and we can get everything changed over into your name."

Kyle nodded numbly. "Am I allowed to tell people he was my father and that's the reason for this sudden inheritance?"

"There's nothing in the language of the will that prevents that. I'd imagine since Marshall left it to you, he was expecting that you would reveal your relationship." Bill buzzed his assistant. "Will you escort Kyle and his wife into conference room B?"

As soon as the conference room door shut, Celia wreathed her arms around his waist and hugged him.

Kyle held on, letting her anchor him. Once he felt reasonably sure he wouldn't faint, he released her.

She fiddled with his collar before searching his eyes. "So, wow, huh?"

"Yeah. I'm havin' a hard time processing anything."

"I can imagine. Do you think it'll sink in when you actually see the place that you own it?"

"Probably not. But I'll admit I'm dying to see it."

"Me too."

"So you're comin' with me to Rawlins?"

"Of course. I'm your wife. All day, remember?" She grinned. "Plus I'm snoopy as hell."

Bill entered the conference room with a stack of papers. All of which seemed to require Kyle's signature. He hoped this lawyer wasn't some kind of shyster because he merely skimmed the legal jargon. It took an hour to get everything wrapped up so they could leave, but Bill warned he'd have more things to deal with once they were through these initial steps.

The biting cold outside snapped Kyle back to reality. He held Celia's door open and contemplated his next move as he walked around to the driver's side.

They'd made it about a mile when Celia said, "I heard your stomach growl, Kyle. You need to eat something."

"We need to check out of the hotel too."

"What about your mother? Weren't you supposed to call her?"

He stared at the red stoplight without answering.

"Kyle?"

"I'll call her and make up a white lie about the lawyer needing me to inspect the property or something, but I can't deal with her today." He looked at Celia. "I know that sounds awful. Ungrateful."

"I think it's better to wait. Time to think things through is rarely a bad thing. It lessens the chance you'll say something to hurt her that you'll regret."

His mind was spinning. Neither of them said much of anything until after they'd eaten a quick lunch at the Flying J truck stop and were back on the road heading up the overpass on I-80.

"Do you want me to drive? You were up late last night."

"I'll let you know if I get tired."

Kyle expected Celia would pepper him with questions, but she was oddly subdued.

He'd made this drive a thousand times, but today it seemed longer than usual. Outside Rawlins they filled up the gas tank, grabbed a few grocery items, and put the coordinates into the GPS. Kyle was pretty sure he remembered how to get there, but it'd been fourteen years and the last thing they needed was to drive around Wyoming back roads in subzero weather.

"I sure hope Marshall left the heat on in his house before he went to the hospital. It'd really suck if you had to face frozen pipes."

He gave Celia a droll look. "Thanks for that."

Kyle turned off the main highway onto a gravel road. It'd been plowed at least once this winter, and that was saying something in Wyoming. The next turnoff was in three miles. He tried to remember what the house looked like, but drew a blank.

In the last twenty-four hours he'd gone back over the conversations he'd had with Marshall that summer. Nothing memorable came to mind. Marshall had to have known he was his son, since it was the year after his motorcycle accident.

The last time he'd run across the man who'd fathered him was at a bar in Rawlins a few years back. Marshall had been drunker than hell and he'd cornered Kyle, babbling about . . . the mark of good stock. He hadn't known what that meant then and it seemed ridiculous to start assigning meaning to it four years later.

Wait. Hadn't the lawyer said Marshall changed the will four years ago?

What were the odds one random conversation in a bar caused Marshall to rethink his will and sign over everything to a son he refused to publicly acknowledge?

"Whatcha thinkin' about so hard?"

"How weird it is to be driving to a place I don't know. A place my father lived most of his life. How bizarre it is to say *my father* in any kind of context at all."

"What would you have said to him if he were alive?"

"No idea."

Chapter Three

$\mathcal{T}$he driveway seemed to go on forever.

They passed a turnoff that led to another ranch, which meant Kyle would have fairly close neighbors.

Celia squinted through the windshield when they crested a small hill and finally came upon the house.

It looked a lot like the house she'd grown up in. A low-slung standard ranch with an attached garage on the left side and a cement slab for a front porch. The house wasn't in horrible shape, but it needed work.

To the left were two smallish structures. One that might've been a chicken coop. Off to the right were two buildings, a barn that matched the age of the house, and a newer metal building. There were no cattle in the pasture or around the stock tank. Snow was piled nearly to the middle of the barbed wire fence that disappeared down the gently sloping hill. She could see a windmill in the distance, which was odd given that the water table in this part of the country was so deep. Was it decorative? But maybe there was a stream nearby. Easy access to water could make or break a ranch.

"Well? What do you think?" Kyle asked after he'd parked by a split rail fence covered in tumbleweeds.

"Let's check out the inside." Celia studied the sagging roofline just a beat too long. When she went to open her door, Kyle was already there, helping her down.

"Careful of those ribs," he murmured. "I've been so self-involved I haven't asked you how they're feeling today."

Sore. "Fine. You don't need to coddle me."

"Maybe I like coddling you."

She tried to catch his gaze but it was already on the house, his anxiety apparent. He held her hand as they skirted snow piles.

Kyle said, "Stay here," and snagged a shovel from beside the front door. He chiseled and scooped until he'd created a walkable path. Then he took her hand and led her up the steps. He inserted the key in the door.

The waft of air from the house was decidedly musty. Celia's first thought was that all houses inhabited by older folks always smelled the same.

The front door opened into the living room. There wasn't much in the way of furniture. An old-fashioned high-backed couch in a hideous plaid pattern and a reclining chair patched with duct tape. Two TV trays flanked the easy chair; one held a remote control and a copy of *TV Guide.* The other had a box of tissues, a glass of water, a coffee mug, and several pill bottles. On the left and right sides of the couch were open built-in shelves, loaded with magazines, knickknacks, shotgun shells, and small hand tools. Both the couch and the chair faced an outdated square-box television. The oatmeal-colored carpet was badly stained. A dirty path led from the front door around the edge of the wall.

Kyle crossed to the first doorway.

Celia followed and peered around his arm. The galley-style kitchen filled the entire length and ended in a large eat-in nook. "I like that."

"Probably be all right once this shit is cleared out." Stuff was heaped on the kitchen counters so she could scarcely tell what color they were. The stove and oven combo was a burnt orangish red, the dishwasher was avocado green, and the refrigerator, which looked fairly new, was white. The double-sided enamel sink was piled to the windowsill with dirty dishes and smelled to high heaven.

"That's disgusting," Kyle said.

"He was a widower. He probably only did dishes when he ran out of clean ones. Maybe when he went to the hospital he expected to be coming back that same day."

Kyle gave her a soft look and kissed the top of her head. "Thanks."

This unsure, sweet Kyle was throwing her for a loop. She headed through the next doorway at the far end of the living room.

Not a traditional hallway at all, but more of a large square, with each door inset and then offset at an angle, which made the area seem spacious. She counted six doors and opened the first one on the left. A smallish bedroom. Packed with crap. The second door opened into a full-size bathroom, done completely in pink and black tile straight from the 1950s. Pink toilet, pink sink, and a pink bathtub.

"Jesus Christ," Kyle said.

"I think it's awesome. Very retro."

"It's awesome if you're a girl who fuckin' loves pink. That is *so* not a dude's bathroom."

"It looks plenty dirty enough to be a guy's bathroom to me."

Kyle laughed.

The third door was to a closet, also piled with junk.

The fourth door led to another bedroom, larger than the first, with a desk, a computer, and lots of boxes.

The master bedroom was behind the fifth door, a surprisingly large space, big enough to hold a king-size bed with room for dressers and a small sitting area. Celia spied another door inside the room and found another bathroom. No bathtub but a decent-size tiled shower, a vanity, and a toilet. She withheld her snicker until Kyle popped his head in. "Seriously? Another goddamn pink bathroom?"

"But this one is pink and turquoise, not pink and black."

"Who the hell ever thought that'd be a good combination?"

"Mrs. Townsend, evidently."

The last door opened to the basement. Nothing had been done to this part of the house besides designating a laundry area. Given what they'd found in the rest of the house, she'd expected the space to be chock-full of stuff, but it was disturbingly barren.

"Kinda spooky down here," Kyle said. "Let's go back up."

Once they were upstairs, Kyle inspected the living room, specifically the temperature controllers. "It's not ice-cold in here, but it's not warm.

And I don't know why one of these reads sixty degrees and the other reads zero."

"Maybe one's a heater control and the other is an air conditioner control?"

"Good thinking, but no. There's another source of heat. Maybe a main source. Maybe geothermal or something." He muttered and poked around.

Celia wandered to the kitchen, took in the huge mess, and shuddered. "Are we staying here tonight or driving back into Rawlins?"

"I planned on staying. But I'd understand if you . . ."

"If you're staying, I'm staying. We'll need to eat. In order to eat, I'll need to fumigate this kitchen. But there's so much stuff stacked everywhere. What do you want to do with it?"

Kyle stared at her for a moment. "No freakin' clue. I'm all ears if you've got an idea."

"We should sort through it, I guess. Make a pile of things to save and one to toss. I'll tackle what I can of the kitchen, if that's all right."

"I feel so guilty for making you help me with this at all, but I honestly don't know what I'd do if you weren't here."

Her heart seemed to skip a beat at his admission. It skipped another ten beats when Kyle moved closer.

"Is this house more or less than you thought it'd be?" he asked.

His eyes were so serious, and that air of vulnerability surrounded him. "It needs a little work, Kyle. Okay, a lot of work. But the space has quirky charm. On the outside it looks like the standard boring ranch house, but inside, there are a few qualities that make it unique. This is your home now. You need to put your personal stamp on it." Celia whispered, "Besides, admit it. You've always secretly wanted two pink bathrooms."

Kyle growled and pulled on her braid to tilt her head back. "Such a smart mouth."

"Like that's a surprise to you."

"No, but this might be to you." Kyle crushed his mouth to hers, sweeping his tongue across the seam of her lips, diving in for a hot, wet kiss.

Her head protested for about a nanosecond and then she clung to him, mouth, hands, body, as he took the kiss deeper with every breath. With every stroke of his agile tongue.

The kiss might've gone on for hours, days even, if not for the loud knocking that wasn't from her knees.

"Hello? Is anyone here?" echoed from the living room.

They froze and broke apart. But Kyle never looked away from her. He uttered a thickly whispered, "This heat between us ain't going away," before releasing her.

Holy crap. Celia's entire body was on fire. From one kiss. She held her hands to her face as Kyle disappeared around the corner. She closed her eyes and found her composure before she followed him.

Kyle was shaking hands with a big guy, probably around thirty-five, who had the mannerisms and carriage she automatically associated with ranchers.

"Come meet our new neighbor, Josh Jones. He lives in the place we passed down the road. Josh, this is my wife, Celia."

She shot Kyle a reprimanding look when he introduced her as his wife. Had she somehow known that her agreement to the moniker *wife* would last longer than a single day?

Josh took her hand. "Nice to meetcha, Celia."

They exchanged banal observations on the weather.

Finally Josh said, "I gotta admit, I'm a little confused on your relationship to Marshall."

"Marshall Townsend was my father, a fact I just found out on Sunday."

Josh looked stunned. "You're kidding me."

"No, sir." Kyle gave him a brief explanation. "So it's been a whirlwind couple of days for us. None of this has really sunk in. We were trying to get our yearly circuit schedules set, and now it looks like we'll be doin' something else entirely. Or at least I will."

"Circuit schedules?" Josh asked.

"I'm a bull rider on the CRA circuit and Celia is a barrel racer."

"No kiddin'? That's gotta be an interesting life. I'm assuming you both have ranching experience?"

"I have some, helping out my ranching friends whenever needed. But

Celia here, she's the real deal. She helped run her family ranch from the time she was eleven up until four years ago when she started barrel racing professionally."

That sounded a lot like pride in Kyle's voice, which shocked the hell out of her.

"Yeah? Whereabouts was that?" Josh asked.

"Muddy Gap. My brothers are Abe and Hank Lawson."

"I've dealt with Abe over the years. How long have you two been married?"

Kyle smirked at her. "What day is it? Tuesday? We've been married since Saturday night."

Another stunned look from Josh. "You weren't just a-woofin' about it bein' a whirlwind couple of days. Hell, the ink ain't even dry on that marriage license."

"We were in Vegas. Decided to get hitched. Poor Celia thought she was marryin' a bull rider and finds herself stuck with a newbie rancher husband instead. I wouldn't blame her if she runs for the hills."

Josh laughed.

So, Kyle was giving her an out. And a way for him to save face when she did bail. She had the perverse need to poke him back. "You might have to kick me out. I'm made of tougher stuff than that, darlin'."

He gave her an arch look. "Guess we'll see, won't we?"

"I did have a valid reason for showing up here besides to satisfy my curiosity. You do plan on taking Marshall's cattle off my hands? Soon? I've been dealing with them since before Thanksgiving, when Marshall went into the hospital. I was happy to do it, because this is the easy time in the cattle business. But I don't have the manpower to deal with his calving and mine. Especially since my wife is eight months pregnant with our first kid and I can't count on her help right now either."

Kyle seemed at a loss, so Celia jumped in. "Congrats on the impending bundle of joy. It's gonna wear on you, though, especially this time of year."

Josh grinned. "That's the problem with them late-spring storms. End up with a blizzard baby. Anyway, I know you guys are pretty much flying blind here, and I'll help you as much as I can now that I know you're sticking around. I thought we could get the cattle sorted first thing tomorrow morning and go from there."

"Are Marshall's horses decent with cattle? Or are they used for something else?"

"Two of 'em are pretty good cow horses."

"I'd prefer to use my own, but mine are boarded at my buddy's place and I don't have so much as a saddle with me. You got tack for us? Or can you direct us to where Marshall kept his?" Celia asked.

"You can use my wife's tack since she isn't riding and I can rustle up something for you, Kyle, if you need it."

"I'd appreciate it."

"Good enough. Let's say seven o'clock?"

"Works for me," Kyle said. "I have a couple questions about this house if you have time. What's the primary source of heat?"

Josh laughed. "Stumped ya, did it? It's wood fired, but the wood burner is outside, and it generates the heat to fire up the radiators. Kind of an unusual thing. But it's basically free to heat your house as long as you've got a store of firewood and the time to keep it fed. Marshall has a backup of electric heat, which was a good thing this time around. Come on. I'll show you where it is."

As soon as they left, Celia returned to the kitchen, moving everything off the counters to get to the dishes. Didn't appear the dishwasher had been used recently, so she washed by hand. Once that was finished, she cleaned out the fridge, dumping the freezer contents except the frozen dinners. Marshall had enough canned food to last the entire winter.

She scrubbed the stove. Cleaned the microwave. Checked under the sink, in the cupboards and drawers for signs of rodents. An unoccupied house was an open invitation to critters. Luckily no signs of mice or squirrel infestation.

She glanced at the time on her cell phone and was shocked to see that an hour and a half had passed since she'd last seen Kyle.

Had he fallen outside? Gotten lost? Panicked, she skirted the boxes and headed toward the front door just as Kyle stumbled into the house and slumped against the wall. "Are you okay?" When he didn't move, she unbuttoned his coat and pulled off his hat.

His face was red, his breathing labored. He croaked, "Water." She raced to the kitchen to fill a glass, brought it back, and he drained it in three fast gulps.

When he seemed settled, Celia asked, "Where were you?"

"Chopping wood. Holy shit, am I out of shape for that kind of physical activity. Josh helped me get the wood burner going, told me how much wood is needed every day. There was none chopped so I split wood until..."

"Until you're ready to pass out." She tugged him to the couch. "You want another drink?"

"Sure."

She handed him the glass when she returned from the kitchen and said, "What's that smirk for?"

"If I tell you thanks for fetching me a glass of water you likely will toss it right in my face."

"Use of the word *fetch* anytime around me might get a bucket of water dumped over your head."

"So noted." He cocked his head. "You make a good wife."

Celia retorted, "Damn straight," like she'd accepted the fact they were husband and wife.

Whoa. When had that happened? What did that say about her?

That you're helping Kyle because you want to. It also means that Kyle was right; part of you wanted to marry him.

Not that she could tell him that, even if the tiniest part of her had started to believe it.

Kyle said, "Appears you made progress on the kitchen."

"You can actually see the countertops."

He stood. "I'll come look because this couch smells like ass."

Celia spread her arms wide. "Ta-da."

"Hey, this space ain't half bad."

"If we get the breakfast nook cleaned out we'll have a place to sit that doesn't stink. But there's no place to put those boxes until *these* boxes are moved."

"Is that your way of tellin' me to get busy hauling stuff to the basement?"

"To be honest, I think most of this is junk. Let's sort through it now and save two trips up and down the stairs."

In seven boxes they found only a handful of useful items. Same situation with the piles in the breakfast nook. While Kyle stacked the trash outside, Celia scrubbed the walls, raised the blinds, and scoured the table and chairs.

Supper wasn't fancy, just soup and toast, but they both ate like they'd never seen food before.

"So what happens tomorrow?" Kyle asked. "And feel free to explain it slowly so this greenhorn can understand."

Celia pushed her bowl aside. "Our cattle are mixed in with Josh's cattle. We'll look at the brand and cull our cows from his herd. I've got experience sorting. I'd prefer to have my own horse, because a good horse can make all the difference. I'll cut the cow out and send her your way. Your job will be to keep the separated ones penned, while getting the new ones I'm moving toward you into the pen."

"Will I be on the ground or on a horse?"

"I imagine Josh will be on horseback too, so it might be easiest for the first part if you were on the ground. You'll need a riding crop to smack the wayward ones back in line."

Kyle stared into his soup bowl.

"Something wrong?"

"Just a lot to think about. Especially for someone like me who's spent the last decade only thinking about my job eight seconds at a time. I hope this dream of owning my own ranch don't become a nightmare." He stood and grabbed her bowl, quickly washing both and setting them on the drying rack. "I'll check the woodstove again and bring in our stuff from the truck."

Next thing she knew Kyle had dumped everything in the master bedroom.

"I take it we're sharing this room."

"No place in the other bedrooms to sleep and I didn't figure you'd wanna bunk on that smelly-ass couch." Kyle held up his hand. "Spare me the rules for us sharin' this bed tonight. I'm whupped. All I wanna do is watch a little TV before I crash."

She noticed he'd brought the TV from the living room and set it on the dresser. "You're welcome to my sleeping bag. I'm good with the blankets I got from the hall closet."

Worry lines etched his forehead and his mouth. Dark circles hung under his eyes. The man was exhausted.

"Set the alarm on your cell phone too so I don't sleep through my first day as a rancher."

Kyle fiddled with the TV until the satellite dish worked. He found pillows and spread them across the bed. He stripped to his birthday suit and crawled into his nest.

From his comments, Celia knew he was struggling with what'd happened today, but she also knew not to expect him to confide in her any further.

Kyle didn't give her a second glance when she wandered in, in her pajamas, unlike last night in the motel room when his hungry eyes had burned away every stitch of her clothing. God. Had that only been last night? So much had happened in such a short amount of time. She slipped into the sleeping bag, twisting to try to get comfy, but she felt like a sausage about to burst her skin.

"Are you always this damn wiggly?"

"I've never gotten used to sleeping bags."

"We can swap, if you'd rather."

Celia blew out a frustrated breath. "No. I'm fine."

"You don't sound fine."

"Neither do you. But I'm betting it's a big fat zero on you spilling your guts to me."

"What would you do, Cele, if I shared every one of my fears about all the shit that went down today?"

"I'd listen."

He snorted and flipped the channel.

"What?"

"You're not any better at sharing this stuff than I am."

His observation surprised her. "I am so better at sharing than you."

"Prove it."

"Fine. Ask me anything."

Kyle shook his head. "It don't work that way. You have to tell me something. Something that's completely new that I did not know about you."

Celia was sure this discussion had a point because Kyle had the sneakiest way of gathering information without her realizing his intent until it was too late. But her pride made it impossible to back down from his challenge, even when she suspected that challenge was rigged. "I was hesitant about committing to travel the circuits with you not because it was you ... but because I wasn't sure I wanted to barrel race at all anymore."

He lifted one eyebrow. "No kiddin'? What would you do instead?"

"I'm thinking about going to vocational school—if I can get a loan. I figure if Abe can get a four-year college degree while runnin' a ranch, I might be able to stand school for two years and wind up with a useful skill besides racing around barrels."

"What would you go to school for?"

"Veterinary assistant. Before Tanna started barrel racing professionally, she went to school for a year in Texas in the same type of program and she said it wasn't that hard. I've always been around livestock, so I'm good working with animals." Part of her expected he'd sneer at her, because that's what the old Kyle would've done. But he looked interested.

"How serious are you? Like checking on start dates and tuition?"

"Yeah. The next semester starts next fall. The tuition ... let's just say even a couple of big event wins won't put a dent in the cost of higher education."

"No one in your family knows about your secret dream to professionally preg-test cows?"

Celia laughed. "Fletch does. He promised me a job if I ever actually followed through and attended school."

"So working as a vet assistant is your dream job?"

"I didn't say that."

Kyle frowned. "Then if you could do anything you wanted and money wasn't an issue, what would you do?"

"Run my own ranch."

He went completely still.

"What?"

"Nothin'." He reached for his beer and swigged. "Get some rest. Been a long day and it'll be more of the same tomorrow."

"And the day after that," she muttered into her pillow.

"What did you say?"

"Ranching is a tough gig. A never-ending, backbreaking round of work."

"Is that why you decided to barrel race?"

Did he believe she was lazy? "No. I never minded the work. I'm not working on the Lawson ranch because after about a year on the circuit there was no place for me there anymore."

"Shit, Celia. Sometimes I'm such an ass. I'm sorry. I didn't mean—"

"Forget it. Good night, Kyle."

Giving him the cold shoulder, she closed her eyes. But she couldn't escape him. Not even in sleep.

She dreamt of him. Intimate snippets. An image of clothes flying. An image of hot skin and hotter kisses. Those intense green eyes staring into hers as his body rose over hers.

She woke with a soft gasp and glanced at Kyle, lost in sleep. Maybe the dream she'd just had wasn't a dream but a fleeting impression of their wedding night. His bare shoulder peeked out from beneath the blanket and she wanted to put her mouth on that smooth section of skin and taste him. Just to see if that kicked any memories.

But he looked so peaceful. She rolled over and went back to sleep.

Chapter Four

*K*yle was seriously fucked with this ranching business.

Seriously fucked and in a panic because he had no clue what he was doing.

Helping out his buddies once in a while didn't come close to understanding what it took to run a ranch on a day-to-day basis.

He and Celia had gotten up at the crack of dawn and knocked back a pot of coffee in near silence. Then they'd tracked down outerwear—coveralls, coats, gloves, hats—and trudged to the stock tank, which was completely frozen. Celia checked the outer metal rim and found a box with two switches. She flipped the top one and a hissing started. "I'll be damned. Marshall set this up to heat the tank with the same woodstove that heats the house."

Kyle wondered how long it would've taken him to figure that out on his own.

Then they headed down the hill to Josh's place.

Josh was outside, pulling tack out of a horse trailer. Four horses stared over the fence in what looked like anticipation.

Celia shouted, "Morning, Josh."

He turned around. "That it is. Nice balmy six degrees, ain't it?"

"Better than six below." Celia pointed to the horses. "So, which one of those beauties is mine?"

"Bugsy. She's the roan on the far left. She's a little feisty, but I reckon you'll handle her. I figured Kyle could have Marshall's horse, Capone. Wasn't sure how much experience you had with horses, Kyle."

"Been on them and around them most my life, but I've never owned one."

"Now you own four of 'em. So how you wanna do this?"

Kyle wasn't the least bit upset that Josh was addressing Celia.

"We talked about it last night. I have experience sorting, so he'll handle the penning. Then we're hoping you can direct us through the right gates so we can get them into our closest pasture."

"No problem. I don't mind helping you guys out, but I'm gonna suggest you study the paperwork that gives the outlay of which property is yours. I know where the land boundaries are on my end that borders yours, but I'm not sure on the other side."

Celia picked up a halter and walked to the corral. Kyle studied the way she approached the horse, talking to it, offering reassuring pats. When the horse shied away, she didn't chase it, merely waited for it to come back. As soon as Bugsy got close enough, Celia slipped the halter on and led her through the gate.

Kyle grabbed a halter. His horse, Capone, didn't move at all; he just stood there and allowed Kyle to slip the halter on. No problem saddling him either, for which Kyle was grateful.

After they were through the gate, Josh handed Kyle a riding crop. "This'll put some of them unruly cows back in their place."

"Or maybe it won't. I swear some of them act up just because they like to feel the sting of the crop." Celia shot him a smirk.

Kyle reined closer to her. "Speaking from personal experience, kitten?"

She laughed. "Wouldn't you like to know?" and kicked her stirrups, galloping away from him.

Oh, little wife of mine, I fully intend to find out when you stop running from me and accept this.

The herd wasn't too far away from Josh's place. But the cows became agitated quickly when three riders started driving them away from their feed. The sluggish animals moved at a snail's pace in the frigid air. When a couple of alpha cows finally took off at a brisk trot, the whole herd followed. Except for a half dozen cows that decided to break away, prompting Celia to chase them down.

Kyle had watched Celia racing around barrels for the last four years. Her style on the dirt was balls-to-the-wall. Not a particularly pretty riding style, but efficient. Whereas out here, in the middle of a herd? Celia was utter poetry. Complete perfection as she showcased the skills that were second nature to her. He would guess she wasn't aware of the power and grace in her movements. Of how regal and right she looked on a horse, cutting through cattle, pushing forward, reining in on a dime. She was born to do this. And the exhilaration on her face told him exactly how much she'd missed it.

That was when he knew he'd fallen hard for her and realized he would do everything he could to make this marriage real. And he knew exactly how to make sure she felt the same. He would give her back a part of herself that'd been missing for the past four years and the ranch of her own that she'd dreamt of.

Besides, even after half a day in the saddle herding cattle, he knew he'd never make it as a cattleman if he didn't have her by his side. And wouldn't that be the best life? Running this ranch together—as husband and wife?

"Kyle, quit goddamn daydreamin' and pay attention!" his lovely bride yelled at him.

He grinned and saluted.

Once they reached the first gate between fences, Kyle dismounted and tied off his horse. Since he'd never sorted cows except during branding, he'd suspected Celia had given him the hardest job. But his job was a piece of cake compared to hers. She had to check the brand on every cow and separate it from the herd, which for animals with a herd mentality was easier said than done. Cows liked to be clumped together, especially when the temperature dipped into single digits.

After a few false starts, Celia pushed the first cow toward him and it trotted into the pen. She shouted, "Look at the marking on the right hip, and make sure the ones goin' through have our brand."

"Will do." He liked that she'd referred to it as *our* brand.

The noise increased the longer they were in the midst of the herd. Celia cut one cow to him with the wrong brand and he almost let it pass. He had to grab the tail to get the cow's attention and it spun so fast it knocked Kyle in the muck. He swatted it with the riding crop and could have sworn he heard Celia laughing at him.

Finally Celia yelled, "I think we've got 'em all. Kyle, do a count."

Count the cows. Right. At least they weren't moving much. He stood on the middle of the fence and counted. Twice. He yelled back at Celia. "One sixty-seven."

"Josh? Is that right?"

"Should be two more of yours. Started out with a hundred seventy but I lost one a few weeks back."

So Celia sliced through the herd, found the last two, and sent them his way. Then Celia and Josh rode over. Celia's face was damp, her cheeks were rosy, and her lips . . . her poor lips looked chapped and windburned.

Maybe you oughta volunteer to kiss them better.

She noticed his smirk but didn't comment.

Josh leaned on his saddle horn. "That only took three hours."

"Only?" Kyle said.

"With a less-experienced sorter it might've taken all damn day. You guys are a good team."

Celia shot Kyle a questioning look and then glanced away.

"Now on to the next fun thing. If you guys are all right with it, I'll ride ahead and open gates."

"That works," Celia said, and deferred to Kyle, almost as an after-thought. "Don't you agree, Kyle?"

"You guys are the experts."

"About how far do we need to drive them?"

"Around three miles. Some of the places between here and there have big snowdrifts, so we'll be takin' the long way."

"You sure this is easier than loading them in a cattle truck and dumping them out right by the stock tank?"

Josh scratched his chin. "I considered that. But the closest place you can get a cattle truck is two miles from here, so we might as well just push them all the way."

"Sounds good." Celia grinned at him. "Kyle, darlin', mount up."

Kyle squeezed her thigh as he passed her. "I've been waiting to hear you say that."

Took another four hours to drive the cattle to the pasture by the house. Kyle had to watch, feeling totally worthless, as Celia started up the tractor and loaded a round bale of hay into the bucket. Josh sliced the netting. Celia smoothed out the roll with the back of the bucket and Josh used a pitchfork to spread the hay for the cattle.

They were quiet on the horseback ride to Josh's place. Kyle was especially mired in his feelings of ineptitude and inadequacy. This was the slowest part of the season in the cattle business. What would he do when it got busy? How would he know what to do?

The last vestiges of daylight disappeared as they finished brushing down the horses and putting everything away. He and Celia were about to leave when Josh's front door opened and a parka-clad woman waddled out. Immediately Josh was by her side, holding her arm to keep her from falling on the ice.

She dropped the hood and smiled at Kyle, then at Celia. "I'm Ronna, Josh's wife. And I couldn't believe it when Josh told me Celia Lawson had moved in next door." Ronna squinted at Celia. "I don't know if you remember me. Ronna Menke? I graduated a year ahead of you?"

"Yes, I remember you, Ronna. We had geometry together."

"That's right. You were so quiet. I don't know if I ever heard you speak up in class."

Celia shifted closer to Kyle. "Math wasn't my best subject."

"So Josh tells me you're newlyweds."

"Guilty. Is it that obvious we're wildly in love?" she cooed, looking up at Kyle, practically batting her eyelashes.

Wildly in love? What the fuck?

"Yes, and I'm happy to see it. You were always so shy."

Again, what the fuck? Celia? Shy? Since when?

"Hitting the rodeo circuit cured me of shyness. Good thing, huh?" Celia hip-checked Kyle. "Or I never would've roped me a hot bull rider."

Kyle wondered if she'd hidden a flask in her boot and had been drinking today. Celia calling him hot? In front of people? He decided to go with it and hooked an arm around her shoulder. "Well, she never lacked for hot cowboys chasin' after her on the circuit. I had to bide my time, swoop in and sweep her off her boots when she least expected it."

Ronna sighed. "So romantic. You are planning on sticking around? Not going to sell? Because the place is worth a lot of money."

Josh flipped Ronna's hood over her head. "Forgive my nosy wife. She's overwhelmed with pregnancy hormones and says the first thing that pops into her head."

"I'm ready to have this baby now," Ronna said, flipping the hood back down. "If Josh will let me out of the house, I'll bake a loaf of pumpkin bread and bring it up."

"That would be much appreciated." Kyle thrust out his hand. "Thanks so much for everything today, Josh. Hopefully you won't regret having us as neighbors with all the questions that'll be coming your way."

"Happy to help."

When Kyle opened Celia's door to help her into the truck, he saw her wince as her back met the seat. Her ribs were probably killing her. Just like her not to mention it.

Neither spoke until they parked in front of the house. "Anything else I need to do with the cattle tonight?" he asked her.

"Make sure the water isn't frozen. If it is, you'll have to break off the crust."

"Okay. I'll load up the woodstove, check that, and then I'll be in to make sure you didn't get cow shit in them stitches today."

"I'm fine. I can help you."

"No."

"Kyle—"

"I know your ribs are killing you, Cele. You shouldn't have been on horseback today. So go inside and take it easy."

"I don't take orders from you."

Kyle got right in her face. "In this case, yes, you do. You're hurt. Now, you either get your ass in the house or I carry you in. Your choice."

That's when the tough girl mask dropped and Kyle saw the pain in her eyes. "Okay."

He almost carried her in anyway.

During the hour it took him to finish chores, Kyle's insecurities about his ability to run a ranch resurfaced, stronger than ever.

You two make a good team.

Yes, they did. He just needed to convince Celia of that fact.

The warmth of the house soothed him. He heard the shower running and smelled something cooking. Grabbing a beer, he stared out the living room picture window, waiting for her.

The sweet scent of her shampoo drifted toward him and his cock pressed against his zipper. Addressing the issues with a hard-on wasn't how he wanted to approach this, but he sure wasn't going to hide how she affected him. Because that was part of this too. He'd never experienced such a burning need for a woman. Not just from lust. He'd been in lust plenty of times in his life. But this? This was different. He'd fallen in love with her before he'd even touched her. Wasn't that a kick in the pants?

Her footsteps stopped behind him and he faced her. She wore her flannel pajama bottoms and an AFR sweatshirt. "How are you feeling?"

"Sore. The ribs didn't bother me while we were workin' cattle, but I definitely noticed them the second we stopped."

"Did you take a pain pill?"

"No. Last time I took pain pills I ended up married to you."

Kyle waited for her to say it was a mistake, or something flip, but she just stared at him with those big, beautiful gray eyes. "Celia, we need to talk."

She nodded.

"Will you be okay sitting on the chairs in the kitchen?"

"Better there than that stanky-ass couch."

Kyle brought them both a beer. They sat across from each other, not really looking at each another. Celia broke the silence first. "I had a voice mail from the secretary at the Big Bend rodeo asking whether I'm competing this weekend."

"What did you say?"

"I haven't called her back." She sipped her beer. "I also had a voice mail from Hank. Bringing me up to date on the diagnosis for Brianna's eye, which is good, by the way."

"Remind me again what is wrong with it?"

"Something with her tear duct. Since birth she's constantly had eye infections to the point that her eye gets matted shut. Now that she's old enough they can do a quick surgery that will unplug the blockage." She shuddered. "I can't imagine watching them stick a metal wire in my baby's eye. I'd go ballistic. No matter how many times they say it isn't painful for the kid."

"I wouldn't be able to watch either," Kyle admitted.

"Abe left a message about their dog, George, who is a holy terror, and said he reminded him of my dog Murray when he was a pup. The last voice message was from Harper. She had a feeling something was 'up' with me and was checking to see if I was okay."

"We have to talk to your brothers tomorrow, Cele."

"I know."

"You have any idea what you want to tell them?"

She shook her head. "I keep hoping Lainie slipped up and already told Hank. He'd tell Abe and I'd just have to do damage control and we could go from there."

"That answer makes me feel better."

"How so?"

"It's better than you sayin' you plan on denying everything that's gone on between us and chalking it up to one drunken night."

"I don't think I can do that, because it would be a lie." She looked at him almost shyly.

Kyle reached for her hand. "I have an idea. Hear me out before you interrupt me."

"I don't interrupt you."

He raised a brow and she hid her smile behind her beer bottle. "I know you want this marriage annulled. Maybe I was poking your buttons a little just to be contrary when I said I didn't want an annulment." *Such a lie, Kyle.* "But everything changed after that phone call from my mom."

Celia silently picked the label off her beer bottle.

"You know everything about ranching and I know nothing. Less than nothing. I felt like a fucking idiot today. And you? You were absolutely in your element. Don't deny it."

"I'm not."

Kyle gathered his courage to get the next part out, and hoped like hell she didn't reject his suggestion. Reject him. "The truth is, I need you. Your ranching expertise. I need you to teach me. I need you to help me. I cannot do this by myself. I don't *want* to do this by myself. And I'd be willing to offer you a deal. Stay and help me for the next six months. After that, if you still want an annulment or divorce or whatever it is at that point, we can call it quits. You mentioned going to trade school—I'll pay for everything starting with the fall semester."

Celia's jaw dropped. "Are you serious?"

"Completely. Because if you don't stay and help me, I'll have no choice but to sell this place."

"You could always hire a ranch hand," Celia pointed out.

"I remember what Bran went through with that. He had no takers. Harper was a last resort. Although neither of them are complaining now."

"True."

Kyle sensed her withdrawal, so he laid it on the line. "You haven't been happy on the circuit the last year. And it had nothin' to do with your relationship with Breck goin' south. You've been struggling for a while. I suspect everything you own is in your horse trailer. You rarely go home to Muddy Gap, a place you've always loved. You don't spend time with your family. I want to know why."

Celia kept her gaze locked on his. "I stayed on the road because I didn't have anywhere else to go."

Happy that she'd given him the truth, Kyle brought her fingertips to his lips for a kiss. "I've felt the same way. Havin' a P.O. box in Rawlins as my home base. Crashing with my mom a couple times a year. Sleeping in my camper or a cheap motel."

"So you do understand."

"Yes. I've been working so fucking hard to make money so I could buy a place of my own and quit the CRA. Now that I've got what I always wanted? I don't know what the hell to do with it."

Celia laughed softly.

"So say you'll help me. Please, Celia. Stay. I need you."

She tugged her hand away from his and drained her beer. "Give me some time to think about it."

"Now?"

"Yeah."

Celia wandered to the living room and he followed her. He leaned against the doorjamb and watched her, a little disconcerted by her abrupt need for space. She pulled on her outerwear and slipped outside without a word or a backward glance.

Then Kyle returned to the kitchen, beating a path in the cracked linoleum from the window to the doorway, watching for her return. Half worried that she would come inside, pack her paltry belongings, and leave for the rodeo in Big Bend.

An hour later the front door slammed. He waited in the kitchen, trying not to look nervous and desperate. Although he was both and she probably knew it.

He glanced up to see her leaning against the counter opposite him, mimicking his stance. "I've thought about it."

"And?"

"And I'll stay for six months. That's it. Then we will have this marriage dissolved. In exchange for my ranching help during that time, I'll take your offer of payment of full tuition for the entire course. Not just the first year. But I have a couple of other conditions."

"I figured you would."

Celia squared her shoulders. "First, you need to trust me with the ranch work. We tend to argue a lot, Kyle, but I need your word that you'll really listen to me. You'll understand that in this, I know what I'm doing."

"That won't be a problem, trust me."

"Good. If we're staying together as a couple, then I want everyone to believe we got married on the spur of the moment because we were wildly in love."

Another problem solved, being he was already wildly in love with her. "Why?"

She looked away again. "I've never been the girl the guys pant after. Listening to Ronna today reminded me how shy I've always been. I never even had a date in high school. With the exception of Harper, I spent more time with my horses than with my classmates. I've come out of my shell the last few years, but that shell is always there, waiting for me to crawl back into it. I couldn't stand for my family or my friends to know the only way a guy like you married a woman like me was because we were drunk."

"Hey." Kyle curled his hands around her face. "Don't say shit like that. You are a beautiful woman, Cele."

"You don't have to say that," she protested.

"I wouldn't say it if it wasn't true." His thumbs stroked her cheekbones before he let his hands fall because he sensed her pulling away.

"So I told you my fear about people finding out the truth about our marriage. What's yours?"

"I'm afraid once people find out I inherited this ranch they'll say you gave up a promising career as a barrel racer to become a rancher's wife because you felt sorry for me."

"What? I don't feel sorry for you. That never even crossed my mind."

They stared at each other for several long moments.

Kyle spoke first. "Did Tanna tell Lainie we were ridin' high on the tequila express on our way to the wedding chapel?"

"I don't think so. She claims our being hammered led us to finally expressing our true feelings for each other."

He couldn't argue with that. "So no one ever has to know that the reason we stood at the altar was from too much free booze at a Devin McClain concert."

"And that I was buzzed on prescription painkillers."

They said, "Unless we tell them" at the same time. They both laughed.

"I sure as hell don't wanna tell anyone. It'll be our secret. As will the fact that we haven't consummated our marriage." He grinned. "Yet."

She retreated and gave him a speculative look. "That leads me to my next stipulation. While we are married, I expect we'll be husband and wife in name only."

"No."

Celia stilled. "No?"

"No." Kyle loomed over her. "Not only no, but *hell* no. *Fuck* no. That is my stipulation. We will be man and wife in every sense of the word."

"Meaning... we'll be having sex?"

"Oh, yes, little wifey mine, we'll be having sex. Lots and lots of sex. Sweet sex, raunchy sex, shower sex, sex on the floor, sex against the wall, sex in bed, sex in the truck, sex in the barn, sex on the tractor, and sex on this table." He smacked it hard.

Her silver eyes went wide.

"And in case that wasn't clear, I'll say it plain. I like sex. A lot of sex. Morning, noon, and night." He leaned closer. "It about killed me, laying next to you the last couple nights, not touching you. Not even able to hold you, *my wife*, in my arms. I want you, Celia, want you like fucking crazy. Make no mistake that I've waited for you for a long damn time and I've held off. But now that you're legally mine and we'll be playing house for the next six months? I won't hold back. We will be intimate on the most basic level. As often as possible." Kyle was breathing hard by the time he finished.

Celia didn't appear to be breathing at all.

"Say something."

"All right. If we're having sex I expect you not to have sex with anyone else."

Kyle bit back a snarl. She really believed he'd cheat on her? Then it hit him. Breck had always played around on Celia. Why wouldn't she expect that he'd do the same? Especially since he'd once had a reputation for being as much of a horn-dog as Breck was?

But this was different. They were married. "Celia, I promise to be faithful to you. You're my wife. Even if this marriage has an expiration date, I would never disrespect you that way. I promise to honor our wedding vows. I'm not like Breck."

"I know that. I just wanted to hear you say it."

He attempted to lighten the mood. "So you're giving me the green light? I can seduce you at will, sexy wife of mine? I can put all my fantasies revolving around you into play?"

"Yes. But I have one other condition."

Don't groan. "Which is?"

"I want a new bed," she blurted out. "And all new bedding that is ours before we have any sex. Because a used bed is just nasty."

Kyle grinned. "Done." He ran his knuckles down the side of her face. "I'm dyin' to touch you. Dyin' to show you how it can be between us. But I can tell every time you move how sore you are. So despite my earlier statement about being all over you, all the time, I won't be exploring this heat with you tonight."

She licked her lips and granted him a come-hither look that made his dick hard. "So now you're being a gentleman?"

"Gentleman?" He kissed the line between her eyes, then her succulent mouth. He brushed his lips across her ear. "Not. Even. Fucking. Close."

She trembled.

Oh hell yeah. Over the last two years, whenever he'd spoken in her ear, she'd trembled. He intended to have her trembling in his arms as often as possible. "Celia," he whispered against the side of her neck, "tell me you want me too."

And rather than squirming away, she offered more of her neck to his exploring mouth. "I want you."

"You smell good. You taste good." He nuzzled the base of her throat. "I could just eat you up, sweet wife. From head to toe and everywhere in between. Especially in between."

Celia stepped back. Her cheeks were such a pretty shade of red. "Stop teasing me."

"But I don't wanna stop."

"Tough up, cowboy, because we can't do anything about it tonight." She crossed her arms over her chest, but not before he caught a glimpse of her hard nipples. "So to recap . . . as far as everyone knows, we're married for real?"

As far as I'm concerned we've been married for real since the second you put on that wedding ring.

"Yep. We'll be all lovey-dovey tomorrow when we talk to your brothers." He crowded her again so his thumb could trace the outline of her full lips. "That won't be hard to pull off. Me wearing the lustful look of a man who can't wait to get his new bride back to bed."

"After that we'll go get my truck and stuff. But I'm leaving my horse until I figure out a place to put him. And you should know that I have four other horses besides Mickey."

Kyle blinked at her. "You're tellin' me we have nine horses?"

"Ten soon, 'cause my mare Blue will foal this spring. But don't worry. I'll deal with the horses."

He shook his head. "I have to learn how to do everything, so there won't be a division of labor between us."

"Okay, if there's no division of chores, that means we have to do a grocery store run in the next few days." Celia smirked at him. "And it's your night to cook supper."

❧

Celia wasn't in their bed when he'd gotten out of the shower, but he noticed she'd made the bed more user-friendly. More cozy.

He dropped the towel and grabbed the remote before sliding beneath the covers. When Celia sauntered in, she stopped, picked up the wet towel, and pointedly held it out.

"Here's a news flash, bucko: I hate wet towels on the floor. And no, I won't hang it up for you."

Forced to leave his warm nest, Kyle hung the towel in the small master bathroom. Celia didn't avert her eyes from his groin and urge him to put on clothing. Which made his cock eager to prove how fast it could go from soft to hard. It pouted when she wasn't impressed.

Once Celia had settled, Kyle made his move. He gently held her chin and kissed her. Starting out slowly. Slicking his tongue across the seam of her lips and feeling her bottom teeth with the tip of it. His thumb made a lazy, sweeping caress of her cheek as he tasted her thoroughly. The kiss would heat up, then he'd turn it down to simmer, gifting her mouth with quick pecks and the soft glide of his lips.

Her body unconsciously arched into his, urging him to take more than a kiss.

Kyle murmured, "Night, sweet wife."

"Night, horny husband."

Just when he thought she'd gone to sleep, she jackknifed up, a wince distorting her face at the sudden pain. "Did you hear that?"

"Hear what?"

"Scratching sounds. Like a mouse. In the wall. Or in a dresser. Or under the bed." She scooted closer to him. "What if there are mice in this mattress?"

"Celia—"

"Listen to me. Mice nest everywhere. They are vile fucking creatures that all deserve to die."

"How do you really feel?" he said dryly.

"Like I cannot wait to get rid of this bed. And scour this house to make sure it's rodent-proof."

"I'll be glad to help you, but not tonight. You're getting all riled up for no reason. Take a deep breath."

"It hurts to breathe."

"I know." He placed his hand on her belly. "That's why I want you to relax. I'd give you a back rub to distract you if it'd help."

"You just want to get me naked."

"That too."

Celia kissed his jaw. "I'll take a rain check."

"Funny thing... I heard it was gonna rain tomorrow."

She laughed.

Kyle could get very used to hearing that laughter every night before he fell asleep.

Chapter Five

There were warm, rough hands gently stroking her skin.

Warm, soft lips dragging kisses across her ribs.

Celia sighed and stretched, basking in the attention. Not wanting to wake up from such a vivid dream.

Her pajama bottoms were tugged down her thighs. She kicked the covers free, allowing her dream lover to completely slide them off.

A male chuckle vibrated against her belly. Those soft, nibbling lips sought a path down her stomach, over the rise of her mound. Then her thighs were pushed apart and a hot, wet tongue licked her from top to bottom.

As she gasped and arched, her ribs sent a stinging reminder of her soreness.

Wait. She shouldn't feel pain in a dream. She shouldn't feel those long, wet laps up and down her slit either. She really shouldn't hear, "Goddamn, you taste sweet," growled against her sex.

Celia opened her eyes and looked down to see Kyle lying between her legs, his hands gripping her inner thighs while his mouth did such amazing things with his tongue. "What are you *doing*?"

Keeping his gaze to hers, he locked his mouth to her clit and sucked.

Her whole body twitched.

He sucked again.

She twitched again.

Kyle lifted his mouth. "Lay back so you don't hurt your ribs."

"But...?"

He rapidly flicked his tongue over the skin covering her clit. "Are you really gonna tell me to stop?"

"No." She lowered herself back to the mattress.

Another chuckle against her sensitive flesh.

Then Kyle set out to make her lose her mind. He tilted her hips to burrow his tongue completely inside her. He pressed soft kisses to the crease of her thighs. He'd lick her clit and stop to blow a cool stream of air over the hot, wet flesh, then return to sucking.

That telltale tingle started, spreading goose bumps from her nape down her spine. Kyle lapped at her slit with long strokes; a growling sound emerged when he dipped his tongue into the entrance to her body. Again and again.

Celia's legs were restless against the blanket. She wanted to grab his head and force him to make her come now.

Kyle raised his face from the delicious assault. "Celia. Show me what you want."

She put her hands over his ears and pressed his mouth over her clit.

He spread her folds apart with his thumbs. He looked at her, lowered his mouth, and sucked once. "Say my name."

"Kyle."

He suckled harder. "Say it again."

"Kyle. Please."

"That's what I wanna hear." He started a sucking, swirling motion with his mouth and tongue that pushed her from teetering on the edge to spinning in the maelstrom.

Her heart pounded, her skin throbbed, white noise roared in her ears as she unraveled. Her fingers dug into Kyle's scalp as he sucked and tongued her through an orgasm without end. When the storm of pleasure eventually faded to a sweet throb, she flopped onto the bed and winced, hissing at the bite of pain in her ribs.

His hair tickled her belly as he kissed a path back up her body. Then his hands were beside her shoulders and he was hanging over her. He grinned. "Good morning."

"That tongue of yours is an awesome alarm clock." It surprised him when she rose up and kissed his lips. But she couldn't withhold another wince at the stab of pain.

Kyle pushed back on his heels. His hands gently covered her ribs and concern replaced his amusement. "How bad do they hurt?"

"Some."

"Don't lie to me."

"I definitely feel it, okay? It was worse last night than right after it happened."

His thumbs followed the edge of her rib cage. "Do I need to take you to a doctor?"

"Time is the only fix. You've had this injury before." Her gaze dropped to his crotch. Kyle was fully erect. "Morning wood?"

"No, you do that to me," he said gruffly. "I woke up with you in my arms and it took every bit of self-control not to . . ." He made a frustrated sound. "You're too fuckin' sore for what I had in mind."

"So you went down on me instead?" *Ooh, listen to you, Celia Lawson, talking so raunchy.*

"I needed to touch you."

She focused on his erect cock and then his eyes. "Left you in a hard spot?"

He shrugged. "I'm used to takin' care of this myself."

"You don't lack for women angling to warm your bed, Kyle. Women happy to take care of that for you."

"We discussed this last night. That's in the past. You're my wife." He started to get up, but Celia hooked her leg around his knee.

"Where you goin'?"

A tiny bit of resentment flared in his eyes. "Why?"

"You're goin' to the bathroom to whack off."

Mr. Dirty Talk blushed.

Be bold. Let him know you're on board for whatever he has in mind. "Show me how you touch yourself so I know what you like."

"Seriously?"

"Yep. And definitely don't be a gentleman about it."

Eyes burning with liquid heat, he curled his right hand around his shaft and started to stroke. "I like it slippery, which is why I do this in the shower."

Fascinated by the rougher way he handled himself, her gaze flicked between his face and his hand.

"You oughta see your eyes, kitten." He groaned and pumped faster.

She felt the effect his self-pleasure was having on her. Her skin tightened. Her pussy heated. Her nipples drew into hard points. She wanted this man so much.

"This…I…won't last long." His broad chest rose and fell rapidly. "Christ. You just licked your lips. Do you have any idea what that does to me?"

"Show me."

Another drawn-out moan.

Although he wasn't squeezing hard, the stroking motion made the veins stand out on his forearm. The muscles bulged and flexed from his wrist to his shoulder. The cords in his neck were rigid, as was his jaw. Her breath caught. Goddamn, he was so sexy. He was such a prime example of masculine perfection and he was all hers.

At least for a little while.

"Fuck. Celia." He threw his head back and came all over his hand.

Holy freakin' hell, that was hot.

She stood and looked into his pleasure-hazed green eyes. "Thanks for the demo."

"Maybe you can return the favor sometime."

"Maybe." She kissed him, finding her taste still lingered on his lips and tongue. "But I'd rather use my mouth."

⁀

They skipped breakfast, dressed for the elements, and started on chores.

Kyle was a quick study in tractor operation. They spread out a roll of hay for the cattle and did a head count. The stock tank needed to be refilled, which required tracking down the water access. While Kyle loaded the woodstove, Celia ventured into the bigger metal building.

It contained miscellaneous farm equipment, all perfectly aligned, all in excellent shape. At least Kyle wasn't faced with immediately replacing outdated, busted equipment. The place was damn near spotless too. Anything resembling junk was stacked in one corner. As she prowled the perimeter, she noticed a switch like the one on the stock tank. This place could be heated with the woodstove also.

She found two older-model ATVs. Trying not to jar her ribs, she climbed on the first one and it started right up. Same for the second one. She had an image of her and Kyle laughing, racing each other across the white landscape.

Romantic nonsense, Celia.

"Celia?" Kyle shouted.

"Back here."

Kyle sauntered into view. He wore stained coveralls, a thick jacket, and an orange knit hunter cap. She'd never considered that look particularly cute on a man, but it worked on him.

"I found two things to show you." Kyle snagged her hand and led her around the back of the building. "I saw the dwindling stack of wood and wondered where the hell I'd get enough to last the rest of the winter. As I'm looking at the treeline, I noticed a section that juts out of this building." They rounded the corner, stopping in front of a long metal building that was practically invisible from anywhere on the property except here.

"What is it?"

"A wood-drying shack. It's full of wood that's already dried, enough for this winter. Looks like I know how I'll be spending part of my summer."

"I wonder if Marshall did this all himself or if he hired out."

"Josh would probably know. But come look what else I found." Kyle towed her through the knee-high snowdrifts to the back of the house.

She squinted. "Is that what I think it is?"

"A hot tub. And it's pretty new."

"Does it have water in it?"

"Not super-nasty water, so I'm guessing Marshall recently changed it. Must be on the same emergency circuit as the heater inside since it didn't freeze. You can get out here from the garage. Cool, huh?"

"More like *brrr*. How can you be excited about sitting in a hot tub when it's four degrees outside?"

"Because I've always wanted one and now I have one." He kissed her nose. "Don't ruin my fun. I'll look for the manual. It'd be good for your ribs."

Celia was absurdly touched by his thoughtfulness. "There's a lot of paperwork we need to look for."

"We'll do it soon as we get back from talking to your brothers and getting your truck."

⟋⟍

After a late lunch, Celia pawed through her duffel bag; she couldn't wait to get the rest of her clothes out of her horse trailer after their trip to talk to her brothers.

Kyle held her hand, rubbing his thumb over her wedding band on the ride to Abe's. "You worried?"

She nodded. "How do you think they'll react?"

"Shock for sure. After that? Who knows? How do *you* think they'll react?"

"I'm hoping they won't pull out the shotguns."

"Jesus, Celia, don't even joke about that."

That was the thing. She wasn't sure whether she *was* joking. Hank and Abe bellowed a lot when they were unhappy with her or a decision she'd made, but they eventually, grudgingly, came to an understanding.

She feared that this situation would be the exception, given the way things had been between them the last few years.

Hank's truck was parked up front next to Abe's. Her brothers ambled out of the barn right after Kyle pulled into the driveway.

He kissed her knuckles. "Regardless of what happens, we're together now. You have me, Cele. I'll always be on your side. You know that, right?"

"I do now." Touched by his fierceness, she impulsively rubbed his rough-skinned fingers across her lips. "Thanks."

"My pleasure." He warned, "Stay put. I'll help you out so you don't hurt your—"

"Ribs, yeah, I know. You sound like a broken record."

LORELEI JAMES   82

"Only because I have some wicked, nekkid plans once you're healed."

Right then Celia considered lying that she'd made a miraculous recovery. Because *wicked, nekkid,* and *Kyle* in the same sentence? Hello, temptation.

"Kyle, what the devil are you doin' here?" Hank asked.

Then Celia stepped into view. "Hey, guys."

"Celia? Didn't expect to see you." Abe grinned and started toward her, probably to wrap her in a bear hug, but Kyle intervened.

"Gotta watch the ribs. She's awful sore."

Hank and Abe exchanged a look. Then they both peered at the bandage on her forehead. Hank demanded, "What the hell happened to you?"

"And why is this the first we've heard of it?" Abe added, glaring at Kyle. "Did you have something to do with her getting injured? Is that why the two of you are here together?"

Celia stepped in front of Kyle. "No. I got hurt last weekend in Vegas. A few stitches, bruised ribs. I'm fine. So back off. It's not Kyle's fault." She'd tried out several phrases in her head on the way over, but nothing had jelled. Best just to say it right out. "We're here together because Kyle and I got married Saturday night in Vegas."

A pause, then Hank and Abe burst out laughing. Their amused gazes zipped between Kyle and Celia. Her brothers looked at each other, then busted a gut again. Adding in knee-slapping laughter. During their fit of mirth, Kyle slipped his arm around Celia's waist.

"Good one, Celia. I needed a laugh. You and Kyle. Together. Right." More snickers.

Their hilarity faded when Celia held out her left hand. "I'm not kidding. Kyle and I are married."

A stunned pause followed.

Then Abe snapped, "Are you pregnant?"

"I tell you I'm married and that's the first question you ask?"

Hank's eyes hardened. "My question is . . . were you drunk?"

Celia's stomach lurched. Her face heated and she gaped at Hank.

"Christ. You were drunk," Hank snarled when she didn't immediately answer.

This was not starting out well at all.

"You watch what you say to her," Kyle warned. "Yes, Celia and I are married. Yes, it happened pretty damn fast." He brought her hand to his mouth and kissed it. "Or we've been headed this way for a long damn time, since we've known each other forever."

"You two have been at each other's throats forever, so I don't buy this *you're in love* bullshit," Abe said.

"Ask Devin if it's bullshit," Celia replied evenly. "He stood up for Kyle at the ceremony."

That comment seemed to incense them more. "*Devin* knew you were married before we did?" Hank bellowed.

"And with the way you're both acting, can you blame Celia for not wanting to tell either of you?" Kyle shot back.

"Because you're too goddamned old for her!" Abe said.

Celia wanted to flee before someone said something hurtful that couldn't be taken back. Because it was coming.

Her brothers' postures were belligerent, their silence disapproving.

"So you're married. What now? You traveling the circuit together?" Hank asked.

"I . . . I dropped out of the circuit."

"What!" Abe and Hank said simultaneously. Then Abe snarled at her, "You're quitting? You're goddamned pregnant, aren't you? Kyle, I'm gonna fucking kill you." He lunged for Kyle, but Hank held him back.

Pissed off beyond measure, Celia yelled, "I don't believe you two! You're assholes. I'm not pregnant! Can't you just be happy for me for one minute?"

"We'd be happy for you except we don't understand what the hell is goin' on. You married *Kyle*? A chance to win a national barrel racing championship is all you've talked about for the last four years, little sis. You're so hell-bent on competing and getting to the next level that you never come home anymore."

That was what they thought? Could her brothers really be so clueless about why she stayed away? Did they really not know her at all?

"But now you'll be traveling with Kyle to support *his* attempt to win a national bull riding championship while you let your own dream turn to dust?"

"No. Kyle and I both quit the circuit."

Shocked silence.

"Then how will you make a living?" Hank demanded.

"More to the point... Where will you live?" Abe also demanded.

Kyle answered, "On my ranch."

"What ranch? Since when do you have a ranch?"

"If you'd stop interrupting and jumping to conclusions, we'd tell you," Celia said.

"Then somebody had better start talking right now."

"Celia and I are living on the ranch I inherited from my father."

Silence. Then, "When did this happen?"

"A few days ago."

"That's what this is about? You suddenly inherited a ranch and knew you couldn't run it by yourself so you convinced Celia to quit the circuit and marry you?"

Celia glared at Hank. No questions about Kyle finally learning the identity of his father? No excitement about his unexpected windfall? Just more accusations? More assumptions?

"I can't believe..." Hank pointed at Kyle. "She deserves way better than you." Then Hank pointed at Celia. "You know this won't last, don't you? Kyle isn't a long-term guy."

All the uncertainty from the last four days, all the hurt her brothers had unconsciously inflicted on her in the last four years, pushed her to the breaking point. A gasping sob broke free and she bent forward to try to stop the sharp, stabbing pain in her ribs and around her heart.

Through the haze of tears, she saw Kyle's shadow move in front of her.

"Celia. Baby. Get in the pickup."

She wrapped her arms around herself, keeping her focus entirely on Kyle as she shuffled backward.

"Where the hell do you think you're goin'?" Hank shouted. "We're not done talking about this!"

She'd never seen Kyle like this. The easygoing man had spun into an absolute rage.

He shoved Hank hard enough that Hank fell on his ass. "We sure as fuck are done because you don't *ever* get to talk to her like that, you hear me?" She watched him struggle for control and attempt to level his breathing. "Celia and I are married. Fucking deal with it. And we didn't come here wanting a goddamn thing from either of you except your congratulations. But instead you insult her, you insult me, and then you make my wife, *your sister*, cry? Jesus. What is wrong with you two?"

Abe helped Hank to his feet. "This has gotten out of hand."

"You're damn right it has. So here's your warning. Stay away from her."

"Dammit, Kyle, knock it off. We're her family."

"No. I'm her family now. Because I'll never *ever* treat her like you just did."

Celia cried harder.

Neither of her brothers tried to stop them from leaving.

At the turnoff to the highway, Kyle said, "Do we still need to stop at Eli's or can it wait?"

"I want my own pickup and if I have to wear these clothes another week, I'll puke."

Beyond heartsick, Celia ignored the phone vibrating in her pocket. She stared out the window. The scenery she'd always loved offered her no comfort at all.

Eli Whirling Cloud was unsaddling a horse when they pulled up. He brushed her down before he approached them. "This is a nice surprise. I expected maybe one of you, but not both of you. But there's only one extra bed, hey."

Celia was so happy to get such a warm welcome from her friend and horse trainer that she almost burst into tears again. "We're not here to crash, but thanks for the offer. We're here to share some news." Celia's heart raced. "Me'n Kyle got hitched last weekend in Vegas."

Eli grinned from ear to ear. "I'll be damned. Congratulations are in order, then?"

"Yep."

"Outstanding." Eli's smile faded. "So why the teary face, sweetheart?"

"We just left Hank and Abe. They were less than enthusiastic about the news."

"Eh, they're both hotheads. Especially when it comes to you. They'll get over it."

"I'll track Mickey down so Kyle can tell you what else has gone on."

Standing in front of her horse trailer, she realized Kyle had been right about one thing. All her worldly goods were contained within it. Three suitcases of clothes. One box of household things and knickknacks.

How pathetic.

Fighting tears, she leaned against the back of the horse trailer, out of view of the house. Her life had become a train wreck. How soon would Kyle regret getting mixed up with her?

Tired of being a fucking baby about her injury, she unloaded everything from her horse trailer herself. She had to take a break after she dumped her suitcases in the back of Kyle's pickup because her ribs were screaming in protest.

She rested against the fence post, watching Mickey in the distance. But her horse didn't gracefully trot up and welcome her home. He tossed his mane and ran farther afield.

You too, Mickey?

His regal head bobbed, as if he'd heard her.

"He's always been a temperamental motherfucker," Kyle drawled behind her. "Don't take it personal."

"It's not like I can ride him anyway."

Kyle swore. "Did you really load and unload all that yourself? Christ, Celia—"

"Please don't yell at me. I can't take any more today, especially not from you."

"Hey. C'mere." Kyle gently enclosed her in his arms. Feeling a little more settled, she pressed her face against his neck, inhaling his scent, and whispered, "Thank you."

He hissed. "Your face is freezing. Let's get you warmed up."

I've got an excellent idea on how we can do that.

Celia eased back until they were nose to nose.

"That's a dangerous look in your eye, kitten. Thinking body friction would warm us both up. Because I'm all over that." Kyle kissed her. Slowly. Teasingly. Making her ache in a new way. Tempting her to whip off their clothes and make naked snow angels. He broke the kiss. "I'm ready to go. Why don't you follow me back so you don't get lost?"

"I never get lost."

"You look a little lost right now."

She teared up once more and he kissed her again. She felt a little more in control, because she understood she wasn't alone. Kyle would be there for her.

"Don't even think about unloading them bags when we get home," he warned.

Back at the house, Celia sat listlessly on the end of the bed and watched as Kyle carried in her luggage.

"Run yourself a hot bath and soak for as long as you can sit still." He pressed his fingers over her lips when she started to protest. "We've had a couple of great argument-free days, so let's not start now."

Celia submerged herself in the pink tub. Too bad she couldn't drown all the voices in her head clamoring for attention.

Kyle knocked twice before he entered. He shamelessly inspected her naked body as he rested on his haunches beside the tub. "You okay?"

No. "Just sore."

"Hungry?"

She shook her head. "But we really need to go to the store tomorrow."

He traced her collarbone and let his finger follow the slope of her breast, dipping below the water to circle her nipple.

Celia studied Kyle's face as he lazily stroked the beaded tip—the hunger in his eyes was undeniable. And exciting. The way he looked at her left her a little breathless.

"So pretty," he murmured.

"So small," she said hastily, curbing the urge to cover herself.

"So pretty," he said again, more firmly. "I like the look of you, Celia. I always have. Lean muscles, long legs, world-class ass from spending your life on horseback."

"I thought you had a thing for busty brunettes."

"Doesn't really matter now because I have a thing for you." He continued that maddening, arousing stroking on her breast.

"Had you ever thought about asking me out...before New Year's Eve?"

"On a date? No."

Her gut clenched.

"Only because I figured you'd say no, or you'd come up with something cutting if I even tried. I'd decided to save myself that humiliation." Kyle looked at her. "Was I wrong?"

"Probably not."

"So it's a damn good thing we skipped that awkward dating stage and went straight to marriage."

She smiled. "Damn good thing."

"Water's getting cold."

"I should probably get out. And I'm sore enough to take a pain pill and crawl into bed."

"That's probably a good idea." Kyle kissed her forehead by her stitches and left the bathroom.

Celia dug out a clean pair of pajamas and downed two pain pills. Sweet Kyle had smoothed out the bedding and plumped her pillows. He even waited until she slid beneath the covers so he could tuck her in.

Her tears surfaced again and she cried until the pain pills kicked in and sent her into a deep sleep.

Chapter Six

$\mathcal{K}$yle woke to the smell of bacon cooking. He considered walking to the kitchen naked and dragging his wife back to bed for a repeat of yesterday morning's wake-up call. The clock read five thirty. Hell, it was still dark outside. And cold as fuck, if the ice on the windows was any indication.

Yawning, he slipped on a pair of sweats.

Celia was placing the cooked bacon strips on a paper towel. She smiled at him. Her eyes were clear and she appeared to be in a happier mood.

Kyle kissed her with more passion than she'd expected. He put his mouth on her ear. "Mornin'. Smells delicious."

"It's just bacon. And biscuits."

"Mmm." He lightly nipped her earlobe. "And the food smells good too." She laughed softly.

"I like to hear that laughter, especially after yesterday." It'd ripped at him to hear her crying herself to sleep. But she hadn't wanted his comfort last night. She'd preferred to handle things herself. That's where they were exactly alike. So he'd reluctantly left her alone. But he'd obsessively checked on her every ten minutes just in case she needed him. In between, he'd tackled two boxes of Marshall's most recent paperwork, including notes from the VA and a home health service out of the local hospital in Rawlins. He had to check it out, see if he could learn anything about his father, even if it turned out to be a dead end. Kyle shoved aside his sense of futility and peered into her eyes. "How're you feeling?"

"Like I had a miraculous recovery. My ribs don't hurt at all." She danced a little jig. "See?"

Sweet wife, your ribs weren't the only things hurtin' yesterday.

Over the years he'd seen her false bravado. He'd seen her injured. Seen her sad. Seen her mad as hell. Seen her devastated. But until yesterday he'd not seen her rocked by all those emotions at one time. He never wanted to see it again. He wanted to hurt anyone who ever put that broken look on her face.

The intensity of that feeling scared him.

"As soon as we're done with chores today, we have to go to town. There's no fresh food at all."

Kyle poured himself a cup of coffee and refilled hers. "Fresh food. What kinds of fresh food? Because I ain't crazy about vegetables. Never taken a liking to fruit, neither."

Celia removed flaky golden biscuits from the oven and slid them onto a plate. "Then we need to discuss what groceries to buy. Living on junk food and fast food isn't an option now." She sat across from him. "Can you cook?"

"Yep." He smirked. "Frozen food, canned food, microwave meals. That's where it appears that I take after my father."

"I can cook some stuff. Since we'll be eating three meals a day together I want to be on the same page about expectations of cooking duties."

"I'm thinkin' your other wifely duties will include sex at least twice a day. Three times on Sunday," he said in a silken growl.

She dropped her fork. "Kyle Gilchrist. I'm serious."

"Me too. I'm hoping you're on the pill so we don't have to use condoms. My annual AFR physical came back clean last month. I haven't been with a woman for nine months."

"You were celibate for nine months?" she said with surprise.

He shrugged. "A quick fuck before I hit the road after a performance stopped doin' it for me."

"Did you arrive at that decision before or after you nailed my friend Lindsay?"

Kyle had wondered when that would come up. "Don't you think you've made me pay enough for that mistake? It's been over a year."

"Fourteen and a half months," she said, then hastily added, "or there-abouts. I really don't recall."

"I'll refresh your memory, kitten. Right after it happened you called me a man-whore in a whole tent full of contestants. Which, contrary to your other accusation, did not boost my cred with the other man-whores infest-ing the world of rodeo."

She focused on slathering jam on a biscuit.

"Then you attacked me again a few days later, calling me names in front of a couple of sponsors. Not cool."

"Know what else wasn't cool? Listening to Lindsay brag about how awe-some you were in bed. In detail. I got a fucking play-by-play of every lick, every thrust, every orgasmic scream."

"So that's why you screamed that I was a mother-fucking son of a bitch ass-wipe fuckwad?"

Celia's cool eyes met his. "I don't remember saying that."

"I do. And I also remember tracking down your drunken ass a few hours later, when you almost racked me, punched me in the stomach, and sank your teeth into my ass."

"You were carrying me upside down like a side of beef! I chomped on your ass because it was the only part of you I could reach to do any dam-age."

Kyle had been livid, forced to deal with a drunk and morose Celia at Abe's insistence. She'd passed out in his hotel room. But not before she'd stunned him with a slurred "Why Lindsay?"

And he'd known immediately she'd meant, *Why not me?*

"How did we even get on this subject?" she grumbled. "We were sup-posed to be talking about groceries."

"I think you wanted to know whether you were supposed to put con-doms on the store list," he said slyly. "So do we?"

Celia rolled her eyes. "No. I'm on the pill. Eat up, greenhorn. It's almost light and the day's a-wastin'."

Sometimes the more times you did something the easier it became. But on day two of chores, Kyle figured that wouldn't be the case with ranching. Ever.

They didn't get back inside until just after noon. Celia unwound a purple rhinestone scarf and ditched her coveralls, coat, and work gloves. She flopped on the couch, trying to catch her breath after helping him haul wood. He perched on the edge of the recliner.

After only a minute, Celia's nose wrinkled. "This thing reeks. We need to get it out of here." She pointed at the chair. "That too."

"So we won't have any furniture in our living room?"

"Better none than this shit." She smiled at him prettily. "Besides, we're goin' to a furniture store to get a new bed. While we're there, we might as well buy furniture we both like and we can actually use."

"Sneaky, wife."

"Don't pretend you haven't been imagining a big-screen TV along that wall."

"Guilty."

She walked the length of the room. "This dirty carpet has to go too."

"A new bed, new bedding, a new couch, a new chair, a new TV, new carpet . . . anything else?"

"A coat of paint. Some bright curtains. And a funky coffee table."

His first thought was he couldn't afford to buy all the household stuff that'd make her happy. Which was followed closely by his second thought: Yes, with help from Marshall's bank account he had the means for Celia to transform this place from a dump into their home. His third thought was that if he let her buy everything her heart desired maybe that would encourage her to stay longer than six months.

"After you take that ugly-ass chair out, I'll help drag out this smelly couch."

Celia was so damn determined he didn't bother reminding her about her injured ribs. After he returned inside from dumping the chair, he tossed her a pair of gloves.

"Am I on the front end or the back end?" she asked.

"The front end bears more weight, so it looks like you're the caboose."

Cheeky woman shook her ass at him and added a husky "Aye, aye, captain."

Kyle lifted his end. When Celia had hers raised, he tilted it slightly to fit through the doorway. The couch wasn't heavy, but the damn thing stank to high heaven and he held his breath until he was out in the fresh air. "Set it down." He maneuvered it around the porch post. "All right. Let's take it slow."

Celia picked up her end and everything was going great. They'd made it to the driveway when she suddenly screamed bloody murder. She screamed like he'd never heard outside a horror flick. Then she dropped her end of the couch, which put him off balance. He lost his grip and the couch hit the ground with a loud crash.

He glanced at Celia, hopping from foot to foot as she smacked her palms on her head, her shoulders, and her stomach like she was slapping mosquitoes, shrieking, "Get them off, get them off, get them OFF!"

"Get what off? Spiders?"

"No. Mice! They skittered out when the couch tipped! They ran up my arms. They were in my fucking hair!" Celia kept beating on herself until he grabbed her hands.

"Stop. You're hurting yourself. They're gone."

"No, they're not. I can still feel them! They scrambled up my arms with their scratchy little mice feet and their furry bodies and their wormy tails slithering across my skin." She shuddered so hard he feared she'd gone into some kind of convulsions.

Kyle pulled her into his arms to try to get her calmed down. And to keep his laughter hidden because in her panic-stricken frame of mind she'd rack him if she heard it.

She finally stopped shaking. She buried her face in his neck and breathed deep. "I hate mice."

"I know you do, baby."

"That whole fucking couch was a mouse hotel. And graveyard. That's why it smelled so bad. It was filled with dead mice."

"Hey, now. It's out of the house."

She sniffed. "I probably smell like mouse piss."

"No. You don't."

"I probably have mouse shit in my hair."

"I haven't seen any. I promise."

One last shuddering breath and she stepped back.

His cell phone rang. He glanced at the number. "Cele, it's the lawyer."

"Take it. I'm fine."

Kyle ambled down the driveway, half listening to the lawyer while keeping an eye on his wife, who seemed . . . too calm in the aftermath of her hysteria.

Celia glared at the offending couch. Suddenly her body seized up. She threw her arms in the air, shouted, "That's the last fucking straw!" and stomped up the porch, disappearing into the garage.

What the hell?

Celia returned. Holding a gas can.

Oh. This wasn't good.

"Bill, I'll have to call you back." He hung up and approached her very, very cautiously. "Celia? Sweetheart? What are you doin'?"

She was muttering to herself as she emptied the entire can of gas all over the couch.

No. She wouldn't.

Kyle watched, his mouth hanging open, as Celia yelled, "Fry, mother-fuckers!" and then lit a crumpled piece of newspaper and tossed it on the gasoline-soaked couch.

A ball of fire shot into the air.

Holy. Fucking. Shit.

She'd set the couch on fire.

In the front yard.

Maybe his kitten wasn't as tamed as he'd thought.

And yeah, maybe he was just a little afraid of her.

Celia turned around and beamed at him. "Will you keep an eye on this while I shower?"

"Ah. Sure, honey, no problem."

Kyle was still watching the flaming couch when Josh's rig pulled up.

Josh stood next to Kyle without saying a word.

Finally Kyle said, "She really hated the couch."

"I guess." Josh pointed to the easy chair teetering on a snowbank. "Is that one next?"

"No. I'm afraid she'll use it as target practice."

Josh laughed. "So besides your flambéed furniture, how are things goin'?"

"Besides the shit ton to do around here?"

"Ready to sell yet?"

"Ask me next month." Kyle sighed. "In the interest of keeping the fire danger down, will you come inside and help me remove the bed from our room?"

"Why? Is she planning to roast marshmallows and weenies on it later tonight?"

"Funny."

"If you don't want it, I'll take it off your hands."

Kyle wondered if Ronna would have the same objections to a used bed that Celia did. "What do you plan on doin' with it?"

"Putting it in the barn so I've got a place to crash during calving."

"It's yours."

The couch was mostly cinders, but they covered the smoking remains with snow anyway before they went inside and dealt with the old mattress.

Right after they'd loaded it into Josh's truck, Celia bounded down the steps in her long black duster, looking as fresh and pretty as a spring flower.

"Ready to go to town, Kyle?"

"I reckon."

"You guys need anything?" Celia asked Josh.

"Ronna wouldn't say no to chocolate ice cream."

"I might need your help wrestling the new bed into our room when we get back."

Josh nodded. "I'll swing up after I see your truck go by."

✌

Kyle wasn't much of a shopper and he inwardly groaned when Celia bragged that she'd compiled four lists.

The first stop was a discount furniture store. After choosing a king-size bed, they sat on, inspected, and price-compared every single living room set in the place. Celia finally decided on a couch, love seat, and chair trio, in a color the salesman referred to as Spanish moss. She also insisted on taking a fabric sample to find coordinating accessories, which threw Kyle for a loop. He'd never pegged tomboy Celia as the type to give a shit about that kind of girly domestic stuff.

She's never had the chance to. She's never had a place of her own.

That thought made Kyle a lot more indulgent at the home goods store.

It also prompted him to participate in the bedding selection process. But he zoned out when she compared towel thickness and colors and debated about rug shapes and patterns. Took two carts full of stuff before she finally quit browsing.

He rallied at the hardware store. While she looked at living room paint samples and bedroom paint—when had he agreed to that?—he picked up a few things he'd need, including the rodent repellent powder Josh had recommended.

Kyle put his foot down when she suggested stopping at a carpet store and an electronics store and a fabric store.

Yet... he admitted he liked grocery shopping with Celia. Not only because she let him crowd her when he pretended to look at the grocery list, but he'd never had this type of intimacy. Buying food and planning to cook meals they'd share for the next week.

At the end of her very long list, she asked, "Can you think of anything else?"

"Do you have stuff to make me cookies?"

Celia looked up at him sharply. "You never mentioned cookies."

Kyle pressed her against the boxed noodles. "I crave sweet stuff, especially if it's warm and sticky. It's your wifely duty to satisfy my craving. To make sure my mouth is always busy. Tasting. Licking. Nibbling. On something."

She went utterly still.

But Kyle noticed the quickening pulse in her neck. The rapid rise and fall of her chest. He couldn't decipher the expression in her gray eyes, though. "What?"

"I want you. So bad I'm thinking about jumping you in the pasta aisle."

So the look was lust, which caused his lust to skyrocket. He kissed her.

Not sweetly. When they finally broke apart, he growled, "We shoulda bought two sets of sheets, because we're gonna set the first ones on fire four seconds after I get you home."

"We've had enough fire-related incidents today. So how about if you . . . fuck me through our new mattress." Celia nipped his jaw. "Twice."

He suspected they hit the world speed record for grocery checkout.

On the way home, he realized she hadn't said anything. "Your ribs are feeling better? Because, kitten, there's no rush to do a little mattress dancin' if you'd rather wait another day or two."

Celia snapped, "Keep up the teasing, funny man, and I'll rip your clothes off right now and not give a shit if you wreck your pickup."

Kyle snickered. And adjusted the crotch of his jeans.

Josh's truck wasn't far behind Kyle's. Celia insisted on carrying in the groceries while they brought the bed and box spring inside. Kyle only half listened to Josh. His entire focus was on the frenzied sounds coming from the kitchen. Cupboard doors slamming. Bags rattling.

Celia hustled into the bedroom and dug through the bags of household goods. She had the puffy white mattress pad spread out on the bed in about fifteen seconds.

"Cele, do you need help—"

"No." She looked up at him, hunger blazing in her eyes. "Josh's ice cream is melting on the kitchen counter. He might wanna get it home right away."

Talk about melting. She was burning him alive with those mercury-colored eyes of hers.

Josh chuckled. "I get it. Don't let the door hit you in the ass on the way out."

Kyle handed the ice cream over and Josh grinned. "Newlyweds. I remember those days. Vaguely. Have a great night."

Kyle locked the door, kicked off his boots, and thought about stripping on his way back to the bedroom, but that'd be hard to do at a run.

Celia had just finished putting on the bottom sheet. She crawled across the bed toward him. Then she was on him, mouth fused to his as she unhooked his belt. Making greedy, sexy noises as she tried to inhale him.

"Celia," he said between kisses, "slow down."

"No. Touch me. Put your hands all over me. Please."

"Hold still." He grabbed the bottom of her shirt, carefully pulling it up and over her head. He groaned at her very girly red bra, dotted with white hearts. Kyle's mouth sought the gentle slope of her breast, kissing along the lacy edge, down to the V and back up the other side.

And Celia was trying to de-pant him.

"Stop. You wanted me to touch you and I am."

"But I wanna touch you too."

"We'll take turns." Good idea. Maybe he wouldn't come at that first thrust if they slowed this down. "My shirt next." Celia focused on the buttons. He tipped her chin up. "Huh-uh. Take it off while you're kissin' me. Because I cannot get enough of this mouth."

Her kisses were sweet, and hungry, and made his cock harder yet. After the buttons were undone, she groaned. "No fair. You're wearing a T-shirt."

"You're wearin' a bra, so we're even." Kyle strung kisses down her neck and dropped to his knees in front of her. Unbuttoning and unzipping her jeans, he slid the denim down the curve of her hips and her long, long legs. He inhaled the scent of her arousal as he pressed his mouth over the black cotton panties. His greedy hands squeezed her butt cheeks, so tight and round and firm.

She impatiently kicked the denim aside and pulled him back to his feet. "My turn." Her palms followed the contours of his chest to the waistband of his jeans. His belt was already undone. He swallowed a groan when she lowered herself to the floor. Keeping her eyes on his, she mouthed his cock through the denim, blowing warm air up the length, then scraping her teeth down. She cupped his package and unzipped him quickly, then hooked her fingers in his belt loops and yanked down his jeans.

Sneaky woman kissed straight up his body, over his briefs and T-shirt until she connected with his lips again.

Kyle clamped his hands on her ass, bringing her groin to his. Damn, she fit against him perfectly. His fingers traced her spine to the bottom band of her bra. One tug and it hit the floor.

Celia broke the kiss. Her hands frantically jerked his T-shirt over his head.

He shimmied her panties down her legs.

She tugged his briefs off.

Celia. Naked.

Him. Naked.

Him naked with Celia.

Fucking finally.

He cupped her breasts, strumming the base of his thumbs over her nipples.

"Kyle. Hurry the hell up. I don't wanna wait. I feel like I've been waiting forever."

"I know, baby. But you've gotta let me touch you a little more." He bent his head. She probably expected he'd suckle those sweet nipples. But his mouth connected with her collarbone and he kissed from one side to the other. "You're so strong. But this part of you is so delicate."

She shifted closer to him.

Her impatience buoyed him to save his in-depth oral worship of her feminine curves until they'd sated this need. "Celia," he whispered against her throat. "Tell me what you want."

"You. Kyle, I want you."

His lips traced the outer rim of her ear, down to her earlobe, where he tugged with his teeth. "So take me."

She stepped back and pushed him onto the bed, releasing a throaty laugh.

He scooted into the middle of the mattress and crooked his finger at her.

His sex kitten pounced on him.

Okay, so this first round would be fast. He was good with that.

Celia straddled his groin, positioning his arms above his head. Mapping his wrists, forearms, biceps with her hand. Squeezing his muscles and releasing a feminine sigh of appreciation. Kicking his lust into high gear with the seductive way her mouth moved on his. Deep, tongue-thrusting kisses. Little nips with her teeth. Choppy breathing he felt against his damp skin.

"I want to touch every part of you," she whispered against his lips.

"Feel free."

She smiled against his cheek. "You must have something in mind for me later if you're letting me have my wicked way with you now."

"Such a smart girl." Kyle touched her face. So damn beautiful with the flush of arousal on her cheeks and her mouth ripe from his. "But you will do one thing for me, right now."

"What?"

"Unbraid your hair."

"Why?"

"You have no idea how many fantasies I've had about you ridin' me, this golden hair surrounding us. Like a curtain hiding us in our own little world."

Her lips curved into a soft smile. "You have a romantic streak."

Kyle refused to be embarrassed that she'd noticed that about him. Few women had.

"I really like that about you," she said, touching his face.

"I'm also a visual guy." His hands caressed her thighs. "And a tactile guy. So this really pushes all my buttons."

"Well, I'm all about pushing your buttons, bull rider." Celia draped the heavy braid over her shoulder. She kept her eyes on his as her fingers unthreaded the strands. At the halfway mark, she let the plait fall behind her back to undo the remainder. As soon as her hair hung loose, she seemed unsure.

"Shake it free. Let me see all of it."

She tossed her head.

"God. You're beautiful. Come here," he said.

Her long locks drifted over them as she bent to kiss him.

Kyle filled both hands with the soft waves, groaning when the honeyed scent of her shampoo teased his nose and her silken hair caressed his skin. He was utterly lost in the feel of her, the taste of her, the scent of her. He wanted to make this moment last forever.

But Celia had other ideas. He felt her hand circle the base of his cock.

Yet she paused. She lifted her mouth from his and he saw that her eyes were heavy-lidded with want.

"Ride me," he murmured huskily.

She scooted her lower half backward, aligning his cock with her warm, slick center. Then she slowly lowered onto him until his hardness filled her completely. Her head fell back and she moaned.

Damn. She was hot, that lithe body so still, yet coiled tight. And wet. Holy fuck, was she wet.

Their eyes met. Held. Celia moved with the ease and grace of an athlete. No wasted motions. She angled forward, using his chest to give her leverage until his cock was buried to the base. Followed by a long, slow withdrawal. Keeping only the head of his cock just inside the entrance to her body, she squeezed her pussy muscles around it.

"That's good. Again." Talk about an understatement. He'd never felt anything that good. That right.

Her body slid against his, belly to belly, her nipples brushing the hair on his chest, her mane teasing his ribs with every sinuous upward glide. His cock never left her snug channel. Her eyes were closed, her teeth digging into her lower lip.

He couldn't take his eyes off her. Keeping his hands on her hips, he urged her to grind down harder, as she created friction against her clit to send her into orbit. "That's it. Show me. Take me with you."

Celia looked at him. "So this is okay for you?"

Kyle touched her face. "Better than okay. It's perfect. You're perfect."

She sucked at his mouth in a bruising kiss as she ramped up the pace.

Christ, the sexy way she undulated her hips might be the death of him. His balls were ready to burst. His skin was so damn tight he thought he'd explode if she ran her hands down his forearms one more time.

Breaking the kiss on a gasp, she adjusted her knees and started to ride him faster.

He pumped his pelvis up to meet her downward motion, sending his cock in deeper. But he sensed her frustration because she was close. He placed her hand over those pale gold curls. "Touch yourself," he softly commanded.

And she obeyed without question, stroking her clit, which almost made him come right then.

He thrust up faster, greedily watching her for that moment when she went sailing headlong into bliss.

"Yes." Celia moaned and arched her back, sending the ends of her hair swishing over his thighs and knees as she rode out the orgasm.

Kyle was beyond desperate to come—his ass cheeks hurt from clenching, trying to stave off his orgasm—but he couldn't tear his hungry gaze away from her. His beautiful, passionate wife.

All at once she seemed to remember where she was. She blinked those pewter eyes at him and a sinful smile curled her lips. "Your turn." With her hands flat on his chest, her hair curtained him as she rode him, bouncing faster but not harder.

"That's perfect. Don't stop." Every hair on his body stood on end as he started to come. Her cunt clamped down, pulling every pulse of semen that shot out of his cock. Every throb made his body shudder. His eyes rolled back in his head and his brain short-circuited.

Celia kissed his neck. Nuzzled his jaw, murmuring unintelligible words as she roused him from the aftermath of his climax.

Gathering that mass of hair in his hands, he brought their mouths together.

She rested her forehead on his. "I may rethink the annulment. That was fantastic."

Kyle laughed. "Yes, sexy wife, it was. I take it your ribs feel okay?"

"Yes." Celia canted her pelvis. "I can't wait to do that again. Although maybe we could skip missionary for another day." She pushed upright. "Let's take a break and eat something. Now that we actually have food to choose from."

"Sounds good." He wrapped one section of her hair around his hand and forearm, stopping her retreat. "But I have one request."

Celia frowned. "I hope it's something I know how to make."

"It has nothin' to do with food. It involves what you're wearing when you're cookin'."

"I'm guessing...just my skin?"

"Nope. I want you to wear my shirt. See, I had this fantasy that when we woke up the morning after our wedding? That I'd see you walking around in nothin' but my shirt." After he admitted that he hoped she wouldn't laugh at him and the odd sentimentality.

She pecked him on the mouth and disconnected their bodies. "I am so loving this romantic side of you, Kyle Gilchrist. I've known you for so long...but it's like I'm finally seeing the real you."

"Meaning?"

"Meaning...I always thought your overabundance of charm was a deadly weapon, but man, it's nothing compared to this sweet and sexy side of you." She touched his face almost reverently. "You are something else. Right now I feel very, very lucky."

He had a chest-thumping moment, hearing her sweet words. Probably made him a Neanderthal, but seeing his seed running down the inside of her thigh gave him another surge of satisfaction.

The front fabric of his flannel shirt hit her at midthigh and the back barely covered her perfect rear, which was perfectly fine with him.

He whistled. "Now that's the way that shirt is supposed to look. Oh, and leave your hair unbound too."

Celia lifted her eyebrows. "Fair is fair."

"I ain't wearing your bra, Cele."

She whipped it at him. "You'd probably fill it out better than I do and wouldn't that be mortifying? Anyway, if I'm minus an article of clothing, you should be too. So, bull rider..." Her admiring gaze flicked over his chest. "No shirt. You just get to wear all them muscles."

"Wanna make bets on whether we finish the meal before we're goin' at it again?"

"Nope. Sucker bet. Because neither of us would mind losing."

Chapter Seven

*A*nother first: cooking without wearing pants.

And Kyle was in a great mood about Celia's state of undress. But he should be in a great mood because they'd rocked the new mattress. Boy howdy, had they ever rocked the mattress.

Being with him... Wow. Her husband was amazing in bed.

He'd been so exuberant in his praise that she knew she would do anything to become the lover he saw when he looked at her so hotly, the uninhibited lover she'd always wanted to be.

One thing they hadn't discussed was her previous sexual experiences, which weren't extensive. She hadn't lost her virginity until age twenty-one, and the guy hadn't known she was a virgin, so she'd come away from that experience feeling jaded. During her first year on the circuit she'd witnessed some wild and kinky scenes, but she hadn't actively partici-pated. She'd let Breck sweet-talk her into his bed. She figured he had enough sexpertise to make up for the lack of hers. Which had proven true.

The fuck-and-run encounters with Breck suited her fine. Trying to find her footing on the circuit discouraged a serious relationship. She'd watched many relationships fail in the rodeo world, and oftentimes that was fol-lowed by career failure.

Like Kyle, she'd verified her suspicions about Breck's bisexuality by accident. Walked in on Breck bending his new traveling partner over the vanity and fucking him.

They'd had a rational discussion, but the bottom line hadn't changed— she liked being with Breck on her terms. She knew he'd liked spending time with her, occasionally between the sheets or more often at a honky-tonk. And she'd demanded that he show her a clean bill of health before she slept with him again.

Then came Michael. Michael inserted himself into Breck's life, which oddly enough, made Breck cling to Celia even tighter. At least in public. He started talking about making commitments, yet she knew in private he preferred Michael's bed to hers. Breck promised her a tropical Christmas vacation, but Michael demanded an invite, so Celia had spent two weeks sunning herself, drinking cocktails, indulging in every spa treatment the resort offered on Breck's dime, while Breck and Michael fucked like animals and fought like cats in the adjoining room.

That'd been the beginning of the end.

Around that time, Kyle had noticed her distraction and he'd cornered her. Urging her to quit living Breck's lie. She knew she hadn't been in love with Breck because it'd been far too easy to break it off with him.

Celia doubted anything with Kyle would ever be easy. He challenged her at every turn.

His arms came around her and he nuzzled the back of her head. "Whatcha thinking about so hard?"

She thought about putting some distance between them, physically and mentally, by giving him a flip answer like how she would miss their sexual compatibility in six months when this union ended. But she refrained. "What to do with these pancakes if I burn 'em."

"You mixed up the batter. I'm not too bad at flipping pancakes. I used to make them for my mom on Mother's Day."

"What a sweet boy." She patted his face. "My, what smooth cheeks you have."

"All for you. I don't wanna leave beard burn all over your skin."

Celia shivered at the words *all over your skin*.

Kyle piled his plate with five cakes, used half a stick of butter and half a bottle of syrup.

She took two pancakes, slathered butter on and sprinkled sugar on top, along with sliced strawberries.

"You don't put on syrup?"

"Nope."

"Ain't they kinda dry?"

"Sugar and fruit makes them perfect. You should try a bite." She held out her fork.

Kyle actually wrinkled his nose. "I told you I ain't big on fruit." He polished off seven pancakes. The man had a big appetite and he'd burn off every calorie tomorrow, probably before noon.

They must've both been ravenous—the food was gone in ten minutes.

She washed the dishes and Kyle dried. When he bumped into her, she jumped. Why was she acting so skittish now?

"Cele? You all right?"

"Uh. Yeah. Why?"

"You've scrubbed that plate three times. I'm pretty sure it's clean."

She laughed. "Sorry. It's just kinda weird, don'tcha think?"

"What? Us having wild monkey sex? Or the fact I'm a man who doesn't mind doin' dishes?"

"Smart-ass. I hate to break it to you, Kyle, but bein' a man who does dishes isn't really all that unusual."

"Oh yeah? You've dated lots of guys with dishpan hands?"

No way did she want to confess her less-than-impressive dating record. "Hank and Abe both did dishes."

Kyle grabbed the plate and rinsed it before he dried it. "They didn't wash dishes until after your folks died. And when Abe was married to Janie the first time, I'll bet you and Janie did all the dishes."

"We did have a dishwasher, so it wasn't a big deal." She plopped the skillet in the water. "But know what's weird? When I was growing up I never saw my dad even rinse out his own coffee cup in the morning, to say nothing of tackling a pile of dirty pots and pans."

"Really? But your mom helped him do stuff around the ranch, right?"

"Yep. Not cleaning machinery or fixin' fence, but she fed cattle and stuff like that. Why?"

He shrugged. "With it bein' just me'n my mom, I learned to do everything. Hated doin' some things, didn't mind doin' others."

Celia took her time using the abrasive side of the sponge on the skillet. She wasn't in a hurry to finish the chore because she found she really liked talking to Kyle. Hearing his stories. Finding out the events in his life that'd shaped him into the man he'd become. She'd watched some of that transformation over the years, but from a different angle.

"Since my mom worked most nights, on the nights she had off, she and I always did the dishes together. From the time I was about seven on. Some of my fondest memories are standing at the sink with her."

Such a sweet boy. Celia was beginning to suspect that sweet, helpful, loving boy still lurked under Kyle's miles of muscles.

She rinsed the pan and handed it over to him. She wiped down her side of the counter, lost in thought about a blond-haired boy helping his mom.

"Got a pretty preoccupied look on your face, wife."

"Only because you missed a spot over there and I'm figuring out the best way to point it out, bein' as we're getting along so well."

A towel snapped close enough to her butt that she felt the whoosh of air. "Hey. Watch it."

"I am. You have the most bitable ass I've ever seen."

Celia ignored him and the renewed quickening in her pulse. As she went to wipe off the table, Kyle picked her up and sat her on it. "What are you doin'?"

"Having an after-dinner treat." He hooked his foot around his chair, dragging it to the end of the table. Then he settled himself between her knees. "Unbutton this shirt that you're wearing," he said in that deep, sexy rasp. "It's in my way."

Celia watched Kyle's eyes as she unfastened every button. He licked his lips when her breasts were exposed and his grip on her knees increased when she was completely bared.

He tugged a lock of her hair free, letting it fall over her breast so just the tip of her nipple peeked out. He did it to the other side and murmured, "So pretty."

Would she ever get used to his offhand compliments? Every once in a while she had to remind herself that this was Kyle, the man who had constantly questioned her femininity over the years, now lavishing praise on those feminine bits.

"Why'd you give me that look?"

She glanced at him and lied because she didn't want to ruin the moment. "Because I bet I look weird perched on this table naked."

"You look mighty tasty to me." His big hands pushed her thighs farther apart. "Scoot down."

"Why here? Why not the bedroom?"

"Because I can finally touch you whenever the hell I want." He rubbed his smoothly shaven cheek between her hipbones. "And I want now."

Even his silver tongue was coated in honey today.

After placing hot, openmouthed kisses on her ribs, he said, "Bring your nipples to my mouth."

Celia straightened, using his broad shoulders to steady herself as she did his bidding, loving that command in his voice, loving the heat in his eyes.

Her hair brushed his face. Kyle didn't bat the strands away; he crushed a handful in each fist. His tongue snaked out to flick the tip of her left nipple. Swirling bigger circles until the top of her breast was damp. Hot. Achy. Then he zeroed in, sucking on that hard crest. When she attempted to pull away because the intensity was too much to bear, his grip on her hair kept her in place.

That tiny bit of pain and his show of control over her turned her inside out. Turned her on in a way she couldn't fathom.

Each lick, each suck, each nip of his teeth made her squirm. She'd never considered her breasts sensitive. Breck spent little time on them and she'd assumed it'd been because they were small. But Kyle's attention was damn close to worship. And she loved every torturous second of it.

Her skin beaded. Her pussy heated. She wanted his fingers there. She wanted his mouth there. She wanted his cock there.

Kyle murmured, "Problem?"

"You're making me crazy."

"It's good for you to be a little crazy for me." He stood and kissed her. Curling his hands around her face, covering her ears so all she could hear was the sound of her own breathing and the staccato rhythm of her heart.

These consuming kisses were on another level of passion. One where her mind was blessedly blank to everything but the next thrust of his tongue, the next glide of his lips as he changed the angle of his head to kiss her deeper.

Kyle backed off, leaving her head buzzing and her mouth tingling. He brushed her hair over her shoulders, running his hands down the length, from her scalp to where it pooled on the table. It seemed to ground him, to soothe him, as he simply stroked her hair. While everything about this man revved her up.

Celia took a deep, quiet breath when he returned to his chair. His taste lingered on her tongue. His scent on her skin. Another, sweeter scent teased her nose, mingling with his male musk.

Strawberries.

His rough-tipped finger traced her slit. "You're wet. I like it that you're wet."

A wicked idea popped into her head and she went with it.

She plucked a whole strawberry from the bowl.

"You takin' a snack break?" he intoned dryly.

"No." Celia ran her tongue around the plump red berry like she was licking the head of his cock. "I know you said you don't like fruit." She pressed the pointed end of the strawberry into her pussy. Then she offered the berry to him. "See if that improves the taste for you."

Kyle's eyes flashed fire and his hand circled her wrist. But instead of pulling it to his mouth, he directed it to hers in a dare. "You first."

Using the tip of her tongue, she delicately licked her juices from the fruit, adding a throaty little, "Mmm," just to see if it had any effect on him.

"More," he said in that guttural rasp.

Yep. It definitely affected him. Celia rubbed the strawberry against the mouth of her sex. She held it to his lips.

He bit into the ripe fruit and juice spurted everywhere.

Her belly cartwheeled when Kyle noisily sucked the juices—hers and the strawberry's—from her fingers. Her stomach bottomed out entirely when he tossed the strawberry hull aside and slid his hands under her butt cheeks.

She whimpered when his tongue rubbed between her pussy lips and connected with her clit. Then he followed the slit to the very heart of her, burrowing his tongue inside completely. So completely she had no idea how he breathed.

Kyle feasted on her pussy. Growling against her tender flesh. His mouth was in constant motion as he drove her higher. Making her thrash and moan. Making her beg.

Finally he focused his oral attention on that bundle of nerves. Quick tongue flicks morphed into rhythmic sucking when she reached the tipping point. She exploded against his mouth. Her cunt throbbed as she gasped through every body-shaking pulse.

He brought her down from that stunning sexual high with soft smooches, tender nuzzles, and gentle sweeps of his hands.

Celia fell back on the table harder than she'd intended and her head made a hard *clunk* when it hit. She barely felt it, as she was still floating in an orgasmic haze.

But Kyle loomed over her immediately. "Baby, you okay?"

"Uh-huh. Well, ah, no." She laughed and knew it sounded slightly hysterical. "You scrambled my brain. I don't know which end is up."

"Luckily I do." He placed his mouth above her belly button and sucked hard. Hard enough to leave a love bruise. "It's this way." He'd already ditched his sweatpants and sported an impressive erection. Before she could comment on it, he started kissing her neck. "Hold on to me as you climb off the table."

She expected he'd take her to bed, but he merely flipped the chair around, sat, and latched onto her hips, pulling her backward. "Stay facing out. Take off that shirt so I can touch you."

His commanding voice was in direct opposition to the calming stroke of his thumbs over the curve of her ass. If she'd thought she was done being turned on by this man tonight, she was mistaken. Once again he had her heart racing and her body softening for his possession.

She scooted back and dropped onto his thighs. He guided all that male hardness inside her and she groaned.

"I know. It feels so damn good." He nuzzled her nape. "Right when I shove my cock into you I wanna fuck you like a madman. But when I feel your pussy so tight and warm and wet around me? I wanna stay all up in you for as long as possible without moving. It's been so long. I've finally got what I've wanted with you and I don't want to rush it."

"Kyle—"

"Don't. Move."

She wrapped her right arm behind his head to clutch his neck. He kept both his hands on her hips, his face against her nape.

They breathed together, their bodies connected but at rest.

His legs were damp with sweat against the backs of her thighs. His every exhalation was a caress on her skin.

"Such sweet obedience," he whispered. "Move on me. Nice and slow. You're awful damn good at a gallop but I wanna keep this at an easy trot."

"How did you know horse analogies turn me on?" Hooking her heels on the bottom rungs on the chair legs gave her some stability and some leverage as she started to move.

He laughed. "Lucky guess." He pulled her body to counter his upward thrusts. Measured thrusts. Nothing fast and furious.

Yet.

Kyle's mouth was everywhere. On the side of her throat. On her ear. Cruising the slope of her shoulder. Bombarding her senses. All while that thick shaft moved inside her.

"Let's kick up the pace."

Celia wasn't sure she could come like this, but she didn't care. This was glorious. Naked and sweat-soaked in their kitchen and their bodies slapping together, his harsh breathing in her ear.

"Celia," he panted. "Jesus, woman. What you do to me." He grunted, shoved deep one last time and his seed filled her.

In the aftermath of such explosive loving, Celia hoped she could satisfy his sexual demands. Such passion existed in this man.

Don't get addicted to his skills because this is temporary, remember? Remind him, remind yourself to enjoy it while it lasts.

His mouth brushed her ear. "Thank you."

"I have a feeling these next six months are gonna be awesome."

"Yeah. I might even learn to like strawberries."

Chapter Eight

*C*ountry tunes played through her iPod speakers. Celia tried to concentrate on repairing the nail holes in the living room wall, but she kept sneaking glances at Kyle. Doing husbandly house stuff. In their house. In his faded, baggy jeans and a long-sleeved long john shirt that matched his green eyes. He'd pulled the sleeves up to his elbows, revealing her obsession: his forearms. An AFR ball cap sat on his head, laced-up leather work boots on his feet. He softly whistled off-key as he lightly sanded the shelves.

The man absolutely rocked her world in so many ways.

He'd woken her with insistent kisses, whispering in that raspy morning voice about how much he needed her. Her body heated at the sound of his voice. Moistened in response to his demands and amazingly thorough caresses. He'd taken her with tenderness as soothing as it was arousing. She loved that he let her see that needy side of him.

As soon as they finished the chores, Kyle joined her in the shower, fucking her mindless. Pressing her against the tiled walls as he took her from behind, he wrapped her braid around his fist, pulling to the slight edge of pain. She'd come so hard she'd screamed. Then he warned her he'd fuck her at least twice more before the day ended.

He'd smirked at her during lunch, but he'd only kissed her and played a little grab ass before they'd started prepping the living room for paint. A necessity before anything else, since on a whim he'd taken her to town and they'd ordered carpet and a new flat-screen TV.

"Kyle? Do you think there's a Sawzall in the garage?"

His back stiffened, as she knew it would. She withheld a snicker.

"Why in the hell do you need a Sawzall?"

"To fix something."

"The thought of you holding a power tool scares the crap outta me."

"I know." She laughed. "I'm thinking if we cut out this portion of the shelving"—she pointed to the center section—"we could put the TV here, and arrange the furniture to face this direction, to improve the flow of the room. That way, no one would walk in front of the TV and we'd save floor space."

Kyle scratched his chin, studying the wall. "There is an outlet over here. We could get a stand for the TV instead of hanging it from the wall. Might have to shore up the base shelf with an extra piece of plywood. We've already gotta paint the whole damn thing.... So, yeah. That'd work."

Celia was surprised that he'd agreed so easily. Her brothers had always dismissed her suggestions to them without consideration.

He faced her. "What?"

"Thank you for not calling it a stupid idea."

"Hey." He set a gloved hand on her cheek. "I ain't gonna argue with you just to argue, Cele. We're past that, aren't we?"

"Yes."

"Good. But, darlin', no way in hell am I letting you run the Sawzall."

He clamped his hand on her butt as he kissed her. He would've made good on his earlier promise if not for the sound of tires spinning up the driveway and two short honks.

They broke apart and peered out the picture window.

Not Josh's truck as she expected, but Lainie's car.

Her stomach cartwheeled.

Lainie exited the driver's side and opened the rear door as Harper climbed out of the passenger's side and her husband, Bran, from the rear.

She and Kyle looked at each other, then back at the people making their way up to the porch.

"Appears we have company," Kyle remarked.

"Is it awful to say I'm glad it's not Hank or Abe?"

"No, kitten, it's not. I'm relieved too."

Kyle held her hand as they opened the door, showing her—and their guests—a united front. "Come on in."

Harper made a beeline for Celia. "Omigod, Celia, congratulations!"

Celia caught Kyle's eye and smiled, before hugging her friend back.

Then Harper whapped her on the arm. "I cannot believe you didn't tell me! You were my maid of honor, for crying out loud. I at least deserved a phone call, especially since no one had a clue you and Kyle were involved."

"And we got such a fantastic reaction when we did tell folks," Kyle said dryly.

Harper hugged Kyle too. "I'm thrilled for you both. Thrilled to the bottom of my heart. And as much as I'd like to claim I saw this one coming, I didn't. Not at all."

"The wild child's been tamed, eh?" Bran blocked Celia's stomach punch and laughed. "Not completely tamed, I see." He thrust out his hand to Kyle. "Congrats, man. I gotta say I wasn't nearly as surprised by this as some people. But I've been watchin' sparks flying between you two for years. Figured there had to be fire under there somewhere."

A whimper sounded and Celia whirled around to face Lainie, holding Brianna. A teary-eyed Lainie passed her daughter to Harper and practically threw herself at Celia. Celia just awkwardly patted her on the back while Harper, Brianna, and Bran disappeared into the kitchen.

Lainie stepped back and took both Celia's hands in hers. "Congratulations. I'm so happy for both of you." Lainie looked at Kyle. "Thrilled to my toes that two of my favorite people in the world found each other. Please believe that. And when I heard what Hank said, how he reacted to this news . . ." She shook her head.

Kyle moved in behind Celia and set his hands on her shoulders. "Thank you, Lainie. I—we—appreciate you coming here. But your husband is an asshole."

"Everyone has railed on Hank and Abe for how they mishandled the situation." Lainie's eyes were still leaking tears. "I won't apologize for Hank, Celia. That's his responsibility. But I had to come and tell you that I don't feel that way. I know deep inside Hank doesn't either; it just caught him and Abe off guard."

"We understand that," Kyle said. "But I'm not letting either one of them near my wife. She deserves better treatment and respect from her brothers. She always has and we both know it."

Lainie nodded. "They were totally unprepared for the backlash. Evidently Janie heard the tail end of your conversation and she couldn't waddle outside fast enough to stop it before it reached the point it did. Her pregnancy hormones took over. She was so incensed she punched Abe in the stomach and took a swing at Hank. Then she called me, so hysterical that I thought she was going into labor, so I hauled ass over there. That's when they told me what'd happened. What they'd said. I lost my mind on them. I was upset, which upset Brianna, and Janie was still yelling...so they had to deal with all three of us. And then Eli showed up."

Celia frowned. "Eli? Really?"

"You know how Eli is always so reserved? He lit into Hank and Abe, angry like I'd never seen. He's the one who told them about Marshall Townsend, Kyle."

"I didn't expect Eli would do that."

"It just got worse. Tanna called to ream my husband. So did Devin, who snapped at them both to grow the fuck up, be happy and thankful that Kyle, one of the greatest guys he knows, ended up with Celia. Then Fletch called because Eli was pissed off enough to share with him what the Lawson brothers had done." Lainie lowered her voice. "We decided to wait a few days before dropping by. Janie would've come too, but she's about to pop."

Celia let go of Lainie's hands. "I'm glad you're here. But to be honest, I don't wanna talk about my brothers anymore, okay?"

"Okay."

"I wanna see my darlin' niece."

Harper and Bran returned with Brianna, who said, "Mamamama-mama," and tried to throw herself out of Harper's arms.

"Come here, kiddo, and say hi to your auntie Celia and your uncle Kyle."

Kyle said, "Whoa. That sounds weird."

Celia held her hands out for Brianna, but she shook her head and buried her face in Lainie's neck.

"So, Kyle, you gonna show me your place and tell me how the hell you ended up with it?" Bran asked.

"Sure. We'll both need a beer. Maybe a lot of beer." Kyle kissed Celia on the cheek before he and Bran went outside.

"I'm ready for the tour," Harper said.

Lainie shifted Brianna. "She's about to fall asleep. Got any place I can sit down?"

"Just the kitchen. The living room furniture was nasty. We're repainting and stuff before the new carpet and furniture come next week."

"I'll catch up with you guys in a minute."

"I'm dying to hear about you and Kyle," Harper said after Lainie went into the kitchen.

Celia gave her the short version of their courtship and marriage because that's all there was.

Harper shook her head. "No wonder I hadn't heard from you. I thought you were mad at me."

"Why would I be mad at you?"

"I don't know. It seems ever since I married Bran you've been distant."

"Just because of distance, Harper." Celia dropped her voice. "Family stuff has been dogging me for a lot longer than this last blowup. You know that. And you and Bran were newlyweds. You didn't want me crashing at your new house and dragging you to Buckeye Joe's to get your drink on."

"You don't have to be knocking back a beer next to me in person to talk to me, Cele."

"True. But it is more fun." She grinned. "I'll take you on the nickel tour."

Harper got a huge kick out of hearing Kyle's reaction to the two pink bathrooms.

Lainie entered the bedroom with a sleeping Brianna. She laid her on her back in the middle of the bed and they all tiptoed out. "She's down for at least a half hour."

"You guys want a beer or coffee or something?"

"I'd love a cup of tea," Harper said.

Celia hadn't played hostess before. She didn't have any dessert-type thing to serve with the coffee, which would probably get her kicked out of the ranch-wives club.

Tea in hand, Harper tugged her into the living room. "Tell me what you've got planned for this space."

Feeling a little shy, because she had no decorating expertise, Celia showed the paint colors. Talked about the furniture. The carpet. Rearranging the space. "Kyle didn't want anything too girly."

Lainie and Harper exchanged a smug look.

"What?"

"Ignore him. Especially since you already have two pink bathrooms. Put whatever colors or patterns in here you want."

Celia couldn't tell them she probably wouldn't be sticking around and didn't want to saddle him with stuff he hated.

Yeah, that's why you picked everything you *like. Because you can't wait to leave it behind. For Kyle's next wife.*

"Speaking of bathrooms... Lainie, could I convince you to take out these stitches?"

"What happened?"

"Run-in with a rogue steer. The doc in Vegas said to leave 'em in a week, so do you mind? Bein's you're a medical professional and all?"

"If I don't do it, you'll do it yourself, won't you?"

"Probably. They itch like hell."

"Come on."

∻

Celia couldn't help but stare at the angry red mark. Good thing they hadn't taken wedding pictures with the Bride of Frankenstein scar.

Lainie looped her arm through Celia's as they walked back to the kitchen. "You're really done with barrel racing and Kyle's giving up bull riding?"

"It wasn't a hard choice—we've both been disillusioned in the last year. We were just talking about how happy we are not to be hitting the blacktop." She looked at Lainie. "I think Tanna's getting to that point too. Although she's winning, she's tired of competing. She's ready to settle down, but she'll never come out and say it."

"It's not PC to admit the appeal of home and hearth, is it?" Lainie asked.

Celia shook her head. "I find it interesting that the girls Harper and I went to high school with, who were lucky enough to attend college, got married right after college graduation. They became housewives and mothers without ever holding down a real job." Her gaze moved between Lainie and Harper. "Both of you guys have jobs outside being ranch wives."

Harper's eyes turned thoughtful. "Are you afraid you'll get bored being Kyle's wife?"

Never. "No. But what if I need something else?" Celia had to stop and think. Was she addressing this now and laying the groundwork for their inevitable divorce? So Harper and Lainie could say they saw it coming early on?

"I don't see Kyle as the type to fault you for that."

Celia sighed. "Do you think the guys are out there talking about this stuff?"

"Chances are high they're discussing cows," Lainie said.

"Cows?"

"Yes, cows are a major topic of discussion. All the freakin' time," Harper complained.

"But Hank and Abe have complained that all Janie and I talk about is babies," Lainie pointed out.

"And Bran reminds me that if we have Renner and Tierney over, all we talk about is the Split Rock Ranch and Resort." Harper's eyes twinkled. "So maybe we oughta talk about one thing that's always on our minds. Sex."

Lainie frowned. "I think I hear Brianna." She scooted out of the kitchen.

Talk about abrupt. Was Lainie uncomfortable talking about this because Hank was Celia's brother? Or because Lainie had been with Kyle during that summer she'd traveled the circuit with Hank and Kyle?

Harper leaned forward. "Spill the juicy details, Cele. You and Kyle."

"The man is amazing in bed. Like gold-medal amazing."

"I bet that was on the plus side of you deciding to marry him, huh?"

Celia spun her coffee cup around. "Believe it or not, Kyle and I didn't have sex until after we were married."

"Seriously?"

"It truly was one of those we-looked-at-each-other-and-everything-just-fell-into-place type of moments." She grinned. "So the fact he has the mad bedroom skills is a serious bonus."

She dropped the subject when Lainie returned with Brianna. Although it kept popping into her head that her husband had had sex with Lainie. Kinky sex. She was starting to wish she didn't know the backstory between her new husband and her brother and his wife. She wasn't jealous. Okay, she was jealous, but how did she bring it up with him?

So... Kyle, is there anything that you, Hank, and Lainie didn't *do together that you wanna try with me?*

Brianna held out her arms for Celia and thoughts of various threesome positions were forgotten. She kissed her niece's head, the coppery ringlets tickling her nose. Brianna had her mother's hair, but her eyes were exactly like Hank's.

Celia wandered to the window and looked out, but didn't see Kyle or Bran anywhere.

Maybe they really were out in the pasture talking about cows.

⟣⟢

Kyle took Bran into the barn and they sat across from each other on the ATVs.

"So you and Celia? I ain't surprised. You've wanted to tap that for a long time," Bran said.

"No lie. Always made me feel like a fuckin' pervert." Kyle grinned. "Still makes me feel like a pervert when I think of all the raunchy stuff I can do with my sexy wife any freakin' time I want."

Bran laughed. "Ain't that the truth." He sipped his beer. "I just gotta throw this out there. Hank and Abe were wrong. And you get props from me for not knocking them both on their asses. I had to stop Harper from goin' over there."

Kyle couldn't help but smile, thinking about sweet-mouthed Harper marching over and giving the gruff ranchers what for.

"They're good guys, but they've treated Celia like she was eleven long after she ain't been eleven. We all kinda did it too, up to a point, but never like her brothers did. And it pissed me off how they threatened us with bodily harm if we ever touched her. Took her a long time to see herself as an attractive girl—woman—and not as a tomboy. I hated that we played a part in that."

Kyle was glad he wasn't the only one who'd seen that. "Me too."

"Hank and Abe will come around. They already have, according to Lainie, but I guess I don't blame you and Celia for needing some time to cool off."

"We sure as shit got plenty to do around here to keep ourselves occupied."

"How shocked were you to find out Marshall Townsend was your father?"

"Ask me when the shock wears off. It's like I'll wake up and find it's all a damn dream. I went from saving as much money as possible to buy my own place to inheriting a place complete with cows, horses, a house, and barns."

"Why do you think your mom didn't tell you?"

"Who the fuck knows? I gotta be honest, I'm too pissed off at her right now to be civil, so I've warned her to give me some time." Kyle shook his head, thinking back to his most recent conversation with his mother and her insistence on explaining things. "I'm pissed off at him too, even though he's dead. He looked me right in the goddamn eye that night at Cactus Jack's. He fucking talked to me and never said a word about any of this."

Bran frowned. "Wait. You mean that time a bunch of us went out in Rawlins a few years back when Hank and Lainie were dating?"

"Yeah. He approached me. Babbled some drunken bullshit, but nothing like, *Hey, I'm your father, lemme buy you a drink and we'll talk.*" Kyle counted to ten. "In the fourteen years since he learned the truth about me, he never tried to get in contact with me. Then he has an attack of conscience on his deathbed and reaches out?"

"Man, that sucks. But at least he done right by you by leaving you this place."

"I guess. It's just weird. All those years growing up, I'd wondered who my father was. I imagine you did too, since we're the only ones of our group who grew up fatherless. But I'd always wondered if I looked like him. Or if he had kids besides me. If maybe he'd died. Or maybe he was famous."

"I had those thoughts a time or two myself. I asked my grandma about it and she was always honest, as much as it pained her. She said my mom hadn't been sure who'd impregnated her because she'd been with lots of guys. So I let it go."

"I thought I'd let it go too, but then this comes from out of nowhere."

"He didn't write you a letter, or anything explaining it?"

Kyle wondered how he could talk about this without coming across as sounding ungrateful. "No. A warning would've been nice. Christ. All those years I helped you guys out on your places? It was like I was playing. I really had no fucking idea how much work is involved in raising cattle."

"And you haven't gotten to the fun parts yet. Two months of limited sleep and frigid nights tracking down an angry mama and sickly calves. Or hot summer days when I literally fall off the rake or the baler because I've been on the machine for sixteen hours straight. Or when you haul cattle to market and lose your ass, but why is steak twelve bucks a pound in the grocery store?"

"I ain't really bitching, you know. I'm just overwhelmed." Kyle grimaced and drained his beer. "And a damn greenhorn."

Bran laughed. "You got yourself a mighty fine ranch hand in Celia. She ain't gonna steer you wrong. She knows more about ranching than her brothers ever gave her credit for. But if you have questions, Kyle, for chrissake, don't have too much pride to call me, okay? You know I ain't the type of guy to make fun of you or make you feel like an idiot for askin'."

"Thanks, Bran. I appreciate it more than you know."

"So, whatdya say we take these ATVs for a spin and you show me your herd?"

After an hour of dinking around, they returned to the house. It loosened something around his heart to see Celia holding Brianna. He'd never seen her around kids; she'd always been the youngest one in their group. Brianna seemed as enamored of Celia as Celia was of her. He knew Celia would make a good mother. Loving. Fierce. Kind. Fair.

Get those kinds of thoughts right outta your head.

"Now, Lainie, I'm gonna respectfully request you take your darlin' daughter away from my wife, so as to not give her any ideas about babies, bein's we've only been married a week."

Celia laughed and nuzzled Brianna's plump cheek before handing her off to Lainie. "She is adorable. But I agree. Let's get through calving season together before we start planning a nursery."

Bran helped Harper on with her coat and Lainie dressed Brianna. She hoisted her daughter on her hip and looked at Celia. "Your brother is going to apologize. Not because I'm making him, but because Hank knows he was wrong. So my question is, will you let him apologize to you?"

She nodded.

Kyle turned to kiss Celia's forehead. Because he couldn't not touch her all the time. He loved that she wanted and accepted his open affection. He'd never had that. Never been with a woman long enough to show that part of himself. He noticed the stitches were gone. "Please tell me that Lainie took these out?"

"Yeah. Sorry it looks so hideous."

"Huh-uh. Every time I look at it I'll be reminded of the day we got married."

Her eyes softened.

"And it sorta does look like a small K, kinda like you branded my initial on your face to forever commemorate the event."

Celia elbowed him. "Jerk."

He laughed.

After Lainie's car disappeared down the driveway, Kyle murmured, "You okay?"

"I'm glad they came."

"Me too." He slapped her butt. "But break is over. We need to finish prepping this room so we can slap on the first coat of paint."

He'd found a Sawzall in the garage and marked off the section of shelving to remove. It bolstered his masculine pride to do something around the house without Celia's help, since he needed her constant supervision when it came to the ranch and ranch chores.

Celia continued filling nail holes and repairing cracks in the walls.

When she finished, she began scuffing the paint on the shelves. Almost violently. She hadn't said anything for a while, which wasn't completely odd. He'd discovered she didn't talk all the time, but when he glanced over at her, she had that stubborn set to her mouth. "Something wrong?"

"No."

Silence.

Then she started sanding harder.

"Come on, Celia, what's goin' on?"

She whirled around. "When you see Lainie do you think of that summer you traveled with her and Hank during Cowboy Christmas? And of all the wild, kinky, crazy sex you had? When you see her do you imagine her naked? Do you remember how it was to fuck her?" Celia's voice escalated so she'd shouted that last part.

Kyle's jaw nearly hit the floor. Then he snapped it shut. "That was a long goddamn time ago."

"Some memories are forever. There are some images you can't erase."

"Like the image of you on your knees sucking Breck off?"

"You're never gonna let me forget that, are you?"

"Like you're not letting me forget something that happened a damn lifetime ago for me?"

She notched her chin higher. "You still haven't answered the question, Kyle. When you see Lainie, is that what you think of? How wild and raunchy and uninhibited she was?"

"You have a high opinion of me, if you believe I'm thinking about fucking another woman when I'm standing next to my wife."

"Oh, don't pull that bullshit answer. I'm not really your wife and we both know it."

Stunned silence filled the air.

"You really are my wife and you really don't wanna push me on this point. I promised you I'd be faithful. For me that means faithful in body and in mind. You owe me the same courtesy."

"Of what? Wishing I had threesome tales to tell you so you could pretend it didn't bother you? Well, fuck that. I'm not perfect like Lainie and I can't just forget about it."

Then he roared, "That's it!" and charged her, throwing her over his shoulder, jerking off her boots so she couldn't kick him as he stormed to their bedroom.

"Goddammit, Kyle, let me down right fucking now or I swear to God I'll—" She gasped when he tossed her on the bed. She gasped louder and swore at him, thrashing beneath his body when he pinned her.

He pulled one wrist up at a time and locked them in cuffs attached to the headboard. Then he rested on her thighs so she couldn't move.

Celia cranked her head, looked at the cuffs with total shock and then glared at him. "What the fuck kind of depraved thing were you planning with these?"

"Something a lot more erotic than this, but you've just plain pissed me off, so we're gonna do this my way. I will make you understand this, Celia. Even if it takes all damn night."

"Let me go."

"No."

"I'm warning you—"

He laughed and reached inside a pillowcase, waving a bandana at her. "Gonna be pretty hard to warn me when you're gagged, ain't it?"

"You wouldn't dare. What the hell is wrong with you? You've hidden these marital aids all over the place? Do you have a stash of vi—"

Kyle stretched the twisted bandana across her mouth and tied it behind her head. "For your sake, kitten, I hope you'd planned to ask if I have a stash of vibrators."

It was hard to smirk with her lips and tongue blocked, but Celia managed to do it. And that's when he knew she was enjoying this lesson just as much as he was.

"Now, we're gonna get a couple of things straight. But first, I'm gonna strip you bare."

She thrashed.

"No need to thank me. It'll be my pleasure." He ripped her blouse open, hearing *ping ping* as the buttons ricocheted off the wall. He tugged the blouse up her arms and tied the fabric around her wrists.

So she hadn't worn a bra after their sexy romp in the shower. Good.

Watching her eyes, he palmed her sweet little tits. Squeezed and played with the firm flesh. Then he dragged the callused tips of his fingers down her body. He popped the top button on her jeans. "Don't kick me. Because if you do? I will take great pleasure in paddling your ass until it's good and red, understand?"

A wide-eyed Celia nodded.

Kyle whisked off her jeans. "I am your husband. That makes you my wife. No pretending. No bullshit games whether we're alone or with other people. We are legally married. You will respect that between us, understood?"

Something flashed in her eyes before she nodded again.

"You have the nerve to throw something in my face that happened so long ago I barely remember it? When for the last two years I've had to watch you with Breck? Seeing you kiss him? Watching you two leave together? Knowing he had you in his bed and didn't appreciate it? That fucking killed me, Celia."

She was trying to speak.

"Listen to me. The only woman I think about fucking is you. But actions speak louder than words, don't they, little wife of mine?" Kyle rubbed the rough edge of his whiskered jaw on her neck, on her chest, on her belly. "How many times do you think I can make you come? How many orgasms will it take for me to prove how much I want you? Only you."

Celia mumbled something around the gag.

"Did you say . . . ten?"

She shook her head wildly.

Kyle squeezed her hips between his knees and lowered his mouth to her left nipple. He bit down hard enough to get her attention and suckled away the sting. He did that twice more. Content to take his time and enjoy the feel of her nipple tight and hard against his flicking tongue. Then he attacked her throat with sucking kisses. He wanted to mark her. So when she looked at her body she saw signs of his possession.

When she closed her eyes, he tapped her on the ass.

"Huh-uh. Look at me. Watch me enjoying your body."

Then he moved between her legs. Grabbing a handful of her ass, Kyle raised her juicy pussy to his mouth and feasted on her. Stabbing his tongue deep inside her cunt. Growling his pleasure at her tangy taste. Then swirling his tongue around her clit. Driving her to the point that she arched, she whimpered, and her thighs went rigid. And he backed off.

Some inventive swear words were coming from behind that gag.

He hung above her body on hands and knees. "I didn't stop to torture you. I stopped so you can look in my eyes. Am I thinking about anyone but you?"

Her breath was decidedly ragged when she slowly shook her head.

"Relax, baby. 'Cause I'm nowhere near done. Seems I have a lot to prove to you."

Kyle whipped off his shirt. He focused all his attention on her skin. Lightly running the rough tips of his fingers down the outside of her legs from the curve of her thigh to the delicate section around her anklebone. He afforded the inside of her legs equal attention. Except when he stroked the crease where pelvis met thigh, he brushed his lips over that hypersensitive sweep of skin between her hipbones.

She whimpered and her whole body twitched.

His gentle strokes and swirling caresses sent goose bumps dancing across her flesh. He placed soft smooches over her abused ribs. He allowed the hair on his chest to rub against her nipples, learning that it made her squirmier than ever.

Kyle's dick protested when he bent forward. He'd be lucky if he didn't shoot in his damn pants before this was done. Touching her like this, when she couldn't do a thing but enjoy the erotic torture, made him hotter than he would've believed.

And it might make him depraved, but he loved how Celia looked tied up. He'd figure out a way to lengthen the chain next time so he could flip her over to touch and taste the back side of her body with just as much attention to detail.

His lips followed the line of her arm from the bend in her elbow, down her muscled biceps, over the inside of her armpit. Then he reversed course, but slowed down. Stopping to lick and suck on spots too tempting to resist.

Celia's eyes were closed and he didn't demand that she open them. He wanted her to lose all coherent thought when he was touching her.

When she started rubbing her legs together and her belly showed a slight sheen of sweat, Kyle eased off. "Be right back. Don't go nowhere." He laughed when she made a garbled noise, trying to connect her foot with his butt before he bounced off the bed. He loved her sass. He secretly loved that she'd shown a jealous streak about Lainie, even when it was misguided. That meant she cared more about him than she was ready to admit. And hell yeah, he could work with that.

Kyle ditched his jeans and grabbed his cordless electric razor.

She tried to lift her head to see what he was doing when he inserted himself between her legs.

He loomed over her and waved the shaver at her.

She shook her head and attempted to scramble backward.

"I'm not gonna shave you, kitten. But since I haven't seen a vibrator in your things, this will do in a pinch." He flicked it on and then off again. "Now, if you can promise not to yell at me or insult me I'll remove the gag."

Celia nodded.

"You sure?"

Another vigorous nod.

He untied it and swallowed whatever she'd been about to say in a ravenous kiss. Basking in her surrender to him. Damn difficult to ignore his body's urging to sink into her. "Am I thinking about pleasing anyone but my beautiful, sexy wife right now?"

"No."

"Say it back to me. Who you are."

"I am your wife."

Kyle clicked on the electric razor and placed the backside of the buzzing object directly on her clit. "Liked me touchin' you?"

"Do ya think?" She moaned. "God. Kyle. Please. I'm already so close."

He latched onto her right nipple and sucked hard, working that tip, until he heard the hitch in her breathing.

Celia cried out as the orgasm unfurled.

With his mouth around her nipple, he felt every throb on his lips.

As the last pulse ended, Kyle tossed the shaver aside, spread her legs wide, and impaled her. Fucking her with short, fast jabs that kept constant friction on her clit. Gritting his teeth against coming right then when another orgasm rocked her.

She actually released a little scream.

The rhythmic squeezing of her cunt muscles around his shaft felt so good he about lost his fucking mind.

As soon as her body slumped against the mattress, Kyle wrapped her legs around his waist with a terse "Hold on," and dropped his hands by her head.

He slammed his cock deep with every thrust. Sucking in gasping breaths filled with Celia's honey-sweet scent. Feeling her warmth and softness absorbing his powerful thrusts.

"So good, God, Celia. It's never been like this. Ever. Nothing that came before you matters." His shaft slid into that hot, gripping tunnel twice more. His balls tightened and he finally gave in to the ear-roaring, blood-pumping, heart-pounding orgasm that wrung him out.

When Kyle could function again, he kissed Celia's throat, up over her chin, and gazed into her sated eyes. He considered trying to come up with something poetic or even romantic. Seemed he could sweet-talk all day long if he was trying to talk his way into a woman's bed. But he'd never meant those words. And now when he did . . . they got stuck in his mouth.

He said the only thing he could think of. "So, what's for supper?"

And his sweet, fiery Celia looked at him and laughed. "It's your turn to cook. Besides, I'm a little tied up at the moment."

Yep. Kyle definitely loved every damn thing about his woman.

Chapter Nine

A loud, "Jesus. Seriously? Today?" brought Celia out of the kitchen.

A woman with a red dye job, wearing lots of makeup and a fake cheetah-print coat sashayed up the driveway.

"Who's that?"

He looked at her strangely. "My mother."

Celia squinted at her. "Cut me some slack. The last time I saw her I was sixteen. And she was a brunette."

"Hell, I saw her at Christmas and she was blond."

"Did you invite her over?"

"And forget to tell you? No. I haven't called her and she knows I'm mad. She better not bitch about sleepin' on the floor if she plans to spend the night with us."

Holy crap. It hit home that she actually had a mother-in-law. A mother-in-law who might be spending the night? She fought the urge to hide in the kitchen as Kyle let his mother in.

"Hey, Mom."

She hugged him fiercely. "My boy. I'm so glad to see you."

"You should've called."

"I did. But you're not answering my calls."

"I've been busy."

"Busy being pissed off?"

"That too."

"I figured. I've given you more than a week and I suspected you'd take a month, so I decided to be proactive." She hugged him again. "You're looking fit."

Kyle snorted. He held his hand out for Celia.

She took a deep breath and stood beside Kyle.

"This is my wife, Celia."

Kyle hadn't even told his mother her name? Her first thought was he was embarrassed to be married to her. Her second thought was he didn't want Celia to get close to his mother because she repeatedly reminded him she wasn't sticking around past the six-month mark.

Her green eyes, identical to Kyle's, narrowed skeptically. "Little Celia Lawson? My God. Kyle used to bitch about you all the time and now you're married to him?"

"Jesus, Mom."

"Sorry." She smiled tightly. "I'm Sherry Gilchrist. Despite all the years my son spent at your brother's place we've never met, have we?" Sherry's voice had the rasp of a lifelong smoker.

"We met a long time ago. But it's nice to see you, Sherry."

"Couldn't've been that long ago, honey, 'cause you ain't that old. Then again . . . now I remember. Good Lord. You still look about sixteen."

Kyle muttered, "I need a fuckin' drink," and bailed into the kitchen.

Celia would make him pay later for abandoning her.

Sherry's gaze tracked everything in the room. "This place is—"

"We're doin' some updates," Celia said hastily. "Everything is kind of a mess."

"So a tour of my son's home is out?"

Intentional use of *my son's* home seemed a little combative. "No. But I'll warn ya. It'll take about three minutes."

Sherry didn't say much besides, "I see Kyle still doesn't make his bed." Followed by, "I imagine Kyle hates the pink bathrooms." Sherry lifted a brow at Celia's pink shirt. "He has an aversion to anything pink."

Smile. "There are chairs in the kitchen if you'd like to sit."

Kyle's glass of whiskey stopped halfway to his mouth. He looked at Celia and Sherry guiltily. "What?"

"Why don't you offer your mother a drink?"

"Nothing alcoholic for me, thanks. I'm driving. I'll have orange juice, which I know is stocked in the fridge because Kyle drinks about a gallon of it a week. He's loved it since he was a boy."

Celia had known about Kyle's juice addiction for years. What bothered her was the almost...jealous aspect of Sherry's comments.

You're being paranoid. This is Kyle's mother. There is no competition.

Kyle parked himself across from Sherry. "You drove to Rawlins by yourself?"

"No. Rick is visiting a friend at the prison."

"Big surprise he's got friends in the slammer," Kyle muttered.

Sherry's, "Be nice," admonishment was followed by a low-pitched smoker's laugh. "I know you've never liked Rick."

"You deserve better."

"And that's why I didn't date while you were growing up. None of them would've passed the Kyle test."

That comment jarred her. Sounds like Kyle had been as protective of his mother as her brothers had been of her.

He smiled. "True. So how long you stayin'?"

"Until we get some things straight. Took me an hour to get my courage up to head up the driveway or I'da been here sooner."

Good thing Kyle's mother hadn't shown up earlier, when her bawdy, bossy son had Celia on her knees in the hallway, hands tied with a bandana as she blew him to heaven. She set the juice on the table. "I'll leave you two to talk."

"Huh-uh. You're my wife. Whatever she says will affect you too, so have a seat."

Sherry wasn't thrilled about Kyle's decree and seemed to study Celia closer than ever when Kyle wrapped one arm around her shoulder.

But her focus returned to Kyle when he demanded, "I wanna know how you got knocked up by Marshall Townsend."

"Kyle, I—"

"Save it. No excuses. We're getting some things straight, remember? So start talking."

When Sherry pressed her hands to her cheeks, Celia noticed the manicure with little red hearts for Valentine's Day. Even Kyle's mother was a girly girl. She curled her rough-skinned fingers into her palms. She'd had a manicure exactly once in her twenty-five years and it was only because Harper did it for free.

Once in a while Kyle would toss off a comment about Celia acting like a man or looking like a man from behind in her Carhartt overalls. She hadn't mentioned it bothered her because she was still finding her footing and discovering verbal boundaries, when in the past everything Kyle had said to her seemed to set her off. The truth was, she wasn't outwardly feminine very often. She didn't devote time to fussing with her appearance when her day was spent outside dealing with livestock. Her clothes were comfortable rather than fashionable, with the exception of the blouses and belts she'd worn in the arena—those had a little flash. There was nothing wrong with living in boots and jeans.

Was there? Did it bother Kyle that she didn't take the time to doll herself up?

When Sherry started to speak she snapped back to attention.

"I've worked in restaurants since I was thirteen. I washed dishes, bused tables, and worked my way up to waitress. When I turned twenty-one I started working in bars. I've either bartended or been a cocktail waitress for the last thirty-nine years."

Kyle wore an impatient look. This was all old news to him. Celia had to wonder why Sherry was rehashing it. For her benefit? So Celia would know how hard Sherry's life had been?

"I'd been bartending at the VFW in Rawlins for a year, trying to figure out what to do with my life. The age group was mostly married middle-aged guys, so they were always flirting with me. Pretty harmless most of the time. Their wives didn't like me 'cause I was hot stuff back in those days."

Celia had no problem envisioning a younger Sherry. Vivacious. Built like a dream. She could probably bullshit with the best of them and mix a mean drink with complete charm. Kyle was a total chip off the old block.

"Marshall only showed up once a month. He was a good-looking man, around forty-five. Respectful. Good tipper. I didn't really flirt with him, but I didn't have to. I knew by the way he looked at me that he wanted me. We talked and I found out he was in a bad marriage. He saw no way out of it since he'd taken over his wife's family ranch.

"One night he'd stuck around while I closed down, and he kissed me. I'd never been kissed with such … I don't want to say desperation, but that's what it was. And it'd been a long time since I'd been with any man, so I said yes when he asked if I'd spend the night with him. We checked into a motel. Without going into too much detail, I think he lived out all his sexual fantasies in that one night. In the morning he'd said if I told anyone, he'd deny it."

"Classy," Kyle said with a snarl.

"I ended up pregnant, which was ironic because he told me he was sterile. I quit my job at the VFW, moved to Casper to work as a waitress. Even at age twenty-eight I wasn't ready for motherhood and I had every intention of putting my baby up for adoption. But the first time I felt Kyle move inside me, I knew I'd do whatever it took to keep him." Sherry's eyes filled with tears and she reached for a napkin. "It wasn't easy being a single mom, working late-night bar hours, trying to find decent child care when I had a nighttime job. But we managed. I stuck it out in Casper for ten years.

"Then one of my old bosses opened up a new supper club in Rawlins and she asked me to train the waitstaff. The money was better, so I returned to where I'd started."

"Did you leave when you were pregnant because you were afraid of Marshall's reaction?" Kyle asked.

"No. Maybe. It was a blur."

"And never once during those years we struggled, did you think to contact Marshall and demand he support me? Support us? You eventually had the proof that I was his kid. Why didn't you do it sooner?"

Sherry took a long sip of her orange juice. "I was a cocktail waitress, Kyle. In a small town. For all Marshall knew, and the way he acted, since I'd slept with him so easily, I'd probably slept with other men that easily all the time."

"Bullshit."

Celia believed Sherry. Harper's mother had also spent her life working in bars. Even before her mother had run off, she had a reputation as an easy piece, which everyone in town believed, regardless if it was true.

"I wish it was bullshit. Marshall and I didn't run in the same circles in Rawlins and we crossed paths only one time. And his wife was with him."

Kyle suddenly sat up and snapped his fingers. "Wait. I remember that. At the fall festival my junior year. I was about sixteen? I'd given up football for rodeo. You volunteered to work the concession stand with me. When they showed up you were really weird. You kept telling me to check the popcorn maker. Like four times."

Her eyes turned shrewd. "You remember that?"

"I just remembered it. You never gave a shit what anyone thought of you, but you were self-conscious in front of them. It was the first time I'd ever seen you like that."

"After seeing him with his nasty wife I remembered why I never told him about you." Sherry dabbed her eyes. "She would've been horrible to you, Kyle, since you were born on the wrong side of the sheets. I'll own up to any mistakes I made raising you alone, but having someone that bitter in your life . . . I don't regret keeping you from that."

"Did he know that night?"

She shook her head. "The night you were in the motorcycle accident I drove out here, pretty hysterical. I said if you needed surgery, he needed to help pay for it because you were his son. He called me every name in the book. Basically threw me out of his house. But a couple of days later he tracked me down and demanded a paternity test."

Kyle got up and grabbed a beer. Instead of returning to his chair, he paced. "So he knew I was his son and did nothing." He faced Sherry, his face a mask of confusion and anger. "Why?"

"I can't answer that. I wish I could. I didn't know him either, Kyle. I had a few conversations with him thirty-some years ago. One night with him. When he found out about you . . . you were an adult, his wife was dead, and he had proof you were his kid. He should have—"

"Since he didn't bother, the responsibility should've been yours," Kyle snapped.

Sherry stood and got in his face. "No, sirree. I will *not* apologize for this.

I've spent my entire life looking out for you and protecting you. I sure as shit wasn't gonna give him a chance to reject you. Didn't matter if you were nine or nineteen or ninety. It still would've hurt you. God, look at you—it's hurting you now." She swallowed with difficulty. "It would've changed you. The ball was completely in his court, Kyle. *His*. Not mine. Not yours. I didn't know he was dying or maybe I would've done something sooner. But the damn man didn't call me until he was on his deathbed. And when he told me he was finally going to make it right with you, I called you immediately."

"So you're saying you wouldn't have done anything differently?"

She stared at him for a long minute. "Honestly? Probably not."

Kyle shook his head. "What you did was wrong."

"And I accept that you feel that way. So I want to know how we can get past this."

"I don't know if we can, Mom."

Sherry looked absolutely stricken.

Celia felt her gut cinch up. She didn't want him to be at odds with his family too.

"There's a reason I haven't called you. I've got some stuff to sort out."

"So now that you're married you don't need me anymore?" Sherry demanded. "Is *she* helping you sort out your problems?"

"Yes. Because she didn't cause them."

"You don't mean—"

Kyle held up his hand. "This is not up for debate. I love you, okay? But if you really love me, then you'll back the hell off for a while." He drained his beer and set the empty can on the counter. Then he leaned over to peck her cheek. "I'll be in touch."

"Where are you going?"

"I have some shit to do in the barn." He left the kitchen and the front door slammed.

Sherry disappeared and Celia expected to hear the door slam as she chased after Kyle. But Celia found her in the living room, staring out the big picture window.

Celia didn't know what she was supposed to do.

"He's never been the type to storm off," Sherry said offhandedly.

"His competitive streak means he usually stays and fights back because he thinks he can win."

"With you too, huh?"

"Things have changed in our relationship, but that is one thing that hasn't changed."

Sherry half turned. "Does he talk to you?"

"Some. Not as much as I'd like, to be honest. Has he always been able to talk to you?"

"Kyle has never opened himself up to anyone. Not since he was a kid. I've tried to break down the walls, knowing I had a hand in putting them up. I hope you can be there for him and be what he needs." Sherry's face tightened. "But be warned. He is my son, my only child, and for a long time the only person who brought joy into my life. He deserves to be that joy in someone else's life, because he has a lot to give."

"I know. He's very sweet and romantic. He's thoughtful. He makes me laugh. He also drives me crazy . . . but it's a good kind of crazy now."

"I'm happy to hear that."

"What would've happened to Marshall if he'd rejected Kyle years ago?"

Sherry flashed a feral smile. "Maybe I'd be in jail in Rawlins right now for attempted murder and Kyle would be visiting me."

Yikes. As much as Sherry frightened Celia, she had to respect the woman for her devotion to seeing to her son's needs above everything else.

"I should probably go."

At Sherry's car, Celia watched Sherry's gaze become fixed on the barn. "Hard to believe this is all his. I've never been able to give him much."

She'd given him so much more, but she wouldn't see it or believe it now. "He's trying to get a handle on all this, Sherry. He needs time."

"Thank you for not bullshitting me and saying he doesn't blame me and that he'll come around."

"Oh, I've no doubt he'll come around. But Kyle has his own way of doin' things. In his own time frame." Celia put her hand on Sherry's arm. "He loves you. You've been the one constant in his life, so you have to know he won't ever turn his back on you. You raised him right, Sherry. He's a good man. Don't forget that's your doing. Not Marshall's."

"Damn straight." Then oddly enough, Sherry hugged her. "Like you said, I've been the constant in his life, the only woman who lasted. Now I'm not. I didn't want to like you, Celia, but it's hard not to. As for Kyle seeming so laid-back . . . he's not. I'm happy to see that you do know him so well. He needs a woman who understands that about him and loves him anyway."

Celia laughed.

❧

At least it was warm in the barn. In his anger he'd forgotten to grab a coat and it was fucking cold outside. So much for his intent to split wood until he couldn't lift his arms.

And then all the work would fall to Celia in the morning? How is that fair to her? How is it fair to her that you just left her with your mother anyway?

It wasn't.

Fuck.

But Kyle had known he would say something he'd regret if he stayed another minute. He knew he'd take out his frustration with Marshall Townsend on his mother. She didn't deserve that.

What had he expected from her anyway? To hear her confess that Marshall had forbidden her from telling him about his parentage? To see her wringing her hands with regret? Maybe he'd wanted a better story than that one night of hook-up sex with morning-after regrets had resulted in his existence.

Jesus. Are you a fucking girl? You thought you'd hear a sob story about them being star-crossed lovers kept apart by circumstances out of their control?

Kyle snorted. Right. He paced around the farm equipment. He had no idea what some of these pieces were even for. Now he had to show even more ignorance with his wife and ask her.

Maybe that was what ate at him. He should've been learning how to do all this ranching stuff from Marshall. Marshall should've contacted him sooner, at least about his intent to leave him a working ranch. Or did he think that Kyle was a greedy bastard who planned to sell the thing outright?

No way. He'd prove that bastard wrong. He wasn't giving up. Not the first week, not the first month, not the first year. This was what he'd wanted his whole life. He could do this. He could make this work. With Celia by his side he could do this.

To take his mind off his anger, he wandered through the barn, marveling at how damn clean it was. Marshall must've spent all his time out here and not in the house. That brought a smile. Bran's barn used to be pretty clean too—he'd bet it wasn't so much anymore. Bran wasn't stupid enough to spend his time around machinery when he had a hot wife waiting inside for him.

The door slammed and Kyle glanced across the shadowy space at Celia. Speaking of hot wife.

Luckily for him she didn't look too hot under the collar.

Celia wandered over to where he sat on an ATV. "She's gone."

"Sorry ... I just ..."

"I know." She hopped up, straddling his lap. Then her hands were in his hair. "Don't think about that." Her soft, warm mouth was gliding over his in a seductive tease. "Think about this." She kissed him. "Just this."

Kyle groaned and held onto her hips, letting her take the lead. Loving that she liked being the aggressor sometimes. Loving that she was equally greedy in her physical need for him as he was in his need for her.

But he knew the need wasn't merely physical anymore. Being naked with her in body helped him trust that he could strip away some of his other defenses. So he lost himself in her, in the kiss that was so much more than just a kiss. His thoughts were of passion-slicked bodies writhing against each other. Of moans and sighs and heavy breathing. Of quenching his thirst for her by tasting the sweat beaded on her skin.

"Brace your hands behind you," she murmured against his tingling lips.

As soon as he leaned back, Celia changed the angle of her pelvis. What a contradiction this was. The delicate, flirty kisses, interspersed with the porn-star way she was bumping and grinding against him.

His heart rate quadrupled when she picked up the tempo. Sliding along his rigid shaft while her nails dug into his scalp and her mouth sucked every bit of reason right out of his head. The weight and pressure of her body, the urgency of her tongue, pushed him from I've-got-an-erection to

I-need-to-come-right-fucking-now. And wasn't that amazing? She could dry-hump him to orgasm in record time.

He broke the kiss. "Celia. Stop."

"Why? Are you close?"

"Yeah. Let's go inside before I shoot in my jeans."

Celia added a pelvis roll and bit down on his lower lip while staring hotly into his eyes. "I'll come in mine if you come in yours."

He sucked in a swift breath when she rode him faster.

"Be my first," she whispered.

"First what?"

"First guy to make me come with my clothes on."

"Seriously? You've never...?"

"Nope. My panties are wet, Kyle. You did that. My clit is swollen and begging for that sweet throb. You did that too." She blew in his ear while she continued to move on him. "Don't deny me. Don't deny yourself. Come on. It'll be fun getting nasty in the barn."

Kyle turned his head, latching onto the tempting skin below her ear, sucking until she moaned. "Do it."

Celia tipped herself over the edge first. She tilted her head back and Kyle felt his gut clench at her beautiful abandon—lips parted, a flush on her cheeks, her hairline damp.

Then her mouth was attacking his neck, sucking on the spot that made him shoot every fucking time. He squeezed his eyes shut and let go as her body pulled the orgasm out of his.

Kyle opened his eyes when sweet kisses peppered his face.

She smiled. Almost... shyly.

He grinned at her. "You can follow me into the barn anytime."

As they headed to the house, Kyle realized it'd gotten to be a habit for them both to use sex as a distraction, as an amusement, as a substitute for conversation. As much as he craved that constant physical contact with Celia, he understood that to truly win her heart, he'd have to probe her mind, not just her body.

"So are you up for a little cribbage tonight? I found an old bowling ball–shaped cribbage board in a box of Marshall's stuff."

Celia stared at him as if he'd suddenly transformed into a unicorn. "What?"

"You play cribbage?"

"Yeah. Why?"

"I didn't know that about you."

Kyle swept a piece of hair behind her ear. "There's a lot you don't know about me. And I'd venture a guess to say I have plenty to learn about you. I can't wait to get started."

"Well, it'd better be the speed version of getting to know me since you've only got six months." She poked him in the ribs. "After I whip your butt at cribbage let's see if we can find a Yahtzee game. Because I am the champion Yahtzee player of the Lawson family."

"Well, I'm the Gilchrist family champ."

She grinned. "Bring it, bull rider. You're goin' down."

Chapter Ten

"*C*elia. Get back here."

"No. I'm done talking to you, Kyle."

"What did I say?"

She whirled around. "Really? You have no freakin' clue what's so insulting about what you just said to me?"

Kyle had a totally perplexed look on his face.

"You don't see how I could possibly be pissed off by you saying, 'Seeing you from the back, dressed like that in men's clothes, it's hard to believe you're even a woman.'"

"But I've said that to you before and you didn't get all bent out of shape."

"Then it's past time I did, isn't it?" She stripped off the overalls and threw them at him. Then she grabbed her coat and her purse, stormed out, slammed the truck door, and sped off.

Jerk.

Everything had gone so well the first week. No small tiffs, no bickering, no big blowups. No exchanges of harsh words in a moment of frustration. The second week? They'd spent every nonworking moment getting naked together. But this third week? They'd been frustrated with each other a lot.

So Kyle's comments, coupled with the fact that he'd been more interested in talking to her or playing board games with her than fucking her at every opportunity, made her wonder if his attraction for her had waned.

Screw that. She'd show him she could look fantastic. She'd make him want her.

But part of her wondered why she even cared about going all glam wife on his dumb ass. She was only going to be around a few months anyway, right?

Didn't matter. Because this was about now. She wanted to make Kyle eat his words and swallow his damn tongue.

That's what propelled her to walk into Wild West Clothiers.

Harper appeared from the back when the chime dinged. "Celia! What brings you here?"

"I needed a break and haven't seen your store in months, so here I am."

Harper preened at Celia calling it *her* store. "We should have plenty of time to talk while you look around. Right after Christmas is typically the slowest time of year in retail. Been especially slow for us, because of the crappy February weather in Wyoming. I've been advertising online to try to clear my stock to make way for spring merchandise. EBay is awesome, so I've been packaging orders. . . . And you don't care one whit about this. I saw your eyes glazing over."

Celia laughed. "I'm glad to hear everything is going well. You've expanded the store into the art gallery."

"It's made a huge difference. We've increased art sales by rotating art in the lodge and guest rooms."

"I saw Braxton's gigantic sculpture out front. That's new too."

"The Split Rock shareholders commissioned that, since Braxton is making a name for himself in the world of western art and he's a hometown boy. He cut us a good deal."

Celia started to wander through the clothes racks filled with beautiful fabrics and vibrant colors. The welcoming way Harper had set up the store tempted Celia to spend all day in here.

She ran her fingers through the silky black fringe on the sleeves of a gray suede leather jacket. Black and silver conchas and multicolored beads added pizzazz but kept the coat simple.

"I'll give you a good deal on that since I'm marking down winter items," Harper offered.

"I'll keep it in mind."

"Are you looking for something in particular?" Harper asked. "For you? For your house? For Kyle?"

Celia scowled. "I'm looking for clothing for me. Been forever since I've bought anything new. Wow me with your expertise, Harper, because I need serious help. You know shopping has never been my thing."

Harper tapped her chin, inspecting Celia head to toe. Then she motioned for her to turn around. "You're not wanting clothing to wear in the barn, right?"

"That kinda stuff I can get at Runnings. Or Walmart. I need something"—*that will make my husband's jaw drop*—"snazzy."

"Excellent. I tell you what. You wander through the store and find pieces that appeal to you. And I'll choose ones I think work on you. Look for separates, not a whole outfit. Pieces you can mix and match. And be daring, Cele. Don't be afraid to try on something out of your comfort zone."

Celia shed the long black duster she'd worn for the last six years and tried on the fringed coat. The flattering cut made her shoulders look bigger, nipping in at the waist and ending at her hips, giving the appearance of curves. With her blond hair and fair coloring she tended to stick with dark colors. With her boyish frame she chose baggy clothes. This jacket fit neither of those criteria.

"You rock that coat," Harper remarked. "I'm not just saying that as a salesperson. It's feminine and western. Perfect. That goes in the *yes* pile."

"I didn't even look at the price tag."

"I said I'd make you a deal. And wipe that look off your face, Mrs. Gilchrist. I'm not looking at you as a charity case. I know what it's like to want something that's out of the price range, which is why I won't pick things you can't afford."

She wanted to throw her arms around her friend and confess how much she loved that a well-put-together, fashionable beauty queen like Harper got Celia the tomboy cowgirl. "Thank you. But I'm not changing my name. I'm still Celia Lawson."

"Really? Why not?"

"Seems like a hassle." Especially since it wasn't permanent. Celia flipped through a rack of long-sleeved shirts. A poppy red one with white piping and black roses caught her eye.

Harper said, "That's the wrong color for you."

Celia found several shirts, but couldn't force herself to check out the skirts or dresses. Not her style. Plus, she didn't have proper girl shoes. She owned one pair of wedge sandals, five pairs of boots, one pair of athletic shoes, and one pair of flip-flops. She'd never been a shoe-crazed girl, which completely flabbergasted both Harper and Tierney.

"All right. Time for the fashion show. I want you to try on everything, and I mean *everything*." Harper smiled brazenly as she threw back the dressing room curtain. "And you're gonna start with my selections first."

Celia groaned halfheartedly.

She nixed the orange and oranger floral shirt. Ditto for the seafoam green number with crisscross straps she couldn't even figure out how to fasten. She didn't mind the green and purple paisley western shirt Harper had paired with a royal purple tank top. And she loved the soft gray sweater that was tighter than she normally wore, with sequins around the scooped neck. And although the navy blue and cream lace tunic looked hippie-ish on the hanger, it looked more prairie-style on her. Chic country.

Chic and Celia Lawson. In the same sentence. Right.

Harper removed the discard pile and brought in Celia's selections. But Harper gave her choices a thumbs-down. Every single shirt Celia had chosen.

When she slipped on the last one, a pale pink thermal with embroidered roses on the three-quarter-length sleeves, Harper shook her head. "I thought you weren't buying clothes to wear in the barn?"

"I give up." Celia slumped into a chair. "Kyle is right. It's hard to tell I'm a woman most of the time."

Harper's eyes pierced her. "Your husband said that to you?"

Celia nodded glumly.

"That jerk. I will be right back."

She heard Harper muttering and the click of hangers.

Then Harper stood in front of her with a smug smile. "These outfits are over the top. But, darlin', that's what you need to make that foolish man … beg."

Celia smiled. "I've missed you." She ducked into the dressing room and slipped on the first outfit. And holy shit, she was afraid to come out.

"Don't make me come in after you," Harper warned.

She took a deep breath and threw back the curtain. "Ta-da."

Silence.

"That bad, huh?" Celia said with a sigh. "I didn't think I could pull this off. It shows way more of my pasty white skin than I'm used to—"

The front door chimed and a voice yelled, "Harper, I just have a quick question—" Tierney stopped. Her eyes were big as saucers behind her glasses as she scrutinized Celia. "I'm glad I didn't try that on. Obviously it was made for her. You are a cowgirl goddess in that smokin'-hot getup."

Celia's mouth dropped open. "Are you serious?"

"She's completely serious. Take a gander at your sexy self in the big mirror."

They were being polite. That's all.

She stepped in front of the three-way mirror. The boot-cut jeans were a faded shade of blue. Tight too. Tan fringe circled the bottom hem by her feet. The outside seam of each leg showed an inch of skin beneath the leather ties, which held the jeans fabric together. The front sat so low you could practically see her hipbones. She turned. The back pockets had sheer lace flaps that exposed more skin. But the jeans did look good. Made her legs look a mile long and her hips look curvier.

The top to the outfit was more outrageous than the bottoms. A vest, the same shade and material as the fringe on the jeans, pushed her boobs together, creating cleavage. The wide collar was crafted of denim. Although the vest reached the waistband of the jeans, it did ride up, revealing a two-inch strip of her belly.

Celia looked nothing like herself. Her gaze met Harper's in the mirror. "It's a fun outfit. But I wasn't looking for something to wear in the bedroom."

"This is not bedroom attire. You look too damn good to limit yourself to the hungry eyes of your husband. You need to wear this out. Let every man in the joint wish he was peeling those skintight jeans down your amazing legs. That'll show him."

Tierney glanced at Harper, then Celia. "What am I missing?"

"Kyle insulted his new bride by questioning her femininity and she's gonna show him she's all woman."

"What can I do to help?"

"Put on that other outfit," Harper said to Celia, "while Tierney and I plot Kyle's comeuppance."

Celia was torn. While she wanted to soothe her feminine pride, she didn't want to humiliate Kyle to do it.

Tierney sauntered over and patted her on the arm. "Don't worry. We're not planning anything mean. But every once in a while our men need a reminder of how lucky they are."

She said, "Okay," but she wasn't entirely convinced it'd work with Kyle. The next outfit was a dress. She yanked it over her head, tugging the clingy fabric down her legs. But there wasn't much fabric to tug. "Harper, you brought me the wrong size."

"Come out and let me see it."

Celia kicked off her socks and headed toward the mirror. "See? The hem is nowhere near my knee."

Tierney rolled her eyes. "I swear the Mud Lilies show more skin than you, Celia."

"I'm modest! It's the way I was raised."

"Sugar, you ain't ten no more. But you are straight up a ten in that dress," Harper said. "Take a look."

She wondered when she'd stepped into an alternate reality. The sleeveless rust-colored dress didn't boast a deep neckline, but the fabric was shirred through the bust area. At the waist, the shirring vanished and the cut became tight to where the dress ended five inches above her knee. Not only did the color bring out the burnished gold strands in her hair, but it gave her normally pale skin a glow. "Well, hell. I don't look like a little girl playing dress-up in Mommy's clothes, do I?"

"Cele, honey," Harper started, "you've seen yourself as that girl for far too long. But look at yourself. That's not a little girl. That beautiful woman staring back at you in the mirror? That *is* you."

Although buoyed by their compliments, Celia remained unsure. "The outfits are great. But honestly, where would I wear them? I don't have a job outside of the ranch. Even if I was still on the road, competing in barrel racing, I don't know that I'd wear them. Which is sort of pathetic when you think about it. And this is a reminder of why I don't go shopping. It makes me feel even more inadequate."

"But, sweetie, don't you think you and Kyle will go out on the town? If only out for dinner?"

"We haven't talked about it. We've been so busy working."

"Here's my take," Tierney said. "When Kyle says, *Hey, baby, let's go out for supper tonight*, you can slip on one of these outfits and blow his mind."

Maybe he hadn't taken her out because he didn't want anyone to know he'd married her. That depressed her even more.

"Or..." Harper stared at her with that devious look Celia had always loved. "Tomorrow night is poker night at our place. Did Kyle mention it?"

"He said he was going. Why?"

"Usually Tierney and I head to Rawlins on poker night and see a movie or eat someplace the guys don't like. But tomorrow night, let's have a girls' night out."

"I don't wanna butt in on your plans."

"Butt in? Wrong. Buck up, little camper," Tierney said. "That was not a request. You're going out with us tomorrow night, getting wild and having fun, even if we have to drag your ass behind Harper's Jeep."

"Show up here at the Split Rock at six o'clock. Have Kyle drop you off on his way to our house and we'll get you all glammed up," Harper said. "But first, I have one more outfit for you to try on. I think it'll be perfect for tomorrow night."

～

Celia left all her purchases at Wild West Clothiers. She couldn't tell Harper the purchases had drained her bank account. Drained it to the point that she'd have to ask her husband for money.

Which set her teeth on edge. She hated asking for money. She'd paid for everything herself since she'd stopped living at home. Since Kyle now had funds from Marshall's account, he'd insisted that all their living expenses be paid from that account.

The problem was, Celia wasn't on the account, so every time she needed to run to town, she had to ask Kyle for money. Or he'd write her a check and she'd have to cash it at the bank before she could go to the grocery store. A couple times she'd just used her bank card to make purchases, but she'd been too embarrassed to ask Kyle to reimburse her. Which meant she had less than fifty bucks to her name.

Her phone buzzed with a text message from Abe. *We welcomed Tyler Alan Lawson to the world an hour ago. Eight pounds of perfection. Mama Janie is doing fine. I'm scared shitless. I'd love for you to meet the newest member of our family, sis.*

Feeling more morose than before she left for the Split Rock, she took the long way back. It was dark when she returned to the ranch, but Kyle had left the porch light on. Not a sweet thought, a practical one. *Don't go assigning romantic meanings to every damn thing he does or you'll spend the next few months looking for other signs to stick around for the long haul that aren't there.*

Kyle came to help her take off her duster right after she walked in the door. "You've been gone a while."

"I was at the Split Rock with Harper and Tierney. We've got catching up to do, so we're going to Rawlins tomorrow night during the poker game." She toed off her boots. "Got a text from Abe. Janie had a boy a little while ago."

"I got a text too. So did you go anywhere else? Like to the hospital?"

"No. Why?"

"A phone call would've been nice."

"I'm not used to answering to anybody." Celia grabbed a beer from the refrigerator and noticed Kyle hadn't started supper. Might be petty, but if he wanted something to eat he could fix it himself.

"Celia, we need—"

"To talk, right? Wrong. I'm sick of talking. I need to take a shower." She shut the bathroom door in his face and locked it. Sipped her beer while unbraiding her hair. The day had left her with a bone-deep sadness she couldn't shake. New clothes hadn't helped. Spending time with her friends hadn't helped. She looked at the empty beer can; booze hadn't helped either. Just when she'd thought she found a place she fit, she'd been given another reminder that she didn't fit anywhere. Even temporarily.

Hot water poured over her. Steam surrounded her. She set aside the soapy washcloth and rinsed the conditioner from her hair. Even though it was barely six o'clock, falling into bed sounded good.

"You can't stay in there all night," Kyle said right outside the shower door.

Damn him. "I locked the door because I wanted privacy."

"No, you locked the door to avoid me and I ain't havin' any part of it." He opened the shower door and stepped inside.

Celia's stomach jumped when his hands circled her hips. But she didn't move. She remained under the spray of hot water.

"Celia," he said silkily against her shoulder.

"Go away."

"You're mad at me."

She didn't respond.

His lips glided across her wet skin. "I hurt your feelings."

She shrugged, as if it was of no consequence, and tried to remove his mouth from her skin.

"I'm sorry."

"Go. I want to finish my shower. Alone."

"No."

"You waiting until I turn around so you can make sure I'm a girl?" Celia turned and stepped back, letting the water spray him in the face. "See? Now go."

Kyle blinked the water from his mesmerizing green eyes. Water droplets clung to the dark scruff lining his cheeks and jaw, dripping down his neck.

How unfair that he looked even better wet. His hair, a mix of different shades of blond, darkened under the stream of water and stuck to his scalp, making him look even more intense. Her gaze dropped to his groin. He had an erection. Big surprise. She whirled around, adjusting the shower spray. She'd freeze him out.

But Kyle was determined. His hands were back on her. His mouth was once again by her ear. "There's no excuse for what I said. None. I'm sorry. Jesus. I'm so fucking sorry, Celia. Will you let me apologize?"

"You can try."

He chuckled. "A challenge. Well, darlin', I live for a challenge."

Celia expected he'd use that silver tongue, telling her how much he loved her body. How beautiful it—and she—was to him. And he did. But not with words. He did it with his steady hands and his mouth in super-slow motion. So she felt his every stuttered breath on her skin. So she felt the heat and hardness of his body as he worshipped hers.

Kyle swept her hair aside, allowing his lips to travel the slope of her shoulder. His callused hands skated up her torso, stopping to caress the underswell of her breasts.

The man was a master at turning her on. But she didn't hear the sexy little chuckle that meant he knew he was getting to her.

His hands slid down her wrists. He placed her left palm on the tile wall and the right palm on the glass door.

The dampness between Celia's thighs owed nothing to the water sluicing down her skin. Her heart thudded. Her brain fogged.

He fondled her breasts, zeroing in on her nipples. Pulling and tweaking the tips, while his mouth was busy biting her neck. Or the tip of his tongue teased her ears. Licking the water from her skin. Making her break out in gooseflesh.

Then Kyle's tongue followed the length of her spine until he was on his knees behind her. His fingertips danced over the outside of her thighs and calves, as he tongued the two dimples above her ass. His voice was a hoarse whisper. "Turn around."

Keeping her eyes closed, she faced her body toward him. She managed to stay steady when he lifted her left foot onto the edge of the tub. And when his beard scraped the inside of her thigh as he kissed higher and higher up her leg. But when his thumbs spread her pussy open for his mouth, and that skilled tongue lapped at her slit, she had to lock her knee to keep it from buckling. Still no little cocky chuckle.

Kyle mapped every inch of her folds with his tongue. Not teasingly, just thoroughly. Then he settled his lips around her clit, alternated sucking and rapidly flicking his tongue over that swollen nub of flesh.

Celia's head fell back. She gave herself over to the divine moment when her entire universe was his mouth sucking on her pussy. When the only thing in her world was the happy throbbing in her sex as the blood pulsed through her body.

Took a minute to regain her bearings. She glanced down at Kyle on his knees, his face nestled in the crease of her thigh.

He reached around and turned off the water. Then he stood and stepped out of the shower, offering his hand to help her. Kyle toweled her hair and dried her off. All actions that might've been mechanical, but he turned every simple touch into pure seduction.

Especially when he lifted her into his arms and carried her to their bed.

There his worship continued. No part of her body was left untouched or unkissed. He slipped inside her and they moved as one. Just as they hung on the precipice and she expected he'd send them both soaring, he stopped moving.

Kyle gazed into her eyes, his look a soulful mix of pleasure and regret. "I know you're not a girl. You're all woman, Celia. And you're all mine." He crushed his lips to hers and slammed home, staying seated deep inside her.

That set her off. It set him off too.

Once she'd found her sanity, she whispered, "Apology accepted."

Chapter Eleven

*A*fter Harper and Tierney duded Celia up, they headed to Buckeye Joe's for girls' night out.

Celia expected the place to be dead. But the Thursday-night special, Jack and Coke for two bucks, kept the joint hopping. The Mud Lilies, the wild group of seventy- and eightysomething women who'd banded together after becoming widows, had scored a table and saved three spots.

Garnet did the wave when they arrived. "About damn time. We started without you." She gave Celia, Tierney, and Harper a one-armed hug, since she held a drink in her other hand. "Cheap drinks tonight, so I intend on bein' a cheap drunk." She whistled for the cocktail waitress. "Another round, barkeep!"

"Garnet is in good spirits," Bernice said, "so watch out."

Harper scanned the group. "Where's Tilda?"

"A Skype date with her grandson who lives in Singapore." Pearl pointed to the dance floor. "And Vivien's already cuttin' a rug with some feller. But he's got wandering hands. I wouldn't be surprised if Viv slapped him."

"Which is why Pearl hasn't taken her eyes off them," Maybelle said. "Ten bucks says she slugs him in the stomach."

"You're on," Pearl said.

They were both sorely disappointed when Vivien just gave the guy a stern talking-to with lots of finger shaking.

Susan Williams, Buckeye Joe's owner, delivered a round of drinks and promised to return and drink a toast.

Garnet held her glass aloft. Her gaze encompassed Celia, Tierney, and Harper. "To these young gals. May their friendships last as long as ours have."

"Hear, hear." Glasses clinked.

That was a sweet and tame toast—from the woman who wore a royal blue tank top emblazoned with GILF in rhinestones. Beneath that, Garnet had on a black lace long-sleeved T-shirt. Her pants were stretch denim covered in glittery sparkles.

And Celia had worried that her outfit was too over the top? She fiddled with the belt to her coat, making sure it stayed knotted. It was always cold in the bar in the winter, so no one thought anything of her leaving her coat on, especially if she wasn't dancing.

Conversation flowed as freely as the booze. Celia wasn't in the mood for either, so she nursed her drink and listened.

An hour passed. She heard about Bernice's upcoming bunion surgery. Vivien bragged on her grandchildren. Pearl talked about starting the Jack Daniel's knitting club. Harper talked about her sisters' military lives. Tierney announced she was throwing a baby shower for Janie and Tyler.

Garnet leaned closer. "See the dude in the beige hat at the bar?"

Celia angled back for a better look. "Gray hair?"

"Yep. How old do you think he is?"

"Between fifty and sixty, closer to the sixty side."

"Practically a baby," Garnet snorted.

"Age is relative. You're the one who taught me that. You oughta ask him to dance."

"I will." She put her mouth on Celia's ear. "Don't tell no one at this table what I'm doin'."

"Why not?"

"Because they'll try to stop me. For my own good. But Lord. I'm tired of being good. Know what I mean?"

"What are you two whispering about over there?" Pearl demanded.

"Nothin'. Just giving Celia sex advice," Garnet trilled. "Pretty raunchy stuff, Pearl. You'd probably blush."

Celia choked on her drink.

"Is that right?" Pearl asked Celia.

"Uh. Yeah. I'm blushing, but it's stuff I, ah, needed to know."

Satisfied, the ladies returned to their conversation.

Garnet murmured, "Thanks for covering for me. I'm off to rock his world."

Another half hour passed. Celia wondered how long she had to stay.

"Boot Scootin' Boogie" blared from the speakers and everyone jumped up for the line dance, except Maybelle and Celia. They volunteered to stay at the table to keep an eye on drinks and purses.

"How's married life treating you?" Maybelle asked.

"Great. We're getting the house set up. Working cattle. Doing all the never-ending ranch stuff. Getting ready for calving."

Maybelle patted her hand. "Celia, dear, that's not what I meant. I wondered if you and Kyle are getting along okay."

Celia bristled. Given their past, did everyone assume she and Kyle would constantly be at war with each another? "Yes, we are. Why?"

"I remember the first few months Earl and I were married. The man drove me insane. I swore I'd made a mistake. Living with him every day was nothing like the rosy world of dating, where he was all cleaned up when he picked me up for a date and he was always on his best behavior. Listening attentively to whatever I said. Buying me little tokens. I was shocked by how fast some of that wooing behavior disappeared after the wedding bells stopped pealing."

"But obviously you worked around it because you were married for over fifty years."

Maybelle offered a sad smile. "Yes. I miss that man every day. But at first it took me a while to admit I liked the real side of Earl better than the idealized dating version. Sure he was a slob. And he had no patience for my dillydallying. We'd fight over the dumbest things. He'd storm off and I'd cry. But he wasn't mad for long. We'd air our grievances and then it was over."

Celia found herself confessing, "Kyle hurt my feelings yesterday. He'd been saying some mean things that I'm probably overly sensitive about."

"What did you do?"

"Stomped off. Bought myself some new clothes. Stayed away from home for a few hours."

"What happened when you went home?"

"He apologized."

"Without prompting?"

She nodded. She probably blushed to the roots of her hair when she recalled how thoroughly he had apologized. Twice.

Maybelle smirked. "I always liked the making-up part too. I'm glad to see you're not the type who holds a grudge or keeps score. That can sour everything in a marriage right quick. You don't want to start your marriage out that way. Always take the high road when given the chance."

That observation jarred Celia because she hadn't taken the high road. She'd actually sunk a little low. Lying to Kyle about her plans tonight. Wearing an outfit that made her feel exposed enough she'd left her coat on. Did she really need to prove to Kyle that other men found her attractive?

No. *Hell* no.

The only man she cared about being sexy for . . . was Kyle. Her husband.

Being here, dressed like this, was a petty, childish thing to do. Kyle deserved a wife who respected him—in public and in private—as much as he respected her.

That was when she knew she loved him. Not Kyle the boy. Not Kyle the bull rider. Kyle her husband. The man who got her. The man who needed her. The man she needed more than she'd ever imagined.

And more than anything, she just wanted to go home to him, hit replay, and do this over. She couldn't do that, but she could keep from making it worse.

"Miz Maybelle, will you excuse me? I need to make a phone call."

Celia scooted outside and huddled against the building as she waited for him to pick up. "Kyle? Can you come and get me and take me home?"

"Aren't you comin' back here after the movie?"

"Umm . . . Yeah, about that. We didn't go to a movie. We're at Buckeye Joe's."

Silence. Then, "I'm on my way."

✑

"Lemme get this straight. Harper, Tierney, and Celia are drinkin' at Buckeye Joe's?" Bran said with an edge to his voice.

"I've seen how Tierney and Celia are when they're drinkin' together." Renner stood. "I'll get my coat."

"I'll get mine too," Bran said, "because I've seen Harper and Celia drinkin' together over the years and it usually ends in a bar fight."

"Looks like your wife is the common denominator of evil," Eli said slyly.

"Fuck off. And back off, you two." Kyle pointed at Bran and Renner. "Celia didn't say nothin' about your wives. She wants me to take her home. Maybe she's sick or something."

"The question is why didn't any of you know your wives were goin' to Buckeye Joe's in the first place?" Fletch asked with a snicker.

Kyle noticed that Tobin, Renner's hired hand, who always talked nonstop, hadn't uttered a peep. In fact, he was mighty interested in his dead hand of cards. "I wanna know how Tobin knows what they're up to."

All eyes zoomed to Tobin.

"What? I'm innocent."

Renner snorted. "That'll be the day, college boy. Start talkin'."

Tobin threw his cards on the table and sighed. "I only know because Garnet contacted me this afternoon. She asked if she got snockered if she could call me to give her a ride home. So I asked what she was doin' tonight and she told me about them meeting at the Buckeye. Sounded like y'all's wives planned on inviting you after they'd cut loose with the Mud Lilies for a few hours. Garnet was pretty pumped that it was cheap-drink night."

Bran groaned. "Those ladies are always in the thick of things, stirring things up."

"That's why I love them old gals. They are far more interesting and fun than any of the women my age I've dated in the last couple years." A grinning Fletch glanced from Hugh Pritchett, Renner's foreman, to Eli. "You guys up for a drink or ten at the Buckeye?"

"Now hold on just a second. What if they planned some kind of surprise?" Kyle asked.

Everyone looked at Tobin.

"Don't look at me like that. How the hell should I know what they've got planned? They're *your* wives."

"Which is why I'm heading there alone," Kyle said. "I'll call from the bar and tell you what's goin' on."

"If we don't hear from you ASAP, we're showing up anyway," Renner shouted as Kyle reached the door.

Kyle drove on autopilot, trying not to come up with worst-case scenarios about why Celia sounded so mortified.

The parking lot was jam-packed.

Just as he started to get out of his truck, his cell phone buzzed with a text from Renner telling him the guys were on their way.

He found Celia in the far back corner of the bar. Wearing her coat and a worried look. Christ. Maybe she was sick.

"Darlin', what's wrong?"

She threw herself at him. "I'm sorry."

"For what?"

"For almost embarrassing the crap outta both of us."

How much had she been drinking? Because she wasn't making a lick of sense. "Come again?"

"Yesterday after you made that nasty crack about me, I went to Harper's store and bought new clothes, intending to prove to you that I am a sexy, hot woman and not some dorky, shapeless little girl."

"Cele. I thought we'd moved on from that."

"We have. I mean, yes, you apologized to me. But I'd already made plans to come here tonight and make myself feel better by wearing something snappy. Then we planned to call you guys to come have a drink with us. You'd walk in and see me lookin' so smokin' hot that you'd immediately regret your mean remark."

"I regretted it the instant I understood it hurt you," he said softly.

"I know." She swallowed hard. "And I regret I'm wearing this slutty outfit. I regret it to the point I haven't taken my damn coat off since I got here."

Kyle's eyes searched hers. "Why not?"

"Because you're the only man I want seeing what I've got on."

"So let me get this straight. You feel guilty about the way you dressed. Guilty enough to tell me about it, but not guilty enough to let me see what you're wearin'?"

She nodded vigorously. "So can we please go home?"

"No. Show me." His tone brooked zero arguing.

Celia peered over his shoulder to check if anyone was watching. Then she whipped open the coat in a fast movement that would've made a flasher proud. "There. You saw it. Now can we go?"

He loomed over her. "Take. Off. The. Coat."

"Why?"

"Because I told you to."

A rebellious expression tightened her face. But he saw it for what it really was. Fear.

This was the perfect opportunity to begin showing her he was proud to have her on his arm, proud that she was his woman, his lover, his wife. That he wanted her to be his wife for a helluva lot longer than six lousy months. He wanted her forever.

Kyle stroked the underside of that stubborn jaw with the rough texture of his glove. "Maybe I want everyone in Buckeye Joe's lookin' at you thinkin', damn, when did Celia Lawson become sex on legs? Maybe I want the men in the bar to eat their goddamn hearts out because all this"—his gaze traveled from her eyes to her boot tips—"is all mine."

She bit her lip. "You haven't even seen the outfit yet."

"I don't need to. I'm sure you look fantastic."

Celia's eyes softened. "Given our history, I'll admit I'm itching to see *wow* in your eyes."

"So take off the damn coat before I rip it off with my teeth."

She pulled the coat open and yanked it off.

Holy fucking shit. Celia hadn't been kidding about being decked out in a sexy-ass getup. He'd always admired her sexy legs. In the past month he'd paid homage to them with his hands and mouth. But he'd never seen her in a short skirt that showed so much of those mile-long legs.

He finally managed to pull his gaze away from the funky buckskin skirt and he let it travel upward. She wore a matching buckskin halter that dipped low enough in front he might've caught a glimpse of nipple.

He imagined her riding her horse, bareback. With those golden locks flowing in the wind behind her, looking so beautiful and free.

"Turn around." Christ. There was no back to the shirt, except for flimsy leather straps that crisscrossed her muscled back. And if she bent over she'd give everyone a peek at that sweet pink flesh between her thighs.

Not happening. Ever. She was his, goddammit. *Only his.*

Kyle went from mildly amused to caveman possessive in three seconds. But he had the urge to show her off. Wrapping her braid around his palm, he tugged her gently until her back met his front. He nuzzled her ear. "Kitten, you are a walking wet dream."

She rubbed her cheek against his in a very catlike move.

He spun her around and made certain she saw the pure male appreciation in his eyes before he consumed her mouth in a blistering kiss. He didn't give a damn that they were in a crowded bar. He wanted her to feed on his lust.

His sweet, sexy Celia held nothing back.

He slowed the kiss. Sweetened it. But it still held that edge of need. He whispered, "Dance with me."

"But, Kyle, you don't—"

"Not a request, little wife of mine. You are dancin' with me. Now." He tossed their coats over the back of the chair and clasped her hand in his. As they snaked through the tables, he nodded to several people he knew, but didn't stop to chat. He stopped right on the edge of the dance floor, hauling her close.

"Umm, Kyle, this is an up-tempo song and I think we're supposed to be two-stepping."

"The good thing about bein' a bad dancer? Ignoring all them pesky rules about how I'm supposed to be dancin'." He murmured, "Besides, the only person who's gonna see that fringe flapping tonight is me."

"And how do you intend to make it flap if you're not spinning me on the dance floor?"

"When I slide this skirt over your sassy ass and pound into you from behind."

A gleam of interest brightened her eyes.

"Can you feel how hard I am?"

"It's hard to miss. For me and everybody else."

He laughed. "Don't be haughty with me. Ain't that the reaction you wanted? Me so hard I can't see straight?"

She pressed a kiss on his neck. "Yes. I like the way you look at me, Kyle. No man has ever looked at me that way. I'm sorry. I . . ."

"It's okay. But I do have one question. Are the rest of the clothes you bought sexy, like this?"

She shrugged. "They're all different from what I normally wear. But, yeah, they show some skin."

"So is that a comfortable outfit?" He slowly spun them into the middle of the dance floor.

"Not really. It's kinda tight, which is hard to believe since it doesn't have much material."

"There ain't gonna be a problem with me tearing it off you?"

"There damn well is a problem with that, Kyle. This wasn't cheap and I—"

He fused his mouth to hers. The kiss, alternating between sweet and fiery, flirty and flat-out lewd, ended when the song did, which was too damn soon for his liking.

"You've proven your point," she panted. "Can we please go now?"

"Nope. You've got that backward. You proved your point. I need to prove mine."

"Which is?"

He offered her a wicked grin. "To show my public appreciation that my wife is a knockout."

"Wouldn't it be better to show your appreciation in private? To me?"

"I plan to. For now, put your arms around me. Dig your nails into the back of my head like you do when I'm goin' down on you."

His sexpot wife blushed and looked away.

"Huh-uh. Eyes on me. If you're bold enough to wear that outfit in public, you can hear all the dirty things I wanna do to you while you're wearing that outfit."

Celia's bashfulness disappeared, replaced by a look of challenge. "Would those dirty thoughts include tying me up? Because you haven't done that near enough for my liking."

Kyle bit back a growl.

"I really thought we'd christen the barn as a sexual playground, because there's lots of rope, and hooks in the rafters."

"Playin' with fire, Celia."

"Mmm. Maybe. Or maybe I need to fan the flames that are already there, since I've been a little … hesitant in expressing my wifely needs."

"Why?"

She kept her gaze on his. "Because this raw sexual need is new to me. And in the last week you've been more interested in talking than—"

"Fucking you until you scream. Well, that's about to change."

"Good." She put her lips on his ear. "Besides the one time Breck talked me into a threesome with Michael? My sexual adventures have been limited and I've been wanting to explore all that uncharted territory with you."

That admission surprised him. "How is it in all the conversations we've had in the last month this hasn't come up?"

She didn't answer. She just looked away.

He trapped her face in his hands, forcing her to look at him. "How limited?"

"Kyle—"

"Tell me all of it. We've been married for weeks." Christ. He hadn't exactly gone easy on her in bed, believing she had the sexual experience to back up her passion.

"I've only been with three guys. Pistol, the guy who popped my cherry—he didn't even know I was a virgin. Breck. I don't count Michael because his part in the threesome was only a blow job. And … you."

Don't show shock.

"I know what you're thinking. On the circuit I wanted people to believe I'd been around the block. I was tired of being the horse-loving, homely hometown girl whose brothers practically enforced her virginity until she was twenty-one. I thought if I acted sexually sophisticated it'd give me confidence to follow through and become that way."

Her teasing and evasive comments hit him then. Over the last few years Celia had only implied she'd been playing musical horse trailers. "Is that why you wanted the marriage to be in name only?"

She nodded.

"Thank God I'm a pushy bastard and wouldn't stand for that, huh? And this news just presents a whole bunch of new possibilities for us."

"So you're not upset?"

"That you've been selective with who's sampled these very fine goods? Hell no. But it wouldn't have mattered to me if you got off banging the entire rodeo team. The past is the past for us, kitten. For both of us." His hands fell from her face and he smoothly slipped his leg between hers so the hard muscle of his thigh connected with her sex.

She hissed, "What are you doing?"

"Dancing with my wife." He rocked them a little more and she gasped. "See? I ain't such a bad dancer after all."

"You trying to make me come right here?"

"No. I'm trying to make you so edgy"—his lips feathered over her jaw—"so needy, that you come on that first, hard thrust."

Celia tilted her head back. Her gray eyes were decidedly somber. "What is going on with you?"

"As much as I'd like to hotfoot it to my truck and take you straight home to bed, I do like bein' out with you. And I thank you for the reminder that I don't expect us to isolate ourselves on the ranch all the time." He grinned. "I cannot wait to see them other outfits you got."

She kissed him. "Thank you."

"But I am gonna whisper dirty nothings in your ear for the duration of the dances."

"I oughta grind my pussy down on your leg and come right now."

"You'd better not."

Celia kicked her heel in, which squeezed his thigh more tightly between her legs. "Oops."

"I'm warning you."

"I'm warning *you*. I've got about one more song dancing with you like this or I'll lose it."

Kyle wondered when he'd lost control of this situation. But he had a really good idea on how to get it back. "Fine. One more song. Now put them sugar lips on mine."

The play of mingled breath and stolen smooches made him damn dizzy. Celia too, if the rapid pounding of the pulse in her throat was an indication. When he bent to lightly suck on that bit of flesh he felt her knees buckle.

Enough foreplay.

He whispered, "Let's go," and towed her off the dance floor. As he helped her with her coat, she said, "I need to say good-bye to my friends."

"They're gone. Their husbands showed up right after I did and took them home. Tobin and Fletch promised to handle getting your wild Mud Lilies pals home."

Kyle pulled her behind him, trying to block the wind. They skirted the edge of the building that faced the back of a hill. He spun her around and pressed her into the metal siding. "You ever been fucked hard and fast up against a honky-tonk?"

She shook her head.

"Take off your panties."

Celia held on to his arm as she slipped them off.

He shoved them in his pocket and crowded her against the building. Watching her liquid silver eyes, he reached beneath her skirt and could feel the heat pouring from her sex. His fingers inched up her inner thigh and delved into her pussy, finding her warm, slick, and ready. He damn near howled that he'd primed Celia's body to this point without touching her.

She whimpered a soft, "Please."

He sealed his mouth to hers as he moved his fingers in and out. Then he unbuckled, unzipped, and dropped his jeans before breaking the kiss to urge, "Jump up and lock your ankles around my waist." Latching onto her tight buns, he hoisted her against the building. He was shaking, but not from the cold. "Reach between us and guide me in, baby."

Her cool fingers brushed his balls, then circled his shaft.

The instant his cockhead touched her molten core, he canted his hips and plunged into her.

"Yes. Do it again."

He withdrew fully and slammed into her fully.

"Don't stop. Hard and fast like that."

He didn't pause to catch his breath. He just fucked her steadily. Pulling her body to meet his demanding thrusts. He went up on his toes to fuck her deeper.

Despite the frigid air, sweat gathered on his brow. Sweat also trickled down the crack of his ass and dampened his balls. He slammed into her, her wet heat easing each hard stroke.

Celia's arms were around his neck, her short fingernails sunk into his scalp, the heels of her cowgirl boots digging into his ass. She panted, her breath indicating how close she was. "Kyle."

"Hold on. I'm gonna tip you forward."

As soon as he did that, she gasped. "Oh. Yes. Like that."

"Squeeze me. Harder." He rested his forehead on her shoulder and jack-hammered into her. Near to that tipping point himself, he gritted his teeth and hoped he could hold on because it felt too fucking good to stop.

She stiffened, her grip on his head increased and she arched back, a sexy wail drifting from her mouth.

The clenching of her cunt around his shaft set him off. He shoved deep and stayed there, managing a hoarse grunt as her body milked his cock until he had not a drop of seed left.

A cold breeze and tickling fingers between his balls roused him. He jumped when he realized it wasn't soft fingers caressing him but the fringe from her skirt flapping in the breeze. He chuckled.

"What?"

"I told you I'd make that fringe move tonight."

Celia drummed his buns with her boot heels. "Smart-ass."

Kyle kissed her. He could've gone on kissing her, if not for the fact she was shivering. "Sorry," he murmured. "Whenever I get a taste of this sinful mouth of yours, I don't wanna stop."

"I don't want you to stop either, but I'm literally freezing my ass off."

"Hang on." Kyle pulled out and paused for a second before putting her feet back on the ground. He attempted to straighten her skirt before quickly redressing. "Let's get you warmed up."

"Aren't you forgetting something?"

Kyle frowned. "No."

"My panties are in your pocket. Give 'em back."

"Nope. They're mine. Besides you'd just be taking them off again in a little while, so I thought I'd save you the trouble." He tugged her coat around her and tied the belt.

"So thoughtful."

He pecked her on the mouth. "I try. Come on, let's go home."

Chapter Twelve

*T*he carpet layers arrived early.

Celia knew it was silly to be nervous, but she'd never picked out carpet before. Kyle hadn't cared—or so he'd claimed—but she really didn't want him to hate it.

Rather than stand around the house and wring her hands because Kyle insisted on doing the cattle check himself, she headed to the horse pasture.

Mickey had designated himself king of her horse pack. Her other horses, Minnie, Coco, and Lazarus were used to Mickey. But Marshall's horses, Bugsy, Capone, Scout, and Pixie were used to Capone being head horse. There was bound to be jockeying for position at feeding time, so she'd separated them. Better to let them get acquainted over the fence line first.

Although the day was bitterly cold, the sun shone brilliantly and not a breath of wind stirred. Celia bundled up—not her favorite thing to be so immobile atop a horse—but the weather demanded it. She saddled Coco and kicked her into a trot. She could spend hours on horseback checking out the lay of the land if there weren't so many other things that needed done. She could spend the next two years getting the place up to snuff.

Too bad you don't have that long.

It seemed her subconscious had taken to warning her of the six-month rule whenever she considered breaking it. Which happened all the freakin' time since she'd finally admitted to herself she was in love with Kyle. She just didn't know what the hell to do about it.

At times it seemed Kyle wanted more. Other times she felt he was eager to do the ranch work on his own and he'd be happy to see her taillights at the end of their agreed time together. So she decided that waiting to broach a possible change in their agreement was her best option. Wasn't like she would fall out of love with him. And maybe if he wasn't in love with her now, he would be in a few more months.

After her ride, she brushed Coco down, fed her some oats, and hung up her tack. She noticed Kyle hanging over the fence, talking to the horses.

She exited the gate and stood beside him. "What's up?"

"Checking out my horseflesh. What did you find out on your frigid horseback ride?"

"There's an old metal shed northwest of here that'd work as a calving shed if we got stuck out there." She looked at him. "Any signs in the herd that we'll have calves soon?"

"Explain signs," Kyle asked without a hint of sarcasm.

"Teats filling with milk. Any cows laying down, getting up over and over, then looking for a place away from the herd?"

"Not that I saw. But to be honest, I wasn't looking for those signs. I'll do a teat check tomorrow for sure." He sighed. "Thanks for not makin' me feel like an idiot because I don't know much about this stuff, Cele."

She patted Minnie's neck. "There's a lot to learn about raising cattle. I'll be the first to admit I don't know it all."

"Seems like you do to me." He raised his hand to pat Minnie too but she shied away from him. "I'd like these horses a whole lot more if we were facing off in the arena and they were trying to buck me off. I might stand a chance with them."

"That's crazy talk. They're all very sweet."

"Which one is pregnant?"

"Blue. She's not here. I left her with Eli."

"Why didn't he bring her when he brought the others yesterday?"

"Since Blue's due date is during calving, I didn't want her to deliver when I couldn't give her all my attention. Mares in the same pasture that don't foal will try to steal another mare's baby."

"Seriously? I've never heard of that."

"It happens all the time. This is Blue's first foal. She's so sweet-tempered and she doesn't have the experience to fight off more aggressive mares. Since Eli has a pasture of pregnant mares, Blue is better off there."

"Who's the sire?"

"Mickey. The randy bastard mounted Blue before we could put her with Xavier."

"Speaking of foaling..."

Celia met Kyle's eyes.

"Let's take a trip to town."

She wondered if he'd bring it up. "I've been dealing with horses all morning. I'm a mess."

"You look fine."

"She's probably tired."

"We won't stay long."

"Why are you pushing me on this?" she demanded.

"Because you'll kick yourself if you don't." He held out his gloved hand. "Come on. I'll drive."

■

Celia and Kyle scoured the hospital parking lot for Abe's truck or Janie's Prius before they entered the hospital.

She knocked on the door of Janie's room, then poked her head in. "You decent?"

Janie was sitting up, a blanket-wrapped bundle tucked in the crook of her left arm. "Celia! I'm so glad you came."

Grateful for the reassuring squeeze from Kyle, she kept hold of his hand as they entered the room. She gave Janie a one-armed hug. "I'm so thrilled for you."

"Thanks. It is a pretty thrilling thing to finally get to see the fruit of my labors—ha ha."

"Congrats, Mama. You look happy."

"And Kyle's here too," Janie said as Kyle kissed Janie's forehead. "Thank you." She shifted to better show them the baby. "This is our boy, Tyler. All eight pounds of him. According to the Mud Lilies gals, all this dark hair is the reason I had heartburn for six months."

"He's beautiful."

Janie flicked a glance at Kyle and Celia's joined hands and then her gaze moved between them. "Congratulations are in order for you two as well."

"Thanks. We're happy." Kyle lifted Celia's hand to his mouth and kissed her knuckles.

"Your brother is a jackass, Celia," Janie said.

"I know."

"He'll come around, but probably not until he's done fussing at me like an old woman and he's got me and precious here locked down at the ranch under his watchful eye."

"Some big changes in your lives, that's for sure."

"Changes we're ready for this time around. Although I worry the one with the biggest adjustment will be George." Janie frowned. "I'm not convinced he needs to be a house dog."

"My mom never would've let me have Murray inside either. I threw a hissy fit when Hank and Abe got me a puppy but wouldn't let me have him in my room."

"I remember that," Kyle said dryly. "You tried to enlist my help."

"And you thwarted me, which was par for the course with us."

"Then," he emphasized. "Not so much anymore."

Tyler fussed and Celia leaned closer to see if he'd open his eyes.

"Would you like to hold him?" Janie asked.

"Yes, please."

Kyle released her hand. "I'll be back. I'm just gonna go check on that one thing."

The door shut.

Janie looked at Celia with surprise. "Was it something I said?"

Celia had no idea what Kyle was up to. "No. I think he's paranoid that if I hold a baby I'll want one of my own. Not that cajoling him into getting what I want has ever worked for me in the past."

"But add sex to the cajoling and he'll probably do damn near anything for you, won't he?"

"The jury's still out on that. Now hand that baby over."

Janie lifted him and Celia tucked him against her body. "The kid does like to be very close to breasts."

"He'll be disappointed in mine." Celia pressed a kiss to his forehead and inhaled the sweet baby scent. "So, Janie, you really ready for motherhood?"

"Yes. I've been watching Lainie and Brianna for the last year, so I'm not as shocked by it as I might've otherwise been. Labor was a bitch though. Holy shit. I wanted to brain Abe when he said, *Just breathe through it.* How about you try to breathe through a busted nose and a broken jaw, buddy."

Celia laughed.

"It is amazing to watch Abe with Tyler, though. He's just so . . . stunned by him."

"He's perfect. I'm thrilled for you guys."

"I know you are, sweetie." Janie drained a glass of water. "So you and Kyle?"

"Yep."

"Typical Lawson response," she muttered. "How did it happen?"

"Kyle and I had been dancing around each other for the last year."

"You and Kyle have been dancing around each other for much longer than that, but go on."

Celia didn't comment on that observation. "After Devin's concert in Vegas, we just looked at each other and knew. So we stopped dancing." She answered Janie's questions about Kyle's inheritance and was relieved when her nosy sister-in-law didn't press for more details on her supposed love match with Kyle. To ward off further inquiries, she talked about shopping at Harper's store and the girls' night out with Harper, Tierney, and the Mud Lilies.

"Sounds like a good time. I fear my girls'-night-out days are a thing of the past."

"I doubt Garnet and Maybelle would let you get away with ditching them." She patted Tyler's little butt when he made a mewling noise. "When will you go back to work at the Split Rock?"

"I'm taking a couple months off. Two at least. Maybe three. Then we'll be in the busy season at the resort. Renner can't run the place without me."

Janie smirked. "Plus I love my job. Lainie is happy with Brianna's day-care place, so I've already reserved a spot for Tyler."

"That'll be handy."

"I imagine when you and Kyle have kids you'll be a full-time at-home mom, like your mom was?"

Celia's mother had been a sweet, hardworking rancher's wife. She remembered that's how she'd always referred to herself—Rose Lawson, mother and rancher's wife. She glanced at Tyler's face. "I guess we'll see. It's a long ways down the road for us."

"Be nice if you had your kids soon though, so they'd be the same age as their cousins."

"Janie!"

She laughed. "I'm kidding. Anyway, you did get an invite to the baby shower Tierney's throwing, right?"

"Yes."

Her eyes narrowed. "You have to come. You and Kyle. Even if you're both still pissed off at Abe. Promise me."

"You want Kyle to come? Aren't baby showers mostly for women?"

"Oh, pooh. That's old-fashioned. These days they're coed."

Celia imagined the look of horror on Kyle's face if he was forced to play baby shower games. She grinned. "I promise we'll both be there."

❧

Kyle approached the information desk. "Excuse me, where would I find the home health care office?"

"Down that hallway and last office on the left."

As he headed that direction, he figured this was a wasted trip. Medical records were confidential. Probably this woman wouldn't remember Marshall Townsend. Or worse, maybe he'd been the same crotchety asshole to her that he'd been to everyone else.

An attractive brunette manned the desk. Her head-to-toe inspection reminded him of the buckle bunnies following the rodeo circuit, contemplating the size of his package behind his belt buckle. "May I help you?"

"I'm here to see Karen McNamara."

"She's on a call right now. Can I give her your name?"

"Kyle Gilchrist. I just have one quick question for her."

"Well, Kyle," she cooed, "could you be a little more specific on your needs? Are you here for"—her gaze swept across his chest and over his arms—"recommendations for sports injury rehab clinics? I'll bet you're some kind of athlete."

He withheld a snort. That lame pickup line would've worked on him at one time. Before he'd stopped fighting his attraction to his best friend's little sister and just accepted the fact he had it bad for the cowgirl and no other woman would do. He smiled at the receptionist. "I'm not an athlete, just a rancher. My wife's sister-in-law suggested I ask about a claim for my ailing father."

Her body language changed immediately at the mention of the word *wife*. "Have a seat. She'll be with you shortly."

Kyle studied the artwork in the small office until the receptionist led him back to an office.

The woman behind the desk offered her hand. "Kyle? Come in. Have a seat. What can I help you with?"

Kyle perched on the edge of the chair. "It's probably pointless of me to ask, but I'm wondering if you can tell me anything about a former patient of yours."

"Former?"

"He died at the VA a few weeks ago. But I found your name in paperwork at his house and it looked like you might've done home health care with him."

"Whereabouts was this?"

"Rawlins. The man's name was Marshall Townsend. He was my father. But I didn't know he was my father until he was dead. The truth is, I know nothing about him. I'm not looking for confidential medical information, just whether you knew him."

She sighed and tapped her pen on her desk blotter. "Yes, I knew Marshall. He came into the hospital early last summer complaining of chest pains. We did a full round of tests and kept him overnight. The test results weren't good. He checked himself out the next day. Because he wanted the visit billed to the VA, our office had to do a home check-in. He didn't return our calls, which forced a home visit. He wasn't particularly happy to see me but he wasn't rude either.

"I asked why he hadn't sought treatment in Rawlins or at the VA in Cheyenne. He said he was as good as dead anyway and he wouldn't spend his last few months trying to change the outcome."

Kyle clenched his teeth. Marshall had known he was dying last summer?

"He'd made up his mind, so there was no point in arguing with him. Do you know how long he was in the VA before he passed on?"

"Two months, I guess."

She frowned. "You really didn't know him?"

"I met him a couple times over the years, but I had no idea he was my father. I wondered if what killed him might be hereditary." Not a believable lie, but he had to learn something about the man.

"No. He had lung cancer. He'd smoked for many years and he'd been subjected to some bad chemicals in Vietnam. To be honest, I'm surprised he lived as long as he did after the diagnosis. I suggested he get his affairs in order. I assume he did?"

"Not besides makin' sure his cows and horses didn't starve." Kyle stood and offered his hand. "I appreciate your time, Miz McNamara."

"You're welcome. Sorry I wasn't more help."

Kyle was lost in thought, leaning against the wall outside of Janie's room, when Celia strolled out. "Had enough of your baby fix?"

"Yep. He started screaming, she jerked open her hospital gown to nurse him, and I took that as my cue to leave."

"I'm ready to go home too."

"We have to stop at the store."

"Can't it wait?"

"Not unless you want to start raising chickens, growing fruit, and milling wheat because we're out of bread, eggs, and orange juice."

He continued to be lost in thought on the drive to the SuperValu. He parked and said, "I'll wait in the truck while you grab what we need."

"You have to come in with me."

"Why? I don't care what kind of juice you buy."

Celia glared at him. "I won't be able to buy *any* juice if you don't come in with me, Kyle, because I don't have any money. None. You hold all the purse strings, remember?"

Made him feel like an ass to see her embarrassment. "Don't snap at me," he said evenly. "This sharing thing, especially about money, is new to me too, okay?"

"I hate asking you for money. It'd be easier if you would..." She turned away. "Never mind. Can we just go in the damn store?"

He grabbed her arm when she tried to flee. "Obviously this has been bugging you for a while. Why haven't you said anything before now?"

Her gaze pinned him "Why didn't you tell me you had business at the hospital today?"

Why did that put a hurt look in her eyes?

Because she's your wife and you're shutting her out.

"Because you're already dealing with enough stuff with your family. I didn't want to add to it when I wasn't sure what I'd find out."

"I recall you telling my brothers that you're my family now. So tell me where you went after you left Janie's room."

Part of him wanted to tell her to mind her own business. But the larger part of him wanted to talk to her. Wanted to open up to her in hopes she'd do the same. He told her about his conversation with the home health care nurse.

Celia remained too quiet for too long after he finished talking.

"What?"

"How long are you gonna do this to yourself, Kyle? What if you never find out anything more about him?"

How could he tell her he couldn't accept that?

She brought his hand to her mouth and kissed his knuckles. "Don't you see his secretiveness benefits you? It frees you."

"How so?"

"You can imagine the best about him, not have proof of the worst. He must've felt something for you, Kyle, even if it was just guilt, to leave you such an amazing inheritance. You need to stop picking apart your good fortune and accept that you'll never know the man. You'll never know why he didn't reach out. The fact he didn't get to know you truly is his loss."

Practical. And sweet. That defined his wife. "Thank you."

"You're welcome. Now can we go in?"

He shook his head. "I wanna backtrack to something you said. It'd be easier if I would . . . what?"

"If you'd add me on the bank account so I didn't have to ask you for money all the damn time. But I know why you don't want to."

"Why's that?"

"Because this marriage is temporary and you're afraid I'll clean you out and take off for greener pastures."

Kyle clenched his jaw. "That's not true. Bill said he'd take care of adding you to everything just as soon as we get a copy of the marriage license."

Celia's eyes narrowed. "I don't know what the holdup is on the marriage license, but it's a moot point. You can add me to your personal bank account without proving we're married. That just shows me that for all your talk about this being a partnership and us being a family, it's not. I can't pay for anything, Kyle. Not even a lousy jug of orange juice. Do you know how that makes me feel?"

He did not want to fight with her about money. Ever. He wasn't worried about putting her on his bank account; she was scared it would be the first step toward making this marriage permanent. That's why she lashed out at him. "Fine. You want money? I'll write you a freakin' check every week. Just like I would if you were my ranch hand."

"Now you're just pissing me off."

Fuck. He could not win when she was like this. Nothing would make her happy. And this stupid argument was like all the other stupid arguments they'd had over the years. They would automatically spout nasty shit to each other, not caring if feelings got hurt, and stomp off. Never learning from their mistakes.

Well, that wasn't happening anymore. She was his wife. He had to come up with a different way to deal with this.

Kyle grabbed her braid and tugged on it.

"Hair pulling in a fight, Kyle? That's a new low, even for you."

He laughed. "That pouty lip of yours is very sexy, Cele."

She faced him. "I don't pout."

"And I don't wanna fight with you about money. So how about until we get the banking situation figured out, we keep an envelope of cash in the house that we both have access to? That way, if you're at the store and you come across one of them sexy nighties and a pair of crotchless panties, you can just go ahead and buy it and not have to worry if it'll affect the grocery budget."

Celia grinned and pushed him. "You're an ass."

"Yep. So does that sound fair?"

"I suppose. Do you want me to put receipts in the envelope so you can see what I spent the money on?"

"Celia. You're my wife. I trust you. You don't have to be accountable to me when it comes to things you buy for our home, okay?"

"Okay." She leaned forward and kissed him.

Happy that they'd circumvented a fight, Kyle surprised Celia with a bouquet of flowers at the checkout. She fussed and said he didn't have to, but he knew she was pleased, since she kept sniffing them.

He remained quiet on the drive home. Still brooding about Marshall. Wondering why a dying man could leave him a ranch worth several million dollars but hadn't picked up the damn phone to tell him about it.

Would that phone call have changed anything?

Yes. No. Maybe.

Celia was right. He had to stop dwelling on this shit. So why couldn't he do it?

"Kyle?"

He looked at her. "What?"

"Are we getting out of the truck?"

Kyle realized they were at the ranch, parked in front of the house. "Yeah. Sorry."

Inside, he hung up his coat, kicked off his boots. He went into the room they'd designated as an office. He noticed Celia had printed out the course requirements and registration information for the vet's assistant program at the community college. If he hadn't already been melancholy, that sure would've done it. Just a reminder that she had every intention of sticking to her six-month time frame.

He stared out the window. He should chop wood. He should figure out how to fix the solar panels by the stock dam. He should be productive, because that's what life as a rancher was all about. But he didn't want to do a damn thing but brood.

And didn't that make him a fucking pussy.

Her soft footsteps alerted him to her presence before that alluring honey scent wafted over him. Celia nestled her face between his shoulder blades and her hands pressed against his pecs.

Kyle closed his eyes. God, he craved her touch. Craved it like nothing he'd ever felt. And didn't that make him a fucking pussy too?

Then Celia's hands were unbuckling his belt. Unzipping his jeans. Her hand slipped into his briefs and she fondled his flaccid cock. But it didn't stay flaccid for long.

"Celia—"

"Turn around."

As soon as he did she pushed him against the wall. "Whoa."

She pulled his jeans to his ankles. By the time she got rid of his briefs, his cock was totally on board with whatever she had planned.

Celia tongued the tip and looked up at him. "Hold on to the window ledge, not my head."

He stroked her cheek with the backs of his knuckles. "I'm agreeing to this even when I oughta turn you over my knee for your cheeky behavior."

"You're not gonna stop and do anything with your dick this close to my mouth." She licked his shaft with the flat of her tongue from root to tip. She parted her lips and swallowed him whole.

"Jesus." He loved the shock as that wet heat surrounded his cock. When she hollowed her cheeks and sucked, his knees damn near buckled every time.

Celia wasn't in the mood to get him off quickly. She was in the mood to tease. To play. She spent extra time laving his balls. She bobbed her head slowly. Sucking him so forcefully when his shaft was fully seated in her mouth that he felt the edges of her teeth digging into the base.

When he began to pump his hips to the rhythm she'd set, she backed off. He groaned, wanting to direct her mouth to where he needed it.

She released his cock entirely and sank her teeth into his thigh.

"Ouch! What was that for?"

"Behave."

"What did I do?"

Celia licked the crease of his thigh. "You're impatient. Good things come to those who wait." She scattered kisses across his lower abdomen and licked the other crease of his thigh. Then she nipped the other quad too.

Kyle made not a sound through his gritted teeth.

"Good boy." She locked her gaze to his as she fed his cock back into that hot cavern an inch at a time.

He couldn't look away from her and the brightness in her eyes from taking control of his pleasure. The wetness and the heat sent goose bumps down his legs. He started to shake. "Don't stop."

She smiled around his girth. She didn't use her hand to jack him. Her fingers lightly teased his balls and her mouth did all the work. A humming sound vibrated around his shaft that made him rise up on his toes.

She pulled off long enough to say, "Watch me when you come."

"Yes."

"Say my name."

"Celia."

Her teasing ended. She used her hand to rapidly stroke his shaft while her mouth parted to receive each short jab of his cockhead.

His groin tightened. Kyle glanced down as the first spurt of come landed on her upper lip. The second spurt hit her tongue as it flickered over the sweet spot beneath the head. The next three pulses coated her mouth, ran off her lips and down her chin. The raunchy visual, the wet marks of his possession, prolonged his orgasm until he was spent, dizzy, and trying to remember how to breathe.

And she still didn't release him. She licked and sucked, nuzzling his groin until his dick was flaccid again.

He sighed and touched her cheek. "Can I just say how much I love that you're a dirty girl?"

"Something as simple as having come dripping off my face puts me in porn-star territory?" Celia grinned and pumped her fist. "Wahoo! That's one life goal achieved."

He laughed softly.

Celia gently tugged his briefs and jeans up while he rested against the wall like a sated lion. She even buckled his belt. Then she stepped back.

He snatched her hand before she could get too far. "Now that my brain is functioning again, let me take care of you."

She shook her head. "Just surprise me like that sometime, okay?"

But he couldn't let it go. "Can I ask why the surprise blow job?"

"I wanted to remind you that I'm okay with whatever raunchy scenario you have in mind in the future. I like that you now see me as a dirty girl."

Kyle studied her, unsure where she'd take this conversation. "Why?"

"Do you remember when you said sometimes you looked at me and had a hard time reconciling the girl I used to be with the woman I am now?" Celia ran her knuckles over his jaw. "Same goes. There are so many more facets to you than I ever imagined, Kyle. I like that you're willing to show them all to me. You are getting better at this sharing stuff."

For the first time in his life, the thought of opening up on more than a superficial level didn't send him into full retreat.

"I particularly like your sweet side. Maybe it's selfish, but do you know why I like it? Because I'm pretty sure you don't show that part of yourself to many people. It makes me feel special."

"You are special, Celia. Not just because you're my wife."

"See? That's the sweet stuff that makes my knees go weak." She pressed her lips to his. "Now, if you'll excuse me, I have cookies to make for my husband."

"Cookies?"

"The thought of cookies perked you up almost as much as a blow job."

He laughed. "A blow job *and* cookies? In the same afternoon? This is turning out to be a fine day after all."

They went straight to bed after supper. Not for another round of slap and tickle, but because their furniture choices were the bed or the table and chairs in the kitchen. Part of him wasn't eager for the couch to arrive. He could get used to slipping into bed early every night with Celia curled into him, nestling her head in the spot between his chest and his armpit that seemed to be made just for her.

⮆

A couple of days later the furniture arrived. Celia insisted on immediately putting the finishing touches on the living room. Kyle installed the new curtain rod while Celia ironed the curtains. Once the gold paisley-patterned panels were hung and framing the windows, she took a moment to admire the room. From the furniture she'd chosen, to the carpet, to the color on the walls. Everything had come together so perfectly. A surge of pride filled her. Maybe she didn't suck at this home-and-hearth stuff as much as she'd feared.

Then she rearranged the few knickknacks displayed on the shelves. Messed with the pillows on the couches. Kyle finally told her to quit fussing while he set up the electronic equipment for the TV.

After taking a shower, she checked the pork roast. It'd be another hour before supper was ready. Celia rested against the doorway separating the kitchen and living room. Her gaze landed on Kyle. Sitting forward on his knees as he fastened cords behind the DVD player. His T-shirt rode up, exposing the lower section of his back. Even that part of him was muscled.

He rolled back until his butt met his calves, keeping his back to her as he wrenched on some piece of equipment. "Still rearranging furniture in your head, kitten?"

"No. I like it the way it is."

"You did a damn fine job picking stuff for this room. Ain't too girly. I won't be afraid to sit on my own couch. It looks like a real home now. Like our home."

Right then, she'd lost any chance of not falling completely in love with Kyle Gilchrist.

Right then, she needed her hands on his body to cement this connection between them.

Celia crossed the room and dropped on her knees behind him. She slid her hands beneath his shirt, greedy to touch all that smooth muscle.

Kyle froze.

She put her mouth on his ear. "I want you."

"Now?"

"Right now."

"Hang on. Lemme put this down." His screwdriver fell to the carpet with a muffled thud.

Then she yanked his T-shirt off and spun him around, pinning him to the floor.

He wrapped her braid around his fist. "What's gotten into you, little wife of mine?"

"Seeing you all manly, wrenching on shit, turns me on."

He laughed. "Evidently. So what are you gonna do with me now?"

"Strip you. Use your body to christen our newly improved living room."

"Good plan. I surrender . . . on one condition."

"Which is what?"

Kyle tugged her closer by her hair. "Can we postpone this for a little bit? I think I've finally figured out hooking up this TV and I need to finish it before I lose my train of thought. 'Cause seeing you naked? It rids my brain of all coherent thought."

Celia sighed. "All right. Gun me down. But it was worth a shot."

He rubbed his nose to hers. "Can I just say for the record I love that you aren't afraid to take the lead when you want me? It's very sexy." Kyle pushed up, slipped his shirt back on, and returned to muttering at the cords coming out of the back of the TV.

She rearranged the shelves she'd rearranged three other times, just to be near him. After about five minutes, she said, "So. What else do you love about me?"

"I'll tell you if you tell me," he teased.

"Okay. You first."

"I love that you're learning to cook more stuff. Not because you're bored with the dishes you can already make, but because you love to challenge yourself."

She hadn't expected him to say anything like that. She'd figured they would exchange sexy banter, then clothes would fly and they'd start putting carpet burns on their bodies. But Kyle was serious, so she seized the chance to be honest with him. "I'm glad you appreciate it. Sort of strange to admit that I finally understand why some women like to cook." A huge part of her motivation in learning new dishes was seeing that smile on his face as he cleaned every bite of food off his plate.

"Your turn," he reminded her.

"Okay. I love the serious look on your face in the morning when the ag report comes on the radio. I'll bet that after only a few weeks you know more about it than I do." Celia dusted the same section of shelving over and over, practically holding her breath as she waited on his response.

Kyle chuckled. "I'll admit hearing about the prices of hog belly futures still confuses me."

"Me too. But it's a reminder that I'm so glad we're not raising hogs." She shivered. "Nasty, smelly things."

"Would you have stuck around if Marshall had left me a hog farm instead of cattle?"

"Not a chance. Not even your handsome face and smokin'-hot body could get me to slop hogs for you." Now there was a lie. Good thing he couldn't see her eyes. "Your turn."

"I love watching how fast you can saddle a horse."

Celia whirled around and looked at him. "Seriously?"

"No lie. It's so automatic for you. I have to keep a mental checklist whenever I do it to make sure I ain't doin' something wrong." He wore a goofy smile. "I timed you once last week."

"You did? How long did it take me?"

"Two minutes and you were off to chase cows."

"I can do better than that," she scoffed and then laughed. "It's funny. Now I have no need to try to beat the clock since I'm not barrel racing, but I still do everything as fast as possible. Like I'm still being timed."

"I hope you didn't take that like I'm judging you, Celia."

"I didn't. It's just crazy how life on the road changes you. Know what I mean?"

He nodded. Then he got a pensive look. "Do you miss it?"

"Not at all. I never understood how lonely it was until I had to travel by myself all the time." She cocked her head. "And what about you?"

"Nope. The only reason I tried to stay at the top was for the money." Kyle gestured to the room. "So I could buy a ranch to call home. Now that I've got it, I lost the reason for being on that blacktop." He pointed at her with a screwdriver. "And I believe it is your turn to tell me something else you love about me."

I love that you get me.

Could she say that without giving too much of herself away?

Another laugh. "You can't think of even one more thing?"

"Yes, I can. I love your loyalty. Even when you're still upset with your mom, you're planning on giving her the money that Marshall left, aren't you? All of it."

"It's not like she won't have to work and I'm setting her up with a life of luxury. It'll give her more options. And it's just . . . I owe her. I am who I am, I'm loyal because of her. Because she beat those values into my head from the time I was a kid."

"Same with Hank and Abe. I resented it so much back then. Not them, just their rules." She still hadn't heard from her brothers. And that hurt like a raw wound that wouldn't scab over.

"Hey." Then Kyle was right in her face. "They're probably waiting until their full body armor arrives before showing up and facing both of us."

Kyle always tried to put a good spin on everything. She loved that he was such an optimist. "Thanks."

"And it's my turn, isn't it?" He gifted her with that rare, secret smile, so she figured this *I love* would be about a body part. Probably her legs. "I love that you starch my shirts. Actually, I love that you don't mind doin' laundry because I freakin' hate it. Maybe it makes me silly, but there's just something special about wearing a shirt that you starched for me."

Whoa. Another answer she hadn't expected. She shouldn't have been surprised that he'd turned what should be a mundane chore into something romantic. "I don't think it's silly at all. I'll admit some selfishness to it because I really like the way you look in them. It's sweet that you appreciate it. That's just another thing I love—"

"Hold that thought, okay? Be right back."

Celia watched him disappear around the corner. Then he returned with a tissue-wrapped package. "What's that?" She squinted at him. "I thought we'd agreed no Valentine's Day presents."

"It's not." He shoved it into her hands. "Just open it."

She ripped the tissue paper off and found a purple long-sleeved shirt nearly identical to the blood-covered one she'd had to throw away after her bulldoggin' mishap in Vegas. She looked at him with complete shock. "Kyle. Where did you find this?"

"I called Harper to thank her for helping you pick out all them sexy clothes." He smiled saucily. "We got to talking and for some reason she remembered your lucky purple shirt and she was happy to track down another one for you. It's not exactly the same—"

"But it's damn close to perfect." *Just like you.* Celia slipped it on over her T-shirt. She had difficulty doing the buttons; her fingers kept fumbling.

Then Kyle's warm fingers were under her chin, lifting it up. Their eyes met. "Do you hate it?"

"God no. I love it. I'm just... touched. Beyond words, really. Thank you." She pressed her lips to his. "I love your sweet, romantic side. Love it like crazy. Love—"

The kitchen timer dinged, signaling that the pork roast was done.

They both stepped back, strangely unsure about what'd just happened.

Then Kyle grinned. "I cannot wait to see what taste sensation you've whipped up tonight. Come on. Let's eat. I'll even set the table."

⚮

After supper, Kyle flipped on the new TV. As soon as she sat beside him on the couch, he scooted closer to her, wrapping his arm around her shoulders. He propped his feet on the coffee table and channel-surfed.

She snuggled into him, trying to remember if they'd ever watched TV together during the years they'd known each other. She couldn't think of a single instance. So it surprised her to discover that he liked dramas and cop shows. She'd pegged him as the type who watched sitcoms.

The events of the day caught up with her. She began to drift off. The next thing she knew, Kyle was sweeping her into his arms and carrying her to bed. "Sorry." She yawned. "I really wanted to christen the furniture tonight."

"It's not like the couch or that reclining chair is goin' anywhere."

"But I was even wearing my get-lucky shirt."

He kissed her forehead. "I thought it was a lucky shirt."

"I'm renaming it my get-lucky shirt. So if I'm wearing it, look out. You'll know what I expect."

"I knew I shoulda bought you a box of chocolates instead."

She whapped him on the arm. She stripped to skin and crawled between the sheets. Four seconds later the bed dipped and Kyle slid his naked body next to hers.

He chuckled softly. "I love that contented sigh you make whenever I touch you. And when I'm laying next to you at night."

"I am content. Very content."

"Good to know."

Celia floated into that happy place between slight consciousness and sleep.

Then Kyle's voice rumbled in her ear. "What did you say? You kinda mumbled."

"That I'm glad to be married to you."

The last thing she remembered hearing before succumbing to exhaustion was Kyle murmuring, "Same goes, kitten."

Chapter Thirteen

$\mathcal{T}$wo days later they'd just finished lunch when they heard a vehicle barreling up the driveway. Celia peeked out the blinds as Abe's truck pulled up.

"You ready for this?"

No. "I guess."

Kyle kissed the back of her head. "I'll let them say their piece, Cele, but I won't put up with disrespect from either of them."

Ridiculous how fast her heart raced when she answered the door and saw her brothers standing side by side.

"Hey, sis. Me'n Abe would like to talk to you."

"We understand if you don't wanna invite us in," Abe said.

She spoke over her shoulder to Kyle. "You gonna throw any punches? 'Cause I'd rather not have bloodstains on our new carpet."

"Maybe we'd best do this in the barn. Just in case the conversation goes south."

Abe nodded and Hank wore a hangdog look she'd never seen from either of them.

"We'll meet you in a few." Then Kyle shut the door in their faces. "Let's pick up the lunch dishes. It'll give you a little time to sort out what you wanna say to them."

Such a sweet, thoughtful man.

Ten minutes later the barn door creaked, announcing their arrival. The barn was fairly dark this time of day. She glanced at Abe, leaning against the workbench, watching Hank pace.

Hank stopped.

No one said a word.

The pause didn't last long. Hank marched right up to her. "Lemme just say this up front. I'm sorry. I'm so goddamn sorry for the bullshit that spewed outta my mouth that day. I don't ... There's no excuse for the way I hurt you. None. And I'm so ashamed of what I said to you, that it's taken me this long to find the balls to face you."

She bit her cheek.

"And it was a hard pill to swallow, realizing how dismissive I've been toward you. When we had that family talk a while back I figured you were just bein' childish about not liking the changes around the homeplace. You asked me where you fit in the future of the ranch and I never responded. I shoved your concerns—and you—aside to focus on my family. Then you stopped coming home, didn't you?"

She nodded.

"I don't know how I forgot that you were my family too, Cele. But I did." His voice wavered and he cleared his throat. "I don't know if you need more time before we can mend what I broke. I just wanted you to know how sorry I am and I'm willing to do whatever it takes to fix it."

Abe ambled over. "I ain't gonna make excuses either for bein' a first-class prick. I hurt you. I hafta live with that the rest of my life. I also hafta live with the fact I was so wrapped up in my life and school that I hadn't noticed you were avoiding coming home. Even before Janie and I got re-married. We're all awful good at pretending everything is fine when it ain't." Abe's eyes roamed over her face. "I look at you and see you're a grown woman. But I also look at you, even now, and see that pigtailed little girl who relied on me for so many years. I let you down, Cele. I hurt you with my careless words. I'm hoping you can forgive me for that. I'm hoping we can wipe the slate clean. Not go back to the way it was, but be better than we were before. Have a real adult relationship and not keep sliding back into those older/younger sibling roles we're used to."

Celia didn't doubt her brothers' sincerity. Their distress was painful to see. This wouldn't be an overnight fix, because it'd taken a few years to reach the breaking point, but it was a step in the right direction.

She started toward Hank and his arms were open before she reached him. He picked her up off the ground and squeezed her. "God, I'm sorry. I love you, sis."

"I know you do. I love you too. That's why it hurt so bad."

Then she was being passed to Abe, who hugged her just as tightly. "We're idiots. But we can be taught, to hear our wives tell it. I'm so sorry. I love you."

She wiped her eyes and watched as her brothers tried to discreetly wipe theirs. She looked at Kyle and knew the apologies were only half done. She held her hand out to him.

His arm circled her waist as they faced Hank and Abe.

"Christ, Kyle." Hank rubbed the back of his neck. "I don't know what the hell to say to you."

"*Sorry, I'm a self-righteous dick who deserves to get my face knocked into the dirt* would be a good place to start."

Hank didn't crack a smile. "Not even that seems like enough. Not only did we treat you worse than some no-account loser, we..." He hung his head as if he couldn't look Kyle in the face.

Abe clapped Hank on the back in a show of support. "You've been a great friend to both of us. Been part of our lives for a long damn time. It just shocked us both that you up and married Celia without warning. Not that you needed our permission or that we're offering an excuse, but we had no idea there was anything going on between you two besides nasty words and dirty looks. It's been that way for years. For it to change overnight?" He shook his head.

"Well, it hasn't exactly been overnight," Kyle said. "But I haven't been lusting after Celia since she was a six-year-old girl, that's for damn sure."

"We know that. We're sorry for accusing you of bein' some kind of user when we both know better," Abe said. "If you make Celia happy... that's all we care about."

"Marriage to me has tamed her wild ways. She's the most docile, eager-to-please ranch wife you've ever met," Kyle said, trying to lighten the mood.

She lightly punched him in the gut. "Jerk."

Kyle laughed. "Not tamed, but still so damn easy to tease."

Abe looked at Celia. "Are we good, then? Because if you wanna talk some more…"

"No. I'm ready to put this behind us," she said.

"Good. Now, Kyle…" Hank started.

Please don't ruin this by going all big brother again.

"What the fuck? Marshall Townsend was your father?"

Celia exhaled a sigh of relief.

"Yeah. DNA verified and everything." Kyle told the story for the millionth time and Celia tuned out the words, listening to the smooth, soothing cadence of Kyle's voice. Letting the constant stroking of his thumb on her hand lull her into a happy place where this would all work out.

Was that what she wanted? To live this life with Kyle for real?

Yes. Because it became more real every day they were together.

"Right, Celia?"

She focused on Kyle. "Sorry. I was thinking about something else."

"I said I couldn't do this without you."

Yeah. She definitely wanted this man all to herself. "Aw, listen to you tryin' to sweet-talk me when I'm already a sure thing."

Kyle gave her a smacking kiss. "Maybe I'll play hard to get tonight."

Celia snorted. "Like that ever happens."

Hank and Abe gawked at them like they'd morphed into alien life-forms.

Kyle flipped the lights on and said to Hank, "As long as you're here, can you tell me what the hell some of this equipment is?"

They walked forward, leaving Abe and Celia to catch up.

"So, Daddy Abe, tell me all about Tyler."

Abe grinned and whipped out his wallet. "I brought you a picture." He passed it over. "He's perfect. Got a full set of lungs, I tell you what. He's fussy, except when he's nursing. But I can't blame the kid—buried in Janie's breasts is a damn fine place to be."

Celia smacked him on the arm. "Janie let me hold him at the hospital." She looked at the dark-haired infant in the picture. She honestly didn't understand why parents showed pictures like this—the red-faced, open-mouthed baby resembled an alien. A pissed-off alien.

"She told me you visited. Sorry I missed you, but I am awful glad you went."

"I won't hold an innocent baby responsible for his daddy bein' a total jackass."

"Good to know. So how are things goin'?"

"Busy. We cleaned a lot of shit piles out of the house. Marshall had been a widower a long time. Getting back into the swing of daily chores and dealing with all the stuff that goes along with raising cattle has been an adjustment for both of us."

Abe leaned close enough to look into Celia's eyes. "But you're happy?"

"Yeah, Abe. I really am. I've never been happier." She felt Kyle's gaze and she looked at him to see a puzzled expression on his face.

"We've brought a couple of boxes we've been saving for you," Abe said.

She fought a groan. She had hoped she'd dealt with her last box for a while. "What's in them?"

"Some of Mom's stuff. I forgot we set it aside for you and I found it when I was in the attic last week."

"Now you've got me curious. Let's go get it."

They left the barn. Kyle and Hank followed.

Kyle carried the three boxes into the guest bedroom before he took Hank and Abe for a tour of the ranch.

She fixed herself a cup of tea and surveyed the guest bedroom. They'd kept the wrought-iron bed and antique dresser. Like the other two bedrooms, this one had beautiful wood floors. She had the fleeting thought that it would make a good nursery.

That'd come out of left field. Must be her brother's fault—after all, he was covered in new-baby pheromones.

Celia opened the first box. The scent of home drifted out. How could a box shoved in a dusty attic for years retain that scent? She focused on the contents. Her toys. Ready to be done with childish things, she'd shoved them in a box a month after her parents had died.

Her baby doll, with shiny brown plastic hair and those creepy doll eyes fringed by fake eyelashes stared back at her. It was in perfect condition. As much as she'd thought she wanted a doll, she'd gotten bored with it within a week.

She'd preferred to play with her stables set. With its twenty varieties of horses, pieces of white plastic fencing, a show ring, a barn, and stables. She picked up the three tiny barrels Hank had given her, so her plastic rider could be a real barrel racer.

Easy to forget all the good times she'd had with her brothers when the last few years had been so difficult. They'd raised her the best they could, practically being kids themselves when saddled with the responsibility of an eleven-year-old girl. Even when all three of them fought like crazy, she'd never questioned their love for her. And she'd never admitted to them or anyone else that she barely remembered their father taking the time to teach her or just hang out with her. He hadn't shown much of an interest in his only daughter. Not like Hank and Abe had. Even before they had no choice.

Which made Kyle's issues with Marshall so hard for Celia to understand. His mother loved him unconditionally. Wasn't that enough?

Fighting melancholy, she dug through the box, finding the only Barbie doll she'd ever owned. Western Stampin' Tara Lynn. Outfitted head to toe in sparkly western regalia, Tara Lynn had a horse named Misty. Her red cowgirl boots left a trail of broken hearts across a piece of paper. Celia smoothed the doll's dark hair and reseated her red cowgirl hat. Funny that the doll reminded her of Tanna.

Celia rooted around and found girlhood trinkets that'd meant so much to her. Purple, red, blue, and white ribbons from 4-H competitions. Arrowheads and funky rocks she'd unearthed in the pasture. A corncob pipe she'd crafted. A book filled with wildflowers she'd pressed. A worn thimble that'd belonged to her great-grandmother. A jar of buttons and the button dog she'd made with her mother on a snowy afternoon.

It'd been years since she'd thought of that day. The two of them sipping hot Russian tea. The strong scent of her mother's Aqua Net hair spray as she'd bent her head next to Celia's, patiently demonstrating how to make a button dog.

At the very bottom of the box was her collection of My Little Ponies. She remembered her horror at seeing them strung up in a tree where she couldn't reach, followed by anger because she knew exactly who'd done it.

Kyle.

Her eight-year-old self would be appalled that she'd married him.

In the second box were odds and ends. Fancy tablecloths and hand towels. A crocheted tissue box cover. Yards of lace and skeins of yarn. Her mother's sewing box. More piles of fabric her brothers hadn't thrown away. She closed the lid, just as unsure what to do with this stuff as they'd been years ago.

Celia knew the last box wouldn't contain her parents' things because they'd given everything away, just another sad memory she'd buried.

The door to their Mom and Dad's bedroom had always been shut, the room off-limits to kids. It'd remained shut after they died.

One afternoon, a few months after their deaths, Abe stormed into that room. He'd ripped their clothes out of the closet and thrown them in the hallway. Then he'd dumped out the dresser drawers in the hallway too. He'd removed every item belonging to them and ordered Hank and Celia to bag it up.

She'd been resentful that she and Hank had to clean up the mess Abe had made. She'd stepped over the piles, intending to give Abe grief, but she found he was already grieving. Her invincible brother was on the floor in their parents' closet, crying silently.

Abe had been so gruff and emotionless after they died. She'd thought he hadn't cared, but that day was when she understood how much Abe *did* care. How hard it was for any of the Lawson siblings to show emotion unless it was anger.

How had she forgotten that?

She'd never said a word about what she'd seen. She'd just quietly and quickly bagged up the leftover physical reminders of her parents' lives. When Abe had claimed that bedroom as his, she'd moved downstairs. Because she couldn't look down that hallway and pretend her parents were away for a while. She finally understood they weren't coming back.

She opened the last box. The wedding ring quilt from her parents' bed.

The fabric had been mended over the years, new patches sewn in where old sections had torn. This quilt had been passed through four generations of women in her family.

Now it was hers. Celia knew she should feel something like pride or thankfulness about this heritage, but all she could muster was sadness. The first three women who'd slept under the quilt with their husbands had been widowed at a young age. Her parents had died far too young. She didn't want to put this quilt on their bed and doom their marriage from the start.

But that was kind of a moot point, wasn't it? Hadn't she doomed it by insisting that it end at the six-month mark? How did she even begin to bring it up with Kyle that she'd changed her mind so early on in their agreement?

She unfolded the quilt, spreading it on the guest bed. It fit this old-fashioned room. She closed the boxes and carried them to the basement. Out of sight, out of mind.

Kyle's voice reached her in the basement. "Celia?"

"Hang on." She bounded up the stairs and found him alone. "Where are my brothers?"

"Janie needed Abe to come home, so they said to tell you they'd be in touch." He wandered to the guest bedroom. "What was in the boxes?"

"Kid stuff. Things of my mom's." She pointed to the bed.

"I remember that." Kyle looked at her. "You sure you want it in here and not our room?"

"I like our bedding." *It's not cursed.*

He curled his hand around her neck and pulled her close. "You all right with everything that happened today?"

"I'm glad they came to us and apologized. I was beginning to wonder if they would."

"Me too."

"Did they say anything else to you?"

"Not really."

She narrowed her eyes at him.

"I swear. We're guys. They apologized. I accepted. End of story. But you…" His thumb stroked the pulse point on her throat. "Seem a little melancholy. Luckily, I've got the perfect cure for that."

"Which is?"

Kyle brushed his mouth over hers. Once. Twice. Then his lips slid to her ear. "It has to do with you handling some hard… wood."

"I'm up for that."

He slapped her on the ass. "Good. Get your warm clothes on. 'Cause there's a pile of logs we need to split and stack."

"You sneaky jerk! I thought we were gonna get naked and wild."

He raised a brow. "During the day? When there's work to be done? Surely an experienced ranch woman such as yourself knows better than that."

"You suck."

Another slap to her ass. "No sassing me. Get cracking."

Chapter Fourteen

$\mathscr{H}$is wife was so fucking hot it was a miracle the snow wasn't melting all around her.

They'd been hauling and stacking wood for the last two hours. Day started to fade, turning the horizon the hazy purple color exclusive to a twilight winter sky. Normally it was Kyle's favorite time of day.

But the scenery paled in comparison to Celia. He couldn't keep his eyes off her. Wearing stained Carhartt coveralls over a girly pink thermal shirt. She'd donned a neon orange Elmer Fudd hat, and pushed the earflaps out, the bill of the cap tugged down so low he could barely see her eyes. Her gloves were new and she kept tugging on them, so every once in a while he'd get a glimpse of her wrists. And his cock would pulse against his zipper.

Which made him feel like an idiot. Celia's wrists turned him on, for chrissake.

"Kyle! Are you even paying attention?" she yelled.

No, little wife of mine. I'm too busy admiring the beautiful flush on your cheeks, and the sexy way your braid swings against your ass.

"Yes. Stop nagging me."

She harrumphed.

During his next two trips to the woodshed, he decided to call it a day. Drag her inside. Fuck her until neither of them could walk. Hope that outstanding sex—lots and lots of body-rocking sex—would keep her interested in sticking around.

Smack. Something hit him in the middle of the back. When he whirled around, a snowball hit his chest, and snow exploded in his face. He stared at her dumbfounded for a millisecond, before another blast of snow hit his forehead. "Jesus, Celia. What the hell?"

"I'm not hauling this wood by myself, while you're lollygagging."

As soon as the word *lollygagging* exited her mouth another snowball hit him in the neck.

"That's it!" Kyle bent down and scooped up a handful of snow, forming a ball as he charged her.

Celia shrieked, and ducked to grab from the stack of snowballs she had stockpiled at her feet. When the hell had she had time to do that?

She let fly with deadly accuracy.

By the time Kyle was within ten feet of her, he looked like the Abominable Snowman.

Laughing, she bobbed and weaved, taunting him, continuing to cover him in snow. She'd run out of ammo and was just flinging handfuls of snow at him.

So she was very surprised when he dove for her feet, knocking her off balance. Celia landed on her butt. Before she could roll away, Kyle pounced on her. Immobilizing her legs, he pinned her arms above her head. Then he swept his free arm across the freshly fallen snow, spraying her face.

"Stop!"

"You started it."

While she was still sputtering death threats, he scooped up a glove full of snow and shoved it down her shirt.

Celia screamed bloody murder, thrashing beneath him like a bull in a bucking chute. "That's cheating!"

"Shoulda thought of that before you declared a snow war."

"I was just trying to get your attention."

"Well, you've got it now." He put his warm mouth against her cold ear. She writhed, attempting to squirm away while gasping for breath.

Then Kyle put his cold nose at the base of her throat where her shoulder met her neck. He opened his mouth on that sensitive sweep of flesh and sucked.

"Oh God. That's not . . . fair."

Her skin was warm, but cooling from the snow melting on her chest. He growled at the taste of her sweat and the heady aroma of her damp hair. He slid down between her thighs and rocked his pelvis into hers as he feasted on her skin.

Celia moaned as his mouth followed the collar of her shirt to the top of her coveralls. He couldn't dip his tongue any farther and she released a frustrated groan.

He pressed kisses along her jaw to her other ear when she arched back, offering him her throat. "I want you all the time, Celia. But fuck, I want you right now." He licked the hollow of her throat. "Say something."

"You're crushing my ribs," she whispered.

"Shit. Sorry."

As soon as he'd relaxed his hold, Celia lifted her hips, twisted her shoulders, and flipped him onto his back, using her considerable body strength to hold him down.

Son of a bitch.

She laughed seductively and then her mouth was on his. Feeding him such hot, openmouthed kisses he could almost forgive her for her trick.

Almost.

Kyle freed one arm and yanked off her hat.

When she raised her head, he gained the advantage, hooked his leg over both of hers, and rolled her.

But Celia was ready. They tumbled across the snow like a couple of runaway logs before coming to a stop with him on top.

He eased back to gaze into her eyes and felt that sharp jab in his gut. Not merely lust but something primal. Helpless against that feeling, he took her mouth in a desperate kiss. Passion that'd been on simmer boiled over. Gloves flew. He unhooked the fasteners on her overalls and she attempted to pull off his coat. He rutted on her and she met each long grind of his pelvis with one of her own.

Kyle tore his mouth from the sweet heat of hers, panting for air. "Now. Goddammit. I need you. Right. Fucking. Now." He pushed back and unzipped his coat, flinging it aside. Next came his shirt. He popped to his feet and lifted a brow in challenge as she hesitated.

"Strip out here in the yard? Where anyone could drive up and see us?"

"Be adventurous, little wife of mine." Kyle removed his boots and started on his jeans.

Celia's eyes were firmly on his crotch as he slid his jeans down. "I love your body, Kyle."

He froze because he had the vague hope she'd intended to say she loved him.

But not another sound exited her mouth.

Brusquely he said, "Same goes, so get up, and lemme see you. All of you."

"You're hard," she said when his briefs were off.

His feet were freezing. He held out his hands and pulled her upright. "Take 'em off or I tear 'em off."

"Help me."

"Baby. You're shaking," he murmured.

She toed her boots off and was jerking her overalls down her legs. "You do this to me. Every time you touch me."

"Are you wet?"

"Besides where you shoved snow down my shirt?" She shivered after she peeled down her yoga pants. "Yes. So wet my panties will probably freeze once you rip them off me."

Kyle unhooked her bra, tossing it aside.

As soon as her underwear and socks were off, he swept her into his arms and walked across the snow to the hot tub.

Celia peppered his cheek with kisses, making needy little moans.

He shifted his hold on her to remove the hot tub cover. Then he gently tossed her into the water.

She hissed as her body absorbed the temperature shock.

Kyle flipped the jets on and hopped in, taking a moment to bask in the heat and steam. When he opened his eyes, he found an owl-eyed Celia watching him.

They stayed on opposite sides of the hot tub as the veil of night fell around them. Reflection from the snow offered the only illumination.

When Celia started toward him, he met her halfway. As much as he ached to return to passion, he needed a moment to savor her.

Celia seemed strangely hesitant to touch him as they faced each other on their knees.

Kyle circled his arm around her waist, bending his head to her neck. "I love the way you taste, right here." His tongue followed the tendon down her neck to her clavicle. "I see that trickle of sweat and I get hard. I wanna put my mouth there and catch every droplet on my tongue."

"Kyle."

"Mmm?" He nuzzled her ear and filled his lungs with her scent.

"Fuck me. Hard and fast. Bend me over. Do me any way you want, but do me now."

Dirty words drifting from that angelic mouth did it for him in a bad way. "Wrap yourself around me, baby, and take me in."

The buoyancy of the water allowed her to hold on to his shoulder with one hand and circle his cock with the other as she guided him inside.

No slow start for his eager kitten. As soon as his shaft was fully seated, she pushed her body up and plunged down until his balls swung into her ass.

Kyle groaned, loving how she'd just taken control, hating how this wouldn't last long for either of them. Her ankles were locked beneath his buttocks and her chest brushed his in a sensual tease as water sloshed over their shoulders.

Her wet lips skimmed his ear and he shuddered at the hot and cold sensation.

He gritted his teeth against his instinct to push her against the edge and plow into her. Kyle reached for the side of the hot tub and held on as she gained momentum. Wrapping her braid around his hand, he tugged her head back to bare the section of skin at her throat that had become his obsession.

The heated water kept their bodies below the surface warm but the air temp, after the sun went down, turned frigid. After lavishing attention on that wet skin, he realized his face was icy, as was hers. Kyle snared her mouth in a blistering kiss. Which increased the frenetic pace of her move-ments.

"More. Harder." Celia changed the angle of her pelvis and rode him faster, rubbing the top of her mound and that sweet little clit against his pubic hair. "So close."

"What will get you there?" he murmured in her ear.

"That. Oh God. Just like that. I swear I can come just from your voice whispering in my ear."

"Fuckin' sexy as hell when you tell me what'll get you off. I'm addicted to that sound you make just before you come."

Celia's nails scored the back of his neck and then she was gasping, her body rigid as her pussy spasmed around his cock.

He was nowhere near close to coming; he greedily watched her face as the orgasm consumed her. She was so beautiful lost in passion. Until she winced.

"What's wrong?"

"Cramp in my right side. Oh shit. That hurts."

He eased out of her and unwrapped her legs from his body. "Lay back in the water. Relax and let me rub it."

She rested her neck against the edge. Her chest came up, her nipples constricted the instant the air hit them. Then she was floating, eyes closed, entrusting herself to him completely.

Kyle found the knotted muscle. Celia groaned when he began to work the spot. He couldn't take his eyes off this complex woman he'd married. There were times when she looked at him that he swore she felt the same way he did. Should he be the first one to take a chance and tell her he loved her?

Right after she said, "That's good, it's gone," he refocused on the phys-ical pull between them. He suckled an icy nipple into the heat of his mouth, rubbed his cheek between her breasts. Then he climbed out and lifted her into his arms.

"You c-c-an't c-c-carry me."

"I am carrying you. No need for you to walk through the snow."

"But our c-c-clothes—"

"Will be fine."

He carried her into the bathroom. After drying them both off, he led her to their bedroom. He stretched her out on her belly with a stern, "Don't move," as he grabbed the lube from the nightstand.

Celia was shivering when he pulled the covers over them.

He layered his body over hers to warm her, nestling his erection in the crack of her ass as he kissed her nape. Then his tongue inched down her spine one vertebra at a time. His fingers slid beneath her hip and stroked her slit with the same teasing motion his tongue used on her back.

She shifted and Kyle gave her a stinging slap on her ass that made her gasp.

"Stay still." His mouth returned to teasing her ear. "I will touch you however I want, whenever I want, wherever I want, remember?" He slapped her other butt cheek. And then dragged her onto her knees, leaving her chest on the bed, stretching her arms above her head. Kissing the edges of her shoulder blades. Her skin had retained the warmth from the hot tub. Every section was so soft. Had he ever been obsessed with any woman's body the way he was obsessed with hers?

No. Celia was an absolute feast for his senses and he wanted to gorge himself on her. Two, three, ten times a day. Every day. For the rest of his life.

Grabbing the bottle of lube, he poured a generous amount on his fingers and gently inserted them into her pussy. His needs teetered between tenderness and roughness—wanting to spread her and impale her, but the thought of hurting her in a moment of lust-fueled haste made him slow down.

He slicked up his cock, circled the tip around her opening and slid home.

Celia sighed.

Kyle watched his cock tunneling into her pussy. Felt the intimate kiss when those inner muscles tightened around his dick. He layered his body over hers, absorbing her every reaction. His chest against her back made her arch closer. His face nestled in her nape sent gooseflesh cascading across her skin. His hands slid up her arms until he threaded his fingers through hers. "Hold on." He eased out and slammed in.

Celia groaned. "Kyle. That feels…"

"For me too." They both loved the quick pace, but he wanted something else for them this time. "I can't hold off any longer," he panted, stopping completely.

"Don't stop. Please."

"I wanna come like this. Us touching from head to toe." Kyle barely pumped his hips. Everything slowed down, but that somehow increased the intensity of their connection.

She turned her head toward his mouth. Their kisses were as languid as the movement of his body on hers, and just as hot. Celia came in a series of strong pulses that left her gasping his name.

That pushed him over the brink and he spiraled into bliss. His orgasm triggered something inside him besides a burst of physical pleasure. And he mumbled, "Christ. I love you."

A beat of silence passed. "Kyle? What was that noise you just made?"

Afraid she might attribute his declaration of love to hot sex, he lied. "Crap. I have a butt cramp."

She laughed. "We're gonna wear out our body parts if we keep this up, Kyle."

"That's a chance I'm willing to take."

Chapter Fifteen

"There are a lot of people here for this baby shower," Celia said to Kyle as they pulled into the nearly full parking area at the Split Rock.

"You sure there's not a ball game goin' on in the lounge?"

"You wish. But there will be plenty of games to keep you entertained." She gave him a smug smile.

"I don't like that look, Celia."

Baby-shower virgin Kyle was in for an interesting afternoon.

Lainie burst outside as soon as they cleared the front steps. "Oh, good, you're here. Let me take that." She snatched the baby gift bag from Celia's hand. "We're running a little behind." She pushed open the massive doors and paused in the slate-floored foyer. "Hand me your coats. Stay right here. I'll be right back to show you to the dining room." She disappeared around the corner.

Celia and Kyle exchanged a look. "Did she forget we know where the dining room is?"

He shrugged. "You're the baby shower expert." He invaded her space and stole a kiss. "How long will this shindig last?"

"A couple of hours probably. Why?"

"Because I've got plans for you." He tipped her head back to nibble on her throat. "Naked plans."

A wave of want washed over her.

"Goddamn, I love that sexy little noise you make when you're turned on."

"I make it a lot around you."

"I know. Means I'm doin' a great job with my husbandly duties."

"Oh, for chrissake, you two. Get a room."

Celia broke away from Kyle at the sound of Abe's voice.

But Kyle merely chuckled, tucking her more firmly against his side. "Great idea. We are at a fancy resort. Wanna check out the hourly rates?"

She elbowed him and faced her brother. Both of her brothers. "Hey, guys. What's up?"

"Lainie sent us to fetch you," Hank said.

"Personal escorts? Is Renner afraid we'll run off with the art or something?"

"You know ... at Bran and Harper's wedding you were eyeballing Braxton's sculpture like it might fit in your purse," Kyle said slyly.

"Kyle!"

He smooched her indignant mouth. "You're still so damn fun to tease."

Abe sighed. "I actually preferred you two flinging insults at each other rather than making goo-goo eyes and cooing like demented doves."

Celia resisted whapping him on the head.

Hank and Abe took the lead as they wandered through the main room of the lodge. They paused outside the opening to the dining room and stepped off to the side.

She'd barely registered the room full of people when they all yelled, "Surprise!"

Both she and Kyle jumped.

Abe said, "Allow me to present ... Mr. and Mrs. Kyle Gilchrist."

Applause and whistles echoed in the room.

Then Harper, Lainie, Janie, Tierney, Bernice, and Vivien rushed forward.

"What's all this?" Celia managed.

"Your wedding shower!" Harper exclaimed.

"But ..." She looked at Janie.

"My baby shower was last month. Since none of us were at your wedding ceremony, nor was there a wild and crazy wedding dance afterward, we decided to throw you a party."

"We figured you could use some household items, since you've both been on the road for the last few years," Lainie added.

"When folks in Muddy Gap heard you guys had gotten hitched? I had dozens of people calling and asking when we were gonna throw you a proper reception," Harper said.

"Except we know improper suits you better," Bernice said with a snicker. "Since me and Viv were friends of your mom's, we asked to be involved."

"Asked?" Tierney snorted. "Demanded is more like it."

Vivien hip-checked her. "Hush, newlywed. When you've been married as long as I was, or as long as Bernice has been, you get to bull your way into whatever party you want."

Bernice, one of the least sentimental women Celia knew, took Celia's hand. "When I heard the news about you and Kyle, it reminded me of something your mama said years ago. Something I'd forgotten because it'd come out of left field. Back in the day, before I started my shop, I was at your folks' place, giving your mom a haircut. Kyle had ridden the bus home with Hank. You and Kyle were sniping at each other. Somehow you ended up chasing each other outside, right in front of the sliding glass door. Your mom said, in that soft-spoken way of hers, 'They fight because there's more between them than they understand at their age.' So I know your mom would be happy for both of you."

Stunned, Celia choked out, "Thank you, Bernice, that's . . ." and turned toward Kyle because she couldn't finish.

He said, "Ladies, can you give me and my bride a moment?"

"Sure."

He blocked her from the room, holding her face in his hands. "What?"

"How is that even possible? What Bernice said about my mom?"

"Can't we just chalk it up to your mother being a perceptive woman?"

"I guess. Perceptiveness sure isn't something I inherited—I didn't have a clue about this shower." Her gaze hooked his. "Did you know about this?"

"Hell no."

"Good." She inhaled deeply. "Because I'd hate to start a fight with you in front of all these people."

"They're used to it from us. So let's defy their expectations." Kyle placed a soft kiss between her eyebrows. "Now buck up and face the music."

When they turned around, another cheer went up.

"Let's get this party started! For the bride..." Harper settled a lace veil on Celia's head.

"And for the groom..." Bran clipped a plastic ball and chain around Kyle's ankle.

Laughter erupted.

Tierney clapped her hands after the hilarity died down. "Okay, people, listen up. We're doing this old school. Men, take Kyle to the bar. Ladies, you know what to do."

Celia tried not to panic when Kyle was ripped away from her without so much as a good-bye kiss.

You're getting too dependent on him, Celia.

"I remember the days when menfolk weren't invited," Garnet said behind her. "Then we could talk about all sorts of raunchy sex stuff."

"Like having men in the next room over is going to stop you from whatever you wanted to say anyway," Maybelle said with a sniff.

"Age does have certain honesty benefits."

Garnet and Maybelle each hooked an arm through Celia's. "We're your official escorts," Garnet confided. "Which I hope means we're either getting booze first or cake first."

Maybelle sighed. "Brace yourself, Celia. It's going to be a long afternoon."

She was hugged about a hundred times. But one person was missing from the crowd. She wondered if Kyle had noticed.

"Why the frown?" Lainie murmured.

"Did you invite Kyle's mom?"

"Yes. But she opted not to come. Evidently Sherry talked to Susan. Susan said Sherry didn't want to spend all afternoon fielding questions about Marshall Townsend being Kyle's father. She said it's supposed to be focused on your marriage. But she did send a gift. So did Tanna."

Women of all ages, some Celia hadn't seen in years, started to fill in the circle of chairs.

Janie sat on Celia's right side and patted her thigh. "Toughen up, cow-girl. This is gonna be some fun."

"You couldn't have warned me? So I had the chance to dress up a little?"

"It doesn't matter what clothes you have on, dear sister, because you're wearing the most important thing . . . the look of a woman in *lurve*."

First time Janie had ever called her sister and it choked her up a little. Which of course Lainie noticed.

Lainie said, "You'll shed a few tears before the day is over, guaranteed."

She steeled her spine, refusing to bawl in front of all the people who'd known her—and Kyle—for most of their lives.

Harper and Tierney stood in the center of the circle and tried to get everyone's attention.

Janie leaned over. "Those two are in their element. I swear the Split Rock should start advertising themed private parties and put them in charge. We could make a mint."

"Aren't you supposed to be on maternity leave?" Lainie pointed out.

"My business brain is still fully functional," Janie retorted. "Now that we have a little mouth to feed, I'm all about increasing our cash flow so we can afford diapers."

"Speaking of . . . Where are your kiddos?" Celia asked.

"With Susan Williams in the first guest room down the hall. Luckily this coincides with naptime."

Tierney pierced them with a dirty look and her sisters-in-law straightened up immediately.

Celia snickered.

"First of all, a toast. But please don't drink until we're all served." Tierney looked hard at Garnet and Tilda. Then she signaled to Fletch and another guy to enter the circle.

Celia asked Janie, "Who's the blond?"

"Tobin Hale. He does a lot around here, but he mostly works for Renner. Both Tobin and Fletch are huge favorites of the Mud Lilies."

Fletch handed out shot glasses and Tobin filled them. But Celia didn't get one.

Harper motioned her into the center of the circle. "We asked your husband to tell us your favorite shot. And you only get to drink it...if he guessed right."

Oohs and aahs rang out.

"Kyle guessed...tequila." Which wasn't her favorite but it was what led them to the altar.

"Wrong. He said your favorite is a *blow job*."

That smarmy jerk.

"But here's where you get to even the score, because he doesn't get to drink if he gets this one wrong. So tell us, Celia, what is Kyle's favorite shot?"

She tapped her chin. "I'll say, a tasty little one called *tie me to the bedpost*."

Laughter pealed through the room.

"And with that, let's all toast to our newlywed."

"Hear, hear!"

"Celia, take a seat and we'll play the first game."

As soon as she sat down, Janie elbowed her. "What?"

"I saved my shot for you since I'm nursing, but for God's sake be discreet," Janie whispered. "I don't want Harper and Tierney, the game Nazis, to catch us cheating." Janie pointed at something behind them; Celia turned to look and drained the whiskey.

Tierney said, "The name of the first game is pass the penis."

"Hot damn!" Garnet shouted, only to be shushed by Bernice and the gang.

"The object of this game, just like in hot potato, is to *not* be holding the penis when the music shuts off. But we've spiced up the rules, adding a second part to the game and another chance to win."

"We'll be watching to see who fondles BOB the best," Harper said, "so even if you're disqualified you're still in the running for a BOB of your own."

"BOB." Lainie repeated. "I hope he comes with a battery pack because the batteries in those things never last."

"Which is why I like the plug-in types," Janie offered.

"Nothing compares to the real thing," Lainie said.

"I cannot wait until I get the all clear to have sex with my husband,"

Janie said. "He had to get inventive during those last months of pregnancy when we had beach ball baby between us. Not that coming up with something new has ever been a problem for him."

"So you *can* teach an old dog new tricks?" Lainie asked.

Janie snickered. "Hell, I can get him to roll over and beg."

"Get used to doing it fast," Lainie advised. "It's the only option when you're horny, the baby has finally gone to sleep, and you just want your man on you and in you *now*."

"Uh. TMI about my brothers' sex lives," Celia said.

Tierney did the hand-clapping thing again. "So let's all stand and gather in a circle."

Harper tugged Celia to her feet. "Our newlywed has volunteered to start the game."

Celia plastered on a smile, allowing Harper to lead her to the other side of the circle, between Betty and Bootsie, sisters who ran the sale barn. Harper handed Celia a long vibrator in the loudest shade of pink she'd ever seen. "How do you turn it on?"

"Twist the rubber ring on the bottom," seventy-year-old Bootsie suggested.

Okay. Celia cranked the bottom section clockwise. The phallus almost vibrated right out of her hand.

"Keep a good hold on that model," Amy-Lynn suggested. "It is pretty intense."

Even Amy-Lynn, a few years younger than Celia, knew more about vibrators than she did? How mortifying.

"Honky Tonk Badonkadonk" blared through the speakers and Celia passed the vibrator to Bonnie, who closed her fist around it and slid it up and down a couple of times. Then she handed it to Amy-Lynn, who brought it up to her lips like she was about to lick it, but she smirked and passed it off to Vivien.

The vibrator made it around the circle one time before the music quit. Bernice was the first one out. The next song, "Brand New Girlfriend," fired up the players, who shouted out *boyfriend* every time instead of *girlfriend*, and both Maybelle and Lainie were lost on that round.

The longer the music played, the raunchier the action became. Celia found herself laughing so hard she wasn't paying attention during "Giddy On Up" and she was caught pink-handed holding the vibrator.

Two players remained. Garnet and Amy-Lynn. They started flipping the vibrator back and forth. Garnet caught it between her knees just as "Friends in Low Places" stopped playing.

Amy-Lynn did a victory lap holding the pink phallus in her hands like a sword.

"Our bride gets to take a consolation prize home." Harper handed her a box.

Amid shouts of, "Open it, open it," she ripped into the big box. Yes, it was a vibrator, but not in an obscene shade of pink—hers was vivid purple with a cherry red head.

Maybelle clapped her hand over Tilda's mouth after she made a crack about Barney the Dinosaur having a sore wee-wee.

Tierney awarded the most lewd use of her hands to Garnet, who turned on her new penis and challenged Amy-Lynn to a dick duel.

That's when Renner walked in. "Looks like y'all are havin' a lot more fun over here."

"Join us and bring all your hot-lookin' buddies," Bootsie shouted, performing a lewd bump and grind that Garnet immediately copied.

Renner's eyes automatically sought out his wife. Tierney bounded over for a brief conversation. When Tierney walked off, Renner's gaze stayed on her ass, which amused Celia. Until Renner caught her watching him and shook his finger at her. "No tequila shooters for you two today, understand?"

Celia and Tierney looked at each other and laughed.

"When are we gonna hear that story?" Vivien asked.

"Never. We've been forbidden from ever discussing it." Tierney winked. "All right, ladies, get out your shot glasses again." Tobin and Fletch appeared with fresh bottles. "The next question for Celia. According to your husband, what's your favorite sexual position?"

Celia fought a blush, but she knew the answer, hands down. "Any."

"That is correct! Pour the woman a shot!"

Thank God. She was tempted to grab the bottle and run.

"Same question back at Kyle. And what will his response be?"

"All," she said without hesitation.

Wolf whistles and laughter followed.

Celia sat and Janie slipped her another shot.

The next game required Celia to wear an apron emblazoned with *Pretty in Pink, Wicked in Spurs*, which had assorted kitchen utensils attached to it. She put on two oven mitts and had to catch various round-shaped fruits and veggies thrown by the attendees and set them in a large soup tureen until she'd completed the circle.

Then Celia was sent out of the room. The guests had to try to name everything pinned on her apron. And all the food she'd stowed in her pot.

Harper walked the perimeter, smacking a pink riding crop with a long feather boa on one end, making sure no one cheated.

"What exactly are you afraid I'll do if you leave me alone?" Celia asked Tierney.

"Nothing. Since Renner and I have been married a year, you're supposed to use this time to ask me any questions about marriage."

"Are you happy?"

Tierney's grin stretched ear to ear. "Sickeningly happy. Disgustingly happy. Especially since Renner is spending less time on the road this year. Sometimes when I look at him I can't believe he's mine. And I know he feels the same because sometimes I catch him watching me with this funny smile on his face. Sounds very sappy and clichéd."

"You guys are a good match."

"Opposites attract and all that. It's been a learning curve for both of us, me never having been married, and him having taken the trip down the aisle twice, but the quickie Vegas marriage doesn't really count in my mind."

Celia waited for Tierney to retract her statement, due to her and Kyle's quickie Vegas marriage, but she continued on.

"Neither of us had a parental marriage to model ours after, or a bad pattern to avoid, which has been a blessing. Renner can't say, *My parents always did it this way*, because his mother died when he was young. So did mine. Our parents' initial marriages left no lasting imprint on either of us."

Sometimes Tierney talked way above Celia's head. Imprinting? Modeling? Wasn't every marriage supposed to be unique to that couple? What worked for one couple didn't mean it was gospel for every other couple? Another thought crossed her mind. Were all the guys giving Kyle husbandly advice on how to handle her?

"I'm sorry, Celia. I'm blathering on and I'm supposed to be listening to you."

"I'm trying to take in the fact I'm actually at my own wedding shower." She cocked her head toward the room where the guys were holed up. "How'd you get them to show up? The promise of free booze?"

Tierney regarded her oddly. "No. The promise of fireworks. Between you and Kyle."

She frowned. "Really?"

"On the guys' side there's a betting pool about how many dirty looks you'll give Kyle once you two get into the same room."

"And the women's side?"

"Oh, the women are more romantic. They have a bet on how many kisses he'll give you to try to wipe those dirty looks off your face."

It made her a little sad that these people believed she couldn't change. That she'd be combative with Kyle as her husband, as she'd been when Kyle had just been an annoyance in her life.

She feared maybe he still saw her as a necessary annoyance. He needed her ranching help. He wanted her physically, almost obsessively. He could put up with her on a temporary basis because there was the benefit of kick-ass sex.

The hollow feeling expanded to think Kyle might be justifying their marriage at her expense.

Kyle wouldn't do that. He's no more the same guy he was years ago when you two constantly butted heads than you are the bratty girl who used to torture him. You need to tell him how you feel. Or at least that your feelings have changed.

"Celia?" Tierney said. "I didn't mean to upset you."

She looked up. "You didn't. I was just trying to figure out how much my brothers bet against me. And if Kyle is in there shooting whiskey."

"Hey, Renner bringing up the tequila shooters incident reminded me of something from that night last year. Right after Kyle showed up at the bar before we started getting wild, he whispered something to you. Seemed pretty intense. Do you remember what he said?"

Don't do this to yourself, kitten. If Breck doesn't know where you've been all week he doesn't deserve you. It's killin' me to see you so damn unhappy. Let's go somewhere. Just you and me, and talk.

If Celia hadn't promised Tierney she'd hang out with her, she would've left with Kyle right then.

She should have. Because directly after Renner and Tierney had taken off, Breck and his cowboy posse bailed. She'd had no choice but to go along because she'd had nowhere else to go. Then Breck and Michael turned in early because they were tired.

Tired of keeping up pretenses most likely.

"Sorry. You don't have to answer that."

Torn from the past, Celia blinked at Tierney. "In a nutshell, he said, *Dump Breck.* Which I did shortly thereafter."

Fletch and a guy Celia didn't know were zipping their coats and appeared to be headed out the door.

Tierney stepped in front of them. "Where are you guys going?"

"We hit a lull and I need Fletch to look at a couple of things while he's out this way."

Fletch tugged on Celia's veil and grinned. "Hard to believe you're a married woman, brat. Married to Kyle, no less."

"Yeah, yeah, yeah, I've heard the *I'm shocked* comment plenty of times."

"I'm not shocked. I'm thrilled you two boneheads stopped fighting long enough to actually talk to each other."

Celia squinted at him with disbelief.

"He wore that same look just now when I said the same thing to him."

"And how did my loving husband respond?"

"That he'd had his eye on you a lot longer than he'd admit. But of course, I already knew that too." Fletch smirked. "I'm an excellent judge of animal behavior."

She cuffed him on the arm. "So have you found an assistant yet?"

"Nope. They last about two months. Then I'm looking again. I've decided it's easier to do it all myself. Why? You know someone who's interested and qualified?"

"I was just thinkin' about your comment that if I ever did follow through and become a veterinary assistant you'd hire me."

"I meant it. But it's not like you won't have your hands full helping Kyle run you guys' ranch."

"Hey, Fletch, the warden granted us some yard time," the man next to Tierney drawled.

Talk about looking like ten miles of bad road. This guy had dark circles under his piercing brown eyes, a scraggly beard covering the entire lower half of his face, shaggy blackish brown hair hanging from beneath his gray cowboy hat. He was a big guy, at least six foot three, and his clothes hung off him like a scarecrow. She guessed his age to be around hers, and he'd be good-looking if he took any kind of pride in his appearance.

After she realized she'd been staring, she thrust out her hand. "I don't believe we've met. Celia."

"Hugh Pritchett. I manage Jackson Stock Contracting for Renner and the tyrant—I mean Tierney—when she lets me."

"Let you. You do whatever the hell you want." Tierney rolled her eyes. "Besides, you look like death warmed over, so no working livestock. It's supposed to be your day off, Hugh."

"Ain't no days off in this business," he said.

"Got that right," Celia replied.

"I've seen you run barrels a coupla times. You're good. Plans to continue that?"

"Nope."

"Your husband said he's done with ridin' bulls too, which don't hurt my feelings none. He rode BB last year, and that's sayin' something, since he's the only one."

Fletch sighed. "You two will talk rodeo all damn day. Come on, Hugh, let's get this check over with so I can get back to drinkin' on *my* day off."

Soon as they were gone, Tierney shook her head. "I worry about Hugh. He'd work twenty-four/seven if Renner let him."

"No offense, but he looks a little ragged."

"Hugh's wife refused to move to Wyoming when Renner relocated the stock business here, and she filed for divorce. Messed him up bad. He's lost seventy pounds in the last year. Calls it the *divorce diet*. He's a great guy and he hates when I mother him, so I do it as often as possible."

"He needs fashion advice from Harper. I'm surprised she hasn't attempted to make him over."

"She's been buying stuff in his size, because the man doesn't need to lose another pound. When she puts her mind to making him look decent, he won't know what hit him." Tierney looped her arm through Celia's. "Let's see who won the prizes."

"More vibrators?"

"Please. Not all the gifts are sexually oriented." She groaned. "But I'm starting to think that's what the partygoers would've preferred."

Celia laughed.

Tilda won the name-the-food game and her prize was a cookbook— which she donated to Celia.

Lainie won the name-the-apron-items game and her prize was a bottle of flavored cooking oil—which she also donated to Celia.

"Okay, this is the last question, Celia, so come up here while Tobin pours the shots." Harper asked, "What do you consider 'your song'?"

The memory came rushing back. At the concert with Kyle, standing in the wings. Devin had looked at them from center stage and said, "This is dedicated to my hometown friends." She remembered her belly swooped when she glanced at Kyle and knew he felt it too. Even through her haze of alcohol she'd known. No wonder she'd ended up married to him that night.

"Celia?" Tierney prompted.

"The song is 'Right in Front of Me' by Devin McClain."

"That's what Kyle said too. Pour this woman a shot."

"The time has come to open presents!" Harper clapped with glee.

Lainie leaned over. "I'll admit I snooped in your kitchen cupboards when we visited. I made a list of what you didn't have and shared it with the shower attendees. Hope you don't mind."

"I'm overwhelmed. Thank you."

The present opening took more than an hour. Celia could not believe the mountain of household items. Garnet referred to a few items as *bood-war* gifts, like the Hitachi "massager" with attachments and a basket of flavored body oils, and a jumbo bottle of lube. No one fessed up to that one and Celia suspected it was from Tanna.

"There's one last game to play and it involves the guys, so ladies, make room while we get Celia ready."

Harper hustled her from the room and led her down the hallway to Wild West Clothiers.

"I don't have to change clothes, do I?"

"No. First I wanted to give you and Kyle your wedding gift from me'n Bran." She unlocked the door and flipped on the lights. "It's up here."

Curious, Celia followed her to the cash register.

Harper picked up a painting leaning against the wall and turned it around. "I saw you looking at this one when you were shopping. The woman in this picture reminds me of you."

The picture was a cattle drive scene. A blond-haired woman on horseback was driving cows across the prairie. The sky was that magnificent color of blue that seemed to be found only in Wyoming. The fences were broken down in places. The ground was so dry dust swirled around the cows' legs. At the forefront of the picture was a man on a horse with his broad back to the viewer as he waited. For just a moment the image came to life. That could be her future with Kyle. The tears she'd sworn she wouldn't cry sprang to her eyes.

"Harper," she said hoarsely. "It's such a stunning gift. I don't know what to say. Thank you doesn't seem enough."

"Now you know how I feel. You sent me to Bran, Celia. I can't ever repay you for that. He's the best thing that's ever happened to me." Then Harper hugged her and they were both crying. And they started giggling because they were crying.

Tierney cleared her throat. "I figured this had happened. You two getting all mushy."

"Oh, shut up, Tierney. I saw you tearing up when you watched them entwined together on the dance floor at Buckeye Joe's a few weeks back."

"Guilty." She pointed to the painting. "I'm glad that's going to your place, Celia. But it makes the Crock-Pot I gave you pale in comparison, huh?"

"But we need a Crock-Pot."

"Such a diplomat. What are we using for a blindfold, Harper?"

Celia froze. "Blindfold?"

"For the last game." Tierney snagged a paisley-patterned scarf from a rack. "This'll work. Turn around."

Everything went black. Then something was smeared under each nostril. A mint scent wafted up. "What the hell?"

"Don't be a baby. It's just a dab of peppermint oil."

Now Celia was really confused.

"Let's go." Tierney led her out.

Noises became louder, but she couldn't make out any individual voices.

"So, everybody, the first couple of games tested how well Celia and Kyle know each other. This game will test how well she knows him by touch. Celia can't see. She can't smell. You all will not give her any hints by making noise. Gentlemen, you will not speak."

"Boo!" came from the back of the room.

She snickered, recognizing Bernice's voice.

"Gentlemen, bare your body parts."

More catcalls.

"Out of ten male arms, you get to figure out which one belongs to Kyle."

This would be a piece of cake.

Tierney placed Celia's hand on the first forearm. Celia started at the wrist and smoothed her hand up to the crease in the elbow. Nope. Not Kyle. Too bony. The second forearm was too hairy. The third forearm too thick. The fourth one was close, but not quite.

But when she touched the fifth forearm, she knew. Strong and meaty, with two big veins that bulged across all that rock-hard muscle. She was tempted to stroke her thumb in the crease of his elbow to see if he flinched, because Kyle always did. But she moved on. Taking her time. Keeping a puzzled expression on her face like she couldn't make up her mind.

"So, do you know which one is your husband's arm?"

"Number five."

"You're sure?"

"Without a doubt."

"Sure enough to lay a big wet kiss on man number five, even when it might not be him?"

"It *is* him."

"Why are you so confident?"

"Because I've been drooling over Kyle's arms for a lot longer than just the little time we've been married."

Catcalls rang out.

"Contestant number five, come forward."

Celia's heart beat a little faster when the blindfold slipped off. She had a brief glimpse into Kyle's gleaming eyes right before he kissed the daylights out of her.

Chapter Sixteen

*T*he smartest thing he'd ever done was marry this woman.

Kyle picked her up and carried her out of the room as he continued to kiss her. He backed her against the wall.

She blinked those liquid silver eyes at him.

"What?"

"A *blow job* is my favorite drink, Kyle? Really?"

He laughed. "I figured we oughta have some fun with it. I also figured you'd shoot back that my favorite shot was a *wet pussy*."

"I had no idea that shot even existed."

He raised his eyebrows. "But you know a drink called *tie me to the bedpost?*"

"I almost said *tie me down and fuck me*," she retorted.

"We'll have to try it sometime."

"The drink?"

Kyle shook his head.

Ooh, look at the flash of interest in Celia's eyes.

"So what did you ladies do? Sounded like you were havin' a wild time."

"Played games. Did some shots. You should see the pile of presents we got."

"Yeah? How come I didn't get to help open them?"

Celia rolled her eyes. "Do you even care that the pot holders from Susan match the hand towels and dishrags from Bernice?"

221 ac ONE NIGHT RODEO

"Point taken."

"What did you guys do?"

"Talked about ranching. Drank beer. Talked about cattle stuff that I always tuned out before, but this time I paid attention. A few differing opinions."

She pecked him on the lips. "The only opinion that matters is mine, right?"

Somehow he'd been afraid she'd say that. He changed the subject. "Speaking of Susan...I heard some interesting gossip. She's considering selling the Buckeye. She's tired of working all the time."

"Really? That'd be weird to have someone else own it."

"We should go dancing there next week," he murmured, crowding her body with his. "We had a good time last time we went."

"You aren't thinking about the dancing part at all. You're thinking about the vertical bop we did against the building after getting hot and bothered on the dance floor."

Kyle tucked the veil behind her ear. Bracing his hands by her head, he focused on nuzzling her exposed skin. Her ears, her jaw, her neck, her temple, her hairline. Touching her...yet not.

"Kyle."

He expanded his attentions to barely-there brushes of his mouth. Soft teases with his breath across her neck, cheek, ear, and temple. A fleeting press of his damp lips.

Celia whimpered softly. "Stop. I can't function when you flip your seduction button on High."

"I'll dial it down a notch. If you do one thing for me."

"What?"

"It involves the vibrator I heard you won."

"Okay."

Kyle peered at her flushed face. "Okay? That was easy. No arguing?"

Her molten gaze hooked his. "You turn me inside out every time you touch me. Why would I ever say no to you?"

He stared at her. Stunned by her acceptance of everything about him. Now was the time to tell her. "Celia. I—"

"Hey, lovebirds," Harper said, stepping behind them. "You cannot skip out on your own party. Quit screwing around. Get back in there and mingle with your guests."

"You this bossy with Bran?" Kyle asked.

"When he *lets* her be bossy." Celia grabbed Kyle's hand. "We're going."

Kyle didn't have to argue with anyone to keep his wife by his side for the rest of the party. Food was spread out. The bar was hopping. Music started. The instant he and Celia found a place to sit, they were surrounded.

Bernice took Celia's right side.

Pearl Tschetter sat on his left. She'd worn a very bridelike getup, white lace from her neck to her ankles, including lace gloves, and a puffy fur pimp hat. She carried a martini glass. A long cigarette holder would've been the crowning touch. "Now, Kyle, this might be overstepping my boundaries…"

Please don't give me sex advice.

"But I wanted to mention I knew Marshall Townsend and his wife."

Not what he'd expected. "You did?"

"Yes. Were you aware my husband owned the implement dealership outside Rawlins?"

Kyle shook his head.

"I did the books, he handled the sales. Anyway, Marshall was a decent fellow, not a particularly happy fellow. We had a Christmas party for our customers and he came every year." Pearl tossed back her martini. "I'll be blunt. I hated when his wife came with him. She was such a shrew. So I'm a little torqued off that he didn't know about you until you were an adult. You might've been the one bright spot in his life, Kyle."

"He could've contacted me after he found out I was his son and he didn't. He left me everything on his deathbed. Not out of guilt, but because he wouldn't have to look anyone in the eye and admit he'd cheated on his wife, even if his wife was a shrew, even when his wife had been dead for years. Saving face was the only thing that mattered. Not finding happiness and not finding me." First time Kyle had said that out loud.

Pearl patted his hand. "Did it feel good to get that out?"

"Yeah, actually, it did."

She drilled him in the chest with a lace-covered fingertip. "That isn't something you oughta be telling me, boy; that's something you oughta be sharing with Celia. Marriage rule number one: She is your confidante. Confide in each other before all others, without exception. Marriage rule number two: Don't be the tough guy with her. She's had enough of that in her life with the way her brothers raised her. Now that you know what's in your bloodline, I came by to warn you. Especially now that I've heard Marshall had the chance to get to know you and didn't take it. Don't be like Marshall. Marriage rule number three: Don't withhold your emotions from her. I'm not talking affections. Because emotions and affections are totally different things. You understand that, right?"

Ah. No, not until this minute, but I think I do now. "Yes, ma'am."

"Good." Pearl picked up her martini glass and floated over to the bar.

Bizarre. He looked over to see scissor-happy Bernice fingering Celia's braid.

"When will you let me take a whack at this mop of hair?"

"Never." Kyle flashed his teeth and plucked the braid out of Bernice's hand.

"A hair fetish. Interesting." Bernice eyed Kyle. "You could use a trim, Shaggy. Stop in next week. I'm running a special." And she was gone.

Then Celia's voice was in his ear. "I could so totally get shit-faced right now."

"Why? What did Bernice say to you?"

"She talked about my mom some more."

"Did she warn you not to be like her?" he said half-jokingly.

Her gaze sharpened. "Were you listening to our conversation?"

"No. But I got the same lecture from Pearl, since she knew Marshall."

"She did? What did she say about him?"

"That I have the bloodline to be a miserable, cheating dick who withholds my emotions. So don't be one."

"Bernice warned me not to give up my dreams just to be a rancher's wife." Celia set her hand on his forearm when he bristled. "She meant don't give up barrel racing if I love it."

Kyle's eyes searched hers. "Do you love it?"

"*Loved.* Past tense." Her eyes held indecision, as if she wanted to tell him something.

"We haven't really talked about this. You know you can talk to me about anything, Cele."

"We did talk a little that night."

"Which night?"

"New Year's Eve. Before you kissed me."

He frowned. "The kiss was mutual."

"I know. You get that cute little wrinkle right here"—she poked the center of his forehead—"when I don't take responsibility for us making out like we'd just discovered kissing."

His thoughts scrolled back. "I remember you said you were unhappy with your performances. I didn't get the impression you intended to quit the circuit altogether."

"That's the impression I wanted you to have."

"Why?"

"Because I didn't want your pity, Kyle. I would've had to drop out anyway unless I started winning big. I was through all the money I won, some I'd set aside before I started competing full-time. Tanna let me tag along with her for the past two events. Because my travel funds were tight, I kept Mickey at Eli's and Tanna let me borrow her super-speed horse. I wish I could say I did loads better on the dirt but I didn't. It's hard to admit that I'm not getting better. I've already reached the peak of my performance level."

"Have I ever treated you with pity, Cele?"

She shook her head. "With annoyance. Sometimes with contempt."

"I'm so glad those days are gone." Kyle touched her cheek. "In fact, I want to tell you—"

"Hey, sis. We're leavin'."

For fuck's sake. Every time he'd tried to tell her how he felt, somebody ruined the moment.

Maybe that's a sign you oughta hold back.

They both looked up at Abe.

"Tyler's fussy. Janie's ready to go."

Hank flanked Abe's right side. "Brianna's doin' her screech-owl imitation, so we're headed out too." Celia seemed surprised when Hank lifted her into a big hug. "Don't be a stranger. You guys should come hang out with us sometime."

"Ah, sure. That'd be fun."

"It's great to have you home around Muddy Gap for good, sis." Abe hugged her. "We'll be in touch soon."

She stared after them.

Kyle snaked his arms around her waist and pressed his lips into the back of her head. "Something wrong?"

"Will it be uncomfortable for you? That things have changed between you and Hank, and you and Abe because of me?"

"Things had changed between me'n them before you entered the picture. To be totally truthful, things were different between me'n Hank after he and Lainie ended up a couple. Not because I was still holding a torch for her. But because I was still on the circuit and Hank wasn't. Then Hank was ranching full-time with Abe and them two got closer, which is as it should be."

She nestled her cheek into the spot on his neck that was made for her. "This might sound stupid. But I like bein' isolated with you on the ranch. It's our own little world. We don't have to share it with anyone. We don't have to worry about other people's preconceived ideas about how we are with each other as a married couple. Especially since we've had a rocky past. In our house, in our bed, I get to be the real me." She kissed his neck. "I like who I am when I'm with you, Kyle. I like who we are together."

That was awful damn close to a declaration of love . . . wasn't it? Here was his chance.

Then Celia lifted her head and looked at him. "So let's go back in and see what else this group has in store for us."

"We can't just take off for home now?" *So I can tell you how I feel without interruption?*

"Nope. Buck up, little camper, and face the music. Literally." She smirked. "I promised Garnet you'd dance with her at least once."

"Jesus."

"The good thing? She's just as bad a dancer as you are."

Chapter Seventeen

❦

*K*yle backed the truck up to the steps and unloaded the wedding shower haul. Celia transferred the gifts to the kitchen, living room, and bathroom.

He'd been so quiet on the drive home she wondered if he'd forgotten about her *anything goes* vibrator promise.

So when she walked into their bedroom and saw him sprawled on the bed, surrounded by four vibrators, and reading the…instruction manual… she couldn't stop the small gasp.

He flashed his *aw shucks you caught me* grin. "I thought you might've been hidin' from me."

Celia pointed to the vibrators and lube. "After seeing all that? Maybe I should be."

"Aw, kitten, it'll be fun. I promise." His gaze flicked over her, head to toe. "Strip."

"But I wanted to take a shower first."

Kyle shook his head. "You'll just have to take another one when I'm done with you anyway. Clothes off. Now."

As soon as she finished stripping, he was wearing that cocky little male smirk. "What?"

"You like it when I boss you around."

The impulse to deny it was strong. She gave him a haughty look instead.

Which just made him laugh. "I'm curious about something."

"What?"

"Don't you already have a vibrator?"

"Why would you assume that?"

"Most women do. Is it hidden in the bedroom someplace? Maybe we oughta play a round of find the vibrator?"

Celia crossed her arms over her chest. "Have a ball. You won't find one, because I don't have one."

That sinful dimple in his cheek winked at her. "Does that mean you have *more* than one?"

"For God's sake, Kyle, no. I used to have a basic model and I—"

"Wore it out?" he supplied.

That's when she pounced on him. Of course, he had the advantage because she was naked. He angled his head and sucked her nipple to distract her.

Then he rolled her and pinned her to the mattress. "Tell me why you don't have at least one vibrator."

"Fine. I had one. I bought it when I started traveling on the road because I didn't have to worry about Hank or Abe finding it in my room. It was a serious eye-opener. It got me off fast."

"Like how fast?"

"Under two minutes."

His eyes widened. "Really? No pressure for us guys."

"It felt good, it was fast, so I started using it a lot."

"Define a lot."

She'd never admitted this to anyone. It was sort of embarrassing. "At least five times a day."

"Holy shit. Really?"

"Yeah. It was getting to be a problem. But what could I do? Call in to Dr. Oz and ask his advice about how to cure my obsession with a vibrating piece of plastic? I knew what he'd tell me to do. So I tossed it in the garbage when it ran out of batteries."

"How long ago was this?"

"Hmmm... Last week?"

Kyle tickled her until she shrieked.

Damn man had always known all of her ticklish spots. "You deserved that!"

He backed off the bed and shed his clothes. His cock was already hard. He grabbed the longest vibrator off the bed. It had a cord and some funky attachments. "This one is actually supposed to be used as a massager." Kyle studied the head, about the size of a squashed tennis ball. "I've never had a vibrator used on me. So, kitten, let's see if that two-minute time frame works on a guy."

"You want me to time it?"

He chuckled. "No, you're gonna use it on me and *I'll* set the timer. So, on your knees."

Her entire body did a happy clench at the possibilities this wicked man could come up with just on the fly.

Kyle plugged in the massager. Then he perched on the edge of the bed, making the muscles and veins in his forearms pop out.

Before he said she couldn't, Celia rubbed her face across those bulging tendons. Rough skin, soft hair, rock-hard muscles, all wrapped up in his musky scent. She let her tongue follow the prominent vein until she reached the bend in his elbow.

He tilted her face up. "As much as I love that, don't get distracted. We're on a fact-finding mission, remember?"

Celia laughed and sucked his cock all the way into her mouth.

"That just earned you time in the naughty chair," he growled.

She let her teeth scrape the length of his shaft as she released it. Then she turned the vibrator on high and looked up at him. "Hit the stopwatch on your phone when this touches your dick." Keeping an eye on his face, she placed the vibrating head on his balls.

"Jesus fucking Christ!" His whole body twitched.

She dragged it over them and back behind the tight sac. Then she slowly moved it up his shaft. When the vibrations reached the sweet spot beneath the cockhead, Celia was afraid Kyle was having some kind of seizure. She pulled the vibrator away; Kyle's hand brought it right back to where she'd had it.

"Leave it," he said gruffly.

Celia held the backside of his cock, letting the vibrator rest beneath the rim of his cockhead.

His breathing turned rabbit fast. His hands were clenched into fists. His head fell back. His thighs quivered. Then he let loose a wail and come erupted from his dick. Some splotches landed on the vibrating head. Some splashed her hand. Then he was done.

She shut off the machine and said, "Time."

Kyle didn't hear her. She grabbed his cell phone and checked the time. One minute and forty-seven seconds.

Heh-heh. Mr. Stamina didn't even make the two-minute mark.

She bent down and brought his cock into her mouth, suckling him gently.

He sighed and patted her head. "Whoa. Never felt anything like that before. My dick is still vibrating." Then he grabbed her hair and pulled her off, giving her a goofy smile. "The weird thing? My ears are ringing."

"You warning me to hide this bad boy so you don't go deaf?"

"No need. Stand up, kitten, and face the wall."

His abrupt change from charming to commanding brought a wee bit of trepidation. But she followed his instructions.

The nightstand drawer behind her opened. What was he getting? Handcuffs? The nipple clamps they hadn't used yet?

He slipped a soft sleep mask over her eyes. "Arms behind your back." As soon as her arms were in place she felt soft rope binding her wrists together.

"How long have you been planning this?"

"Since I saw your eyes heat when I mentioned tying you up."

"I have a crappy poker face."

Kyle's breath skated across her ear. "I know."

"Is that why you showed up at Breck's poker games? Because you knew I'd be an easy mark?"

"No. I showed up so I could be in the same room with you, watching you, and no one would think anything of it."

Her breath caught. "Really? Why?"

"Because I've wanted you for a lot longer than I let on, Celia. And now? I've got you right where I want you."

"Tied up?"

"*Naked* and tied up." He tugged her backward to settle her on the bed, pushing her thighs apart and tracing her slit. "Naked, tied up, and wet."

"What are you gonna do to me?"

Kyle chuckled and then his mouth was cruising down her belly. "See how many times I can make you come with those vibrators."

Celia jackknifed. "No! Kyle. You can't."

A firm push on her chest and she was flat on the mattress again. "I can so. You gave me free rein, remember? You said I could do anything I wanted with them. All four of them."

"Oh God."

He moved away. She suspected that if she tried to break free, the demented man would tie her legs to those hook things she'd seen that he'd added to the bottom of the bed frame.

Then he was back. "Let's try this one first." He turned on the one she'd used on him—she recognized the sound—but it didn't stay by her ear for long.

Kyle gripped her left thigh and set the buzzing head directly on her clit.

She arched her hips, not sure if she was trying to throw it off or dig it in deeper.

"Steady. Let it happen. Because, kitten, it's gonna happen."

Her heart pounded. This wouldn't last long. She might even beat his time.

Then the whirring sound increased. "I turned it to high. Just in case you were curious." And he added a mean little chuckle.

"Kyle! You jerk."

"Now, now, little wife of mine, is that any way to talk to the man who can keep you on edge for hours and not let you come at all?"

Dammit. He had a point.

Before she could retort, her pussy muscles tightened and she came in a blinding rush. The vibrations intensified with each throb. She sighed with relief when he removed the vibrator.

"Breathe, baby."

Celia inhaled and realized Kyle had been right. Her ears were ringing too.

"How was that, besides fast?"

"I think my crotch is numb."

"Really?" A long, wet tongue licked straight up her sex and she groaned. "Not totally numb."

"Thanks for clarifying that for me."

"Anytime. Any other comments on the Super Duper Orgasmi-tron 2000?"

She laughed. "The pulses were intense, but didn't last as long as when you give me an orgasm. It's just fast. But I like that slow buildup you do so well."

Kyle kissed her for a good, long time. Then he murmured, "Let's give the purple pussy eater a spin."

"You really intend to try every one of those vibrators on me tonight?"

"Yep."

And he did.

Celia needed recovery time between trials. Kyle had very inventive ways of keeping her occupied. He was in turn sweet, sexy, funny, raunchy, and demanding. Very demanding.

After the last vibrator received the thumbs-down, Kyle got rid of her blindfold. He untied the rope. He plastered his body to hers so not an inch of space remained between them.

He made love to her slowly. So slowly that by the time they reached the end of that long climb to pleasure, they were soaked in sweat.

After she returned to sanity from that orgasmic high, she said, "Throw the vibrators away. I don't need them. I don't want them, when I have you."

Kyle stared into her eyes. "You have me, kitten. For as long as you want." The kiss he bestowed on her lips nearly brought tears to her eyes.

She was in so deep with him. Because she wanted him forever.

Chapter Eighteen

*K*yle wasn't the most tech-savvy guy, but he'd managed to track down the right department at the Nevada Marriage Bureau to get his questions answered, since no one ever answered the phone at the Trade Winds Wedding Chapel.

Being on hold sucked.

This was the third time he'd been transferred, and a bad feeling started to take root.

A voice came on the line. "Sorry for the wait. Please spell your last name for me again?"

"G-i-l-c-h-r-i-s-t. First name, Kyle."

"What was the bride's last name?"

"Lawson. L-a-w-s-o-n. First name, Celia."

Clickety-clack sounded through the receiver. He paced, but the dread weighting him down made the movement seem sluggish.

"You said the ceremony took place at the Winds of Change Chapel at the Trade Winds Casino?"

"Yes, ma'am."

A sigh echoed. "No wonder. I haven't received any paperwork from that venue for the last two months."

Kyle froze. "Excuse me?"

"No marriage certificates have been requested or filed with the State of Nevada since November."

"But we filled out the paperwork! We signed it, the witnesses signed it, the officiant signed it. Everything was done before we exchanged vows and I paid the bill."

"Do you have a receipt?"

"For the rings. I didn't figure I needed a receipt for the damn marriage!" He inhaled. "Sorry. This is a nightmare."

"Yes, sir, I'm sure it is. But at this point there's nothing else I can do for you, except direct you to the state's wedding licensing and permit division. They can check to see if the Winds of Change Chapel is currently licensed or if their license somehow lapsed or expired altogether."

Kyle sat down hard on the office chair. "Lapsed? How is that even possible?"

"Wedding chapels have a yearly licensing fee. If it isn't paid, then they're operating without a valid license and any ceremonies performed on the premises aren't legally recognized by the state. Once the fees are brought current, then that paperwork is allowed to be filed. Unless..."

"Unless what?"

"Unless the state license has lapsed for more than sixty days. In that case, most owners opt to apply for a new license rather than pay the hefty penalties and reinstatement fees. But don't worry. I've never seen that happen in the five years I've worked here."

Kyle's thoughts flashed back to the *Under New Ownership* signs that'd been all over the casino and the wedding chapel. His sense of dread exploded into full-blown panic.

What if he and Celia weren't really married?

"Sir? Is there anything else I can help you with?"

"I don't suppose you've got the number handy for the state licensing commission?"

"I'll just go ahead and transfer you to that department."

"Thanks." He started to feel light-headed as he waited for the next representative to come on the line. He forced slow and steady breaths. So by the time his call was answered, he felt a little calmer.

Until he heard the news he'd feared. The Winds of Change Chapel had no valid permits. Not only that, but two days after they married, the state gaming commission had stepped in and closed down the entire Trade Winds facility, locking away all paperwork as evidence.

When Kyle pressed the phone rep to offer advice, his was simple: No marriage certificate meant no legally recognized marriage.

At that point Kyle had to put his head between his knees.

Celia wasn't his wife. He had no claim to her.

He swallowed convulsively until the dizziness subsided.

He loved her. If he was completely fucking honest with himself, he wouldn't have married her at all if he hadn't been in love with her.

Why couldn't he admit that to himself?

Why couldn't he admit that to her? That he'd hoped at the end of the six months she'd be as crazy in love with him as he was with her?

Fuck.

He needed more time to make sure that happened. Each day, hell, each hour he spent with her in the last month made him fall even more in love with her. And he suspected she'd grown more attached to him the more time they'd spent together.

So if she knew they weren't really legally married? Celia would honor their verbal contract and stay to help him through calving. But on an intimate level? She'd retreat. She'd be embarrassed by the oversight, especially after the huge shower the community had thrown for them. Especially after the issues her brothers had raised.

No way could he run the ranch without her. He didn't *want* to run it without her. It was as much hers as his. He closed his eyes, reminded of the words Breck had tossed off the day after their marriage. That Kyle had nothing to offer Celia. His inheritance had changed that in so many ways and he finally felt like a man worthy of her. Because he knew what she wanted and he could give it to her. Not life on the road as a barrel racer, but a home of her own. A ranch. A life with him—a man who loved her body and soul and understood her completely.

And now he was supposed to tell her . . . *Hey, we aren't married because we were both too shit-faced to check the freakin' permits.*

Yeah, that would go over well.

Don't be a jackass. Tell her the truth. Tell her you love her. Tell her you want to marry her for real this time. A real wedding ceremony that she'll remember, with her family and all your friends in attendance. With a wedding dance, a honeymoon, the whole shebang.

No. Celia would rather save face than admit the marriage wasn't a love match.

But still, he'd have to tell her the truth soon. The devil on his shoulder poked him hard.

Or would he?

Kyle was awful damn good at playing dumb—not that it was always an act. Since their discussion about money, Celia hadn't mentioned needing the marriage license to change her name on her driver's license or her Social Security card.

So, realistically, he could pretend that with all the crap they had to deal with regarding the ranch he'd just "forgotten" all about getting a copy of their official marriage license ... until she brought it up. Or he could bring it up at the six-month mark. Then they could discover together—snicker—that the paperwork had never gotten filed. That would give him a perfect opening to confess his love for her, and ask her to marry him for real, forever, because he couldn't live without her.

That could work.

That *had* to work.

❦

Kyle was in a foul mood.

Celia had known it would happen sometime. Except for the couple of times she'd caught him brooding in the barn, he had been far too even-keeled about his ranch heritage and the massive changes and responsibilities in his life in the last six weeks. Naturally his anger issues had to happen on a day when she was feeling less than confident about the changes in their relationship. He'd gotten quiet when she'd brought up the financial deadline for fall class registration.

He'd been pissy about a lot of stuff the last few days.

So she got pissy right back. "For the third time, Kyle. What do you want to do with all this stuff?"

Kyle scowled at the pile of clothes on the bed. "How the fuck should I know? I've never cleaned out my dead father's closet before."

She was tempted to mimic him. Instead she just tore off an oversize garbage bag and started jamming clothes inside the thick plastic.

"What are you doin'?"

"Stuffing a turkey, what does it look like?"

He made a snarling noise instead of laughing. "It looks like you're throwing it away."

"I am. I made an executive decision. You don't want this shit, I don't want this shit, so I'm tossing it."

Kyle stomped over and ripped the garbage bag from her hands. "I didn't say I wanted to just shitcan it. I said I don't know what to do with any of it. Can't we take it to a shelter or someplace?"

The shelter comment reminded Celia of the bags of clothing that had filled the basement of Abe's house for months and then had mostly ended up in the trash anyway. She retorted, "A bum wouldn't even wear this crap."

"Nice shot, Celia."

"It's true." She snatched a brown-and-yellow-checked flannel shirt from the pile and shook it at Kyle. "Do you really see yourself wearing this? Even for chores? It's missing buttons. It's got rips in the elbows, not to mention it's freakin' huge. It hangs to your damn knees."

"Are you sayin' I'm a shrimp or something?"

She stared at him as if he'd lost his mind. "Sensitive much? Obviously Marshall was a rotund guy. You're not."

He mumbled and turned away.

Oh joy, he was muttering now. "Does that mean you don't want my help?"

Kyle shrugged.

Instead of giving into her increasingly violent temptations, like whipping a hanger at the back of his head, she chose to take the high road. Let him stew in his own crabby juices for a while. She headed for the room they'd set up as an office. In the closet she'd found more boxes of worthless crap. Why would anyone keep broken eyeglasses? The bottom of one box was filled with boxes of rubber bands. All the same size. Maybe there'd been a huge sale on them. A long time ago if the disintegrated condition of the rubber was any indication.

Celia threw away faded receipts. Newspaper articles. Yellowed recipe cards. Green Stamps booklets and coupons that had expired two decades ago. Had all this stuff belonged to Marshall's wife? It looked like he'd dumped out several junk drawers straight into the box and shoved it in the closet.

She found nothing of a personal nature, which made her sad, and she saw no reason to keep any of it. With that mind-set she was able to get through all but two boxes before Kyle came looking for her again.

The hard set to his mouth indicated that his mood hadn't improved a bit.

It wasn't like she hadn't tried to make it better. Cajoling hadn't changed anything. Silence hadn't changed anything. Being rude hadn't changed anything. She hadn't tried smacking him upside the head with a cast-iron frying pan either, but if he kept it up she might be tempted to do just that. At some point during her mental back-and-forth, Celia realized it wasn't her job as his wife to make that change in attitude happen. It was his problem.

She reminded herself that married people fought. It was the ebb and flow of finding the fine lines in a relationship. How could she know which line not to cross if she didn't step a toe over that line once in a while? Things were bound to come to a head between them because they both seemed to sport that attitude. So chances were high if they continued testing those lines they'd be in for a helluva fight.

Bring it.

"The bedroom closet is cleared out if you wanna hang your stuff in there."

"Thank you." Celia kept sorting papers. Nothing salvageable. But thank God she hadn't found any mouse droppings, although it might be easier to set fire to this stuff than sort it.

"What now?"

He was asking her for direction? "Pick a room. Unless you'd rather do this while I do one of the other ten billion things that need done around here."

"It's not my fault he was a packrat, Cele."

"I didn't say it was, Kyle."

"Why're you bein' like this?"

Celia looked at him. "Like what? Helpful?"

"No, like you can't stand to be around me unless I'm fucking you."

That did it. She rolled to her feet and wiped the dust from her hands. "Maybe because you're an asshole when we aren't fucking. And you can just forget about me fucking you anytime soon, buddy."

Kyle grabbed her arm as she sidestepped him. "Where you going?"

"To get more garbage bags. Is that all right? Or do I need your permission?"

His eyes narrowed. "Got a whole mouthful of attitude today, don'tcha?"

"Like that's a big shock."

The muscle in his jaw twitched and he stared at her with those stormy green eyes.

"Did you need something? Or are you just pissing with me, lookin' for a fight? 'Cause I'll give you one."

"I know you will." He jerked her against his body. "That's one of my favorite things about you." Then his mouth crashed down on hers with a brutal kiss. No buildup, just heat and hunger.

Just to be ornery, Celia tried to shove him away.

He let their mouths part long enough to release a mean little chuckle before he pulled both her wrists behind her back and pressed her against the wall, his mouth hungry on hers again.

Dammit. He wasn't supposed to have the power to do this. Make her so crazy with lust she'd lose her head the instant he touched her. Even when she was mad at him. How could he always have the upper hand?

Because you give it to him. Because you like that he has a sharp edge beneath that easygoing facade.

Kyle was relentless with his soul-stealing kisses. He would not relinquish his hold on her.

Need and sexual greed rode her hard. She bucked and pushed against him, wanting him to stop teasing and get on with it.

"Now," he half growled. "Right fucking here, right fucking now."

"Fine. But no talking."

"Fine."

At least she hadn't been a total pushover. Besides, she'd always heard that angry sex was on a whole other level of hotness. Might be sadistic, but she wanted to find out, and it wasn't like she'd rather be cleaning out boxes instead of getting it on with her sexy husband.

He released her hands. Then he was peeling her sweatpants down her legs. His mouth returned for more violently hot kisses.

Somehow Kyle ditched his jeans. Somehow he lifted her and pinned her to the wall. He pushed her knees wide, burying his mouth in her throat.

Celia hissed when the tip of his cock rubbed across her clit—three, four, five times before his cock sought entrance to her body.

He paused for a moment, letting his hardness fill her.

She clutched him, one arm wrapped around his neck, her other hand twisted in a fistful of his shirt. She squeezed her inner muscles around his cock as a signal she was in the moment with him.

Then Kyle's hands gripped her ass as he pulled her down to meet his forceful thrusts.

Every time, she didn't think it could be better than the last time and every time it was.

Celia wanted to let her head fall back and feel his passion overtaking her, trusting that he would propel them to the point of detonation.

But Kyle's mouth didn't leave hers. His kisses were packed with heat and passion and an almost desperate need.

By the way his strokes quickened and his body tensed, Celia knew he was close. She broke the seal of their mouths to whisper, "Grind into me. You know how I like it."

"I thought you said no talking."

"I changed my mind."

He canted his pelvis to hit her clit on every up thrust and growled, "Say something dirty."

"The office closet."

He snorted a soft laugh and put his mouth on her ear, knowing that it drove her wild. "Give me real dirty talk. You know you want to."

"Fuck me harder. Fuck me through the goddamn wall."

Kyle reared back, rammed into her with enough force to knock a picture to the floor. He jackhammered his hips, grinding into her with the precise amount of friction that made her come undone.

He plunged into her relentlessly through her orgasm. Then he stopped. His mouth was on her lips. The kiss was surprisingly tender for as hard as his body shuddered against hers.

Celia moved her hands to cradle his head. She tried to soothe him. He seemed almost bereft as his climax faded. When he panted against her shoulder, she murmured, "You okay?"

"No."

When she tried to force him to look at her, he wouldn't allow it. "Kyle?"

"I've been an ass the last couple days."

"Ya think?"

"I came into the office hoping you could help me find the romantic streak in me that's been missing the last week. I wanted to rewind at least to this morning before we got snippy with each other. I wanted to seduce you, give you the sweetness and the…damn devotion you deserve. But when I see you, Celia, all I can think about is burying myself in you so fast and hard that you don't have a chance to think about anything but how much I want you." His mouth skimmed her cheek. "How much I always fucking want you. Christ. It's beyond scary how much you mean to me."

She froze.

"Say something," he demanded softly.

"If you tell me you're sorry…I will kick your ass."

Finally his eyes met hers.

"That is the single best compliment I've ever gotten." Celia traced his lips. "Don't wreck it, okay?"

"Okay." He pulled out, let her down, and tossed her sweatpants over. She gave him her back as they got dressed.

Before she could face him, Kyle wrapped his arms around her from behind. "I don't want to wreck it either. But I do want to explain at least part of the reason for my lousy mood the last couple of days. I was feeling so lost when I was goin' through stuff that belonged to him. In every room there's more of his things and I realize I'm not gonna get to know him by keeping his ratty-ass shirts, or by reading his cash register receipts from thirty years ago. None of this feels like mine. But then I saw you ... and you feel like mine."

Celia closed her eyes and let his words wash over her. He'd definitely reconnected with his sweet, romantic side. He'd definitely given her an opening to admit her feelings had changed. Did she have the guts to do it? Just as she opened her mouth, Kyle kissed the back of her head.

"So, thank you. I'll be outside."

Chapter Nineteen

*K*yle adjusted the scarf against the arctic wind seeping beneath his jacket collar. He slowed the ATV down and his eyes scanned the herd, huddled together against the cold.

One cow stood off to the side. The little black blob on the ground beside her couldn't be a calf. This group wasn't set to calve yet. Unless...he'd somehow missed sorting this one into the group of "heavies."

Entirely possible, given the fact that he still needed advice when it came to separating the cattle into different groups.

He'd managed to hide his surprise from Celia when she'd explained that cattle producers kept heifers—first-time mothers—away from the other pregnant cows. Evidently some heifers freaked out about the birthing process, either seeing other cows suffer though it or going through it themselves. And some were clueless about what to do with the calf after expelling it from their body. So pregnant heifers required extra attention during the birth process and after.

Once a cow's teats were full, earning the nickname *heavies*, they were culled from the herd and placed closer to the cow barn in preparation for birth. Then those pairs would be turned out and the next set brought in, which meant plenty of trudging though the outlying pastures.

Kyle climbed off the ATV, intending to approach the mama out of her line of vision. But her big head whipped around and she mooed a warning.

That didn't deter him. He needed to check to make sure the calf wasn't dead, so he cut off to the side, as if he had business in the herd.

Mama cow wasn't buying it. She pawed the ground.

He stared at her in disbelief. She pawed the ground? Like a pissed-off bull? Yeah, she wasn't leaving that calf anytime soon. He pulled out his cell and called Celia, not turning his back on the protective mama.

"Hey, I'm checking the herd in the southeast pasture and we've got a calf. Uh-huh. I can't get close enough to see if it's alive. It ain't moved since I've been here and the mama is pissed off that I'm in the same pasture. I wasn't aware I needed them. Are the ear tags in the ATV compartment?" Kyle held the phone away, wondering if she'd blister his ear for being such a damn greenhorn. But Celia's tone didn't change as she explained the necessity of checking that before taking off, as well as having a notebook to keep track of births and carrying antibiotics. She told him she'd pick up the necessary supplies and head in his direction.

After she hung up, Kyle was grateful for cell phones. Granted, they didn't get service everywhere on the ranch, but it was much better than the old way of tracking down your ranching partner on foot, horseback, or ATV.

Kyle did a quick check of the rest of the herd, just in case he'd missed another calf. Then he settled on the ATV to wait, keeping a close eye on the unmoving calf. Hoping the thing wasn't dead. Not only would it be a loss of income, he'd feel guilty and inadequate that it'd died on his watch.

The mama mooed and began to lick the calf's head and lo and behold, it moved. The little bugger struggled to stand. Mama continued lowing encouragement. Finally it stood, butting its head on the underside of the mama's belly searching for food. That hungry mouth latched onto a teat, sucking almost violently.

He heaved a sigh of relief.

The drone of an ATV drifted to him and he turned to watch Celia's approach. She parked alongside him, her gaze on the pair.

"Did you assist in getting the calf up off the ground?"

"Nope. Why?"

"Just checking. It's a good idea to keep notes on stuff like that." She smiled at him and jumped off the ATV. "I'm gonna see if she'll let me get close."

Kyle wanted to warn her to be careful, but the words stuck in his throat because unlike him, she knew what she was doing.

She approached the mama head-on. He heard her talking, but not what she was saying. The cow mooed a warning and Celia froze when the mama started pawing at the ground again. His wife backed away slowly, much to Kyle's relief.

"That's gonna be a fun one to tag tomorrow. No sense in trying to do it tonight. Mama ain't gonna let us any closer and that calf ain't letting loose of the feed bag anytime soon."

"So now what?"

"You find any other ones?"

"No. But I only looked from the outside."

"Let's wander through the ladies and see what's shaking. They're all cold, so they probably ain't gonna move a whole lot. And it'll get them used to us, because we're gonna be messing with their babies over the next few months. If they see us outside the tractor delivering feed, hopefully they'll be less likely to charge us."

Kyle followed Celia's lead. She rarely approached a cow from the rear, always from the side or head-on. She touched them. Talked to them. Getting close enough to check udders and the back end, without spooking a single cow.

When she'd finished her check, she glanced up at the sky. "Damn low-pressure system. We'll have another surprise birth before the night is over." Celia nudged him with her shoulder. "Congrats, cattleman. We're officially in calving season."

"And you sound giddy about that."

"I am. It's a lot of work. A lot of fretting. A lot of lost sleep. But seeing those sweet baby faces? Seeing the mamas so protective of those babies? This is what ranchers live for. Defying the odds and delivering healthy calves." She grinned at him. "We'll stock up on strong coffee. And note-books. Just because Marshall knew the ins and outs of his herd and didn't feel the need to write anything down, doesn't mean I'm gonna let you get away with that from the start."

"Do Abe and Hank keep notebooks?"

"They keep records, but a lot of the info is in their heads, which didn't help me when I was trying to sort through problems."

Fascinated by his wife's take on things, Kyle asked, "What kind of problems?"

Celia flipped her braid behind her back. "Not necessarily problems with the calves, but issues with the dam—otherwise known as the mama. Sometimes they're just so mean after giving birth until the calf is weaned that it's best to get rid of them. Summer stuff on the ranch means you get so busy that you'll forget unless you can go back and look through the notes. It'll especially become important if you increase the size of your herd."

"What did you want to change at the Lawson ranch?"

"I wanted to keep a better eye on the sires, instead of just turning the bulls loose in the pasture and trying to figure out after the fact which bull sired which calf. They always said recording birth weights when we weren't running purebreds was a waste of time, especially when they said they could see whether a calf was gaining weight. But I at least wanted to try it with a couple of the heifers and see if their calf weights went up every year."

"What would it take to do that here?"

Her eyes turned shrewd. "You're serious? So you're really gonna listen to my ideas? And not just discount them?"

"Yep. I wanna start everything out right."

"You'd need a portable scale."

"The thing with the sling in the barn is the regular scale, right?"

"Yep." She glanced at the sky again. "Let's get the feed and then spread the straw. It'll be damn close to dark by the time we get back here to spread it out."

Kyle rubbed his chin with a gloved finger. "Remind me again why we're spreading out two bales?"

"One to feed their bellies. The old, crappy stuff we'll use to cover the ground. It'll give 'em some warmth, especially important if we have any more surprise births tonight. And if they get really hungry, they'll eat the crappy stuff. It's hard to chew, and chewing and digesting is part of what keeps them warm."

He couldn't help but kiss her. "I had no idea about any of this stuff. Every day you blow my mind with something new. You are so damn smart."

"It's pretty much common knowledge."

"Not for me. You've done way more of this cattle-raising stuff than even I realized. You know what works and what doesn't. I won't argue with you just to argue."

"Oh." She nearly blinded him with her beautiful smile. Then she nearly knocked him on his ass when she threw her arms around his neck. "Thank you for listening to me. It means more than you'll ever know."

Kyle slapped her butt and kissed her again. "You're welcome. But, kitten, I get to drive the tractor."

❧

Over the next twenty-four hours, Kyle didn't have a chance to talk to Celia about anything that didn't concern calving. He helped her pull a calf. Leading the distressed mama into the birthing equipment and hobbling her legs. Talk about a new experience. As was donning a long obstetrical glove and inserting his arm up to his shoulder in a birth canal to reposition the large calf. Then watching as Celia expertly used the OB chains to pull and tug the calf a little at a time until it slid free.

Even after ripping the amniotic sac away from the mouth, the calf still wasn't breathing. Celia jerked it by the hind legs, hanging it upside down until fluid cleared the lungs in a wet gush and it breathed on its own. They placed the pair in one of the empty stalls in the cow barn and watched as mama and baby got acquainted.

The next two days a blizzard raged. Kyle spent his time on the tractor, clearing pathways in the pasture. Clearing a path to the creek for the part of the herd that'd taken shelter from the storm in a low-lying copse of trees. Clearing a path from the cow barn to the house. Clearing a path from the house to the old barn where they'd brought the horses. After he'd spread feed and straw to the three separate sections of the herd, he plowed the road down to Josh's place, in case an emergency arose and they needed Fletch's veterinary assistance.

Then he mucked the cow and horse stalls at night—that Celia had mucked that morning. They split up the every-three-hour cattle checks. They worked together to get the cattle fed twice a day in the snow. He and Celia took turns catching a catnap here and there. In this frigid weather they burned a lot of wood, which required constant tending.

In the two weeks since that first calf dropped they'd added forty-seven calves to the herd. They had no choice but to move the mamas and babies back outside within twenty-four hours of the birth because the number of births was increasing every day.

Forty-seven down, one hundred and twenty-two to go.

After being up all night, at dawn Celia sent him to bed.

Kyle woke at nine o'clock—according to the alarm—and, disoriented because the bedroom shades were pulled, he had no idea if it was morning or night. He set his feet on the floor and noticed he'd fallen into bed fully clothed.

Not the first time that'd happened.

The sounds of a conversation drifted through the crack in the door. He recognized Celia's voice and stood to listen.

"...Was afraid I'd have to send her to stay with her mother for the rest of it."

Ah. Josh. The acoustics in this house funneled everything into the hallway, so he heard every word perfectly.

"I'm guessing Ronna argued?"

Josh sighed. "Yeah. She reminded me she's a ranch wife. Since she wasn't helping take care of the cattle, it was her job to take care of me while I take care of the cows."

"Hard to argue with that logic, huh?"

"Impossible. I know William has been fussy and then we had the snowstorm and she's been locked in the house with a cranky baby and an absent or a comatose husband for two weeks."

"Maybe you oughta cut her a break. Let her plow the road. It'd give you time with your son and show her that you do need her help."

Kyle grinned. His wife was so damn intuitive. He wondered if anyone else had appreciated that about her.

You keep forgetting she's not your wife.

His happy mood vanished.

"You know, Celia, that's a great idea," Josh said.

Just as he reached for the door handle to join them in the kitchen, he heard Josh say, "That husband of yours is a hard worker."

"You sound surprised."

"I'm not. Okay, maybe I am a little. Most rodeo guys I've known are showmen. Guys born into the ranching life are aware of how much work it entails. I've got buddies who couldn't wait to get the hell off the ranch. So bein's Kyle wasn't raised a ranch kid, it's odd he hasn't put the place up for sale."

"If you had the chance to sell your place, would you?"

"Hell no. I wouldn't know what to do with myself. Ranching is all I've ever known."

"Same here. It's honestly all I've ever wanted to do. Running his own ranch has always been Kyle's dream."

"He's lucky to have you to show him the ropes. He never would've figured out a lot of this stuff by himself."

"Oh, I don't know. He's bright. He has been exposed to some of this over the years. But mostly he's determined. I've known Kyle for almost twenty years. He's good at whatever he puts his mind to."

No mistaking the pride in Celia's voce.

Josh laughed. "Spoken like a newlywed in love."

In love? Really? His heart skipped faster. Was it possible she'd already fallen in love with him?

"It's a welcome change for us, having neighbors our age close by," Josh added. "Between you and me, Marshall was . . . a hermit."

"So you didn't drop by for coffee to swap calving traumas?"

"No. Marshall was an intimidating old fella. I have no idea how he dealt with a herd that size by himself at his age for as long as he did. I was floored when he asked me to take over his livestock after he'd finished shipping last year's cattle so he could deal with his health issues. I was even more floored when he offered to pay me pretty well to do it. With a baby on the way, the drought, and the uncertain cattle market, well, I ain't stupid."

"We certainly appreciate how well you took care of them. We've had uneventful calving so far."

Kyle heard her knock wood.

"Us too."

Louder knocking on wood and they both laughed.

"I gotta get. Just wanted to check in."

Footsteps echoed from the living room and he slid behind the door, which was idiotic because they couldn't see him.

Kyle crawled back in bed, and as he expected, Celia checked on him.

The instant she pulled the covers over his shoulder, he groaned. "What time is it?"

"A little after nine. In the morning. Sorry. I didn't mean to wake you. Go back to sleep."

"Probably my turn to make the rounds anyway."

"We're good for a little while." Her fingers traced the day's worth of beard on his cheeks. "Rest while you can."

"I have a better idea." He grabbed her around the waist, rolling her to her back on the bed. Then he smothered her surprised shrieks. Dragging her into the kiss from the first touch of his tongue to hers.

Celia was as starved for him as he was for her. Six days was too damn long to go without touching her.

Then she ripped her mouth from his and put her hands on his chest, pushing him away. "Kyle. Stop."

"Why? The cows can wait fifteen minutes." He nuzzled her ear. "I'm dyin' for you, Celia."

"I . . . we can't."

He pushed up. "What's wrong?"

Her cheeks were bright pink "I got my period."

"Oh. So that means I can't kiss you? Grind on you a little? Do you have cramps or something?"

She blushed harder. "Can't we just drop it?"

"Why are you embarrassed?"

"Just stop looming over me. You're making me self-conscious."

Kyle rolled until they were on their sides facing each other. "Don't be self-conscious. We've had our arms up a cow's birth canal together. We can talk about this stuff."

"That'd be a first."

"Really? Why?"

Celia briefly closed her eyes. "After my mother died, I had no one to ask about that kinda girl stuff when it happened to me. I finally got up the courage to tell Abe and he got all embarrassed. He drove me to Kmart in Rawlins, handed me twenty bucks, and told me to stock up on female supplies. I doubt he ever mentioned it to Hank."

"That was fuckin' stupid and insensitive of him. It's part of life for women and men who live together. My mom went to bed with a heating pad, a bottle of Midol, a stash of chocolate, and a bottle of wine after her bar shift during that time of the month. She never hid it from me because she said I'd have to deal with it. She never sent me to the store to buy tampons, but it wasn't some dirty secret either."

"Things were a little better when Janie lived there," Celia admitted. "But I was back to ignorance with other female issues after she left."

"Like what?"

She glanced down at his chest. "Like girl clothes. Bernice cornered me to tell me to stop acting like a tomboy and start wearing a bra. Problem was, I didn't own a bra. I was so small-chested I didn't think it mattered. And the last thing I wanted was to draw attention to my lack of curves and become even more self-conscious that I didn't look like Harper."

"Hey." Kyle nudged her face up to look into her eyes. "I teased you about that, didn't I?"

"You never called me tiny tits or anything, but you made cracks about whether I was even a girl."

He rested his forehead to hers. "Jesus. I'm sorry."

"I know. I also know you didn't do it because you secretly had a crush on me, which in hindsight, would've made it worse. You were just being a

251 ONE NIGHT RODEO

guy, jerking me around like you always did. I would've been more suspicious if you'd stopped."

Kyle's lips forced a path down her neck. Happy she'd worn a shirt with snaps, he popped them one at a time and dragged openmouthed kisses over each bit of exposed skin.

And looky there, she hadn't worn a bra.

She made a soft noise when he licked her left nipple.

He cupped a breast in each hand and pressed the flesh together to tongue both nipples. "Put your hands up my shirt. Play with my nipples like I'm playing with yours."

Celia's cold fingers made him jump and she responded with a low, sexy chuckle that he felt beneath his lips.

Her hands were all over him, sending goose bumps across his arms and down his back. She brushed the ridges of his abs. She mapped the planes of his chest with her palms, her fingertips, not just focusing on his nipples.

He scooted up to kiss her in the same unhurried manner that he caressed her. Exploring her mouth. Sinking deeper into the moment. One last nuzzle and he eased back to look at her. Her face was flushed, her eyes a soft silvery gray.

Celia set her hands on his cheeks. Her thumbs followed the arc of his eyebrows, trailed down his temples and jaw. "You're so damn good-looking, Kyle. Such a perfect mix of rugged and handsome."

Kyle blushed.

"I'm sorry if I don't say that enough. But I am thinking it. Every day when I look at you."

"Thank you." He kissed the inside of her wrist and changed the course of the conversation. "I love touching you, Celia." His hands mapped her face the same way hers had mapped his. "I love that I can touch you whenever I want."

"Same goes." She yawned. And looked embarrassed by it. "Sorry. You touching me is far from yawn-inducing."

"I'll stop hogging your sleep time." He kissed her forehead and pulled the covers under her chin.

She said, "Kyle. Wait," when he'd reached the door.

He turned back around.

"Don't go. There's nothin' that needs done for a little while. And I really like being curled up next to you. I've missed that the last few days. Will you crawl back in here for a bit?"

Oh, sweet woman, what am I gonna do without you?

Kyle hoped he would never have to find out.

Chapter Twenty

$\mathcal{C}$elia was so damn tired she thought she might be hallucinating when Abe's truck pulled up. Paranoia slammed into her when both Hank and Abe trudged up the driveway.

She stepped outside. "Please tell me you're not here because of bad news."

Hank gave Abe a little shove. "See? I told ya we should've called first."

Abe gave Hank a one-handed shove right back. "We can't drop by and see how our newly married little sister is doin'?"

"I guess. It's just sort of weird."

"Actually, we came by to talk."

Celia held the door open and warned, "Boots off."

"Like that ain't already been drilled into my head at my house," Hank grumbled.

After shedding outerwear, they followed her into the kitchen and sat at the table.

"Coffee? Beer?" she offered.

"Nothin' for me," Abe said.

"Me neither," Hank said. "We can't stay long."

This was freaking her out. They both wore their serious faces. "What's on your mind that can't be said over the phone?" Or in front of Kyle?

"After our blowup or whatever it was with you, me'n Abe got to talkin' about some stuff."

"What kind of stuff?"

They exchanged a look, then Abe focused on her. "The kind of money stuff that can tear families apart. You never brought it up."

"You're surprised? That's not our way. You guys raised me. You oughta know that."

"We do. Which is why this is important, sis, so listen up," Abe said.

"First off, you are aware that all our friends gave us what for after what we said to you and Kyle. But no one came down on us harder than Bran," Hank said. "It didn't have anything to do with your friendship with Harper. He said we were idiots. That we should've expected you'd want a stake in the Lawson ranch. It's just as much your heritage as ours."

Abe sighed. "I know I'm gonna come across sounding like a dick, but I've always considered the ranch mine since I was the oldest and to some extent it was on my shoulders to keep it going. Those years Hank was gone off and on bullfighting, when you helped me with the work? I thought of you more as a hired hand and a bookkeeper. Then when Hank came back home full-time, and you were chasing your dream on the circuit, the ranch felt like mine and Hank's."

For once, Celia was glad to keep her mouth shut.

"I wasn't any better," Hank said. "I built my new house on Lawson land. With Abe's blessing. I don't know what the devil has been wrong with us, sis. We cut you out. Completely. Not only being ignorant as to why you stayed away from home, but being clueless that your decision didn't have a damn thing to do with loving barrel racing and constantly being on the road. You haven't asked for a penny from us in the last four years. And we didn't offer."

"So what we're tryin' to say . . . is better late than never."

Her gaze snapped to Abe's. "What do you mean?"

"You do know you could sue us, right? Demand your third of the value of the ranch."

"But that means you'd have to sell it," she pointed out. "I'd never de-mand that—you know that, don't you?"

Hank nodded. "Obviously we ain't keen on doin' that. The best way we've come up with to make it fair to you is to offer you a cash settlement."

Celia looked between her brothers as if they'd lost their minds. "A cash settlement?"

"For your third of the Lawson ranch. We can't pay you it all at once. But we arranged with our banker to put the first payment in an account for you."

"What's the catch?"

They exchanged another look and Abe nodded to Hank. "No catch. Except we wish you'd keep it and the money to yourself for a little while yet."

"You mean keep it from Kyle." Why did that annoy her?

Abe reached for her hand. "Don't give us that surly look. Kyle just had a life-changing windfall. And we're not suggesting your marriage ain't gonna last. This money isn't a windfall for you, Cele; it's your heritage. If you want to share it with Kyle down the road apiece, feel free. But we're asking you to wait a bit."

"Have you told your wives about this?"

Hank shook his head. "Lainie has her own money from her father's foundation and her job at the hospital. We have a joint household fund we both contribute to, but she doesn't have nothin' to do with the ranch income or expenses. So this is our business. Lawson business."

"Same with Janie. She's got her own money, a stake in the Split Rock and her job there. We decided to keep some separation between our finances and our relationship this time." Abe locked his gaze to hers. "Our reason for doin' this, little sis, is to give you some financial security. You deserve it."

Her belly fluttered with panic. Had her brothers somehow guessed that she and Kyle were a temporary couple? That she was only sticking with him long enough to get the money he promised her so she could go to school?

Keep telling yourself that, Celia. Convince yourself you're not in love with your husband.

"Talk to us," Hank said, startling her.

"I don't know what to say."

"Maybe you could start by askin' how much money it is."

She looked at Abe. "How much?"

"One hundred and twenty-five thousand dollars."

Celia's jaw dropped. "Are you fucking kidding me?"

Hank laughed. "Pay up, bro."

Abe dug in the front pocket of his jeans and flicked a crumpled twenty at Hank. "I bet him you'd say, 'Are you fucking serious?' He argued you'd say . . . exactly what you did. Anyway. It's your money now."

"You guys aren't like, hurting yourselves financially by doing this?"

"No. But even if we had to tighten our belts, it's no more than what you've done out of necessity. And since we've come clean with you, Celia, come clean with us."

Shit. "About?"

"How much longer you would've been able to stay on the road," Hank said.

"Not all season," she confessed. "That's why Kyle and I arranged to meet in Vegas during the expo. We talked about traveling together this season."

"As husband and wife?" Abe asked sharply.

Celia looked Abe in the eye and lied. "Yes. Kyle and I had a change in our relationship a while back. We kept it under wraps for our own reasons. Then everything changed, practically overnight. So if we weren't here running this ranch together, we'd be on the road together."

"Fair enough." Hank stood.

"We probably better get. I'm on diaper duty so Janie can try to rest up."

She followed him back into the foyer. "So what do you do with Tyler while mama's sleeping?"

Abe grinned. "Try to get him to sleep so I can nap too. Between calving season and havin' a new baby, I'm exhausted."

"That's what Josh says. Kyle's checking Josh's herd so he can get a few hours of shut-eye. His wife has been sick, so he's been on diaper duty too."

"Mighty neighborly of Kyle to help out."

"Josh's gone above and beyond for us, so it's the least we could do."

Hank handed her a thick manila envelope. "Here's everything you'll need. We already put the money in your account. Next year there will be another deposit for the same amount. Then we'll reevaluate."

Like a quarter of a million dollars over the next year wasn't enough.

"Thanks. I'd say something more poignant but I'm stunned. Seriously stunned."

"Take care, sis." Then they were gone.

Celia went into the office and sat at the desk. She spread the papers out.

She'd gone from having forty-one dollars and twelve cents in her checking account to having one hundred and twenty-five thousand dollars. She looked at the balance but it didn't feel like it was real money.

And until they were through with calving it wasn't like she could spend any of it anyway.

As long as she was by the computer, she transferred the information on the last few births from her notebook to the spreadsheet. She checked her e-mail.

But her gaze kept flicking to the papers on the desk.

Hadn't we promised each other no secrets?

Yes. But this was different. Hank and Abe weren't telling their spouses either, so it was more of a business decision. Still, guilt ate at her. She shoved the papers into the envelope and hid them in the bottom drawer of the filing cabinet.

Chapter Twenty-one

$\mathscr{K}$yle had just finished helping Josh fix a section of corral nearly leveled by an angry cow, when he saw Abe Lawson's truck coming down the hill from his house.

He should've been happy that Celia's brother was making an effort to keep in contact with her. But for some reason, Abe's visit when Kyle wasn't around pissed him off. He knew it was stupid and petty, but he couldn't help his resentment.

His resentment increased when he had to hear from Josh, for the one millionth time, how freakin' lucky he was to have Celia to show him the ranching ropes. Like he was a total dumb ass. Maybe he hadn't been born to this lifestyle, but he'd been around it for years. And some of the stuff ranchers considered secret knowledge was just plain common sense. He didn't appreciate being made to feel like the resident idiot.

When has your wife ever treated you like the resident idiot?

Never.

Wife. Right. That was just another issue weighing on him. He wasn't responsible for the chapel's licensing issues, but he was responsible for not telling her about the legal glitch when he'd discovered it. Confessing his reasons—hoping she'd fall in love with him for real—seemed like a lame excuse to keep her around as his ranch hand.

It's more like you're her ranch hand.

He'd been feeling that way for the better part of a week. Always looking to Celia for direction before performing a task. Always asking her questions before doing anything so he didn't fuck it up.

Bottom line? Kyle needed to man up. He needed to be the master of his domain. He needed to figure out some of this shit on his own and not rely on her. 'Cause sure as hell, when she found out they weren't really husband and wife? She'd be long gone. One thing that hadn't changed about Celia— when she was upset, she ran.

As a kid she'd run off into the woods or by the creek.

As a teenager she'd raced off on her horse.

Now she just hopped in her truck and left.

Kyle remembered the night she'd run to him, a week after she'd broken up with Breck. In that moment he'd wanted to be the one man she always ran to. The one man she could count on. And he'd set out to become just that man.

"Kyle?"

He looked at Josh. "Sorry. What did you say?"

"I just asked if Celia had a brand preference for tubes."

Kyle frowned. "What do you mean?"

"Ever had to tube-feed a calf? It happens when the calf is too weak to suck. Shove a tube into the esophagus and force-feed it until it can suck on its own. Some folks like stiffer tubes, some like the softer type."

"She hasn't mentioned a preference and we haven't needed them so far. Why?"

"I know Marshall bought the stiffer kind. That's what I use. I figured if Celia liked the softer ones, I'd swap her. Ronna bought the wrong kind." Josh shook his head. "That's why I don't send her to the ranch supply store."

"Everyone makes mistakes."

"Bet Celia never buys the wrong damn thing," Josh grumbled.

No, but I probably would. Not that Kyle would admit it to Josh or anyone else. "Why don't you return it to the store?"

"No refunds or exchanges."

"Not even for unopened merchandise?"

"Nope."

"That sucks. Guess I'd shop somewhere else, especially if you've been a good customer. I'd also point out to the store manager that you can probably buy the same stuff online, but cheaper. And if they wanted to keep you as a customer, they'd relax their policies."

Josh gave him an odd look.

"What?"

"For a second, you reminded me of Marshall."

Kyle didn't know how to take that. He shrugged. "I don't tolerate that kinda bullshit." He stepped back and squinted at the corral. "Anything else you need a hand with before I take off?"

"Nah. Thanks for helping today. I appreciate it."

"You've helped us plenty, so I'm happy to return the favor."

Rather than dragging his piss-poor mood inside, he grabbed his gloves and headed for the woodshed. Chopping wood cleared his mind, worked his body, and was one thing he didn't need to ask direction on.

Celia honked as she cut through the pasture on the ATV to do a round of cattle checks.

As soon as he'd chopped a few days' worth of fuel, he stoked the wood burner. He climbed in the tractor and stacked three straw bales next to the gate where the heifers were penned. Then he scooped and packed more snow along the north side as an additional windbreak. By the time he finished it was full-on dark. He was starved and exhausted, but his night wasn't close to over.

Kyle didn't bother to shower. He'd be back out in the elements covered in manure and birth fluid before too long. He hung up his outerwear and settled in front of the TV with a beer and a box of Triscuits.

Celia returned a little more than an hour later. She wasn't her usual chatty self, so Kyle should've suspected something was up. The cupboard door slammed. The refrigerator door slammed.

Yep, something was definitely up with her.

She stood in front of the TV. "So we're not having supper tonight?"

"Why you askin' me?"

"Because we're supposed to share the household stuff. I thought maybe since you were inside first you would've started supper."

Maybe since she'd been inside since after breakfast she could've planned supper. Not that he could say that to her. Kyle held out the box of crackers. "I'll share my supper with you."

She glared at him. "Funny."

"Suit yourself."

"When was the last time you cooked supper?" she demanded.

"I don't remember." Kyle swigged his beer. "But I imagine you do. And I imagine you intend to remind me too."

That comment earned him a half growl. Then she stomped away from the TV.

Good.

He heard her rattling pans in the kitchen. Any other day he'd have followed her, trying to coax her into a better mood by acting in the annoyingly charming manner she couldn't resist. Tonight he let her stew. He didn't budge when he caught a whiff of eggs and toast. Not even when his stomach growled.

After she ate, Celia sat in the recliner, but she wasn't watching TV. She had a couple notebooks open, switching back and forth to write in them.

"What are you doin'?"

"Composing love letters," she muttered. "What does it look like I'm doing?"

"I don't know. That's why I asked."

She tapped the pen on the notebook. "I'm recopying my notes while they're still fresh in my mind. Then I'll put them in the spreadsheet on the computer."

So she'd been on the computer all damn day. He drained the last of his beer. "I saw Abe's truck drive past Josh's place."

"He and Hank stopped by."

"Both of them? What did they want?"

Celia continued scribbling in her notebook. "Nothin' really. They had to go to Rawlins on a diaper run and checked to see how we were doin' during calving."

Right. So they didn't need to talk to him? Just Celia? Because obviously he didn't know what the fuck he was doing.

"Why?" she asked.

"No reason. Just thought it was odd you didn't mention that both your brothers showed up."

"So I have to report everything to you now?"

Kyle's eyes narrowed on her. That was a little defensive.

"It wasn't a big thing," she insisted. "And they didn't stay long."

"I'm not sorry I missed them. I'm sure they would've gotten a huge kick out of asking me specific questions just to see if I knew the proper rancher answer. So, yeah, sorry I missed that fun time."

Her mouth dropped open. "What has gotten into you?"

"Nothin'." He stood. "Forget it. I'll deal with the livestock tonight. If you don't think I'll fuck it up too badly."

"I don't think that," she said softly. "You don't have to do it all yourself. We're a team."

"I want to do it all myself. It's your chance to get some rest. Take it. 'Cause I guarantee I'll be dog-tired and worthless for most of tomorrow. But like that's different from any other day around here."

Celia didn't say a word as he dressed in his outerwear.

Just as Kyle opened the door, Celia said, "Wait."

He paused.

"I don't know what Josh, or my brothers, or anyone else has said to you to make you feel this way. I've been as supportive as I know how to be. And I've never tried to make you feel inadequate, because I know exactly how it feels when it's been done to me. It's not my fault you don't have experience with this, Kyle."

When Kyle turned around to apologize for being a dick, she'd already walked away.

❧

His first five births went like clockwork. Easy delivery. Mama cleaned the calf immediately. The baby wobbled upright and began to suck. So he'd gotten a little cocky. He could do this. He'd even dozed off for half an hour.

Invigorated by his nap, he slipped into the cold, moonless night. The near stillness of the air at night was a welcome change from the harsh winter winds slapping him in the face earlier in the day. He ducked into the heifer pen and saw one cow off in the corner away from the feed. As he got closer he noticed one side of her belly stuck out farther than the other. He snagged one of the ropes draped over the fence posts, fashioned a loop, and dropped it over her neck, all the while patting her and speaking to her in the soothing, encouraging tone he'd learned from Celia.

She lumbered along without protest. Didn't kick up a fuss when he locked her down in the birthing equipment. She was straining to expel the calf, and if her lethargy was an indication, she'd probably been at it for a while.

Why hadn't you noticed it?

Ignoring the gnawing feeling of guilt, he hobbled her back legs. Pinned her tail out of the way. He'd slipped on a glove and checked the position of the calf. It appeared to be right side up.

So he'd gone to the next step, trying to deliver the calf. He'd attached the chains below the calf's dewclaws and had pulled the front legs free far enough out of the birth canal to see the head. Twice he'd gotten close; twice the calf had slid back inside.

Kyle's body was bathed in sweat. He was out of breath. One person pulling a calf was a helluva lot of work. But every time he stopped to rest, he lost ground. So he didn't stop.

His pride had kept him from running up to the house to wake Celia for help. He justified his decision by telling himself he needed to know how to handle this stuff on his own. And the only way to do that was by immersing himself in it.

And talk about immersed. This was one messy birth.

Three hours passed without any progress. He was exhausted. His muscles ached. And because he was tired and suffering from muscle and eyestrain, he didn't notice that the chains had caused damage to the heifer's birth canal until blood began pouring out of her back end. Kyle was forced to admit this type of birth was out of his level of experience. His hands were so slimy with fluid, blood, and shit that his cell phone slipped out of his hand three times before he got a decent enough grasp to call Fletch.

Luckily Fletch was close by. He didn't offer advice besides to hang tight.

He also didn't ask if Celia was around helping. He probably assumed she'd be by Kyle's side, being as she was the one with experience, not him.

That was when Kyle understood the gravity of his mistake.

Half an hour later the barn door slammed open and Kyle glanced over to see Fletch stomping his feet. He carried a medical bag, official in his role as August Fletcher, DVM. But Kyle's anxiety was high, knowing his friend would see firsthand how he'd fucked up.

Kyle noticed the dark crescents beneath Fletch's eyes and saw that several days' growth of whiskers dotted his windburned face.

Fletch pulled off the wool hat and shoved it in his pocket, shaking loose his long hair. "Show me whatcha got."

"Back here."

He stopped at the back end of the cow and used a penlight flashlight. Then he pulled on a rubber glove and inserted his arm; his harsh breathing echoed as he maneuvered his arm around inside the too-still heifer. After ditching the bloody glove, he stepped around to peer at the cow's face. "Son of a bitch."

"What?"

"There's no saving her. She'll be dead within the hour."

"What about the calf?"

"It's been dead a while. Give me the rundown on what happened."

Kyle talked quickly, but tried to relay every minute detail until Fletch held up his hand.

He glanced around the barn. "Where's Celia?"

"Sleeping. She's had a long day so I've been dealing with the night issues."

"So she didn't assist with this at all?"

Kyle's cheeks burned with shame and he shook his head.

Fletch swore. His dark hair fell across his face as he aimed his focus on the floor. He clenched his fists at his sides as if fighting for control.

In that moment, Kyle realized just how big Fletch was. At six foot five in his work boots, with enormous shoulders and chest, the man was a monster. A monster Kyle had always considered a gentle giant unless he was crushing opponents on the football field.

When Fletch finally looked up, his brown eyes were black and hard as stones. "We've been friends a long time, Gilchrist, so I ain't gonna sugar-coat this."

Kyle nodded.

"Your pride or stubbornness or whatever chip you've got on your god-damn shoulder about your inexperience as a rancher is what led to that animal dying. It's your fault. No ifs, ands, or buts about it. That animal was in your care. Which means you suck it up and ask for help from someone who's been through this type of birth before if you don't have the first clue about what to do.

"I don't give a flying fuck if you and Celia had a big fight before you came out here. When you saw this heifer was in distress? The very first thing you should've done was slammed a lid on your pride and ran up to the house to ask Celia for her help. We both know Celia would've hauled ass down here had she been aware of the seriousness of the situation. But you kept that from her. Why? I didn't think you had a huge male ego that doesn't allow you to admit to a woman that something is beyond your skill set. Jesus. Don't ever exhaust yourself to the point your inexperience kills an innocent animal when you have the chance to save that animal."

He had no response. He felt sick.

"You are a smart guy. You don't have to figure this shit out by yourself. Don't let the macho attitude that comes from being a professional bull rider permeate this part of your life. You don't gotta be the toughest one on the dirt here."

That stung.

"You are responsible for the lives of a couple hundred animals. The only person who expects you to know everything about this...is you. That's an unreasonable burden to place on yourself. And here's a news flash. Even if you live to be a hundred you'll never know it all about ranching. Listen. Learn. Ask questions. Ask for help. And quit using your feelings of inadequacy against Celia. She is your wife. Be goddamn grateful she is your wife."

"I am."

"Good."

"Although it's too little too late."

"For that animal. Not for the rest of them. I don't envy you cleaning up this mess. And I'm gonna go against all my previous advice and suggest you don't involve Celia in disposing of the carcass." Fletch propped his hands on his hips and gave Kyle an arch look. "Any other questions while I'm here?"

Kyle's initial response was to say nope, but he bit it back. "So as far as the cleanup . . . I just get the tractor through the big barn door and scoop the cow into the bucket?"

"That'd be easiest."

"And then I dump it? Where? The ground is too hard in most places to dig a hole."

Fletch ran his hand through his hair. "I suggest you dump it in the closest pasture the tractor can get to, that's farthest from the herd."

Kyle remembered from a conversation with Josh that it was important to control where the coyotes would find the carcass to try to keep the nasty scavengers from the nearly helpless calves. "Thanks for the advice."

"Let's get her out of the equipment." Fletch pointed to the heifer, now dead.

Fletch left, leaving Kyle to deal with everything alone.

He loaded the cow without issue. Slow going on the ice, in the dark. Each bump and skid jarred the whole tractor with the heavy weight the front end carried. After he cleared the fourth gate, he found a spot by a steep incline. He lowered the bucket and rolled her out, over the fence into the ravine. Then he headed back. Two and a half hours had passed since he'd started the gruesome journey. One final check on the mamas close to the house, and the heifers again, and he closed it all down just as the very edges of the sky began to lighten.

The house was quiet. Kyle stripped where he stood and stumbled to the bathroom. Not even the sweet scent of Celia's shampoo roused him from the feeling of despair as he washed away the grime.

Although he was exhausted, and naked, he couldn't crawl into bed next to Celia yet. He stared out the bedroom window, wishing he could roll the clock back twenty-four hours.

"Kyle?" she murmured sleepily.

Funny how just the sound of her voice soothed him. Filled him with a feeling of shelter. Would he break down when he told her his pride had cost the lives of two animals?

"What's wrong? Omigod, are you hurt?" The covers rustled and her feet hit the floor.

He didn't deserve her concern. Not after the way he'd acted today. "I'm not hurt." On the outside. On the inside? Different story. "Go back to sleep, sweetheart."

But Celia wouldn't allow him to hide. She ducked beneath the arm he'd braced on the wall, getting right in his face. "Talk to me."

"I'm sorry." He gathered her into his arms and held her against him.

"Sorry about what?"

"Everything. You . . . you deserve better than what you got from me today. I fucked up."

"Kyle. You're shaking. What the hell is goin' on? You're scaring me."

So he told her. Without holding anything back. Without trying to put a spin on it so he didn't come off looking and sounding like a stubborn fool. When he finished, his face was wet. His voice was hoarse. But his conscience was nowhere near clean.

Celia stepped back, away from him. He didn't blame her. But when she lovingly, sweetly ran her fingers down his arm to tug on his hand, he felt like an idiot again. He should've known she wouldn't leave him when he was like this, no matter if he deserved it.

"Come on. Crawl in bed and let me warm you up."

He allowed himself to be led like a child. Beneath the sheets he reached for her, resting the side of his face on her chest, his arms circling her waist.

She pulled the covers up and locked her legs around his. Celia didn't speak at all. Not to patronize him. Or chew his ass. Or add more guilt to the pile he already carried. She just held him and let him clutch her like the lifeline she was.

The shakes stopped when he felt consciousness fading. "Thank you."

"For what?"

"For showing me once again you're the better person than me in so many ways."

"Kyle."

"I'm serious. You're intimidating as hell, Celia. You're so freakin' smart. Although I don't tell you that twenty-four/seven, because I don't want you to get a swelled head."

"Usually you're the one with the swelled head. I ain't talking about this one." She tapped his forehead.

"I'm too tired to do anything about that right now."

"That's a first. Now get some sleep."

As he drifted off, he said, "Don't leave."

"I won't. I'm right here."

"No. Don't ever leave me. Not now. Not in six months. Not in sixty years. Be my wife forever."

"Kyle. You're exhausted and upset. You have no idea what you're babbling about."

"But I do. I'm perfectly…capable of…telling you…that I…" He chased the thought until sleep overtook him.

Chapter Twenty-two

With the birth of the last calf, things slowed down some. If the first six weeks of their marriage had been a whirlwind, the last six weeks were a tornado. Losing three calves wasn't good, but it could've been so much worse.

It'd ripped her up, seeing Kyle's devastation the night that cow had died on his watch. Hard lesson to learn, the importance of vigilance, but one he would never forget. She considered how different the season would've turned out if she hadn't been here. If Kyle had had to muddle through everything on his own. What would he have done if she hadn't been around to guide him?

As much as she'd made herself indispensable, she didn't want her husband looking at her and seeing a ranch hand. She wanted Kyle to see her first as his wife, second as a good ranching partner. Especially after he'd begged her not to go when he'd said he wanted her as his wife forever. At the time she feared it'd been exhaustion talking. But over the last few weeks, things had changed between them again. Their bond had strengthened. She'd never been happier in her life and she wanted Kyle to know it.

As Celia curled against Kyle's side last night, content in the aftermath of his very thorough loving, she came up with a simple, small way to prove she wanted this marriage to be real in every sense of the word too—she would change her name. On her driver's license and her Social Security card. She'd make it official.

After checking the herd, Kyle jotted down a list of supplies. Normally Celia tagged along when he went to town, but she opted to stay home and he left after a late lunch.

In the office, she pawed through the binder they'd started for keeping track of important paperwork. They would soon need a better system because papers and receipts were already getting jumbled together. She sorted through copies of their birth certificates, vehicle titles, Marshall's will, and the land plat survey. But no marriage license.

Hadn't Kyle mentioned taking care of that weeks ago?

What the devil had he done with it? Maybe he'd put it in a different place. They were supposed to keep everything together for easy access.

So why is your bank statement still hidden?

Why hadn't she told Kyle about it? Because it was an escape hatch? Because she didn't want to share the money with him?

No. As Kyle's wife she was entitled to fifty percent of his inheritance. So while the amount her brothers had given her was generous, it was a drop in the bucket compared to what this ranch was worth.

She grabbed her bank statement and the course requirement printout from her hiding spot behind the stack of *Cowboys & Indians* magazines. She stared at the dollar amount, still shocked she had that much money. Leaning against the window frame, she looked out across the snowbanks, which had started to melt, revealing lots of fences to fix this spring. Other ranch and household improvements loomed. Kyle didn't need this money to make those changes happen. Would he see her offer to put the money in a joint account as a sign she wanted to meld their lives together on all fronts? Yes.

Celia set the bank statement and college information on the ironing board to keep it separate from the other paperwork. After a half an hour of fruitless searching, she figured Kyle had gotten so busy he must've forgotten about obtaining a copy of the license. She went online and tracked down the phone numbers to request that a copy of the marriage license be sent to their current address.

Took ten minutes until a real live person came on the line. Celia explained the situation—twice—and bit back her frustration at being transferred again.

"Miss Lawson? Sorry to keep you waiting. I did some checking and nothing has changed with regard to Trade Winds Casino since the facility was closed. Since the sixty-day grace period for permits had passed, unfortunately right before your ceremony, the marriage is invalid."

She froze. "Excuse me? I must've misunderstood. I heard you say the marriage is invalid."

"The marriage is invalid," she repeated. "Just like I explained to Mr. Gilchrist when he called—"

"What? Kyle has been in touch with your office? When?"

"According to the case file, over a month ago. Since your marriage certificate wasn't the only one affected by the Winds of Change permit lapse and subsequent closure of the Trade Winds Casino, there's an active file on it, and all inquiries are directed solely to me."

"So you're telling me Mr. Gilchrist knew about this?"

"Yes, ma'am."

Kyle had found out their marriage wasn't valid and he'd somehow forgotten to tell her?

Bullshit. He hadn't told her because he wouldn't have made it through calving season without her.

A very sharp pain stabbed near her heart.

Was he really that calculating? Throw in the constant mind-boggling sex . . .

"Is there anything else I can help you with, Miss Lawson?"

"No. Thank you." Numb, she hung up and wandered out of the office.

She stopped in the doorway of their bedroom. Seemed foolish, her happiness this morning that he'd made the bed without prompting.

She managed to keep her tears in check until she entered the living room. She'd been filled with so much pride that her first foray into home decorating had turned out so well. The comfy furniture, the carpet, the vibrant curtains. Even the western painting on the wall made the space so indelibly theirs.

Celia clapped her hand over her mouth to stifle the cry and dropped onto the loveseat. She'd thought of this house as her home the first week they'd moved in. Had she really believed she could shake hands with Kyle at the end of six months and walk away like they'd completed a business transaction? When they'd been as intimate as two people can possibly be?

She loved him. So what was she supposed to do now? Confront him? Ask what he was waiting for and why he hadn't told her about the invalidity of their marriage?

There was that stabbing pain near her heart again. She had no claim on him. She didn't care about having a claim to his inheritance if they weren't married, but she'd really thought of him, and this place, as hers.

She had no one to talk to about this. No one. Everyone believed their marriage was real.

She'd never felt so alone in her life.

Celia couldn't face him. Not when her emotions were so raw. She went to the guest bedroom closet and found her duffel bag. Almost on automatic, she shoved a couple changes of clothes inside and added the toiletries she'd need for a night away, even when she had no idea where she'd go.

Don't run. Stay and fight.

No. The old Celia would argue, accuse, talk without listening. The new Celia needed time to sort through this.

With heavy footsteps and a heavier heart, she climbed into her pickup. She couldn't look at her horses, standing by the fence. She'd have to remind Kyle to feed them tonight.

At the Stop sign at the end of the gravel road she really seemed to be at a crossroads. Right took her to Rawlins. Left took her to Muddy Gap. Neither choice seemed right. Part of her wanted to spin around and head back to the ranch. Pretend nothing had changed. Because they were happy together. Weren't they?

But the fear that Kyle might look her in the eye and tell her it was over kept her from turning around. She needed to toughen up and prepare herself for that possibility.

Ultimately she turned left. Toward Muddy Gap.

Her stomach growled as she drove through town, but facing the diner regulars in her frame of mind wasn't happening. The Closed sign hung on

273 ONE NIGHT RODEO

the front door of Bernice's Beauty Barn, but Celia noticed the back end of Bernice's Chrysler Imperial sticking out in the parking area, so she pulled in.

Bernice opened the metal door a crack, and barked, "What?" at Celia's knock before she poked her head out. Her scowl morphed into a smile. "Hey, girl, come on in. I was just catching up on orders." She flicked her half-finished, still-smoking cigarette butt into the snow. For a second, Celia thought about diving for it to keep that precious tobacco from going to waste.

Pathetic, Celia.

"You comin' in or what?" Bernice barked.

"Yeah." Celia let the door slam behind her.

"What brings you to town?" Bernice rubbed her hands gleefully. "You finally gonna let me cut that hair? Or would Kyle have an issue with that?"

She almost said, "Who cares what the fuck Kyle thinks? Let's do it." Facing a major life trauma was no time to enact such a huge change.

Bernice led her to the sitting area. "So, sugar, not that I'm not happy to see you, but you don't look happy. What's up?"

Celia, who prided herself on not being a crybaby-type of woman, burst into tears for the two-millionth time. Maybe not that many, but it sure seemed like it. She didn't babble or blurt anything out, she just sobbed.

Bernice handed her a box of tissues and didn't speak until Celia's tears subsided. "That first fight as a married couple is always the hardest," Bernice said softly.

Celia dabbed her eyes. That was as good an explanation for her hysteria as any. She expected Bernice would offer surprise that she and Kyle hadn't fought before now. But Bernice said nothing along those lines, and Celia knew she'd done the right thing coming here.

"I remember my first married fight with Bob. He'd said something stupid off the cuff because most men are clueless dumb asses and it takes a while to train them. Anyway, I thought my world had ended, even as I was wondering if I could get away with killing him for hurting my feelings."

"What did you do?"

"I didn't want to go home to Mama and give her reason to think the marriage was goin' south so soon. It was summertime and so I went to my favorite fishing spot. Brought a sleeping bag. Planned to spend the whole night out there. Shocked the shit outta me when Bob showed up at ten o'clock. He'd been all over the place, trying to find me. The man didn't know what he'd done to upset me; he just knew that he'd done something and he needed to make it right. We've had our fair share of rows since that day thirty-some-odd years ago and we've always worked it out." She patted Celia's knee. "Does Kyle know there's a problem?"

Celia shook her head.

"I'm sure you don't wanna go to your brothers' places or to Harper's?"

"No. I need some time to think. I'm not being a brat hoping he'll track me down either."

Bernice patted her knee again. "I understand. Why don't you stay here tonight? There's a TV and a cot in my office. I'll grab you some grub from the diner."

"Thanks, Bernice."

"You're welcome. But I do have a condition for you staying here. If Kyle does track you down, you listen to him. You talk to him. No hiding, all right?"

Celia had no intention of telling Kyle where she was. "All right."

Bernice stood. "Be back with your food."

While Celia ate, Bernice got rid of all the cigarette butts and almost empty cigarette packs to keep Celia from temptation. She texted Kyle that she was babysitting overnight for Hank and Lainie, reminding him to feed the horses tonight and in the morning.

As soon as Bernice locked her in, Celia shut off her cell phone. She stretched out on the cot and watched mindless TV without seeing any of it.

❧

Kyle received Celia's text message after he pulled into the driveway. He'd been delayed in town later than he'd liked, and something about her message seemed . . . off.

He unloaded his supplies. Checked cattle. Fed the horses. The house was dark and gave him a weird feeling that this would be his life if Celia wasn't in it.

Kyle fixed a plate of leftovers and ate over the kitchen sink, just like he'd done in his bachelor days. He checked for more text messages before he got in the shower. He checked for more text messages after he'd plopped on the couch to watch TV.

About halfway through the episode of *Top Chef,* he noticed a blue light glowing in the hallway. He checked the office and saw Celia had left the computer on. Weird. She always shut it off.

He nudged the mouse and the State of Nevada's marriage license information Web site showed up on the screen.

He was pretty sure his heart stopped. His gaze took in the papers spread across the desk. Celia had been looking for something and he didn't need a magnifying glass and a tweed hat to know what she'd been searching for.

And she hadn't found it because it didn't exist.

Kyle scrubbed his hands over his jaw. What the fuck was he supposed to do now? Panic like he'd never felt knocked him to his knees. She'd left him. And he'd bet a hundred bucks she wasn't at Hank's. He dialed their home phone while he paced in the office.

"Hello?"

"Hey, Lainie."

"Kyle! What's going on?"

"Not much. Just wondered what you guys were up to tonight."

Silence.

Maybe he'd been wrong. *Please. Let me be wrong.*

"Sorry. Brianna just threw her spoon at her father. She's teething and being a total pain. She can't go to bed soon enough for us. We are plain exhausted from dealing with monster child."

His hopes plummeted.

"So you're not hiring a babysitter and slipping on your dancin' shoes once the monster is down for the count?"

Lainie snorted. "I'm in my sweats covered in spaghetti. So . . . no."

"I won't bug you. No big reason for the call. I just wanted to touch base with Hank. He can give me a ring tomorrow."

"I'll tell him. Give our love to Celia."

I'd give her my love too if I knew where the hell she was.

Next he called Abe. Shot the shit. Asked a random question about ATV maintenance. As he said good-bye Abe told him to say hey to Celia.

Strike two. And if Harper was harboring Celia she wouldn't tell him, so he didn't bother to call her.

Where the devil could she be?

Kyle checked the bathroom. Her toothbrush was gone. She'd only told him to feed the horses tonight and tomorrow, which hopefully meant she planned to be home tomorrow. He called her and the call went straight to her voice mail.

Not taking his calls. Big surprise.

He wandered back to the office and stacked the papers strewn across the desk. On a whim, he clicked on the history tab to see what online sites Celia had visited. Nevada State government sites today. Ranch supply sites yesterday. Nothing unusual for the last three weeks. Not needing to see anything else, he shut down the computer.

Angry, frustrated, worried, heartsick. Scared. Holy shit was he scared she'd walk away.

Yeah? What are her options? You're not legally bound to give her anything since she's not your wife. She doesn't have enough money to get back on the circuit full-time. She doesn't have a place to live. After the blowup with her brothers she'd never ask them for anything. Maybe she'll hit the road with Tanna? Or move to Texas permanently?

The fuck that was happening.

Kyle moved from the window and accidentally bumped the ironing board. A few papers fluttered to the floor. He thumbed through them and froze.

A bank account statement. A statement for an account that contained one hundred and twenty-five thousand dollars. Celia's bank account.

Celia had that much money?

Since when?

Had she been lying to him all along?

He flipped through the papers, stopping when he came across the information for veterinary trade school in Cheyenne. Test dates, registration criteria, and deadlines.

Had she meant to leave this out for him?

Kyle would find out the truth. But he'd have to find her first.

~

His phone rang at seven thirty in the morning just after he'd parked the tractor. And it wasn't Celia. He barked, "What?"

"Come and get your wife."

"Who is this?"

"Bernice. Celia's been at the Beauty Barn since yesterday afternoon. I've got customers coming in and I'd really thought you wouldn't be an idiot and let her sulk all freakin' night."

"I'm on my way."

Chapter Twenty-three

The morning wasn't as cold as it'd been earlier in the week. Celia wondered how Kyle was faring doing chores alone.

As much as she'd tossed and turned on the crappy cot last night, she hadn't come up with a way to talk about the marriage issue. Or the nonmarriage issue.

She cleaned herself up and unlocked the back door for Bernice. She'd just finished her second cup of coffee when the back door slammed. "The coffee's fresh if you want a cup."

"Don't mind if I do."

Celia spun around. A very ragged-looking Kyle approached her wearing his pissed-off face.

She said the first thing that popped into her head. "A bit early for the full salon treatment, isn't it?"

"Funny. Maybe I should ask if you get a special rate since you spent the night here?"

No snappy retort for that.

"Jesus, Celia. I was worried sick when I figured out you weren't babysitting for either of your brothers."

"You called them?"

"What the hell do you think? You didn't answer your cell phone. I spent all night pacing, wondering if you'd gotten in an accident...."

She wanted to snap she hadn't been thinking straight because she'd found out—oh, they weren't fucking *married*—but she knew shutting off her phone had been childish. "I'm sorry you were worried. So they know?"

"That you lied to me and spent the night God-knows-where? Not exactly something I wanna share with anyone, let alone your brothers."

Celia marched up to him. "You wanna talk lies? How about the lie that we were married?"

"We were married. The chapel in Vegas let their license expire, which neither of us could've known at the time."

"So why didn't you tell me? Why did you let me—us—continue to live together as husband and wife?" Everything they'd done, everything they'd been to each other, had been based on a lie. "You didn't tell me because you needed me as your goddamn ranch hand. You needed me to help you through calving."

"That's really how little you think of me, Celia? I'm that shallow, heartless, and calculating?"

"You tell me. You've known about the bogus marriage for weeks. Yeah, I talked to the lady in Nevada too. I know the whole license/permit issue is completely out of the norm. But isn't it ironic that you found out the truth before that first calf dropped?"

Kyle didn't say anything.

And Celia was so worked up she feared she would say something she'd regret. She was afraid she'd revert to that little girl who goaded him. So she walked away from him, to the sitting area, where she'd left her purse. She turned on her cell phone and scrolled through the missed calls. Thirty-some calls from Kyle over the course of the last twelve hours.

Celia frowned at the number of missed calls from Tanna.

Kyle barreled around the corner. "Goddammit, Celia. We're trying to talk about some of this stuff—"

She held up her hand. "Tanna has called me fourteen times in the last twenty minutes."

"By all means, call her back right fucking now. I'd hate for her to miss your advice on her love life when our marriage is falling apart."

"There is no marriage," she snapped. "So don't pull that *I wanna talk about this now* bullshit attitude on me when you should've talked to me weeks ago—Tanna? Hey. What's going on?"

Tanna was close to hysterical.

Finally Celia calmed her down enough to decipher the phrase she kept repeating. She lowered herself onto the couch. "When?"

She vaguely heard Kyle ask, "What's wrong?"

"Take a deep breath because I can't understand you. Oh God. I'm so sorry." She listened to Tanna falling apart and she tried to hold it together. "No, that's okay. I'll have it on me at all times. Yes. I promise."

Celia dropped her phone to the carpet. She put her forehead on her knees, hoping to muffle her sobs. What horrible news.

Poor Tanna.

Celia felt Kyle's hand rubbing her back, offering support, and that made her want to cry harder. "What's going on?"

She sat up. "Tanna's mom, Bonita, had a stroke."

"Is she gonna be okay?"

"They don't know. It doesn't look good."

"Ah, dammit, Celia. I'm so sorry. I know you spent a lot of time with her."

She thought of Bonita's sweet smile as she bustled around the kitchen. The way she twirled her dish towel and her dog, Smoochie, started dancing.

"She was so much like my mom. After Murray died, she was the only one who didn't tell me to get over it. She was so sweet and motherly and I didn't realize how much I missed that." The last part came out on a sob.

Celia found herself hauled into Kyle's arms. He let her curl up in a ball on his lap, and held her as she sobbed. Which made it worse because he had the ability to soothe her like no one else. How could this all be a lie?

She cried harder.

Her phone began to vibrate on the floor. She practically leaped out of Kyle's arms to scoop it up.

Tanna. Again. She hastily wiped her face. "Hey, T. No. It's okay." Celia began to pace as she listened to Tanna's nonsensical ramblings. "Of course. You don't even have to ask. Seriously. It's a three-hour drive. I'll let you know as soon as I get there." Celia couldn't look at Kyle. "Kyle has this ranch thing down pat. He won't miss his ranch hand at all."

Kyle made a growling noise behind her.

"Cell service in Wyoming sucks, so don't panic if you can't get ahold of me, okay?"

She couldn't afford to break down now. She had to focus on Tanna. Be strong for her friend. She grabbed her duffel bag from Bernice's office and slipped her coat on. She felt Kyle's burning gaze on her so she met it head-on.

"Goin' someplace?"

"Texas."

"You're going to Texas now?" he said incredulously. "How are you getting there?"

"I'll drive to Denver and fly to Dallas."

"So you're just gonna jump in your truck and leave without talking to me about any of this first?"

"Tanna needs me. Her family has been my family for the last four years. And there's nothing for me here anymore."

"Celia," Kyle said sharply. "You can't just drop everything and go to her."

"Says who?"

"Me."

"And who are you? Right. You're the man who's not really my husband. You're the guy who kept me in the dark about our marriage being a lie."

"It wasn't a lie, goddammit. The way I feel about you isn't a lie. What we had—what we still have—isn't a lie either. You know that."

"It doesn't matter." She raced out the door.

Two seconds later Kyle had caught her and latched onto her biceps. "It's the only thing that matters. Look at me, Celia."

She shook her head.

"Please."

She might've snapped at him if he hadn't softened his tone. Softened his hold. If he hadn't said *please*. Against her better judgment, she looked into his eyes and saw the same misery she felt.

"These last three months have been the best of my life. I don't want to lose you. Not because I need your ranching expertise but because I need you."

"Why are you telling me this now?"

He broke eye contact for a second. "Because you wouldn't let me tell you before."

"It just proves you didn't try very hard to tell me anything, did you?" Celia jerked out of his hold and made tracks for her truck.

But Kyle didn't let her get far. "Fine, you're right. I've been a closemouthed jerk. I'll come with you and we'll talk about it on the way to Denver."

"I don't know how long I'll be gone and you have a ranch to run."

He snarled, "I don't give a shit about the ranch right now."

She wheeled around after throwing her duffel bag in the back of her pickup. "Don't ever say that. Those animals depend on you. They are your responsibility. This is your life now. You can't just up and take off whenever the hell you want."

"And you can?"

"It's not *my* ranch, Kyle. I have no claim on it." *I have no claim on you.* "And don't worry about giving me any of the money you promised me when I agreed to stay married to you. I don't want it."

"You certainly don't need it anymore, do you?" he shot back.

Celia stiffened.

"You wanna talk about a secret? How about the amount of money in your bank account? Was your claim that you were too broke to buy even a jug of juice a total lie?"

"No! I was that broke. I've been so broke for the last year I couldn't have competed if it hadn't been for Tanna." Was that part of the reason she'd felt so obligated to go to Texas? Because she owed Tanna?

"Then where did you get that much money?" he demanded.

Tell him it's none of his business. "From Abe and Hank. You got your inheritance and they gave me mine."

"Were you going to tell me?"

Celia stared at him, refusing to feel guilty. "It's pointless now, isn't it? You have your ranch and I have the means to go to school. We both got what we wanted."

"So we're done? You don't need my money, you don't need me, and so you're not sticking around? We played house for a few months and that's it?"

"What do you want me to say?"

His eyes searched hers with such intensity she couldn't look away. "Say that the time we spent together meant something to you."

No matter how upset she was, she couldn't lie to him.

You don't have to be an idiot and blurt out the truth either.

But Celia found herself doing just that. "Yes, it meant something to me, asshole."

Just like that, his miserable posture changed. He erased the distance between them with four angry strides. "You want to know the honest-to-God truth, Celia? I love you. For chrissake, woman, I've been half in love with you for the last two years and you haven't even noticed! So what if we were impaired the night we got married? Marrying you was the best thing I've ever done in my life and I won't apologize for it."

Her mouth dropped open. "Then why didn't you just tell me that?"

"Because I was afraid this would happen! You'd get pissed about the marriage license screwup and not believe me when I said it didn't matter to me. I wanted to be with you anyway. With you as my wife. I'd decided to give myself every single fucking minute of those six months you promised me because that might be all I'd ever get with you."

"Kyle."

"I love you. Do you hear me? I love you." He shouted the last part. "Only you. Only ever you, Celia. From the moment I knew I'd made pledges to you I've considered you my wife. *Mine.* Even now, when I know the rings aren't legally binding, I won't take mine off. Because it means something to me. You mean everything to me. You know in your heart that what we have is real. No little piece of paper should have the power to change that."

Now that he'd finally opened up to her, telling her everything she'd wanted to hear for months...she had to leave? But she had no choice. Tanna, who took great pride in not needing anyone, had begged her to come to Texas. And Celia wouldn't let Tanna down when she so desperately needed someone to help hold her up.

But what if her leaving at such a crucial time put everything with Kyle in jeopardy? What if he gave her an ultimatum?

He must've sensed her indecision because his eyes were gentle even when his tone stayed firm. "I know you need to go to Tanna. I'm not asking you to slap your friend's hand away when she's reached out to you." He paused. "But don't slap mine away either."

She remembered saying that to him and it'd been a turning point for them.

"I'll stay here and hold down our ranch. Not mine, *ours*. I will be waiting in *our* house, sleeping in *our* bed, waiting for you to come home to me. You belong with me. You're happy with me."

Kyle didn't touch her. Didn't beg her to keep in contact with him. He just looked her dead in the eye and said, "I'll be waiting for you. As long as it takes, Celia. I love you."

Then he turned and walked away.

✒

Kyle had hoped for a declaration of love from Celia after he'd yelled out that he loved her in the parting lot of Bernice's Beauty Barn, for chrissake.

But somehow . . . her calling him an asshole was close enough to an admission of feelings to prompt him to come clean with her about everything. He'd laid himself bare for her. He hoped it would be enough to make this right.

He just had to put his head down, keep the ranch running, and hope like hell she came back to him.

✒

Day one without Celia sucked ass.

Day two without Celia sucked ass.

Day three without Celia sucked ass.

By day four without Celia, Kyle was ready to sell the whole damn ranch.

So when his mother's car pulled up to the house, Kyle was so happy to see her he opened the door even before she knocked.

He watched her climb out of the car, the smart, strong woman who'd raised him on her own. She'd had no family, no one to count on but herself during her pregnancy and throughout his childhood. It'd always been the two of them. It'd always been enough.

If he truly thought about it, he hadn't been overly concerned about discovering the identity of his father growing up. Once in a while he'd ask his mother, never really expecting a serious response. He'd become obsessed with the male who'd given him half of his DNA only since he'd received the inheritance from that mysterious man.

Genetically, Kyle didn't know if he'd inherited any of his father's features. He'd not found a single picture of Marshall in any of his belongings. So because he had only a fuzzy mental image of the man, he had no idea if he and Marshall had the same hands or the same eyebrow shape or the same shoe size.

But Kyle knew what his mom had looked like as a child. As a teenager. As a young mother. He knew how she'd felt at all those different stages of her life. He knew he'd inherited her eyes, her mouth, and her good nature.

Her work ethic.

Her capacity to love unconditionally.

Over the past few days, he'd had all the time in the world to think and no one to talk to about his realizations. Maybe revelation was a more apt description for what he'd finally grasped: Marshall Townsend had lost out.

Kyle understood that he would not find a letter of explanation from Marshall in the boxes of papers about why he'd made no effort to get to know his son. He wouldn't find a secret scrapbook Marshall had compiled with newspaper clippings of Kyle's triumphs in the world of rodeo.

At last count his mother had thirty-two scrapbooks. One devoted to every year of Kyle's life. And she made an effort every day to be part of her son's life.

That's what counted.

Kyle could spend the rest of his life second-guessing a dead stranger's motives, or he could do as Celia had suggested weeks ago. He could let it go. Be happy with his windfall. Be grateful Marshall had given him some land, cattle, and money. Be grateful his mother had given him so much more.

Two weeks ago he'd authorized the lawyer to release the money

Marshall had set aside for her, plus extra from his account. She'd called him immediately, completely in shock. When she'd started crying, he'd lied about having chores to finish and quickly ended the call. He'd had no idea how to deal with her gratitude.

Looks like he'd have to come up with something on the fly.

Sherry Gilchrist bounded up the steps and hugged him. "My boy."

He hugged her back. Hard. "Hey, hot Mama. Come on in."

"What's this? You actually seem happy to see me."

"I am."

"So, how are you?"

Lonely. "Hanging in there."

She glanced up. "Don't lie to me, Kyle Dean Gilchrist. You look like hell."

"Thanks for the confidence booster."

"You'd be disappointed if I started sugarcoating my maternal responses to you now."

He grinned. The woman who'd given birth to him definitely had her own way of doing things. And he appreciated more than ever the easy rhythm to their relationship. "What brings you by?"

"I've got appointments in Rawlins and I wanted to talk to you face-to-face so you couldn't hang up on me."

"Am I in trouble for that?"

"No. But I'm pretty sure I raised you better than that." She kicked off her stiletto boots and wandered through the living room. "Oh, Kyle, just look at your home. It's so nice. Not too fussy. Warm and welcoming. It's perfect for you and Celia."

"Thanks. I owe all the decorating and stuff to her."

She sat on the love seat. "Where is your lovely wife?"

"Texas. Her best friend's mom had a stroke, so she went down to be with the family."

"That girl . . . She really is a sweetie, isn't she? So thoughtful. So genuinely helpful." Then she frowned. "Wait. She left you here to handle the ranch by yourself?"

He only bristled a little. "We're through with calving, which is the worst part. I'm just fine on my own." *Liar.*

"I'd hoped to talk to both of you on this family matter, but since I'm limited on time you'll have to fill her in when she gets home."

If she ever comes home. Kyle took the chair opposite her, secretly pleased that his mom already accepted that Celia would be part of their little family. "Fill her in on what?"

"A couple of things. First, I'm leaving Rick."

"About damn time." Then his gaze turned sharp. "He didn't hurt you or anything?"

"No. He wasn't particularly heartbroken about the breakup either. It just was easier to stay than to go for both of us. Second, I'm moving. Checking out places to live in Rawlins and in Muddy Gap."

"Why Muddy Gap?"

"That's where I'll be working. Came about in a strange way. When I called Susan Williams to let her know I wouldn't be attending your wedding shower, she remembered me from years back when I applied for a bartending job at Buckeye Joe's and she hadn't hired me. She thought I might run off with her husband." She smirked. "So we're shooting the breeze, talking about all the changes in the bar industry over the years, since we're the same age."

"Really? Because you look way younger than her."

His mother preened. "I'll take that compliment, you rascal charmer."

Kyle grinned again. She'd called him that ever since he'd talked his way out of detention at age ten.

"Anyway, she's burned out since her ex-husband bailed with that cocktail waitress. She wants to have a life away from the bar." Her eyes gleamed. "So when you told me about the money Marshall left me, I called her and bought in. You're looking at the new partner of the Buckeye!"

Stunned didn't come close to describing how he felt. "Mom. That's awesome."

"I know. Isn't it great? Susan wants me to start tonight. Introduce me to the regulars, that sort of thing. She's letting me stay with her until I get my own place. After all the years I've slaved for others, this is a dream come true for me." She laughed. "Being part owner in a bar. I almost can't believe it!"

Her enthusiasm was infectious. "So that means free drinks whenever I stroll into the Buckeye?"

"You wish. But I will admit part of the appeal for me was moving closer to you. And any future grandbabies you and Celia might wanna give me."

"Neither of us is ready for kids." He scratched his jaw. "But I was thinking about buying her a dog." That's how desperate he was to lure Celia home. He'd contacted half a dozen different breeders in case she didn't want another mongrel blue heeler like her beloved dog, Murray.

Kyle was going crazy without her. A minute at a time.

"Well, son, as much as I like dogs, I draw the line at calling a dog a grandbaby."

"Understood." He watched her fiddle and fuss with her buttons, which meant she had something else on her mind. "What else is up?"

"One other thing I wanted to talk to you about."

"Shoot."

"I was happy Marshall did one thing right in his miserable life by providing you with a place to call your own."

"But?"

"But you've been so angry since this inheritance happened. At me. At Marshall. At yourself. Even at Celia."

He looked away.

"I'm worried about you. This isn't like you, Kyle. You've gone from being a happy kid to a happy teen to a genuinely happy adult. You never were resentful that I couldn't give you all the things other boys your age had. You just made the most of what you *did* have. Now that you have everything you ever wanted . . . you're not happy. And because you weren't a morose kid I had to pry secrets out of, I never pressured you to open up to me. In hindsight, maybe I should have."

"Why?"

"So we wouldn't be at an impasse. I want to know what you're thinking. I want to know what I can do to earn your forgiveness."

During his alone time, it had come as a shock to recognize he hadn't applied the "the past is the past" philosophy he'd taken with Celia to his mother. Should she have told him Marshall Townsend was his father? Probably. But letting his mother's long-ago decision ruin their future relationship? Stupid, petty, and shortsighted. And mean. God. He'd been a whiny little prick to her these last couple of months. She deserved better from him too.

As hard as it was to do, Kyle looked her in the eye. "First, I'd ask for your forgiveness for acting like a bratty kid."

"Done."

"As far as I'm concerned, there's nothin' to forgive. You did what you thought was right at the time. You stuck by it. I admire that. I have a lot of admiration for you, in case you didn't know. And it sucks for Marshall that he didn't get in touch with me, because I am a cool kid. Or so you've always told me."

She whapped him on the knee. "Oh, you're gonna make me cry."

When she sniffled, Kyle stood and tugged her into his arms. "Mom. I love you. I am happy." Or he would be as soon as he straightened out this situation with his woman. "I just had to figure some of this stuff out on my own."

"That's what Celia told me," she said. "She knows you so well. You're lucky, son."

"I know I am. I'm hoping in your new life as bar owner you'll make time to hang out with me and Celia. She hasn't had a mom for a long damn time, and I'm more than willing to share mine with her because you're the best mom ever."

She cried harder.

He let her.

Then she stepped back and wiped her eyes. "Thanks. I needed that."

"Me too."

"When is Celia coming back?"

"I don't know."

Her green-eyed gaze turned sharp and mom-like. "Is everything all right between you two?"

It'd be easy to lie and slap on a happy face. But he couldn't. His mother knew him equally as well and she would ferret out the bullshit eventually. "Not really. We had a big fight right before she got the call from Tanna. Then she left. I haven't heard from her since."

"At all?"

Kyle shook his head.

"Well, you know what you have to do, don't you?"

"Ah. No. Not really. That's the thing."

She poked him in the chest. "You get your butt to Texas and bring your wife back home where she belongs. You want her to think you don't care? Will you let your very first fight change the course of your marriage? No way, buster."

"But it's different now than when I was ridin' bulls and could do whatever the hell I wanted. I've got livestock to take care of. And the last thing Celia said to me was to own up to my responsibilities with the ranch."

Another two hard pokes in his chest. "And Celia is one of those responsibilities. The biggest one. Don't you let her get away from you. She loves you. She looks at you the way I'd always hoped the right woman would. So you talk to your neighbor, or hire someone, or hell, even tell me what to do and I'll take care of the dang cows. But don't you let this go another day, Kyle. Not. A. Single. Day."

The thought of his mom ankle-deep in muck in her high-heeled shoes made him smile. The thought of getting in his truck, driving to Texas, and having Celia in his arms in thirty-six hours made his smile even wider. "You're right. Thanks for the kick in the butt when I need it."

She kissed his cheek. "Honey, that's what mothers do best."

☙

Ten minutes after his mom had left, Kyle was about to head down to Josh's to beg for his help for a couple of days when Lainie's vehicle pulled up.

He had to lock his knees against the fear that something had happened to Celia. Was that why he hadn't heard from her? He threw the door open. "Lainie. What's wrong?"

"Let me come inside. It's cold out here and I've been on my feet all day." Lainie unwrapped her scarf. She looked like she'd been crying.

Kyle managed a calm, "Tell me what the hell happened before I lose my fucking mind."

She sank onto the couch. "Tanna's mom died yesterday."

Yesterday?

"Have you heard from Celia at all?" He shook his head again and Lainie sighed wearily. "I was afraid of that."

Had Celia confided in Lainie about their fight? Or about their marriage? "Of what?"

"Stupid cell phones." She held hers out. "See? Even I don't get service here. And Tanna's folks' house is one of the few places in Texas where there's limited cell service. So between the spotty service in Wyoming and you and Celia being without a home phone, I figured that's why Celia called me—because she couldn't get ahold of you."

So Celia hadn't told Lainie about the fight or the marriage license problem. Good. He'd let Lainie believe that crappy cell phone service was the culprit for Celia and him being out of touch with each other for four days. "What did she say? Is she okay?" *Does she miss me? Is she coming home?*

"She's . . . coping. She told me the funeral is the day after tomorrow."

"That soon?"

"Yes. I guess grief has done some crazy things to Tanna's dad and he just wants the whole thing over with." Lainie glanced up at him. "You are planning to go to Texas? Because Celia sounded a little . . . lost."

That twisted his heart and his stomach into a gigantic knot. "I was just on my way to ask Josh if he'd take care of things here for a couple days so I could go get her."

"Well, not to overstep our bounds, but Hank and Abe have volunteered to pitch in and take care of your livestock. They figured it'd be all right even if you needed a full week."

Stunned, Kyle just stared at her.

"What? Would you prefer to have Josh do it? That's okay with us too."

"No, I don't know what to say. I didn't expect the offer . . . not after all that happened. . . ."

"You thought we'd just let you handle this on your own? Huh-uh. Family doesn't work that way. Both you and Celia need to understand that. You both need to get used to it."

He cleared his throat. "Well. Thanks."

"You're welcome. Admit you've always wanted a buttinsky sister-in-law, and pushy brothers-in-law. So for better or for worse, you're stuck with us now."

Kyle said, "I'm glad," and meant it.

"Oh, and Bran said he'd help out. As did Renner and his foreman, Hugh. So we've got you covered."

Again Kyle just stared at her.

"What are you waiting for? Shoo, man. Get yourself packed. It's a long drive to that part of Texas."

"But what if . . ." *She refuses to come home? What if she's decided now that she's got money to compete she'll hit the road with Tanna again? How could I return to Wyoming without her?*

"But what if . . . what?" Lainie prompted.

Kyle couldn't voice his fears to Lainie. He remembered Pearl's advice to always talk to his wife first about things. And that's what he intended to do. As soon as possible. "Nothin'. I appreciate you bein' the go-between, Lainie. But I'll handle getting ahold of Celia from here on out, all right?"

"She said something along those lines too when I told her I'd relay the message." She flapped her hand at him. "My God. You and Celia are two peas in a pod. Stubborn. Both wanting exactly the same thing."

"A national CRA championship?" he joked.

"No, you're both looking for a place to call home. She loved racing around barrels for a while, but she never intended to make that her life. Same with you and bull riding. It was a means to an end. Now you both have what you want. She loves you, Kyle, as much as you love her. I've seen you two together and I know you were meant for each other."

"Damn straight."

Lainie danced a little jig around him. "Besides, I get to say I told you so. I told you one day you'd find a woman who loved and appreciated every-thing about you. And you did. I just didn't expect it to be Celia."

Then you weren't paying attention. Because it's been her all along.

Chapter Twenty-four

❦

*I*t was one of the worst weeks of Celia's life.

The somber mood in the Barker household. Tanna and her brother Garrett's devastation was made worse when their father, Milt, handed down edict after edict. Bonita's best friend, Rosalie, refereed between father and children, in addition to coordinating the food, handling phone calls and visitors.

Celia helped as much as she could. Staying busy kept the memories of when she'd lost her parents locked down tight. She'd taken over feeding the cattle and the horses to allow Milt, Garrett, and Tanna to deal with the most pressing issues. It also allowed her time away from Tanna's grief, which was overpowering and all-consuming.

Talk about all-consuming. She missed Kyle. Missed him like she'd left part of herself with him. Maybe the best part. She missed the home she'd made with him. Missed the life they'd begun to build together regardless if they were officially husband and wife. There was so much she wanted to tell him. In person.

And Celia had wanted Kyle so badly today, she'd sworn she'd seen him at Bonita's funeral. Sitting in the back row at the church, wearing a black hat and a dark green sport coat. But she hadn't seen him during the processional out of the church. Nor had she seen him at the cemetery. Obviously he'd been a figment of her needy imagination.

After the funeral Celia changed out of her dress clothes and put on work clothes to deal with the livestock. She lingered outside, trying to glean joy from the beautiful spring afternoon. As much as she appreciated the milder Texas weather, she missed Wyoming. Missed the spring snow that this time of year turned everything into a mud bog. She missed the cold air and the big sky and the constant smell of wood smoke. She missed the sound of calves bawling and the sound of Kyle whistling as he worked.

How long did Tanna expect her to stay? Because if Celia had her way, she'd hop a plane tomorrow morning and she could be home by suppertime. She imagined pulling into the driveway at twilight. Kyle running out of the house to greet her. Sweeping her into his arms, peppering her face with kisses, and making her promise she'd never, ever leave him again.

Romantic nonsense. Next you'll have him riding up on a white horse. Carrying a puppy.

After two more quick swipes with the brush, she patted Daisy-Mae on the rump and returned her tools to the barn, hanging up the chinks and straw hat she'd borrowed from Tanna's stash.

But even after she left the pen area, three horses hung over the fence trying to get her attention. She wandered over. They took off when they realized she didn't intend to feed them.

"You know, I shouldn't be surprised I'd find you out here with the horses."

Celia spun around, her heart racing. Not a figment of her imagination this time. Kyle was here. Really here. In his black hat and a green sport coat. "Kyle?"

"Glad to know you haven't forgotten my name in the last six days, nine hours, and twenty-three minutes."

She didn't think, she just acted. She hopped over the fence and threw herself into his arms. "I can't believe . . . I thought I was seeing things. You really were at the church."

"Yeah. I kinda slipped in and snuck out. I knew you were with the family and I didn't want to distract you." He gestured to the pasture. "If you'd waited I'da done a cattle check with you. Someone told me recently I ain't all bad on a horse." He smiled.

That charming smile did things to her knees and other parts of her body. "How long have you been here?"

"Only since about an hour before the service started. I drove straight through. Found a hotel, got cleaned up." Kyle curled his hands around her face. "Stayed away from you until I couldn't stay away any longer."

Celia closed her eyes when his lips met hers.

"Christ, I missed you. I hated that you left with things hanging between us. But I understand why you did. You are Tanna's friend; she's been there for you so many times when you felt you had no one else. You owed her and she needed you. But I need you too, Cele." Kyle tilted her face so he looked directly into her eyes. "I love you. You've been my wife in my heart and soul since the morning we woke up wearing wedding rings. And yes, I should've told you when I learned about the marriage license issue. I'm not proud to say I didn't tell you because I thought you'd leave me. See, you've never needed me as much as I need you." His small smile was there and gone. "I wasn't worried about losing my ranching expert, Celia. I was ter-rified of losing you."

"You didn't lose me. After you told me you loved me, even when you knew I had to leave, it gave me so much hope and . . ."

"And what?"

"And I can finally admit that I love you like crazy."

"Thank God for that." He held her for several long moments. One hand twisted around her braid, the other hand covered her heart. "The thought of not having you in my life, by my side, every damn day for the rest of my life makes me die inside."

"Don't say that."

"But it's true. I never knew I could love anyone the way I love you. It scares me, Cele."

Her tears leaked out the corners of her eyes and ran over his hands. But she didn't even try to stop them. "I missed you so much, Kyle."

"Oh shit. Don't cry. I freak the fuck out when you cry." His fingers started to wipe the moisture from her cheeks.

Celia put her hands around his wrists. "They're happy tears. You make me happy. Ever since last year, when you told me I deserved better than Breck, when you convinced me that if I walked away from him I'd give myself a chance to find a good man who loved everything about me. I'm so thankful that man is you." Celia squeezed his wrists. "I think part of that bratty little girl who annoyed you always secretly loved you."

He laughed. Then he kissed her. With sweetness. With his heart. With his soul. The passion would come later when they were alone. Celia let herself fall into it, fall into him.

Took a good, long while before they finally broke the kisses, and even afterward, their hands stayed clasped, their bodies gravitated toward each other.

"Will you stay with me at my hotel room tonight? I'm dying to touch you."

"Yes. God, yes. I missed that about us too." She buried her face in his neck.

But he wouldn't allow her to hide. "So why the sadness in your eyes?"

"I feel guilty. I'm so happy right now. And Tanna's inside, so devastated."

"She's lucky you could drop everything and go to her, but she'll have to stand on her own now. You realize that, right?"

"Yes. Speaking of dropping everything . . . who's taking care of the livestock at home? Josh?"

"And your brothers. And Bran. And Renner and his crew. They said they owed me for all the years I helped them out. They were more than happy to return the favor for a few days. But I suspect our sisters-in-law had a lot to do with makin' that happen."

"My meddling family members making you crazy yet?"

"Nope. I sort of like it, to be honest." He briefly pressed his mouth to hers. The man could not stop kissing her. And she really loved that about him. "My mom has some news too. But it'll keep. First things first."

"What? After I left during our big fight, you want assurances from me that from this point on you'll come first in my life?"

"Yep, that's a start. And you'll come second in mine, right after the cows." He laughed when she swatted at him. "Kidding. I figured that's what a real cattleman would say. But if that's the case, I'll never be a real cattleman, because you'll always come first. Always." He wrapped her braid around his fist and tugged. "But if being a cattlewoman isn't enough for you? The offer to pay for your school still stands. I want you to have your dream, Celia. No matter what it is."

"You … this life we've begun to build together … that's my dream. It's more than I ever hoped for. More than I ever thought I'd deserve." Celia touched his jaw. "Part of me is afraid this *is* a dream."

"It's not, baby. It's as real as it gets."

"I can't believe you came after me."

"I can't believe you thought I'd ever let you go."

They looked at each other and laughed. "We're so sappy."

"Sappy, happy, sloppy in love. That's us, kitten." He slung his arm over her shoulder and they walked along the paddock.

"Did you tell Tanna or anyone about the marriage license screwup?"

"No. Did you?"

"Are you kiddin'? After the way your brothers acted the first time? You think I wanna give them a real reason to beat the shit outta me for living in sin with their baby sister? No way." He stopped and faced her. "So no more living in sin. I have a couple ideas how we can fix this." Kyle dropped to his knees. "Celia Rose Lawson, I love you. I can't live without you. Will you marry me? Again?"

"Yes!" She jerked him to his feet and said, "Yes. Yes. Yes. Yes. Yes. Yes. Yes," punctuating each *yes* with a kiss.

He laughed. "We have two options. The first: Hop in the truck and drive straight to Vegas. We'll find a chapel with an up-to-date permit and we'll tie the knot again, and make sure we leave with all the proper paperwork. So we'll have proof we're really married."

"That sounds perfect."

"Ah, but I'm not done. I know that tequila-fueled ceremony wasn't the wedding of your dreams. So the second option: Have a hometown preacher marry us in front of our family and friends, so you can wear a fancy dress and have a big party afterward. If you want that, I'm good with that. I'm good with anything that makes you mine as soon as possible."

She liked his possessive side as much as his sweet side. "Something about us getting married in boots and jeans fits us. Something about keeping the ceremony about us pledging ourselves to each other in private suits us too. So thanks, but I'll take the quickie Vegas wedding."

"You sure?"

"Yes. Because I already feel like I'm married to you. It'd just be a formality."

Kyle kissed her. "This time we'll be sober when we repeat our eternal vows to each other. This time I'm putting a big diamond on your hand. This time when we seal the deal with a kiss, I'll take extreme pleasure in knowing that I'm the first man who ever kissed you as well as the last man who'll ever kiss you."

"And there's that romantic streak I've been missing something fierce," she murmured.

"Then we'll rent one of them fancy bridal suites and I'll spend the whole night proving how much I love you." He grinned and waggled his eyebrows. "I guarantee we'll both remember our wedding night."

She touched his face. "I love you, Kyle. So much. Who knew me asking you to keep me from doing something stupid turned out to be the best thing I ever did?"

"One night turned out to be a lifetime. I'm good with that."

Lorelei James is the *New York Times* and *USA Today* bestselling author of contemporary erotic romances set in the modern-day Wild West. Her books have won the Romantic Times Reviewers' Choice Award, as well as the CAPA Award. Lorelei lives in western South Dakota with her family... and a whole closetful of cowgirl boots.

Did you miss the first book in the sexy
Blacktop Cowboys® series?
Read on for an excerpt from Lorelei James's

Available now from Signet Eclipse

"*S*crewing two guys doesn't make you a slut."

Lainie Capshaw darted a quick glance at the crowd in Bucky's Tavern. Luckily none of her coworkers—her male coworkers—lurked about. "Maybe you could've said that a little louder, Tanna. I don't think they heard you on the dance floor."

"*Puh-lease.* The men in this joint are too busy gawking at the cocktail waitress with the watermelon-size tits to be eavesdropping on us." Tanna sucked down a healthy swig of beer. "Twenty bucks says ol' monster jugs pops a strap in the next ten minutes."

"No dice. If I take that bet, you'll sneak up behind her and slice the damn strap just so you can win."

"You're no fun." Tanna sighed dramatically. "I'm bored."

Lainie rolled her eyes. A bored Tanna was a dangerous Tanna.

"So let's talk about Lainie's lewd love life."

"Let's not."

Tanna wagged her finger. "Ah, ah, ah. Suck it up, chickie. You walk the walk, you gotta talk the talk. Besides, who cares if you're boning two guys? Cowboys are notorious for having a different buckle bunny every night, in every podunk rodeo town on the circuit. It pisses me off there's still a double standard for women."

"True. But…"

"But what?" Tanna looked at her quizzically. "You aren't feeling guilty, are you?"

She shrugged. "Maybe. Wouldn't you?"

"Hell, no."

Bull. Lainie called Tanna's bluff. "So if the buff babe in the yellow shirt sauntered over and said, 'I wanna screw your brains out against my truck right now,' you'd follow him out into the parking lot without question?"

"Or hesitation. Well, besides checking my purse for condoms."

"Even when you're already making time with that studly bulldogger from Austin?" Lainie challenged.

Tanna planted her elbows on the table. "I'd do it in a heartbeat, Lainie. What would *you* do if both your men showed up here tonight?"

Wet myself. "Umm . . . I'd probably run."

"Like a contest to see who wanted you more? Whoever catches you first wins?"

Good Lord. Talk about an overactive sense of drama. "No. More like running from my problem."

"Doesn't sound like a problem to me. Two sexy men angling to thrill you between the sheets." Tanna smiled brazenly. "Or against the bathroom stall, in Kyle's case."

Whoo-ee. Just thinking about the hot tryst with Kyle still fried Lainie's circuits. Never in her life had she warranted an I-need-you-right-fucking-now bout of raunchy monkey sex. So yeah, it'd earned her bragging rights. Even been-there-done-that Tanna had been impressed by Lainie's balls-to-the-wall behavior.

Tanna's cell phone vibrated on the tabletop. She squinted at the number and snapped, " 'Bout time, you dumb bastard," before she flounced out the side door, chewing the caller's ass.

Lainie hunched over the table to discourage any cowboys from asking her to dance. Probably an unnecessary precaution, since tantalizing Tanna usually garnered that type of male attention, not her.

Which was why it was so twisted that Lainie had captured the interest of not one, but two men. Two very hot, very alpha men on two different circuits.

Lainie liked working the rodeo circuits, even though the pay was crap. As a med tech for Lariat Sports Medicine, she split her time between the two largest rodeo organizations: the Cowboy Rodeo Association, known as the CRA, and the Extreme Bull Showcase, known as EBS.

The CRA was comprised of rough stock events: bareback, saddle bronc, and bull riding; as well as timed events: calf roping, team roping, steer wrestling—also known as bulldoggin'—and barrel racing. The EBS had just one event—bull riding.

The CRA bull riders didn't compete in the EBS and vice versa. Which was how Lainie ended up with a hot cowboy hookup on both the CRA and the EBS.

Fraternizing with cowboys could be career suicide for a woman in the male-dominated sport, especially when her job was to examine those glorious bodies. Lainie prided herself on avoiding the sexual temptation for damn near two years.

Until she'd met Hank Lawson.

She'd encountered the intense CRA bullfighter after he'd pulled his Achilles tendon during a CRA event and grudgingly limped into medical services. After she'd fixed him up, he asked her out on a date. Lainie refused—tempting as it'd been. Not only was Hank a hundred percent real Wyoming cowboy who handled bulls with ease and panache, but at six-three, with inky black hair and ruggedly masculine features, he embodied tall, dark, and handsome.

She kept refusing until Hank invited her to dance at a sponsors' dinner. A simple dance—what could it hurt?

If she appreciated Hank's moves in the arena, his moves on the dance floor were equally fine. Whenever hard-bodied Hank studied her with those eyes the color of new denim, she experienced a rush of adrenaline that must have been equal to spending eight seconds astride a two-thousand-pound bull.

Two weeks later, Hank asked her to two-step at another rodeo event. Too much wine and too much Hank went straight to her head. One slow dance led them directly to Hank's motel room for a little mattress dancing.

Revisiting that romp with Hank caused Lainie's thighs to clench with want. Intense concentration and instinctual reaction were the hallmarks of good bullfighters, and Hank had both in spades. No surprise his single-mindedness carried over into the bedroom.

The man took his own sweet time making love; it was as maddening as it was arousing. Leisurely undressing her. Running his work-roughened fingers over every inch of her bare skin. Kissing everywhere his hands roamed. Wringing at least two explosive orgasms from her before he rode her hard and fast, or slow and sweet.

As phenomenal as the sex was, Hank rarely deviated from missionary position. Even if Lainie started out on top showing off her excellent riding skills, she'd end up underneath Hank at the big finish. She'd shoved aside her niggling doubts about Hank's lack of sexual spontaneity because he made her come so many times she saw stars.

So why had she hooked up with bull rider Kyle Gilchrist from the EBS circuit? True, Kyle and Hank were opposites. Physically, Kyle was wiry rather than overly muscular. His green eyes sparkled with mischief, not intensity. With Kyle's blond locks and golden facial hair, he resembled a Viking.

After taking a year off due to knee surgery, Kyle returned to the EBS with a vengeance. He'd started dropping by the sports medicine room to chat, in the guise of having his previous knee injury reexamined. Very polite. Very much interested in showing her in explicit detail how a modern-day Viking would utterly ravish her.

Her resistance lasted two months. The square-jawed, sloe-eyed sweet talker had literally charmed the pants right off her in a bathroom stall at Denny's outside Chula Vista. That first weekend she'd had sex with Kyle six times—not once in missionary position.

It'd been freeing. Fun. Hot as sin…until the weekend ended. Away from the temptation of Kyle's consuming kisses, she questioned whether she'd become as loose and easy as the buckle bunnies trailing after the circuit cowboys.

But mostly Lainie wondered whether she could juggle both men at the same time.

She and Hank hadn't discussed exclusivity. For all she knew, Hank could be sleeping with half the barrel racers on the CRA circuit. Kyle hadn't demanded promises either. Given Kyle's charm and good looks, she doubted he spent his nights alone watching Country Music Television.

So it wasn't the "cheating" factor that bothered her. It was the fact that she really liked both men and she didn't know who she'd pick if she had to choose.

Luckily, Lainie was in the catbird seat for a while. In the big world of professional rodeo, the EBS and CRA circuits rarely intersected geographically. Chances were slim she'd run into Hank if she was with Kyle or vice versa.

Feeling a little cocky, she sipped her beer.

Lainie's smugness lasted all of thirty seconds before two rough-skinned hands covered her eyes and a deep, sexy male voice murmured, "Guess who."

∽

Kyle Gilchrist could not believe his luck. Mel was here. Right here. Her wild curls tickling his cheek. Her powdery scent teasing his nose. The sight of her lithe little body hardened his cock.

And to think he'd dreaded spending the eve of his CRA debut in some dive bar in Lamar, Colorado.

Cool fingers circled his wrists. "Kyle?"

He removed his hands and spun the bar stool, forcing Mel to face him. "Hey, sugar. Surprise."

"Oh, my God. It is you. What are you doing here? This isn't your circuit."

"Came in to have a beer and coerce a pretty woman into dancin' with me. And look who I found first thing—the prettiest lady I know." Kyle's palms slid down her bare arms to grasp her fingers. "Come on." Allowing her no chance to argue, he tugged her to the dance floor, right into the thick of the crowd.

"Kyle, this isn't a good idea. What if—"

"It's the best idea I've had in weeks. Come on. Admit it. You missed me."

"Maybe." She smiled against his throat.

He wasn't much of a dancer, so he employed every seductive tactic he'd stockpiled over the years to draw her attention away from his two left feet. Brushing his thumb at the base of her neck. Gradually easing his thigh between hers. Swaying to the beat of the music while their bodies moved to a rhythm uniquely theirs.

The final chord of the tune rang out. He spun them until her back was to the main part of the bar.

She tried to push him away. "Kyle. Let go."

"Not until you give me a kiss."

"But I can't. Not here where everyone can see—"

Kyle settled his mouth over hers, treating her to the lazy kisses that always distracted her.

A soft protest exited her mouth, which he swallowed in another kiss. She thought too much. Worried too much. The best way to turn off her overactive brain was to turn her on in a whole 'nother way.

As luck would have it, that was one thing Kyle was very good at.

∽

Hank Lawson paced in the shadow of the sleazy honky-tonk. "No, sir. I understand. Yes." He grinned at the phone. "I'm committed to the next three weeks. Uh-huh. Well, sir—all right, Bryson—it's a good opportunity for me to work with some of the rankest bulls in the CRA. No. I'll cut it short if I have to. Absolutely, I'll be there. Tulsa. Looking forward to it." He clicked the phone off and pumped his fist into the air.

"Yes!" Hank couldn't wait to tell … He stopped. Wait a second. He couldn't tell anyone. Dammit. That sucked. Biggest news of his career and he had to keep a lid on it.

Bullfighting. In the EBS. It was a callback from his pretryout test last month at a second-tier event.

As much as Hank loved bullfighting in the CRA, for a bullfighter, the EBS was the big time. More money. TV coverage. More sponsorships. Fans. And he wasn't supposed to tell anyone? Screw that. Hank scrolled through his contact list and hit Dial.

"Hank?" she answered breathlessly. "What's up?"

"News, but promise me it'll stay under your hat."

"Fine. Spill it fast because I'm short on time."

The noise in the background sounded like she was at a rodeo. "I scored another audition with the EBS."

She squealed. "Seriously? That's awesome! When?"

"A couple of weeks. Once I'm done with Cowboy Christmas."

"They couldn't get you in sooner?"

"Bryson asked if I'd be available for the Huntington Beach event next week, but I can't. I've already committed to—"

"God, Hank, why can't you let Gilly navigate the CRA trail on his own? It ain't like he's a rookie."

He scowled. Would she ever get over her beef with his buddy? Probably not. The girl held a grudge like nobody's business. "I'm not goin' on the road as a favor to Gilly. Truth is, I'm doin' this for me."

"For the money?"

"Partially. But the more bulls I can get on the next three weeks, the better my chances in the EBS."

"Unless you get stomped by one and blow your goddamn big chance," she retorted.

"Thanks for the confidence, sis," he groused.

"I have the utmost confidence in you, bro. It's the bulls I don't trust. That said, I really *am* excited for you."

"I know you are. Remember, you can't tell anyone."

"Not even Abe?"

"I'll tell him."

"You'd better. But I'm afraid he won't be as thrilled. Come to think of it, if you do get picked, it'll be more work for me at the ranch. Maybe I oughta be rooting for the bulls."

Hank laughed softly.

"Glad I amuse you. Shit. I'm up. Later."

He said, "Up for what?" to the dial tone. He glanced at the time. Damn. He'd been outside for thirty minutes. Not only hadn't he said hello to Lainie yet—and wouldn't she be surprised to see him—but he'd left Gilly hanging. Too bad he hadn't introduced them before he'd taken the call. He headed back inside.

The flashing lights from the stage show inside the honky-tonk screwed with his eyes. Hank blinked a couple times, scanning the tables. The band wailed a decent cover of Billy Currington's latest love song.

He stopped at the bar and ordered three Coors Lights. Hank felt like a fish swimming upstream, juggling three bottles of beer as the people rushed off the dance floor after the tune ended. He'd made it to the table he'd spotted Lainie and her friend sitting at earlier, but there was no sign of her now.

Huh. Hank looked around the bar. No sign of Gilly either.

His gaze wandered to the dance floor. One couple hadn't left yet, oblivious to the fact the music had stopped. They were twined together, mouths fused, body pressed to body.

Hank squinted. Hey. Wait a minute. Was that…?

Holy fucking shit. That *was* Lainie—his Lainie—in a clinch with some happy-handed cowboy.

Fury filled him. He'd fucking lay the bastard out cold. *Come on, asshole— show me your face so I can figure out where I'm gonna put the first bruise.*

Then the loser in the cowboy hat kissing Hank's goddamn woman lifted his head.

Not just any cowboy had his hands and mouth on Lainie; *Gilly* had his hands and mouth on Lainie.

Hank's stomach dropped. And so did the bottles of beer.

Lainie and Gilly looked at him at the same time the raucous crowd broke into applause at his clumsiness.

The cocktail waitress snapped, "Maybe you oughta think about drinkin' one at a time, buddy."

But he couldn't tear his eyes off them. Tempting to punch his buddy in the kisser for kissing her. Equally tempting to pull Lainie outside and ask her what the hell was going on.

The couple stopped right in front of him.

Hank calmly said, "Lainie, sweetheart, I was gonna introduce you to my good buddy Gilly, but I see you two have already met."